I AM JOHN TITOR

I AM JOHN LITOR

I AM JOHN TITOR

NIAMH ARTHUR

SEAN PLATT

While based on a legend, the contents of this novel are entirely fictional and any similarity to an actual person is coincidental.

This is what we *wish* had happened.

Part I

Part 1

Chapter One

2036

THE MAN SPRINTED as if trying to outrun his fate, gasping for breath as he leapt up the final few crumbling concrete steps, his feet pounding hard enough to bruise both heels.

He chanced a glance behind him, spying the silhouettes of his pursuers. A rag-tag group of dangerous-looking people, except for the closest, the only one he really needed to worry about, and not rag-tag at all.

The man pushed himself harder, ran even faster, closing the distance between himself and the Chevy.

He dove inside and jammed the key into the ignition, shoving aside the wiring for the c204 Unit. The ancient Corvette was his only chance for escape, but even after a third attempt, he heard only a dull clicking amid his whispered disappointment.

His hands trembled as he pounded the wheel with hardened fists, inhaled sharply, filling his lungs before blowing the air back out in a gust and testing the engine again.

It sputtered to life as a second engine roared like a gas-powered lion behind him.

He yanked the wheel sharply to the right, careening down the parking structure in the Corvette, hauling ass down several flights as his motley crew of pursuers gave chase behind him.

The man was nearly at the bottom. Almost home free.

But then a third engine screamed to life behind him.

No matter, he was almost at the—

Disaster was like a lightning strike to the Chevy as tires squealed across the concrete, his exit barred by a new enemy, a brigade of military vehicles and a group of gruff-looking men who looked like they had been born with itchy trigger fingers.

He made a sloppy left into another part of the garage, his car a heat-seeking missile in search of the nearest exit.

But that was also blocked.

Same for the exit after that.

And now he was running out of options.

He was stuck in the approximate center of the ground floor, with enemy vehicles racing toward him, a beat to shit Mustang in the lead.

Pure panic rippled through his body. Was he really going to do this?

Time was disappearing on him, so he had no other choice. He had to turn on the machine, and that meant flicking on the Variable Gravity Lock system, then entering a code.

Once done, he heard a loud chirp from an angry alarm, then a small light to trigger the short countdown as he secured himself in his seat and energy began to crackle around the car, a bright blue bubble of electricity as he stared out his windshield. Then the Mustang squealed to a stop several feet in front of him. The driver's face — one the traveler had known forever — looked stricken.

But that was all according to plan.

I'm sorry, the man mouthed.

The Chevy shimmered, streaks of rainbow light radiating out from the metal frame.

The air grew heavy with the scent of burning rubber and ozone as a high-pitched whine echoed throughout the garage, like a vacuum cleaner on the fritz.

And then the world disappeared.

Chapter Two

RJ – 2024

RAMON JIMENEZ — RJ — mopped his brow, but that only smeared more sweat onto his hand.

Heat radiated from the Florida swampland in thick waves that made it harder and harder to breathe as their small boat bobbed through the shoulder-high grass, mud still soaking up the back of his jeans from a misstep while boarding.

This was all bullshit. Not just the sweat trickling down his neck, but the situation itself. A begrudging realization of what his life had become sent a chill through his body despite the oppressive heat. Goddamned Gitter Boys.

He swatted the air in frustration. Goddamned mosquitos, too. His arms were already red and swollen, even though he'd spent half his day swatting at the buggers.

Otis and Buck has been bickering back and forth all day, same as always. The father and son duo were supposed to make for compelling documentary television, but RJ had yet to see their appeal, no matter how many times Michael tried cajoling him into liking the idea. RJ went along with it all like a good boy, until *Gator Gitters* became a project on their actual slate instead of another line on the whiteboard.

Otis was seriously overweight, loudmouthed, and slovenly, and he was missing three teeth. His son, Buck, was several cans short of a six-pack, with pecs like deflated balloons. He always looked and sounded like he was slowly descending from some sort of high, including right now.

"Dang." Buck usually started his stories with *dang*. "I've been wanting to tell ya 'bout this slice of peach pie I had last night. Didn't even need no whipped cream."

"Yeah?" Otis was interested.

"Green eyes." Buck laughed to punctuate his misogyny. "Greenest green you ever seen. Like the color of green God would'a laid on a gator." He nodded, as if comparing his dalliance to a dangerous reptile was a good thing.

"I had a little firecracker with green eyes myself. Couple'a weeks ago. Hair like a head full of black Spanish moss."

Buck seemed surprised by his father's admission and appeared to chew on a thought.

The cameras were already on it. Both the ones in RJ's boat and Lou, sharing his vessel with the Gitters. The director made a motion for everyone.

"She got long legs?" asked Buck.

"I guess they all got long legs, except for the short ones."

"What did her tits feel like?"

"I don't know, son." Otis shrugged. "They felt like tits."

Buck brightened, having finally reduced his equation to the lowest common denominator. "Did she have a tattoo on her belly of two butterflies fucking?"

Realization washed over Otis. "Well, *shit.*"

RJ's crew was clearly amused, but he was pissed, already anticipating the long conversation that would border on an argument with network executives as to why he should not include that colorful little exchange in the final cut.

He and Michael had sold *Gator Gitters*, their newest docuseries, as an adrenaline-pumping inside look into the lives of fearless father and son gator hunters, navigating treacherous swamps and marshlands, bog warriors braving the elements and facing off with massive reptiles. Thrilling chases, dramatic showdowns, and nail-biting close calls, all showcasing the unique beauty and inherent danger of the Florida wilderness.

But in truth it was a reality show, where staged drama, performative moments, and fastidious editing told a more compelling story than the technical truth.

RJ could barely stand how fake the show was becoming. But the network was the network, Michael was Michael, and RJ would have to keep doing what RJ had been doing for long enough to be unfortunately used to it by now.

The sky was quickly losing its tangerine glow on the way to dusk. The low sun cast long shadows across the swamp, draping both reeds and water in an eerie orange-blue glow. They were losing the light fast and just getting started.

Alligators were most active at night, so their best footage would come after dark.

The gurgle of frogs was getting louder, same for a chorus of crickets and the humming cicadas, emerging from an unsettling silence cut only by the inanity of the Gitters; nature herself singing a lullaby as twilight drew near.

But the Gitters refused to let her have it, erupting into an argument as Buck violently shook his head like a wet dog drying off. "It was the same piece of ass, Pa. You just didn't know what to do with it and can't remember her name."

"I knew what to do enough to get 'er done twice," Otis asserted.

"Like I believe that shit." Buck shook his head again. "You probably did 'er doggy so you could keep it up while watching *Massage Creep*."

"I was making girls scream hallelujah a decade before you was spunk. And her name was Lula."

"Lila," Buck corrected.

"Maybe it was two different girls."

"Or maybe you have Oldtimer's."

"It's called Alzheimer's."

"I'm glad you could remember that." Then to highlight his cleverness, Buck added, "Dang."

"You just—" Otis stopped at what must have been the telltale sound of gators in the distance, splashing through the water in search of prey.

Gators were quiet critters until they attacked, but the Gitter boys could hear a gator slipping into the water like a preternatural skill.

But then it was right back to the argument, with Buck cutting into their moment of silence with something Lula/Lila must have told him that he'd obviously just remembered. "She said I looked an awful lot like this one customer. She also said that the old man needed a bunch of dirty talk before he could finish."

"I didn't pay her!" Otis protested. "And not all the girls at Dixie Delights is prostitutes, you know."

"I ain't saying you paid and don't care that you did."

Buck held his belly as he chuckled. "But Lila told me all about that dirty talk. Pretty specific—"

"You best shut the fuck up, son."

Otis got a look on his face that RJ knew a little too well and thought that maybe he too could hear the splashing getting louder. Suddenly RJ and the camera crew had multiple reasons to squirm.

Even knowing better, Buck jumped up to make his declaration.

Otis followed, leaping to his feet and shouting his son down before Buck could get his purported dirty talk out. But he jumped up too fast and jostled the boat.

Buck windmilled his arms to recover.

Otis fell to a squat and grabbed the boat by her sides, one in each hand as he regained his balance.

But it was not enough. The movement sent Lou into the drink, camera still in hand. RJ was terrified for Lou with what must be a wall of gators snaking in around them.

The director shouted new orders, but RJ couldn't decipher his directives amid the cacophony, or accurately read his gestures directed at the second cameraperson, probably telling her to focus on the gators. Like she needed the instructions.

Buck and Otis both sprang into action, leaping into the bow of their own boat and grabbing their weapons — long poles with metal hooks at one end — before turning the predators into prey.

RJ dragged a panicking Lou out of the water while the cameraman screamed his lungs raw at the alligators, still invisible in the water Lou had occupied just a moment before. Not that RJ could blame him. He wanted to scream himself, even though he was still relatively safe in the boat.

"You're fine," RJ assured Lou as the cameraman panted and heaved on the boat floor. "You're safe now."

An orchestra of mayhem blared behind them as cameras captured the Gitters loudly leaping off the boat to wrestle the gators. RJ could easily imagine the accompanying score.

"*I'm safe now?*" Lou repeated, sounding six kinds of pissed. "I'M SAFE NOW?"

RJ swallowed. "Yeah, man, you're—"

"I QUIT!"

"Wait a minute, Lou. Just think about—"

"I don't need to think about anything! You're lucky if I don't sue you!"

"We can make this right," said RJ with a calm he only wished he could feel. "Just—"

"You better be glad that camera didn't belong to me."

RJ stole a glance to confirm what he already knew from pulling it out of the swamp. Lou was wet, but the camera was destroyed.

The whooping and hollering had settled, so RJ assumed that everyone was okay when he turned around, expecting to see at least one Gitter-dominated gator.

Instead Otis was pulling Buck off of his enemy — a large rotting log — and dragging him back into the boat. "Her name was Lula, and you didn't hear shit about nothing."

Buck grumbled something, finally coming down from his high.

The director put out his hand to lower the second camera.

RJ sighed, wondering when life might send him back into an actual story.

Chapter Three

RJ – 2024

RJ STARED at the road through his windshield as Florida wilderness flew by on both sides.

He kept his hands on the wheel and his mind on a life that clearly needed some rethinking.

He longed to feel good about his work again, waking up inspired and falling asleep at night eager to get going again. But he might as well be missing months from his memory given how much he cared about what was happening right now. That shitshow back there should never have happened.

This was his fault. He had been in the backseat of his own life for too long now. Three misses in a row (none of them really RJ's fault), and now Michael made all the rules.

But how long was RJ going to let that continue without demanding the chance to try again?

Crypto Crazies had been promising, but after that last

crash, and most subjects' unwillingness to disclose personal financial information, it ended up as a no-go.

Deep Web Dwellers was supposed to explore the lives of people involved in the darknet. But Legal didn't like the implications of documenting illicit activities.

Undercover Billionaire (*not* what RJ wanted to call it) was about a Canadian Man named Marco who spent millions each year housing political refugees. Marco himself lived in a 1900-square-foot home, drove an eight-year-old Prius, and lived on a minimum wage budget for one month each year. Despite the man having the most interesting things to say, there had been public backlash, accusing the show of trivializing poverty and creating spectacle from a serious socioeconomic issue — which missed the point of what RJ wanted to say with that docuseries. Ironically, not a single person complaining about the show seemed to have actually watched it, and if they had, they likely would've agreed with what it had to say.

Again, not RJ's fault.

His headlights pierced the ribbon of asphalt in front of him — an artery slicing through marshy wetlands on either side. The sky was deep blue, now dotted with stars. Lights from oncoming traffic were like battalions of fireflies flying by in the darkness.

His phone started to ring with "Yakety Sax" — the calliope of fast-paced whimsy that had once served as the theme song from *The Benny Hill Show*. Michael's custom ringtone on RJ's phone used to be "Never Gonna Give You Up," both because he was like a dog with a bone when it came to getting his way, and because sometimes talking to Michael felt like the universe itself was Rick-rolling him. RJ changed the ringtone after Michael had called RJ, trying to find him in a bar when he was sitting two stools away. Michael had been sober enough to take offense and demand that RJ give him a less offensive ringtone — and drunk enough to never follow up.

"Answer call," RJ told Siri.

"Yo—" Michael started.

"Yo nothing. Did you hear what happened on set? About Lou?"

There was a long pause before RJ continued, "*Gator Gitters* isn't a docuseries, dude; it's a prime example of everything wrong with streaming."

"It's not about streaming or not streaming. Never has been. This show hits the target for a specific audience. That's what you're not getting. People want to be entertained, and the Gitter Boys are definitely entertaining."

"They are *not* entertaining."

"So what if FlixIt wants to call it a docuseries instead of a reality show so that viewers can feel smarter about themselves while watching—"

"It's the televisual equivalent of chewing on tin foil while getting a root canal."

"—means more viewers for us and—"

"We're not making art, Michael. We're making fuel for the content mill. When did—"

"Of course we're feeding the mill. Since when were we supposed to be doing something different? OH! I know, why don't we drag *Undercover Billionaire* out of the closet and see if we can—"

"Reality Check."

"What?" Michael said.

"We only got flack for that project because it was called *Undercover Billionaire*. I wanted to call it *Reality Check*."

"And they rightly hated that title because it said nothing while trying to be clever. It was the Comic Sans of docuseries titles."

"This is supposed to be fun, Michael."

"You're not having fun?"

"*Gator Gitters* is a masterclass in scraping the bottom of the entertainment barrel, so no."

"Okay, I get it, you hate the Gitters more than *The Happening*. But can you be more specific? What is it about today that's making it sound like I need to get you a puppy?"

"Suzanne doesn't want a puppy."

"That's not even close to an answer. Is this about Lou?"

"It's not just about Lou."

"Tell me what happened." Michael was putting on his soothing parent voice.

"Our best footage today was Buck wrestling a rotten log. Except for that colorful little exchange that the network's gonna love, about a father and son apparently giving it to the same girl with a tattoo of two butterflies fucking — I mean, *what does that even look like?*" RJ ranted. "There's the fact that we're down a director, and one cameraman. I'm also pretty sure that Buck was high."

"Seems like a safe assumption."

"And that doesn't bother you?" RJ snapped.

"Do you remember *Tiger King*?"

"Of course I remember fucking *Tiger King*. Please don't tell me that's the bar here."

"I'm not saying it's the bar, RJ, I'm just saying that we're already *in* the Gitter business, so let's see the project through and—"

"I can't even get a moment to breathe with all the bull-shit here, Mikey."

RJ only called him Mikey when he really needed his partner to hear him. He drew a deep breath while awaiting Michael's response, glancing to the right side of the road at a clapboard gas station, its neon sign advertising cigarettes flickering like a beacon in the dark.

"A few more days," Michael replied. "Then we wrap the project and figure out what's next."

"You're not hearing me, man. I don't have a few days. I seriously don't think I can do this."

"What are you suggesting?" Michael finally sounded appropriately concerned.

"Put Damon on it."

"Damon is—"

"*Put Damon on it.*" RJ gave Michael a long beat to marinate in his request. "I'm telling you, I just can't do this anymore. I've hit my limit, and I need you to hear me. I understand that putting Damon in my place is inconvenient while simultaneously insisting that making the move is necessary."

"Let's make sure we're solving for the right problem here and not creating new ones."

"The problem is that I am a creative asset who feels like his talent is being wasted on yet another meaningless project, and that's making me feel like our work no longer matters. I need out on this one so that I can give you my best self for everything else we do."

"I hear you…"

RJ kept quiet as he sped by two men walking down the road. He craned his neck to look back at them, both mostly silhouettes from behind, but one clearly carrying a gas can.

A blink later, he passed an old Chevy Corvette abandoned on the roadside. The sight sparked something inside RJ the second he saw it, though he never could have said what or why.

"Is this really about the series?" Michael finally asked. "Because we pick the next one. Same as it's always been, one for the money and one for us. So tell me, what's different this time?"

"It doesn't feel like it's been one for the money and one

for us, man. It feels like you're always steering the ship now and mistaking passion for dollars."

"That's not fair."

"I think it is. List our last five projects and tell me which one of them I was over the moon about."

"Is this about Suzanne?"

"No. I don't know. Maybe."

"I really do hear you," Michael assured him. "But I don't want to be rash. Let's talk it out. Get a good night's sleep and I promise to listen with an open mind tomorrow. I just want to make sure that you're thinking clearly before we do something expensive and possibly foolhardy. This is awfully sudden, and not like you."

"I've not always been the best about raising my hand and admitting when I need help, but that's what I'm saying to you right now, Mikey. *I feel like I might be breaking and that means I need to—*"

The double beep of a dropped call felt like a punch to the gut. RJ had no idea how long he had been talking to himself. He plucked the phone out of its cradle to see if he could call Michael right back, but that beat of looking away from the road meant that he spied a litter of debris in the road too late.

RJ swerved but plowed over what looked like a piece of broken chair anyway. The phone went flying from his hand.

He pulled over — like he had any other choice — then picked up his phone from the footwell to see that the screen was cracked and the power was gone.

RJ stared down the road, anticipating his trek through an inky darkness filled with alligators and snakes on either side.

He started walking.

Chapter Four

RJ – 2024

RJ WAS desperate for a tow truck, or anyone who might help him get home before he started punching trees. But even if he could get service out in the middle of nowhere, his screen was cracked and the phone still refused to turn on.

He was shit out of luck in the dark, with a long walk before he made it back to that neon sign a few miles back. The night air should have been healing, even sticky as it was, but his brisk steps kept him stewing in an unease he couldn't explain, even more bothered by his situation with the Gitter Boys.

A canopy of trees blocked the moonglow to cast shadows across the black road, like bars across a jail cell. Mosquitos buzzed all around him. The highway was dark, until the rare car whizzed by to cast a thin ribbon of light into the horizon.

An oncoming car lit the Corvette, still abandoned on

the roadside a hundred yards or so in front of him. So he was probably halfway to the gas station. Not too bad.

He picked up his pace, feeling inspired by the sight, but then RJ stopped altogether when he heard a car slowing down behind him.

He turned toward the vehicle — a Ford F-150 — as the passenger side window rolled down to reveal a group of rowdy teenagers, their obnoxious banter barely audible over the deafening blare of Luke Combs singing spring break country through their speakers.

"Hey, man! You need a lift?" asked the driver, who looked like he might not be old enough to shave and was clearly trying to suppress his chuckle.

"I could sure use a ride to the gas station just ahead."

"Well, hop in." The driver returned his nod with a grin.

RJ took a step toward the truck. "Thanks."

"LATER, LOSER!" the cabin full of assholes yelled in a chorus as the F-150 pulled away.

Then the truck was swallowed by darkness.

RJ felt compelled to stop at the Corvette. Even though he also felt exposed, wishing he had his phone to use as a flashlight, he peered into the car's windows. In scant light, the interior looked nothing like the inside of any Corvette RJ had ever seen, boxy with a thick coiled wire coming out. It looked a bit like one of those old CB radios truckers use. Black leather with the Corvette insignia stitched into the headrests, and a dashboard full of retro charm with analog dials and gauges.

RJ could not describe or define his emotions, let alone understand why he was feeling them. Looking into the Corvette was for some reason upsetting his stomach. There was something acutely familiar about it, inside and out. But no matter how long he stared at the vehicle, RJ had no idea where that familiarity might be coming from.

He dismissed it as déjà vu and forced himself to start walking again.

2,191 steps later (according to his watch), RJ reached the gas station. He still couldn't see the name of the place from the outside, but upon entering, he noted a proud looking plaque that announced the shop as Homestead Gas & Goods. A friendly promise the convenience store kept, decorated with memorabilia from the 50s and 60s, vintage metal Coca-Cola signs and adverts for Burma Shave. Plain concrete walls and checkered linoleum floors. The corner jukebox looked recently polished.

There were two men inside, in addition to a friendly-looking clerk. The first man had dark skin, hair, and clothing, his posture rigid, and his manner seeming measured and controlled. The second man had a mop of frazzled brown hair and wild, haunted eyes. RJ made eye contact with the clerk.

"Excuse me, sir, do you have a phone I could use to call a tow?"

"Right over there." He tugged on his beard and nodded to a pay phone on the wall that looked even older than the jukebox.

"Thanks." RJ walked over to the phone, where he experienced something truly out of time, looking through the Yellow Pages for the first time in what had to be fifteen years, at least. He dropped the quarter and dime he was lucky enough to have in his pocket down the slot.

"Excuse me," came a voice from behind him. "Do you have a moment?"

RJ turned around to see the man with wild eyes just as his call started ringing.

"I'm sorry—" RJ started, just as a woman answered his call.

"Cho's Towing."

RJ held up a finger to the stranger.

"I need a tow." RJ turned around to take the call. "I had a blowout."

"Sure thing. Do you know where you are?"

"I'm outside of Homestead Gas & Goods," RJ said, though he couldn't help but perk his ears to the conversation starting between the two other patrons of the mercantile.

"*Wild Wild West* is a masterpiece," said the wild-eyed man.

"You have to be kidding," his companion replied. "That movie is *terrible.*"

"A steampunk western with Denzel Washington, Bill Murray, and Gary Oldman? It's another Spielberg classic."

WHAT?

"*Wild Wild West* had Will Smith and—"

"Will Smith from *The Matrix*?"

Again: *WHAT?*

RJ wanted to hear more, but the person at Cho's towing needed his attention. "Are you on the highway? Do you know the mile marker?"

Goddammit. RJ felt embarrassed. He had barely been driving, letting Siri lead the way, same as he had simply been following Michael.

"I'm sorry. I'll have to ask. I normally just look at my phone." RJ covered the receiver and called out to the clerk, "Excuse me — can you please tell me what the nearest mile marker is?"

"141," he answered with a friendly nod, just as the wild-eyed man turned to his buddy as if affronted.

"The doorknob in *The Sixth Sense* was *blue*, not red."

The man with perfect posture replied, "Red. Same as Cole's sweater and Malcolm's door." He looked to RJ.

Of course the guy was right, so RJ gave him a thumbs up.

"Do you have AAA?" the woman on the phone asked.

"I do!" Finally a win.

"Do you know your membership number?"

"Would you be surprised to learn that I keep it in my phone?"

"Not in the least."

After finishing his transaction, he hung up the phone. Only then, while looking around Homestead Gas & Goods, did RJ realize that the man with the wild eyes had left, along with his buddy.

Then he remembered that those same men had been walking away from the Corvette and his night could not have felt more surreal.

Chapter Five

RJ – 2024

RJ WAS anxious for the tow truck to finally arrive. Not just in a hurry to get the hell home and on with his night, he was dying to know more about the Corvette. He had a ride and the other men didn't, so it would help if his wheels would hurry up and get here. Maybe he could kindly ask the driver to make a short pit stop on the way back to his RAV4.

He'd been thrilled when the woman at Cho's Towing promised that a driver was in the area and his wait would only be 10-15 minutes. He was also fool enough to believe her, bouncing on his heels when Stan's truck spit gravel onto the blacktop a half-hour later.

He ran to the cab, climbed in, slapped the dashboard with an open palm as he identified himself, and boldly asked if they could get going and sort the details later. Stan, a rotund man of at least 350 pounds squeezed behind the steering wheel, appeared delighted by RJ's excitement.

Stan was friendly enough, but an unreliable narrator, at first apologizing for his tardiness by saying that it sometimes seemed like his GPS was replaced by a Ouija board, but then let it slip less than a mile later that he had actually found himself stuck in a "never ending game of Tetris."

RJ started to worry that perhaps they had already passed the Corvette. Everything looked the same and he had no way of knowing. "It's probably not safe to drive much faster than this when it's so dark, right?"

"Vroom-vroom! You wanna go faster?" Stan stepped on the gas. "So what were you doing out here when your tire went kablooey?"

"I was working over in Sawgrass."

That seemed to surprise the hell right out of Stan. "What were you doing in Sawgrass?"

RJ sighed, really not wanting to talk about it. "I'm making a docuseries."

"Oh yeah? Is it about the Civil War? I saw a docuseries about the Civil War one time. It was pretty good. What's your show called?"

None of your fucking business.

"*Gator Gitters*," RJ said without pride. "I'm the producer."

"NO SHIT!" Stan slapped the steering wheel. "I'm buddies with both of 'em! Otis and my old man used to co-host the Mud Olympics senior year of high school, so me and Buck have been like Twinkies and cream since forever."

"Oh."

"You ever thought about having a third on the show?"

"It's called *Gator Gitters*. You're not a Gitter."

"Good point!" Stan slapped the wheel again, thrilled to

have just the open door he was looking for. "What about a reality show about the interesting characters one meets as a tow truck driver?"

"I'm not sure—"

"You'll never believe some of the crazy folks I towed. Once there was this paranormal investigator, looked like Inspector Gadget without all the gadgets. He used one of them old VW things as his ghost hunting mobile or whatever and — OH! There was also this traveling musician and he didn't have no money or Autoclub, so he didn't call, but I saw him on the side of the road and he offered me a concert in trade for a tow. It was only a couple of miles, and the music was pretty good."

They had definitely passed the Corvette. RJ could see his SUV in the distance.

He was more disappointed than he should have been.

He pointed. "That's me, right there."

"Really, it would be like having a bunch of reality shows in one. You got shows about paranormal investigators and maybe even traveling musicians, but in Tow Truck Troubadours, you would get both."

Stan had clearly been thinking about Tow Truck Troubadours long before now. He pulled up behind the SUV and turned to RJ.

"Maybe there could be a quirky beekeeper whose truck is filled with buzzing bees that escaped from their hives during transit."

"Did that really happen?" RJ was humiliated that he felt compelled to ask.

"I said *maybe* there could be one," Stan clarified.

RJ drove home feeling suddenly exhausted, and bothered by the Corvette for reasons he couldn't explain to himself, no matter how many times he turned that question over in his mind throughout the drive.

"Everything okay?" Suzanne asked as he entered, clearly concerned because RJ was two hours later than she expected, without a text.

"Fuck this day twice."

"Can you be any more specific? Or is that and a grunt all I get?"

"Sorry." RJ walked over and kissed her. "I got a flat tire, and that was after we lost Lou."

"How did you lose him?"

"First, over the side of our boat when Buck and Otis were playing dumb and dumber, then again when he quit and threatened to sue the production."

"Did he actually use that word?" Suzanne asked.

"He said we'd be lucky if he didn't sue us, so yes."

"Then you might be needing my services again soon."

"Let's hope not. I love giving you the business when we have it, but I would greatly prefer not needing an attorney right now."

"Do you want to go out and eat?"

"Isn't it kind of late for that?"

"We have leftovers, but getting out of here might help you to calm down."

"I've been dying to get home. Please don't make me leave."

Suzanne laughed. "How about a movie?"

"Sure."

"You sound *super* excited. Would it help if you got to choose?"

"YAY! A movie!" RJ clapped.

"Much better. Any suggestions?"

RJ was about to say no, but then a movie blinked into his mind. "*Back to the Future*."

"*Back to the Future*?" Suzanne repeated. "I love the choice, but it doesn't sound like you."

RJ loved the original, but Suzanne was right in that he usually preferred movies he hadn't seen yet over old favorites. And they had a mountain to watch in their pile. But that Corvette with nodes and wires in the console had apparently put the classic back in his head.

"*Back to the Future* it is," she said when RJ still hadn't replied.

"Hey, do you happen to remember ever seeing a picture of a Corvette with wires and weird shit inside or anything like that? I think I might have seen a replica of something from a movie. Or maybe the actual prop."

"Is that what you're so bothered about?"

RJ nodded. "Do you?"

Suzanne sighed as she looked at him. "Why are you asking?"

"I saw this Corvette on the side of the road about a mile from where I broke down. I peeked inside when I was passing it, because you know I can't help myself, and there wasn't exactly a Flux Capacitor in it, but there was some strange, wired shit in there, and it felt familiar somehow … is this sounding familiar to you at all?"

Suzanne sighed again. "I can't believe you don't remember."

"Are you going to tell me what it is that I don't remember?"

"Only if you promise not to bring my mother into whatever it is you're planning right now."

The truth plowed right into him. "It was John Titor's car."

"A *replica* of John Titor's car. Probably from some deranged fan."

She sounded suddenly colder, perhaps even on her way to pissed off, like she always was when it came to her mother.

The two men in the gas station and their crazy conversation about movies.

Which maybe wasn't crazy after all, if one of them was a time traveler from an alternate timeline. Except that *no*, the men were obviously *playing* Titor because anything else was batshit crazy.

"I'll take a raincheck on the movie." RJ was already on his way to the office. "And leftovers sound great!"

He sat at his desk, found images of Titor's Corvette online, then a few keystrokes later, his heart pounding with a new yet familiar excitement, he gave his partner a call. The Titor story had always been undoable because it didn't have an end. But with that strange conversation in the gas station and the wild eyes on that man … What if …?

"Dude," RJ said when Michael answered, "I need you to meet me for a drink."

Chapter Six

RJ – 2024

THE SEAHORSE WAS an old bar with a facelift. It still had wood paneled walls and rustic furniture, now made ironic with modern touches like handsome art and neon signs. A bar lined with craft beer on tap and a back shelf filled with rarer bottles. The jukebox and pool table were both unblemished, polished and gleaming beneath strings of exposed lights that crisscrossed the ceiling.

Approximately equidistant from their homes, with a warm but never overwhelming atmosphere, this was RJ and Michael's place. But tonight Michael had brought Damon along. Normally, RJ had zero issues with their new producer, but tonight he needed to talk with his partner.

"Hey, Damon. Good to see you." RJ's tone and body language conspired to say otherwise.

"It looks like you two might have something to talk about, so I'm going to order a Miami Vice." Damon offered RJ an uncertain smile and walked off toward the bar.

"It's half strawberry daiquiri and half piña colada," Michael explained.

"I know what a Miami Vice is."

"Maybe you should order one. You seem *muy* agitated."

"Don't do that." RJ shook his head. "I hate when you do that."

"State the obvious?"

"Your Spanglish bullshit. It's insulting."

"You do it all the time," Michael argued.

"My parents were born in Juarez—"

"How about a margarita?"

"Is that a joke?" RJ asked.

"Depends on if you think it was funny. You said you wanted to meet for a drink, but I got the distinct impression then, and am still getting it now, that you actually wanted to meet so you could bitch about something. So please, bitch, I'm listening."

"I don't want to 'bitch' about anything."

"You mean right now this minute? Because the other night you doubled-down on bitching, so—"

"Is it *bitching* for me to tell you how I'm feeling?"

"No. But it was bitchin' when we were still at film school making plans for our future together, and we agreed that I would handle the business side and you would handle the creative, because that's where each of us can shine the most."

"It was different back then."

"What was different about it, RJ? Please tell me."

"The work meant something, and I believed that you cared about that."

"I do care about it," Michael argued. "But that doesn't mean I have to care about it in the same way that

you do. *Reel Deceit* did exactly what it was supposed
to do."

"Get us kicked out?"

"Get us into the festivals and onto distributors. We
were on a nice run until we hit that snag, and then that
other snag, followed by—"

"I know the history of Genuine Lens Productions,
thank you. But I think we should have a conversation
about—"

"*Another* conversation."

"—where Genuine Lens is going."

"You act like I'm dragging you through our projects."

"Do you think that maybe that's how I'm feeling? All
you want to do is more 'women in trouble' true crime
bullshit—"

"It doesn't have to be bullshit."

"—or even worse dreck like *Gator Gitters*."

"RJ. Tell me what the fuck you want and we can have a
conversation about it. You didn't want true crime, so I got
us an alternative. We have to pay the bills before we can
grow Genuine Lens."

"I used to be proud of our name. It embarrasses me
that *Gator Gitters* is—"

"Give me a pitch, compadre."

"*Me gustaria que te crecieran un par de cojones y algo de autoes-
tima. Compadre.*"

"Is that your pitch?" Michael asked with a shrug. "It
sounds pretty cool."

"I want to do John Titor."

Michael laughed, but the sound wasn't pleasant. "I
have to say the same thing now as I said the last time you
pitched this: Titor is a non-starter. That story has been
done more times than *A Christmas Carol*. And despite all the
projects out there, nothing new has ever been uncovered,

unless you're telling me that Suzanne's mother is finally willing to—"

"No. That one's a non-starter for me … I want to work on something that doesn't make me feel like my life is going in the wrong direction. Something that I'm not going to wish I could travel back in time to erase when I'm on my deathbed."

"Then hit me with another pitch. *Otra vez por favor.*" Michael raised his eyebrows. "Is it Spanglish if the entire sentence *es en Español?*"

"It is if your Spanish is only the meat in a torta with English as the bread."

"You mean *el pan.*"

"So, just to clarify," RJ redirected, "we're not even going to discuss the possibility of a John Titor project, even though I'm telling you that I have a new angle."

"Unless you've persuaded Suzanne's mother to talk, then, yes, this is the end of it."

"End of what?" Damon asked, back with his Miami Vice.

"The end of a conversation that never got started," RJ replied.

Damon took a sip and tried again. "About what?"

Michael rolled his eyes. "About John Titor."

"Who's that?"

"Uh-oh." Michael made a face. "You should probably buckle up. This is going to take a while."

RJ kept a long story with endless details mercifully short to prove his partner wrong. "John Titor is the name of a man who made some forum posts in the early 2000s claiming to be from the year 2036."

"But they didn't have iPhones in their future yet," Michael interjected.

RJ ignored the interruption. "Titor told of a tomorrow

where Americans went through a civil war, which was followed by a world war. The U.S. was so destroyed that our culture became closer to life at the OK Corral than the future we have *with iPhones* today."

"You mean the present," Michael corrected.

Damon stopped sipping, seeming seriously interested. "If it was like the Old West, then how did they have enough technology for time travel?"

Michael rolled his eyes on cue. "You're encouraging him?"

"Good question." RJ nodded. "According to what Titor posted in the forums, even though the general population went backward in time, there were still some massive breakthroughs in science."

"Why did he travel back in time?"

"Jesus Christ." Michael laughed.

"Titor was part of a time travel program. He supposedly went back into the 1970s to get a particular computer that he said would help rebuild the infrastructure of the country."

"An old computer from back when computers sucked was going to help rebuild America's infrastructure?" Damon looked dubious.

Michael nodded in approval. "Now you're getting it."

"And if he went back to the 70s, why was he posting in the early 2000s? Was he an old guy by then?"

"Because he made a stop on the way back to his own time to connect with his family and prepare them for the wars to come."

"Wars that never happened," Michael said.

"Because the alternate world lines—"

"The thing was one hundred percent a hoax."

"I think I saw his time machine. The Corvette. When my tire blew the other night."

"Have you lost your mind?" Michael exploded.

But RJ couldn't stop, now that his confession was underway. "I walked to this gas station that was stuck in a 1950's time warp, and they were arguing about *Wild Wild West*. One guy was saying it was a Spielberg movie starring Denzel Washington, and the other guy—"

"Stop. Just stop." Michael glared at RJ. "I get it, *Gator Gitters* is driving you loco, amigo."

"Fuck you." He wished now that he hadn't said anything. He could make this documentary on his own.

Damon broke the awkward silence by slurping the last of his Miami Vice.

RJ stood to leave.

But then Michael said something that seemed to surprise all three of them. "Help Damon take over *Gator Gitters* and find a way to get Suzanne's mom involved. If you can do that, I promise our next project can be about John Titor."

Chapter Seven

RJ – 2024

RJ KNEW the true work on this project involved countless hours sitting at his desk.

But first he wanted to revisit Homestead Gas & Goods to ask about the two strangers, seeing as the most expedient way of debunking his theory would be to discover that the guys were crazy locals, though of course RJ was hoping for the opposite.

The clerk shook his head. "Never seen 'em before."

"Can you tell me where they were going?"

"I could. But I won't."

"I'm sorry?"

"No need to apologize. And that goes for both of us. You have your reasons for asking, and I figure since I don't know you from them and they might not want me to say anything, it's best if I don't."

"What if I said it was important?"

The clerk shrugged. "Couldn't help you anyway. Don't know where they went."

"Fair enough," RJ replied after a long moment where he could think of nothing else.

"Have you tried the Gator Bits?" The clerk nodded to a display of bags filled with caramel-colored snacks by the register. "They're great for munching on the go."

They also looked great for accelerating the onset of diabetes.

"No, thank you," RJ replied.

ONE DEAD END CONFIRMED, RJ returned to his computer, where he knew he'd spend the rest of the day.

Following a full read of Titor's posts, RJ felt the tickle of ambition and creativity rubbing together, that inspired feeling he hadn't had in far too long. He did what any decent documentarian would do while attempting to untangle an enigmatic story involving a time traveler from the future by starting with whatever archival footage he could possibly find. He spent far too many hours watching old news clips about the Titor story, though none of them came even remotely close to saying anything new about the legend — Michael was right about that.

RJ kept going, undeterred as he sifted through YouTube, hoping to uncover fresh perspectives or perhaps unearth some previously tucked away gem from the digital mines. But he'd already seen most of it the last time he'd jumped down the Titor rabbit hole, and it had all been debunked or proven unprovable.

John Titor's military symbol had first surfaced on the Time Travel Institute forums on November 2, 2000, from a poster calling himself TimeTravel_0. In January 2001, the pseudonym emerged, when TimeTravel_0 began posting on the Art Bell BBS Forums as John Titor. His last post was at the end of March, 2001. Across an ungodly amount of entries between those dates, Titor consistently alleged that he was an American soldier from the year 2036, stationed in Tampa, Florida, as part of a government time-travel project, sent back to 1975 to secure an IBM 5100 computer: a simple piece of technology that ran both APL and BASIC programming languages, the unit was essential for fixing numerous legacy computer programs in 2036 that led to the UNIX year 2038 problem.

According to Titor, he was specifically chosen for the mission because of his paternal grandfather's direct involvement in the assembly and programming of the original machine. He offered detailed information about the computer's unpublished features, leading to some speculation that a computer scientist might have been manufacturing the intrigue.

RJ looked up the names of the team members, but none of them had the last name Titor. He made a note to find out their children and grandchildren's names in his research notebook.

Titor said his stop in the year 2000 was for personal reasons: to recover photographs lost in a future civil war and to spend time with his family, a topic dear to his heart and frequently discussed. But he'd never given enough details to track them down.

He stopped on a YouTube thumbnail of an old man donning a literal tinfoil hat, his eyes wide and manic. The caption read: TRUE FACT: I MET JOHN TITOR IN PERSON: 2001 CENTRAL PARK ENCOUNTER. Even if Temporal Tom's story was totally ridiculous (and how could it not be), the thumbnail alone made it a no-questions *click*.

RJ listened intently as Tom spent twenty minutes

setting the stage. RJ was afraid to skip ahead and risk missing a moment. Tom finally got to the point, telling his 74 subscribers that he met Titor first in a seedy bar, and then later with a group of fellow miscreants in Central Park. According to Tom, he and Titor had deep conversations about an impending civil war, quantum physics, and hidden truths of the universe.

But then RJ had researched Tom's past, and it turned out he had a criminal record. But not just any criminal record: he had been part of a heist to steal the IBM 5100 in 1975, which was exactly what Titor claimed to be doing.

RJ wondered why no other reporters had covered the story, until he saw that Tom had only started posting his videos three months ago, meaning he might be the only one onto this angle … so far.

The video ended and RJ was about to click the next one. But then Suzanne entered the room and saw what was on his screen and he felt a full-bodied flush of embarrassment. He'd told her about the conversation with the two men in the gas station, and while she hadn't laughed outright at him, she hadn't exactly been convinced by RJ's theory that one of them was Titor.

People have bad memories. They do drugs. They have mental illnesses that cause them to hallucinate. Or they're just downright weird, and they don't care what other people think of them.

Suzanne caught sight of his screen and started laughing. "Seriously? Tinfoil hat people? Have you considered that you might have hit a dead end?"

He chuckled along with her, trying to downplay his interest in Temporal Tom. "It hasn't been all tinfoil hats, you know." It was a weak defense, so RJ laughed at himself.

"Did you find what you were looking for?"

"Nothing definitive." Although he wasn't sure what

would be definitive, at this point. Only that the tingle in his gut that told him he had to keep digging.

"Why don't you tell me about some of the non-tinfoil stuff that you found. Even if it's old. I want to hear the stuff you can't ignore."

"I just really love some of the things he posted." He was still a little embarrassed, but clicked over to his notes and read from the top of where he'd collected some of his favorite Titor quotes anyway. "Like, *You do not rewrite history. I can only affect what happens here just as easily as you can. Why do people in this time period worry so much about time travelers destroying their worldline when they have no problem doing it themselves every day?*"

"Well, he does have a point." Suzanne smiled. "We are excellent at messing up our own world and sure as hell don't need any help from any time travelers."

"*My goal is not to be believed. Most people do not take news of the war very well, but I find that everyone believes it's inevitable. Even in your own history, are not great inventions and discoveries made during a time of war in your effort to kill and maim in new and more efficient ways?*"

"Dark but true." She nodded. "What else you got?"

"This one is because he supposedly worked for GE and—"

"I'm well aware of the story."

"Sorry." RJ offered her a sheepish smile. "Anyway, Titor said, *No, I do not work for GE or any other company. Are 'stock tips' really the first thing you want to know about in the future? As a representative of your time period, do you realize what that says about you? You should probably know that this time is not remembered for its selflessness, charity, or ability to work together.*"

"Another solid observation from future boy." Suzanne sat next to RJ and rested her head on his shoulder before she said, "More ..."

So RJ read as the sky darkened outside, painting a picture of the enigmatic figure claiming to be John Titor, despite Suzanne's familiarity with his blend of prophetic warnings, philosophical musings, and intricate technical details.

It was kind of her to support him. Not only did Suzanne know everything there was to know about Titor, that case had ruined her mother's career. Her being there with him, supporting RJ despite his choice of topic, was special.

But still he couldn't wait for Suzanne to leave, so he could click on that next video from Temporal Tom.

Chapter Eight

RJ – 2024

RJ SAT much straighter in his seat this morning, but he was still having a hard time making his argument to Michael, considering it contradicted the core of everything he had been saying about the Gitters since the very beginning.

"Damon has it." RJ glanced at the GPS and saw the same thing as his last glance: still on track, still seventeen more miles to go. "It's not that big a deal."

"You keep saying that. Both that Damon has it, and that your sudden absence isn't a big deal, same for our new producer handling what you keep promising won't be a problem — even though you've also been complaining about how hard the Gitters are to control from day one."

He wasn't wrong, and RJ couldn't really argue, so Michael kept going. "It also seems like a hearty coincidence that you were *just* telling me how fed up you were with everything, and asking if Damon could take over production. So why don't you level with me, RJ? Tell me where you're going. Because we both know it has some-thing to do with Titor. The conditions of that project included you helping Damon get acclimated on *Gator Gitters*, not just dumping him there and running off!"

Of course it had something to do with Titor.

RJ was on his way to meet Temporal Tom in person. He'd been up before the sun, and on the road for a full hour and a half before he finally stirred up the courage to give Michael a call.

"I'm following a lead."

"Is it Suzanne's mom?"

"Her name is Cecilia. If you're going to keep constantly bringing her up, you should probably start using her name."

"So that's a negative. You know that whatever you found on YouTube isn't really a lead, right?"

"You make it look so easy, rolling two assumptions right into the one."

"Did your lead come from YouTube?"

"Even if it did, that doesn't mean—"

"So that's a yes. Why can't you just be straight with me?"

"Because you say shit like, *You know that whatever you found on YouTube isn't really a lead, right?*"

"That's not how I sound."

"Sorry," RJ said with another unnecessary glance at the GPS. "I'll work on my asshole impression."

"I'll help Damon with the Gitters. For today. Now can you please tell me where you're going?"

"I promise you a full report when I get back. But I'm almost there and I need to clear my head."

"Doesn't Suzanne do that for you?"

He answered Michael by killing the call.

Pulling up to the house, RJ wondered how much he

would really be telling his partner. Tom's shack was old and neglected, with peeling paint and a slanted roof with piles of trash and discarded junk — from broken furniture to cardboard boxes and other detritus — scattered about a yard overgrown with weeds and blocking his path to the entrance.

It got worse after RJ made his way to the porch. He didn't even get to knock before the door exploded open and Temporal Tom, looking even more grizzled than he did in his videos, threw his gaze across the yard like a fly fisherman casting his line into the river. And though it was not exactly unexpected, RJ still felt deeply disappointed to see that Tom answered his door while wearing an honest to God tinfoil hat.

"Were you followed?" Tom asked after he finished coughing up a lung.

RJ shook his head. "Definitely not."

"Hurry up." Tom ordered him inside as he started to violently cough again.

RJ entered and felt another uncomfortable wave of *Michael might be right.*

Tom shut his front door and handed him a tinfoil hat.

RJ shook his head. "I'm not sure I need that."

"No one thinks they need one until they find themselves in the crosshairs of an international battle for control." Tom turned to a stuffed parrot glued to a perch in the corner, as if expecting it to agree.

"Is that where you are?"

"I wear a hat." Tom walked into the living room and swept a tall stack of binders off the nearest loveseat and onto the floor. "Are the cameras still coming?"

"There are no cameras today. Just me."

"I thought you said you were making a documentary. That's why I agreed to talk." He tugged on his beard, looking over at the parrot again in frustration: *Can you believe this shit?* "I don't just give away conversations for free."

"It's a docuseries. And discovery is the first step. Cameras come later."

"This is for the Discovery Channel?" He brightened. "I was sure they hated my idea."

"Discovery is what we call this part of the process, happening right now, where we determine whether your story is credible."

"Who's *we*? I only see you."

"My partner, Michael."

"Partner like you're gay?"

"Partner like we run a production company together."

"I don't give a shit where you put it, I'm just trying to discover you too." Tom pointed to the freshly cleared loveseat after stealing a glance at the parrot. "Go ahead and sit so you can decide if I'm lying."

RJ took a seat. "You said in your video that there were things you couldn't put on YouTube."

Temporal Tom pointed to his tinfoil hat for confirmation.

"Great. Would you like to tell me any of those things now?"

"I was recruited by John Titor." Tom offered RJ a definitive nod and started coughing again.

"Yes. You said that in your video. Do you have anything additional?"

"Titor claimed to be from the future. He told me I'd get caught for a crime I hadn't committed yet." Tom finished with a hard stop.

After a long pause, RJ said, "That's the story you told in your video. Is there anything else?"

"Shit." Another look at the parrot while coughing. "Of course there's more."

"Like…"

"You're the one asking the questions!"

"Why did you believe him? That he was from the future."

"He knew my name, even though no one had called me that in forever."

"You mean Tom?"

"No. Everyone used to call me Goober when I was a kid."

RJ didn't understand. "That sounds like the past instead of the future."

"He said people would start calling me that again. And sure enough they did, whether I wanted them to or not. It was even on my arrest record."

"Goober?"

"That's right."

RJ wasn't really understanding. "What else do you—"

"I was the driver in his heist."

"When did you know that the man you met in New York was the same John Titor who was posting on the forums all those years later?"

"You ever meet *two* John Titors?"

"I've met more than one Goober." The other goobers just didn't usually call themselves that. "Any other reason?"

"Both guys talked the same way. Especially all that stuff about our second civil war here in the States, starting around 2005. Something to do with 'order and rights.' Civil unrest during a presidential election that led to some Waco-type event every month. Things kept getting worse until the whole world was at war a few years later. America got split into five regions after that."

"And the details were the same?"

"Exactly," Goober said.

Intriguing, but all of it was still public knowledge.

"He said the civil war supposedly raged for ten years," Goober added.

"What happened then?" Of course RJ knew.

"World War III." He tried to whistle, but it led to him coughing. "Went fast."

"Except that it didn't. None of that happened."

"Probably cuz Titor stopped it."

"Right." RJ nodded. "And how did all this motivate you to steal a computer?"

"He paid me to steal the computer."

RJ could hear Michael saying *I told you so* in the back of his head. He ignored it.

"Did Titor tell you the cause of the third World War?"

"He didn't really say nothing about it in person, seeing as he was mostly focused on heisting IBM. And he was vague in his posts, something about hostilities led by border clashes and overpopulation."

RJ nodded again. "But none of that happened, because Titor stopped it."

"That's what I'd like to believe, seeing as I did my part, but Titor also claimed that the Everett-Wheeler model of quantum physics was correct."

RJ was stunned that Tom had even heard of the Everett-Wheeler model of quantum physics, let alone that he'd remember the name to say it. "You're talking about multiverses."

"The many-worlds interpretation," Tom agreed. "According to Titor, time travel causes a new timestream to form. He called it a worldline."

"That sure makes his claims impossible to disprove. Everything that doesn't happen the way he predicts, it's because he changed it in this one." Now RJ sounded like Michael.

"He ain't looking for you to believe 'im." And Goober sounded like RJ. In theory.

"Tell me something about Titor that you've never told anyone." RJ didn't like how close he was to begging. "What was he like? As a person?"

"He sure was into movies," Tom said. "He was constantly quoting them."

There it was. "What kinds of movies?"

"We thought he was crazy. Talking about these movies that didn't exist. But turned out most were things that came out later, in the Eighties and Nineties." Tom grinned. "I went to see every one he mentioned after I got out of jail."

"Were they the same as he described them?"

"Apparently his worldline didn't have Keanu Reeves in it."

Which didn't prove anything. So he tried one more question. "What did he look like?"

"Some kinda light-skinned brown — like you."

"Latino?"

"Curly, brown hair, looked like he almost never combed it," Goober said. "Dark circles under his eyes, even though he was charming as hell. And there was something … haunted about him."

All RJ could think was: *I met John Titor.*

Chapter Nine

RJ – 2024

FLORIDA WAS a hotbed for Titor conspiracists (that was apparently why Temporal Tom lived there), and RJ had another planned stop on his way back. One he would be happy to tell Michael all about, even if he ended up keeping the visit with Goober to himself. He was fifty-fifty upon leaving the shack, but the closer RJ got to the university, the closer he was to only mentioning his second stop and making it sound more epic than whatever it turned out to be. Worthy of a full day away from the Gitters.

Professor Jeremy Fisher opened the door to a pristine wood-paneled office. The man was in his sixties and every bit the cliché as Goober, albeit in a flavor with fewer nuts. A distinguished man in a tweed jacket and bifocals. An overstuffed chair sat behind a wooden desk surrounded by shelves of books and personal knickknacks amid many potted plants.

"I'm excited for our chat." Fisher invited him in with a

smile, but RJ didn't think it would have looked any more performative even if the cameras had been rolling. The professor surely knew what discovery was, but also saw their conversation as an audition.

The author of *Behind the Vortex: The Science of John Titor* was a documented publicity hound.

RJ couldn't help laughing as he sat on the subordinate side of Fisher's desk.

"Care to share?" The professor offered RJ another performative smile.

"I was just thinking about what a difference this office is from the last place I visited."

"Another Titor scholar, I presume?"

"Something like that." RJ laughed again.

"Do you mind if I ask who?"

"Just someone on a video."

Fisher looked at him … waiting.

"His name was Temporal Tom," RJ said.

"Ah. The uneducated ramblings of a man who can't parse conspiracy from backwater ignorance."

No laughing from RJ that time. And also, fuck Fisher.

"I was hoping you can tell me what your research says about who John Titor was personally."

Fisher laughed like a man kindly not pointing out that he had been asked a stupid question. "Titor was an enigma, and he worked hard to keep it that way."

"But he talked about his family, his one true love, his life in the future."

"He was careful only to reveal enough to paint a picture of the future that would inspire us in the present." Fisher leaned forward and laced his hands together on his desk. "Think about it. The Butterfly Effect. His mission had to be surgical, changing the minimum needed to create the future he was aiming for. Extraneous information, no matter how innocently offered, could've had devastating effects."

"Did he ever mention anything about movies in his posts?"

"Movies?" Fisher looked insulted. "What do you mean?"

"Movies," RJ replied, standing his ground. "Like *Casablanca*. *The Matrix*. *The Breakfast Club*. One of my sources said he liked talking about them."

Fisher stared at him for a moment. "I thought you were a documentarian."

"I'm coming at it from a different angle than most."

"No matter what your angle, you'll need to explain to your viewers how time travel works." He leaned back in his chair with gleaming eyes. But unlike Goober, he had no beard to stroke.

"The C204 time displacement unit, a fascinating concept indeed. According to Titor, this technology was developed by General Electric in 2034. It works by creating a 'vortex' or 'singularity'" — Fisher made the air quotes while over pronouncing each one — "in space-time through the use of a circulating beam of protons. By manipulating the energy and gravity of this vortex, one can travel both backward and forward in time."

Smarmy bastard. But RJ decided to keep him talking. Maybe he'd accidentally let something slip that would actually be useful.

"So, this time machine was powered by two micro singularities, right? Created by feeding atomic particles into a 'miniature black hole'?" RJ made the air quotes too.

"Exactly!" The gesture seemed to delight him. "These micro singularities produce a significant amount of energy, which in turn allows the time machine to achieve faster-than-light speeds — a crucial element for time travel."

"And do you find Titor's theories credible?"

Fisher paused as if deep in thought about a question he had answered countless times before he finally exhaled. "As I stated in my book, while Titor's ideas may sound far-fetched, the concepts themselves are not beyond the realm of possibility. Theoretical physics has explored the potential for creating artificial black holes, and manipulating space-time is an area of extensive study."

"But science has so far seen no practical application or tangible evidence, correct?"

"There was no human flight until after the Wright Brothers."

"What about Titor claiming to time travel by car. Can you explain that, or was old Johnny inspired by Robert Zemeckis?"

Fisher chuckled, tickling his own butt with the seat of his chair as he wiggled around in the spotlight, probably imagining how this would all play out on the little screen later.

"Yes, that is certainly an unusual detail. Titor described his time machine as being installed in a 1967 Chevrolet Corvette, which is a rather peculiar choice. But it's important to remember that the vehicle itself is not the time machine, but rather serves as the housing for the 'C204 time displacement unit.'" Again with the finger quotes. "In theory, any vehicle or container could be used. It would just have to accommodate the necessary equipment."

"So, it's not about the car itself, but the technology inside it."

"Correct. The car is merely a vessel for the time displacement unit. Titor's vintage choice might have been a personal preference, or perhaps to avoid drawing attention as he traveled through various periods."

"So, if the Earth is moving around the sun, why

doesn't the time machine end up in space when it moves to a different day or year — what if there is a building in the exact spot he's traveling to? Does he end up inside a wall?"

"Ah, excellent questions!" Fisher might have gotten a boner. "Titor's time machine was supposedly equipped with a 'variable gravity lock' system designed to allow the unit to remain stationary relative to the Earth's gravitational field, even as it traveled through time and space."

He leaned forward. "Titor claimed that this system was necessary to ensure that the unit did not appear in a different location on Earth when traveling through time. No materializing inside a wall or getting stranded in space."

"And how did this 'variable gravity lock' system work?" RJ made air quotes again, sure that Fisher had no idea he was being mocked.

"It was controlled by a set of computers programmed to maintain a bubble of null gravity around the time machine, allowing the unit to remain stationary, relative to the Earth's surface, even as it traveled through time. So, by essentially pinging forward, the system could tell if there was a gravity change in the destination, like one created by a building, and return to the last safe location on its journey. Quite a clever way to ensure a safe arrival between epochs, wouldn't you agree?"

"Honestly, it's a bit too much science for me."

Fisher laughed. "Let me put it this way: Titor used black holes to travel through time and gravity to stay safe."

"What would that look like?"

"Of course." Fisher grinned. "I believe what you're looking for is the cool bubble around his Chevy that picked up some of the ground beneath him upon departure, meaning that our time traveling hero was always leaving a bad-ass crater behind on his way."

Fisher paused for a moment, then added, "Speaking to the masses requires a certain level of ... oversimplification."

RJ wanted to go before the guy tried to sell him a book, but he had one more question, same as the one he asked Goober. "Have you ever come across any descriptions of his appearance?"

Fisher looked at him like he was a moron. "He traveled through time to stop World War III."

"I'm just wondering—"

"Plenty of crackpots claimed to have seen him, but Titor would've disguised himself. He was too smart to let anyone recognize him."

"How would they have recognized him if he hadn't been born yet?"

"He knew that any evidence he left behind — even an observer's description — had the potential to change history in ways he couldn't predict. I address all of that in *Behind the Vortex: The Science of John Titor*. Would you care to buy a copy?" Fisher laughed. "You'll be lucky enough to have an autographed edition, no extra charge. Might be worth even more after your docuseries comes out."

Or not.

Chapter Ten

RJ – 2024

RJ WAS BACK ON SET, wishing he was anywhere else, assuming that anywhere else was a place where he could dig deeper into the Titor story in peace.

Damon was putting in a valiant effort to fill his shoes for sure, hands-on and proactive in the best possible way, asking excellent questions and acting on whatever answers RJ was willing to give him. But RJ was having a hard time showing up for Damon — he couldn't help stealing minutes to read what he could from Fisher's book, hoping to find some other detail whose significance Fisher didn't recognize but that RJ somehow might.

A dangerous thought — considering once RJ acknowledged a single nugget as reality, he might as well admit to the possibility of a glittering mine full of truths. So he wasn't yet ready to admit his thoughts about the project to Michael, but for the first time, RJ was feeling an inkling of impossible certainty.

Not that he could take the show there. For their docuseries to have any serious weight, he would for sure have to play the hoax angle.

It worried him that he didn't want to. He knew better than to drink the Kool-Aid that his interviewees offered. But seeing that car by the road, and that out of time conversation about *Wild Wild West* (and *The Sixth Sense* as a comedy?) — what if he'd seen the proof that the whole world had been looking for?

"You're doing great," he assured Damon as the new producer prepared to take the crew out, filming for the day. RJ planned to stay in his temporary office near the edge of the swamp, mapping out a timeline on the wall. Not that Damon needed to know that. "Michael and I couldn't be happier that you're here."

"Thanks," Damon replied, sounding like he wanted to say something else. Maybe a few things.

RJ would make it up to him, once he got the timeline out of his head. It was starting to squeeze him like a vice.

Five minutes after finishing, while he was still standing in front of the Titor timeline and studying his work, Suzanne entered the office.

He was delighted to see her.

"You look happy."

RJ grinned. "I am happy."

"Is that because you're working on things that you're not supposed to be working on?" Suzanne glanced at the timeline. "Like that."

"I talked to the author of *Behind the Vortex: The Science of John Titor* today. He was a Frasier Crane with none of the punchlines, but I started reading his book and the science is interesting."

"Yes." Suzanne agreed, but not really. "Science fiction can be interesting."

"You're not taking me seriously."

"I'm surprised that you're taking *this* seriously." Another glance at the timeline. "I don't want Michael to be right any more than you do, Ramon, but it looks to me like you might be making it easy for him."

"It's not my fault that the resources for this story are so limited. I would love to be interviewing true scholars on the subject instead of crackpots and pompous assholes. I have no hook … maybe if—"

"No, RJ."

"You didn't even let me finish."

"Are you going to surprise me? Or do I know exactly what question you're going to ask next?"

"I could surprise you."

Suzanne stared at him.

"Would it really hurt to ask her?" RJ finally said.

"We have a job to do. Lou has filed a lawsuit. We need to make a plan. I understand the obsession, believe me, I've seen the show, and you know how it can be with my mother."

"Fine." But RJ was fully deflated.

Enough to unseat Suzanne. She drew a breath after a short but awkward silence. "I do have somebody I can give you. Not Mom, but a family friend."

"Have you met this family friend before?"

"A few times. Mom met him during the investigation."

"And you never told me about this guy?" RJ was grinning.

"I'm sure you can understand why." Suzanne didn't return his smile.

"Maybe you could explain it to me."

"Jesus, RJ." She clearly didn't want to discuss it. "We were constantly fighting because you wouldn't stop hinting about talking with my mom. And I'm pretty sure you still have no idea how annoying those 'hints' were getting."

"I have an idea," RJ admitted.

"And you were hitting the crackpot angle much too hard at the time for me to introduce you to a family friend. We had just started dating. It was too much, too fast."

"Thank you. And sorry. I appreciate the connect. Who is the guy?"

"He was one of the admins on Art Bell's post to post forum. His name is Bennie Moore."

"How does he fit in? What's his story? Or should I just wait to hear it from him?" RJ smiled at Suzanne again, hoping that this time she might smile back.

She finally did. "Talk to Bennie. He's not a crackpot or a scientist, but he was there for the whole thing. Bennie's not the kind of guy who's likely to change, so I'm sure he'll enjoy telling you the truth as he sees it. I do get the paradox of this story, and why it can't technically be disproven, regardless of how ridiculous the assertions might be. So I also get that you need a good hook. Hopefully Bennie can help you find the angle you're looking for."

"Thanks, Suzanne. That's—"

"Where's the medic?" Damon exploded through the office door in a panic.

"What's wrong?" asked RJ and Suzanne in unison.

"Buck is acting stranger than usual, and—"

"He's high," RJ explained. "Buck is always high."

"Please don't acknowledge that out loud," said Suzanne.

Damon shook his head. "He's not high. This isn't just stranger, it's different. I don't think it's from the drugs at all … though I doubt they helped with his dehydration."

"He probably has heatstroke. Let's go." RJ left Suzanne with a kiss on the cheek before following Damon out the door.

It slammed shut behind them as Damon said, "And a gator ate one of the drones."

Of course it did.

Chapter Eleven

RJ – 2024

IT WAS dark by the time RJ and Suzanne closed the front door behind them.

They were both exhausted from dealing with what had turned into a full afternoon of chaos. The kind of moodily humid night when neither one of them would want to do anything other than order some DoorDash and crawl into bed.

"I'm opening a bottle of wine," Suzanne announced on her way into the kitchen. She kept talking, calling out as RJ made his way into the living room and clattering about in the kitchen for a corkscrew. "I think I understand it better now … your ennui."

"Thank you?" RJ sat on the couch.

Suzanne entered the living room and took a seat next to him, giving them each a generous pour into a fat bottomed goblet. "What do you say we give Bennie a call?"

"You mean right now?"

"No time like the present. Unless you're John Titor, then you can be polyamorous with the past and the future as well."

"I'm glad you're starting to see the appeal. I usually send an email or something first. It feels rude to just call, even if you have the number."

"I love that you're such a considerate man, which is just one of the reasons why I texted Bennie earlier today and asked him if he wouldn't mind giving my overly curious boyfriend who has no plans to drop the Titor topic any time soon a few minutes of his time tonight."

RJ laughed. "Just a few minutes?"

"We have a Zoom link." Suzanne took a sip, then grabbed her phone and swiped a few times, smiling at her man as she said, "I love how excited you look right now!"

His phone buzzed with the link, then he grinned while he grabbed his laptop and logged in. A few blinks of buffering, then a man with a wide grin and a graying beard appeared onscreen.

"Bennie!" Suzanne exclaimed, with far more glee than RJ had anticipated. "It's great to see you!"

"Your mother told me about those kidney stones a few months ago." Bennie shook his head. "I'm so sorry."

"It was total bullshit. Do you have any idea how much water I drink?" Then at RJ's look, she mumbled, "*I told you we were family friends.*"

"Thank you for agreeing to meet with me, Mr. Moore—"

"Bennie."

"—but Suzanne said that you might be willing to answer some questions about John Titor and all of that nuttiness on the Art Bell forums back in 2000."

"Those were exciting times for sure." Bennie leaned back in his seat with a glow of nostalgia. "The internet was just taking off, giving us human interaction in truly anonymous spaces for the first time. Of course, that also opened the door for plenty of nonsense."

"Nonsense like what?" RJ asked.

"Hoaxes, people pretending to be all sorts of things. I could be a purple dinosaur made of mushrooms or the Flying Spaghetti Monster if I decided to be, and if I posted enough times with enough conviction, there would eventually be folks posting to champion my claim."

"Is that what happened with Titor?"

"Whether or not John Titor was who he claimed to be, he had plenty of supporters on the forums."

"How did you end up there?"

"I had been an occasional listener of Bell's show for years. Until I heard a story about a guy who claimed to have a bottomless hole on his property. Mel's hole. You heard of it?"

RJ slid a look at Suzanne, but she just kept looking at her clearly close friend.

"I got hooked from that episode on. So I guess you could have called me a reluctant fan."

"Were you there for Titor's first post?" Suzanne asked.

"Nope." He shook his head. "Just missed it. He initially posted as Time Travel_0, but I was there for every one of the days he was online during his three months on our forum. Like I said, exciting times."

"What made them so exciting? I get that it was a different time, but it wasn't *that* different. What made the John Titor character so ... magnetic?"

Bennie smiled. He looked almost wistful. "I guess it was that he seemed *so credible*. A lot of us thought his line was bullshit, but we were all having so much fun with it anyway. Titor answered every question about the future without ever getting rattled. Cool like Samuel Jackson licking a snow cone."

Suzanne laughed. "I love you, Bennie."

"You too, kiddo." He gave her a wink.

"Did you ever believe him?" RJ asked.

Bennie laughed. "I don't quite know how to answer that. Because on one hand, of course not, but on the other one, after those first few months…" He laughed again. "Ever heard of Ong's Hat?"

Yes. "What's that?"

"It's this conspiracy theory about a group of renegade Princeton professors conducting quantum physics and chaos theory experiments and supposedly discovering a new theory for dimensional travel using a device called 'the egg' as a result. The professors ended up in a parallel world."

"Are you saying that John Titor is just another internet tall tale made all the more exciting because you were there at the time of its conception?"

"Exactly." Bennie nodded. "Ong's Hat went from being a rumor to a proven hoax, to much more than that. An online experience. *Almost* a game. The goal was to manufacture a lie credible enough that a growing number of people would believe it to be true."

"Like *The Blair Witch Project*?" RJ asked.

"Better. The Blair Witch could be disproven with just a little digging, but the underlying logic of what John Titor was putting forward could not be so easily dismissed."

He shrugged and kept going. "I'm sure that John Titor was someone's spark of an idea or elaborate story, made into an interactive experience for users who were new to the internet. His story was so elegantly told that it lives on today."

Suzanne put her hand on RJ's knee and refilled her

glass, topping him off before returning the mostly empty bottle to the coffee table, still smiling at RJ, probably at how 'excited he looked.'

"After all that time on the forums, you must have a favorite theory." RJ said it almost like a dare.

Bennie took it. "Indeed I do."

"Here we go." Suzanne laughed as she took a sip.

Bennie nodded. "I think someone in Hollywood was behind it."

"You mean a writer?" RJ could see that.

"Sure. And a director, set designers, whatever. Maybe a couple of guys—"

"Could have been gals," Suzanne interjected.

"—or maybe a whole team, I don't know. But the images Titor posted always looked professional to me. Like they were designed." Bennie shrugged again. "I don't know a better way to explain it than whoever John Titor was, *they*—" He must have been looking right at Suzanne, but it was hard to tell through the Zoom. "They knew an awful lot about telling a story in an entertaining way."

RJ asked a better question. "What about the IBM 5100? Titor supposedly knew things that he couldn't really have known, right? Doesn't his specific knowledge about that unit lend his story a bit of credibility?"

"You could argue that, sure, and believe me, I have." Bennie laughed, this time to himself. "But if anyone knew these things, then everyone could know them with access to the right people."

"Do you have any theories on who that person might be? You mentioned Hollywood. Is there anyone specific that you think might have done this?"

"I don't have a clue." Bennie shook his head. "I just feel like I got one of those sneak preview passes where you have to answer some questions about why you did or didn't like a movie, but you get to see it before everyone else. Looks like I'm still filling out the form."

"And was it a good movie?"

Bennie smiled, "Best I've ever seen."

Then Suzanne took over with some small talk before signing them off for the night. RJ closed the laptop feeling gutted, but gave her a Grade-A grin and said, "I guess I'll go back to *Gator Gitters*, since it looks like John Titor is—"

"No." Suzanne shook her head, unwilling to let him finish the sentence. "I'll call my mom. The John Titor case ruined her career. She's been maligned as a crackpot for years. Let's figure out what more there is to this story."

Chapter Twelve

RJ – 2024

RJ COULD FEEL Michael's eye-rolling like a waft of hot air as they approached Sunny Acres Nursing Home, where Suzanne waited to bring the boys in for an off the record conversation with her mother. The place was brick with white columns and manicured lawns, flower boxes fixed to all the front windows, and a double row of trees along the entrance. Hardly cinematic, but RJ knew Michael was location scouting it anyway.

RJ held the door open for him.

"*Gracias*," Michael said as he passed.

"*Chupa me verga*," RJ replied.

Suzanne was already walking up to them.

"How is she doing?" RJ asked.

"You mean how will you be doing with her?"

He shrugged. "Sure."

"She's good. We made a deal that she wouldn't be in the docuseries *at all*, and that you would only be using whatever she tells you today as a way to get yourself pointed in the right direction."

"Of course." RJ nodded and swept his hand in a *forward* gesture. "After you."

Suzanne turned around and started past the reception desk with a nod of allowance to security in regard to her guests.

RJ followed as Michael muttered next to him, "We're in a fucking nursing home right now. There is zero chance of making this place look in any way cool or edgy. It doesn't fit with our aesthetic. *Muy feo.*"

"Do Otis and Buck fit with our aesthetic? Talking about sleeping with the same girl while Buck is high all the time?"

"They slept with the same girl?"

"We can't even film in this place anyway. We literally just promised that."

"Good. It's creepy. I bet they get like one death a day. Or maybe four a week."

"You should be excited," RJ said. "You said we could do the project if Suzanne's mom agreed to be involved. Now we're about to get that one thing that nobody has ever had before: an interview with a former member of the FBI—"

"Who can't be in our docuseries."

"—who was actually assigned to the John Titor case. That's a *huge* get!"

"It would be amazing if she could be in this."

"She can't," Suzanne snapped before turning around at her mother's door and locking her eyes onto RJ. "Please."

She didn't need to say anything more.

Suzanne opened the door.

Cecilia gave her daughter a warm smile before turning

on RJ and Michael with an icy stare as they crossed the threshold into the tidy room. Family photos adorned the walls and furniture, several featuring Suzanne, from toddler to just last Christmas. A few well-placed knickknacks were arranged like props to make the place feel like home: a table covered in partially assembled puzzles pieces, a mantel full of Cecilia Trainor's awards and commendations from the FBI, and a small but impressive library of true crime books and memoirs. *I'll Be Gone in the Dark* and *Just Kids* sat atop the pile.

Cecilia sat in an armchair, upright, her eyes sharp, betraying none of the physical decline that RJ knew had befallen her body. She stared him up and down, a hint of a sneer playing at the corners of her mouth. "So, you're the one."

RJ smiled. "It's a pleasure to see you again, Cecilia. Thank you for taking the time to speak with us."

Cecilia swatted the air. "You're here to discuss the only one of my cases that anyone ever wants to talk about these days, or any days. So go ahead and ask me whatever it is you came here to ask me."

She turned to Michael. "You here to record this? Because I don't plan on repeating myself. And you look like the kind of Sneaky Pete who thinks he can persuade an old lady to change her mind and get me to sign off on using our interview in your little production." Cecilia shook her head. "It won't happen, and you'll be sorry if you try."

"We understand," RJ assured her.

"You have questions, or shall I get started?"

"I just want to say that I really appreciate you taking the time to speak with me. I understand what a privilege it is, and I'm eager to hear all that you have to say. So, please, start the story wherever you feel is most appropriate."

Cecelia nodded and got started. "I grew up thinking

there was nothing more fun than solving a good puzzle…" But then she stopped and stared into space.

Michael gave RJ a look: *She's too old.*

A beat later she got going again. "I never much cared for TV, unless it was a show with mysteries, or a show that tried to explain them. I was also ahead of my time. There weren't too many women in the bureau back in the 70s, especially not in the field. Too bad I blazed a trail that led me right off a cliff."

She took a performative breath and then finished her thought. "I already solved this case for you. I've known who John Titor was for years…"

Cecilia paused, obviously baiting them.

RJ bit down on it. "So, who is he?"

"It's not that easy, and I'm not that fast. The price of that information is listening to another story first."

"Another story?" RJ repeated, buying a beat to bury his obvious irritation. How could Cecilia announce that she knew Titor's identity before redirecting him somewhere else? He glanced at Suzanne, who obviously wasn't surprised at all. He turned back to the former FBI agent with a smile. "I can't wait to hear it."

Michael rolled his eyes and muttered under his breath.

Cecilia pretended not to notice. "It was 2005 when the FBI got intel on a bomb threat from an informant in—"

"Wait." RJ interrupted the second he registered his own confusion. "I thought Titor went back to his own time in 2001?"

"Do you want the information or not?" Cecilia asked.

"Sorry. I promise not to interrupt again." RJ looked over at Michael, now surreptitiously checking his phone.

Cecilia offered RJ a nod and continued. "Our informant said that his brother-in-law was a member of a small group of people who were planning to blow up several buildings in Omaha, Nebraska—"

"That was the new capital, after the civil war, according to Titor," RJ interrupted, already breaking his promise.

"It was." Cecilia nodded, not seeming to mind. "We, my partner and I, went to hunt them down. But the brother-in-law realized that he had been found out before we got there, and he was already in the wind."

"And that guy was John Titor?" Michael asked.

Cecilia looked at Suzanne, then back at the guys. "You're going to need a little context first..." She eased down into her armchair as her eyes took on a distant, almost dreamy quality. "Let me paint you a picture of Titor's world. His 2036 is different from the future it looks like we're headed for, more like the Old West than anything we've seen in science fiction."

Westworld, Firefly, Outland, etc., but RJ knew what she meant.

Cecilia went on to describe a rural life where "high technology" still existed but was used mainly for communication and travel. People otherwise lived a more rustic existence, raising most of their own food and performing more farm work than the average American had seen in more than a century and a half. Life revolved around community, with people working long hours and coming together to support one another.

"What about the internet?" Michael asked.

"The internet still existed, but it served a different purpose. People spent more time talking and interacting with one another in person, forging stronger bonds in their communities."

"Do you find it strange at all that you're speaking about a future that never happened in the past tense?" Michael asked, and again RJ couldn't tell whether or not he was fucking with the former FBI agent.

Cecilia smiled. "Not at all, young man. It's all past tense for me."

"So who was John Titor then?" RJ tried.

"You mean besides someone who was asking people to open their own eyes?" The question was rhetorical, so Cecilia kept talking. "Titor said the same thing happened in our world when the power went off that happened in his."

"And what's that?" Michael's turn to take the bait.

"We shifted to a world where people tend to leave their homes and actually spend time with their neighbors. A world with a lot more personal trust and far less paranoia. Titor suggested that the bad parts of his timeline might find us too, if his mission failed, but that perhaps we could take the best parts of his timeline to improve our present."

"Who is John Titor, specifically?" Michael tried harder than RJ.

Cecilia smiled. "I'm about to tell you."

Chapter Thirteen

THREE DAYS EARLIER ...

THE TWO MEN were nearly finished with their business at Homestead Gas & Goods when a frazzled looking Ramon (RJ, according to his business card) entered the gas station, desperately needing to use the phone.

He looked wildly around, noted the two possible patrons before fixing his gaze on Hollis, the heavyset and fat-hearted man who had been working at Homestead since he was a pre-teen sweeping the floor for candy. He'd started running the place after he knocked up Louisa Farr during her senior year of high school and was now just a few months shy of finishing his second year of junior college himself.

"Excuse me, sir, do you have a phone I could use to call a tow?"

"Right over there." Hollis nodded to a pay phone across the way while tugging on his beard.

"Thanks." Ramon smiled, then he opened a phonebook and started searching with his finger as if he was having an out of body experience. He dropped his change in the slot to make his call as the curly-haired man approached him.

"Excuse me. Do you have a moment?"

Ramon spun around, startled by the man and his wildly haunted eyes. "I'm sorry—" He held up a finger to the stranger, turning back around to take his call. "I need a tow ... I'm outside of Homestead Gas & Goods."

The curly-haired man left Ramon at the pay phone and approached Hollis at the counter instead. "Excuse me. Do you have a moment?"

"Too many of 'em, buddy. How can I help you?" Hollis smiled. "I'm not sure that you need any more gas than you've already got."

"I was hoping you could give me directions. I'm looking for a Coral Snake Road."

Hollis laughed. "Way less dangerous than it sounds. Take the highway to Dillard West and then take that road up to the mountain. You'll see Coral Snake up at the top. Right or left, depends on your address."

"That's very helpful. Thank you." He nodded at Hollis.

"Might want to get some snacks for the drive." Hollis pointed to a package of caramel-colored nuggets. "The Gator Bits are good."

"What are they?" The man was clearly both interested and repulsed.

"Like caramel corn and fairy dust," Hollis replied with a pat to his belly. "I can't eat them no more because my wife says they're bad for me, but it's a melt-in-your-mouth kind of snack." A wistful sigh. "I envy anyone trying Gator Bits for the first time."

The man nodded. "Two cans of gas and one bag of Gator Bits."

"Sure you don't want a bag for each of you?"

"We'll share."

The two men exited Homestead and stepped back into the oppressive Florida night, heavy with humidity and the buzz of insects from the swampland yawning on either side of the road. They carried their gas cans toward the Corvette, abandoned up the highway and thirsty for fuel, falling into a game meant for passing time on their way.

"Best picture, 1994?" Curly Hair asked.

"*Forrest Gump*. Should have been Pulp Fiction." His companion made a face. "What movie features the line, 'I'm King of the World'?"

"You should probably try a couple of hard ones." Curly Hair knew it was a softball, but all the traveling could jumble things in his head, so really, he was buying time.

"Is that your answer?"

"*Titanic*." He remembered just in time.

"Who made *Black Swan*?"

Curly Hair stopped walking. "We agreed, nothing past 2005. That's cheating."

"Fine. Who played Morpheus in *The Matrix*?"

"Depends who's asking," he replied.

"I'm asking."

"In that case, Laurence Fishburne."

They reached the Corvette and gassed up in silence. Falling into easy conversation as they drove up the mountain, they made a left at the top onto Coral Snake Road. Their destination was a cabin in the woods, nestled in a quiet glen surrounded by tall, lush trees. The chimney sent spiraling smoke into the air as they parked.

"Are you ready?" The straight-laced man asked his out-of-time companion.

"As I'll ever be," John Titor replied.

Part II

Part II

Chapter Fourteen

2036

JACK ANDERSON HID with his best friend Cameron behind an ancient once-red pickup truck, faded enough to flirt with pink and darkened by an array of rust spots pocking the surface. Its frame was caked in mud and dust, the windows tinted a murky gray. The tires were flat and cracked; the antennae had long ago snapped off. Even so, the pickup was still better than the parking garage itself, crumbling in too many places, every wall drenched in graffiti, the entire structure sagging in defeat as a reek of oil clung to the air like a fog. Both the pickup and the parking garage were picture-perfect representations of this part of the broken world. Not that people took many pictures these days.

A few pigeons flew by, wings flapping as Jack looked out at the gang of men huddled around a campfire, laughing loudly enough for Jack and Cameron to hear in the parking garage.

"What do you think is so funny?"

"Once he gets going, Farley can get his boys laughing about anything." Cameron shrugged. "Seriously, one of them probably farted."

"They don't look much like boys." Jack took inventory of the gang. A dozen bodies in total, including Farley, and only three among them could be considered anything less than full-grown men.

"They used to be boys."

Jack nodded, pleased to see they were obviously morons. "Men with such a juvenile sense of humor shouldn't be too hard to outsmart."

"I never said they were smart. I said they were brutal."

"I believe the word you used was 'unflinching.'"

"Fine. Unflinching." Cameron looked back at the red 1967 Chevy convertible and the impossible machine nestled inside that old metal dinosaur.

"You sure about this?" Jack asked.

"Do you want me to say no?"

"We do this, and we'll make a permanent enemy out of Farley."

Cameron looked from the Farley boys (men) huddled around their campfire before glancing over to the Chevy again, then back at his chosen brother. "I only have one family."

Jack swallowed, pleased by the answer yet understandably nervous. His training would kick in, but the butterflies in his stomach were still in mid-rebellion, and in moments like this, they fluttered the hardest, building up enough of a gust to keep him alive through the battle.

"So we're good to go?" Jack was just making sure.

Cameron nodded. "On your count."

Jack swallowed again. "3 … 2 … 1—"

Cameron hit a button on his walkie-talkie. "GO."

The stairwell door exploded open behind the gang, followed by a deafening roar, ominous and deep, reverberating and intensifying as the men scattered about, bellowing in curses and shouts from every direction.

The hairs on Jack's neck were all at attention as he and Cameron sprinted out from their hiding place.

Chapter Fifteen

RJ – 2024

"WHO IS JOHN TITOR, SPECIFICALLY?" Michael asked.

"I'm about to tell you." Cecilia smiled, then glanced at her daughter.

"How about I get us all a cup of coffee?" Suzanne offered as she stood. *In case you're feeling too tired to pay attention.*"

She shot a look at Michael, whose lips were pressed tightly together.

RJ turned back to Cecilia. "Please, continue."

Cecilia leaned back in her armchair, her gaze crawling back into yesterday. "We tracked down the brother-in-law after our leads led us to the home of one of his friends. We were lucky enough to talk our way right into the house. That might not have been so easy if the brother-in-law had been home. But he and his buddy were out, and the missus was much more amenable."

Cecilia paused, letting RJ's suspense and Michael's

obvious annoyance hang in the air like a silent proclamation. "We started with a few simple questions. Like the frequency of the friend's visits, where—"

"Was the friend John Titor?" Michael interrupted.

"—they might be at the moment, and any other friends they hung out with. Common, harmless questions." Cecilia leaned forward. "Until she asked us something we never expected."

RJ leaned forward too, in perfect contrast to Michael's detached disposition. "What did she ask?"

"'Is this about the time travel stuff?'" Cecilia quoted, an echo of that old surprise still alive in her eyes. "She mentioned the name 'Titor' as if talking about what sounded good for lunch. We questioned her further, probing around to find out what she meant by 'time travel stuff' without tipping her off to the fact that her insight might be a big deal."

"Was Titor the friend?" RJ asked Michael's question again, but without interrupting.

Cecilia shook her head. "No. The woman tried her best to brush it off. Her husband and his friend were both obsessed with what she referred to as a 'silly conspiracy theory.' We asked her to tell us more about the theory, and she explained that John Titor was a time traveler who supposedly prevented World War III. The basement was apparently filled with a massive collection of materials on the subject — articles, obscure magazines, you name it."

She shook her head again. "But we didn't see any of it. No warrant, or reason to get one based on the Titor intel alone. Her demeanor changed the second we asked to see the collection. It was like flipping a switch. She asked if her husband was in trouble, and I reassured her that we were simply looking for information about a case and that her husband might possibly be able to assist us with. But she was understandably spooked and demanded that we leave."

"Did the men know Titor personally?" RJ asked.

"No, but they were profoundly influenced by him, almost like disciples. But that's not the end of it." Cecilia offered a wry smile, her eyes sparkling with withheld secrets. "I never heard about Titor until that day, even though I still take it personally that no one passed the story on to me when it came through the FBI a few years before and was quickly solved. After stumbling into that den of what to me were new mysteries, I couldn't wait to see what would happen next."

Michael couldn't help himself. "So what happened next?"

"We next went to the second friend's house. And that's where things got really interesting."

Chapter Sixteen

JACK – 2036

THE ONCE-PROUD HALLS of the university turned fort stood with an air of defiance, almost as if the military dared time itself to disregard its prestigious past in favor of this new and dangerous present. The walls bore the scars of a tumultuous era, grand architecture now clad in the utilitarian garb of necessity. Shadows across the campus seemed almost alive.

Jack stood at attention, garbed in an amalgamation of army attire and coveralls. A patch adorned his chest, its intricate design a symbol of the path he'd promised to never stray from, and a testament to the thin line between safety and the realm of the divine. It was a depiction of a Kerr singularity: a haunting eye surrounded by gravity waves, with a pair of spiraling paths coursing through its core. Emblazoned along the bottom of his badge were the numbers 107 and the words *Temporal Recon*.

His heart was a staccato drumbeat of anticipation and

trepidation. He had trained tirelessly for this moment, honing his mind and body for the arduous journey ahead. Now, with the final briefing looming before him, the enormity of Jack's task settled upon his shoulders like a leaden mantle.

He was to travel back to the year 1990, to a time before humanity's insatiable hunger for progress led them to taint their sustenance. Jack was tasked with gathering seeds, unblemished by the genetic modification that grew to plague crops like a cancer. Nuclear devastation in the 2010s had turned large swathes of land barren and infertile, but unmodified seeds held the answer to growing crops in the patches that still remained viable.

The breath hitched in his chest, nerves frayed amid the gravity of his mission. He was a soldier of time, traversing eons to mend those fractures that threatened to tear his world apart. Or he could be, if everything went right.

Despite rigorous training designed to keep him out of such thoughts, Jack couldn't help but wonder: *If I fail, then does that mean the future will fall?*

It was a pointless question. There were contingencies within contingencies without even counting the alternate timelines. If those weren't enough…

Jack's job was to focus only on what he could control.

A difficult childhood on the farm made this personal. He knew precisely what the future was facing with soil getting worse. Jack pictured his father sifting once-rich dirt like sand through his fingers, tortured and lamenting as he looked up at Grandpa's nearly identical expression.

After the wars, the land had turned harsh and unforgiving, the soil stubborn and unyielding despite desperate efforts. Genetically modified crops were the first to give out. Corn had all but vanished from the fields, the endless golden stalks that had been vital to the American diet surrendering to stubborn weeds that refused to be tamed. Root vegetables had become scarce. And orchards that once bore the sweet fruits of smart labor were barren and forlorn.

As crops grew scarcer, the livestock suffered too. Animals that roamed the pastures and grazed on the plenty soon struggled for sustenance, until their weakened bodies finally collapsed.

The weight of his mission was colossal, but Jack had made significant sacrifices to be here, surrendering his dream of raising horses, leaving Mom to tend the animals all by herself. But this mission was bigger than his dreams, or any one individual. He had the chance to save his planet. His people needed food.

Commander Jessup was a stern, weathered man who brooked no bullshit and had a reputation for molding the best soldiers in Temporal Recon. Jack straightened his posture as the commander halted in front of him.

"Anderson." Jessup's voice was gravel and glue. "Do I need to ask if you're ready?"

Jack locked onto his commander's gaze to give himself an anchor. "Not a shred of doubt, sir."

"Any concerns about your mission?"

"None that can eclipse my determination, sir."

"Got the jitters?"

"Absolutely, sir. But it's the same shiver that got me here."

"Good lad. Honesty in the gut makes the mind sharper." His smile took Jack by surprise, a rare warmth spilling over the icy terrain of their relationship. He landed a robust pat on Jack's midriff before making a double tap at his forehead. "Keeps the control room upstairs ticking right. We rendezvous at the launch point at dawn."

Jessup made an about face and started walking. Jack

trailed him through the scabs of formerly grand lecture halls repurposed into briefing rooms and training facilities. Soldiers scurried past them until the commander and Jack finally arrived at a large set of heavy doors.

They swung open to a room without windows, and Jack's breath hitched in his throat at the sight of an ancient 1967 Chevy convertible.

"My vehicle for the mission?" Jack confirmed.

"We've made some modifications, but yes, she's all yours. We thought the Chevy would be fitting, given your destination. More of the cars from the 60s survived because they were built to last. So long as you don't have one from post-1990, you're good."

"The car is incredible, sir." He almost felt reverent. "I'll finish my mission with honor."

"I've no doubt, son." Jessup sounded almost affectionate as he clapped a hand on Jack's shoulder. "Rest up, and I'll see you at the launch point in the morning. We're all counting on you. I thought you'd enjoy taking it to the launch site yourself. A driver will be waiting when you get there to give you a ride home."

"Thank you, sir." Keeping the grin off of his face was painful. "I won't let you down."

"I know you won't."

Jack's heart was racing as he got behind the wheel and started the engine. It pounded even harder as he pulled out of the room and onto the road.

But not on his way to the launch site.

Jack had one stop that he needed to make first.

Chapter Seventeen

JACK – 2036

THE TRIP WASN'T LONG, but the ride itself a far cry from the gentle rhythm that rolled through Jack's body when he was on horseback. Not that Jack could deny the thrill of the rumbling seat beneath him as the landscape unfurled before him as a stark reminder of the world he was fighting to save.

As the Chevy rolled over the broken terrain, Jack looked out at the once-vibrant countryside, succumbing to time away from mankind's constant intrusion. Tendrils of wild grass crept over abandoned fields, and skeletal remains of dead orchards loomed like specters as he passed them.

He drank in the sights, knowing that come tomorrow, he might never see any of it ever again.

Except that Jack needed to stop entertaining the possibility of failure. His mission wasn't accomplished until his cargo was safely in a Temporal Recon transit facility.

Commander Jessup had encouraged him to acknowledge his nerves, not stir doubt about the odds of his success.

Jack navigated the treacherous roads until he finally arrived at the treehouse, perched high in the boughs of an ancient oak, the finest one on their farm, nestled on the bank of a muddy river prone to flooding. A wraparound deck in her branch-laden sanctuary boasted stunning vistas of the world he'd promised to change.

He got out of the Chevy and whistled up at the treehouse, beckoning his mother to come out and see the marvel for herself. Not that his call was necessary. She'd heard him rolling up and came bounding outside, her eyes widening with awe as she took in the gleaming convertible.

"Is that for your mission, or from your mission and you're already back?" She grinned, looking hopeful.

Jack smiled back at her. "It's for you to come down here and look at."

Mom clambered down the ladder, ignoring the last several rungs as she jumped down to the ground and ran over to marvel at the Chevy.

"I can't believe they're letting you drive this thing." She ran her fingers along the vehicle's sleek lines. "It's so pretty! These were already old when I was young, you know. Can we go for a ride?"

Jack shook his head. "I'm lucky they even let me bring it home. I shouldn't."

"Can you show me the time machine part?" Her eyes sparkled so bright that he couldn't say no.

He grinned as he opened the door.

Mom looked inside, casting a furtive glance around the cabin.

"How does it work? Do you start it with your fingerprint or something? So that not just anyone can hop in the thing and start joyriding through history?"

"I have to put in a code."

"Good thing I don't know it. I'd be tempted to steal it and take it back to the Sixties, to see the Beatles play live."

"If I succeed, I promise I'll take you to a Beatles concert before I turn it back in. Besides, you already know the code."

"I do?"

"It's your anniversary. You and Dad's."

She wiped the tear that started as he finished his sentence.

"You okay, Mom?" Jack asked.

"Of course." She smiled. "I'll be right back."

Mom sprinted back up the ladder, leaving him alone for the two minutes it took for her to return with a worn copy of *The Talented Mr. Ripley*. She looked through the book, its pages packed with her doodles and scribbles. She came to a simple necklace tucked into it somewhere near the end, then nodded in satisfaction as she snapped the book closed and handed it over to Jack.

"Take this with you."

Jack shook his head. "I can't take this."

"So I'll know it's you."

He took the book and tucked it under his arm. "Can I take care of the horses for you?"

"I was hoping you'd offer." She gave him another lingering smile, then turned around and started back toward the treehouse as Cameron came striding toward him. He was wearing his usual mischievous grin and that mop of unruly hair. A leather case was slung over his shoulder, slapping at his side as he walked, faster and faster as he quickly closed the distance between them.

Mom was back up top looking down at Cameron when he arrived. "Hey there, Cameron!"

Instead of answering with the usual *Hello*, Cameron

sang the first few words of a song that Mom had been handcrafting for years.

"*Oh, time, you relentless river, you wax and you wane. Unseen hands upon the clock, in sunshine or in rain…*"

"*Oh, time, you're the healer and the thief in the night. Stealing moments as you mend, in shadows or in light…*" she sang down at him. "I trust you won't be getting Jack into any trouble."

Mom didn't wait for Cameron's answer before disappearing inside.

He came over to Jack, eyeing the Corvette like a seasoned collector admiring a priceless work of art. "Sure is—"

"It's not for you." Jack found that it was often best to cut Cameron off before he got started.

"I didn't even—"

"You did." Jack laughed. "So what have you been up to? And if you start reciting passages from another book I can't understand and won't ever care about, I might have to find myself a thick beam and a strong rope."

"Vivid." Cameron nodded in admiration. "But a hollow threat. You're too much of a good soldier to kill yourself before the big mission."

"You're right about that." He nodded with a sigh, then gave Cameron what he wanted. "Go ahead, I know there's some book you're dying to tell me about. Are we onto repeats now? You must have already read everything in the library at least once by now."

"It's called *Between the Gears: Explorations in Arcane Engineering.*" Cameron was delighted to reply, ignoring the rest of what Jack had said. "It's all about the world of esoteric mechanics."

"I assume you're going to tell me what that means."

"It's about how ancient and mystical principles have influenced the field of engineering throughout history."

"What are the ancient and mystical principles that make time travel work?" Jack asked like it was a serious question.

"You wanted to know what I was reading."

"Maybe a better question is *why are you reading it?* How does that possibly help you with your job?"

"Work isn't my only reason for reading, Jack."

Cameron was one of the best mechanics Jack had ever met — he'd earned enough to keep him in movies and books by working for a company that maintained wireless internet nodes. Most of his free time was spent poring over history, assembling missing pieces and making sense of whatever he could find.

Cameron grinned as he turned to Jack and touched his arm. "Do you have a moment?"

"Yes." He nodded. "But I can already tell that I'm going to regret it."

Chapter Eighteen

Jack – 2036

"WHY DOES it look like you don't believe me?" Cameron asked.

Jack narrowed his eyes, holding a stare on his best friend for several long seconds before finally replying with an indirect answer to his question. "You're the best mechanic I know. Hell, you're probably the best mechanic any of us know."

"I'm sure your Commander Jessup would disagree."

"What's your angle?"

"Are you saying you don't want to give your best buddy a hand?"

"I'm asking why you need one," Jack clarified.

"I already told you."

"No, you said that the axle broke on Arvel Stafford's truck."

"Right. And from this point forward I'll stop arguing when you say that you're clueless when it comes to cars."

"What's that supposed to mean?" Jack asked.

"Broken axles are a two-man job."

"And I'm the person you want help from. The night before my Temporal Recon mission to save the world.

"It'll be fast. And your fancy pants mission is the reason I'm asking you. We might never see each other again. Sad, but true."

Jack couldn't argue with that.

"You could get help from someone else tomorrow."

"There isn't another Jack in this world." Cameron grinned. "And I promised Arvel that the work would be done today."

"On the night before my mission. Got it." He nodded. "How long is this going to take?"

"Two hours. Maybe four, given that you're the one helping me."

Jack laughed. "Asshole."

"Maybe you'll be awesome and we'll get out of there in two." Cameron nodded at the Corvette. "Can we take her?"

Ah. The angle. There it was.

"Of course we can't."

"It's been years since I've seen one," Cameron said. "And never one that looked like that."

"Are you going to admit that was your plan all along?"

"My plan was to milk one last little round of labor out of you before Jack Anderson bids us all bye-bye and drives onto what might be a one-way trip to yesterday. But getting in the car is an excellent bonus."

"What do you want me to say, Cam?"

"Yes. Obviously."

"I'm lucky that Jessup let me bring the unit home. He'll kill me if he finds out."

"No he won't." Cameron shook his head. "He needs

you for the mission tomorrow. And it's a 1967 Chevy Corvette, not a 'unit.'"

"It's both of those things. And I bet that Jessup's trust has something to do with the fact that I'm not dumb enough to let my idiot friends drive the time machine."

"You said I was the best mechanic around, so I'm for sure not an idiot." Cameron ticked a point on his finger before raising another one. "I'm happy to sit shotgun, so there's no threat of me taking the wheel. And finally…" He ticked another finger to make the number three. "Even if I was driving, there would be zero chance I could actually use the car as a time machine, because I don't know the code. I'm just asking for a ride in it. One last hurrah. Just the two of us."

"Fine. Jesus." Jack laughed. "It's going to be a sweet relief driving decades away from you."

Cameron blew him a kiss.

Jack said, "I'm going to bring in the horses."

"Great. That gives me a chance to give a proper hello and goodbye to Kat."

Of course Jack should be telling Cameron to fuck off instead of going along with his shenanigans. But he had been gone for months-long stretches going on several years now. It was lonely in the military, and time with Cameron felt like home. Besides, no one would be dumb enough to sneak around Arvel's place, because if they knew about the old man, then they also had to know about Hank. His place was also on the way, so Jack could get the hard part done with Cameron fast, then leave him to finish things while Jack double-timed it toward the launch site.

Jack inhaled the warm scent of hay and horses on his approach to the barn, savoring the aroma before he kissed it goodbye. Whinnies and snorts greeted him like old friends as he entered.

Sun streamed through dusty windows and washed the mounts in its golden light. Jack's hands moved deftly, unbuckling harnesses and securing the horses for another night.

"I will miss you," he whispered to each of them.

Cameron had perfect timing, descending the treehouse ladder as Jack was leaving the barn.

They met at the Chevy.

"Get in." Jack opened his door and got behind the wheel.

"Your manners have always been great, but the military has really polished them to a shine." Cameron closed his door and Jack started the car.

"Is it your birthday?" Cameron asked about a mile down the road.

"What? No."

"The code. For the time machine. Is it your birthday?"

"No. Also, go to hell. I'm not playing this game with you."

"We both know that's not true," Cameron argued. "We're already playing."

"*You're* playing."

"Every time you talk, it means you're playing."

"That's not—"

"See. Still playing." Cameron grinned. "Is it the day we first met?"

"Jesus. No. What makes you think the code would have anything whatsoever to do with you? And better question, even if it did, why would I remember the day we met?"

"You don't remember the day we met?" Cameron sounded hurt.

"Of course I remember the day we met. My sister…"

Jack couldn't finish, and Cameron shouldn't have

brought it up. So he guessed something else to redirect the attention. "8-8-34?"

"What's that?"

"The night you almost gathered enough sack to ask Monica to—"

"No. And we can play all you like now that it's clear you have no capacity to guess the actual code."

"Is that a challenge?"

Jack shook his head. "Simple statement of fact."

"1-1-00."

"Alright." Jack nodded. "Legitimate guess, but no, the code has nothing to do with Y2K."

"12-4-04?"

"Nope."

"11-16-05?"

"Definitely not."

"2-3-08?"

"It has nothing to do with the civil war."

"How about World War III? You could save me some serious time guessing if you just say no."

"No."

"2-29-20?"

"No, it's not the signing of our constitution or anything to do with the government."

"Time travel itself then. When did CERN crack the time travel nut? Was it July? I'm pretty sure it was some-time in summer."

"It was August 19, 2034. And no."

"Does it have anything to with your mission?"

"I think that's been 20 questions."

"You never said we were playing to 20, and besides, it hasn't been even close to 20 questions yet, and fuck you if you try including shit like *Was it July?*"

"I don't do that." Jack shook his head. "*You* do that."

They rebooted the game after taking an accurate tally and agreeing to keep the limit at 20 questions total. Cameron had been spending too long musing over his final attempt at an accurate answer, and likely lamenting all of his stupider guesses.

"We're like a minute from Arvel's. I think you forgot how fast cars go."

"Is it Amelia's birthday?" Cameron asked.

Jack laughed it off. "And that's 20."

"Her death day?"

"I said that's 20." Jack's reply was dry, now all out of mirth. "And fuck you."

"So I'm right?" Cameron smiled, trying to lighten the mood now that he'd darkened it.

"Do you seriously think I'm dumb enough to base the time machine code on a date?" Jack scoffed, as if he would ever do something that ludicrous. "The codes are randomized."

"So then it's not the number of times you've sworn that you would never let me get you into trouble again?"

Jack killed the engine and opened his car door without answering Cameron, throwing a hearty wave to Arvel as he closed it.

"Looks like you brought help!" Arvel called out to Cameron before turning to Jack with a nod at the Chevy. "And what a beauty she is."

"Good to see!" Jack called back. And then he remembered. "Is Hank properly restrained?"

Arvel laughed. "What kind of a fool do you take me for?"

Chapter Nineteen

JACK – 2036

ARVEL SAT on his wraparound front porch, elevated on sturdy lumber stilts, looking out at Jack and Cameron working on his old pickup like a lord looming over his kingdom. A copse of lush trees swayed gently behind him, their branches weaving a dappled pattern of shadows onto the ground.

"Don't you think you should be using a bigger wrench for that bolt?" Arvel called out.

Jack looked up, replying with the same varietal of reply he had been giving the old man for the last hour, every time he saw fit to critique their work, which would even have been a lot if Jack were being compensated instead of simply inconvenienced. On his last night in 2036.

"Just using the one I was told to use."

"It's the right one," Cameron assured Arvel.

The old man's face was weathered with wrinkles, his skin almost like a hide. Bushy white eyebrows framed small gray eyes and a hedge of wispy whiskers covered his face. His threadbare cardigan covered a long-sleeved shirt that probably used to be red, with its fabric pulled tight across his bony frame.

Arvel stayed quiet for no more than a minute. "Be careful with that jack stand, Cameron. I don't want my truck falling on you boys."

"I'm sure we want that even less," Cameron replied.

Jack chuckled under the truck.

"Making you laugh is usually like ice skating uphill, and that wasn't even a joke," Cameron said, just loud enough for his buddy to hear.

"You have no idea what ice skating is like. I was laughing at something stupid."

"Was it that show *Farmer Fiona*? Because I don't get why everyone keeps talking about ten-minute episodes with lighting that makes me squint, when I'm already squinting at the terrible acting."

"She shoots the show in her basement. What do you want it to look like? And she's not acting. That really is Farmer Fiona."

"It's a comedy, but the show is about a woman growing Swiss chard in her basement."

Jack laughed again. "So you only saw the first episode."

"Do I really need to see more?"

"Only if you're interested in knowing what the show is actually about."

Cameron shook his head. "No thanks."

"Fiona doesn't just 'grow Swiss chard in her basement.' The plot is that she's running a bootleg vegetable business. From micro greens to mushrooms. But she plays herself. It's really funny."

"I was totally wrong. Watching a woman cultivating fungi in her underground lair does indeed sound like comedy gold. A root vegetable racket? Hysterical. Covert kale operations? It's what I've been missing all my life. Nothing makes me lose my shit like contraband cucumbers. Also mushrooms are a fungus. And out of curiosity, which episode has mushrooms, and what kind of mush—"

Arvel started shouting.

Then Cameron yelled, "FUCK!"

And Arvel bellowed, "HANK! STOP!"

And then most terrifying of all: "RUN!"

Cameron was already out from under the truck and running as Hank the mammoth crocodile charged them.

But Jack wasn't fast enough and needed to roll the other way, back under the cover of the truck, just out of reach from the creature's massive snapping jaws.

Jack was safe, but only because the crocodile was too big to fit under the truck. He had inches of grace between himself and the beast. A rough cough and Hank could bite into his foot and drag him out all the way.

The crocodile thrashed around to the other side of the pickup, probably to see if he could eat Jack alive from the opposite end.

Jack rolled the other way, almost home free before his shirt snagged on a piece of metal and kept him from escaping the monster amphibian's reach.

Arvel was suddenly behind Hank, whooping and hollering as he jabbed a long stick with a dead rabbit skewered on the end at the croc.

Hank tore into the rabbit, spewing blood and gore across Jack's face.

There were loud shouts and semi-familiar yelling in the background from voices that didn't belong.

Arvel whistled sharply, and the croc seemed to calm, backing out and away from under the truck.

Jack heard an unmistakable roar from the Chevy's

engine amid the chaos and looked up just in time to see the vehicle being driven away by someone he recognized. Panic swelled in his chest as he watched the Temporal Recon's time machine disappear down the road.

Cameron sprinted after the Corvette, stopping only when certain defeat became painfully obvious.

Together they stared down the road where the vehicle had vanished, hearts racing with shock and adrenaline.

"*Fuck*." Cameron turned to Jack. "Do you—"

Jack's fist plowed into his nose.

Cameron staggered back with both hands over his gushing nostrils. "What the fuck?"

"WHAT THE FUCK IS RIGHT!" Jack was pure rage, his trembling lip just inches from Cameron's face. He took a heaving, calming breath, but it wasn't enough. "I can't believe you did this shit to me!"

Jack tried to punch him again, but this time Cameron was ready, ducking fast, then tackling his friend and sending them both hard to the ground.

Arvel kept shouting for them to quit it as they grappled around on the ground, fists flying and dirt churning underneath them, his bellows barely audible over Jack and Cameron's ragged breathing and the dull thuds from traded punches.

They rolled over one another, each desperately working for the upper hand.

Cameron finally managed to pin Jack to the ground, straddling his chest and restraining his flailing arms. Sweat dripped from Cameron's brow onto Jack's face, blending in with the dirt and blood.

"Just fucking listen to me! It wasn't me. I had *nothing* to do with this."

"Oh yeah?" Jack challenged him. "You spend the whole ride here trying to get the code out of me!"

"It was a game. I wasn't serious."

"I saw who stole the Chevy, Cameron."

Arvel might as well have been holding the proverbial bowl of popcorn while they argued.

"Who took the Chevy?"

"You can't play dumb. You weren't the one stuck under the fucking truck."

"No," Cameron was calm now. "But I was trying to wrestle a goddamned crocodile from behind to save my best friend."

"It was Rabbit."

Cameron drew a hard breath, clearly now getting why Jack had made his accusation. "I haven't talked to Rabbit, or any of Farley's boys, for years. And that's the God's honest truth."

Jack felt furiously helpless, and sorrowful that his best friend in the world might have betrayed him. He couldn't help but think about that conversation they'd had after Amelia—

No. He wouldn't. Not after everything they'd been through together. Not even for her.

Would he?

"You have to believe me," Cameron said.

"You're the best liar I know," Jack finally replied.

"Ouch. And also thank you." Cameron stood straight. "Look. We both know the Corvette would still be in your possession if I had never talked you into coming out here and helping me with Arvel."

"Thanks for that." Arvel nodded, deadpan.

Hank continued to feast on his dead bunny.

"I can help you get the car back," Cameron promised.

"How?" Jack asked.

"I know Farley and all of his tricks. I also have a damn good idea about where the gang would go."

Cameron was right — working together was Jack's best chance of getting the unit back in time to complete his mission. Unless Cameron was back with the Farleys and this was a trap, intended to stop Jack from reporting the theft to Jessup and calling in the cavalry.

His heart didn't want to believe that Cameron would betray him, but Jack's head told him that he was an idiot to simply trust his old friend on faith. Not when this much was at stake.

Jack stayed silent for a long while before he finally sighed with his answer. "You've done enough."

Then he walked away from Cameron.

Chapter Twenty

J ACK – 2036

"BUDDY?" Cameron called after him.

Jack ignored him, still walking away but now turning to Arvel, anger and frustration radiating off of his body like heat from a fire. "Hank needs to be put down! You know it's illegal to keep him."

"Sorry to tell you, son," Arvel chuckled to make it clear that he wasn't really sorry at all. "But it's *gators* that are illegal. There ain't enough crocodiles left for us to kill 'em all off."

Jack clenched his jaw and kept walking, not even bothering to make a retort. Not only had his (mission critical time traveling machine) car been stolen, he didn't even have a horse. This was too much, even for a soldier like him.

His hands balled into fists, then he shook with anger, the breath leaving his lungs in shallow pants, his feet stomping with fury as his curses gained color and volume from within the tornado of emotions tearing through him. He was having a grown man's version of a toddler's tantrum.

Cameron looked like he was trying not to laugh, which made Jack want to sock him again.

Arvel sounded almost oblivious. "There's a green bike in the shed you can use."

"Thanks." *For nothing*, Jack didn't add, though he did say, "Fuck you, Cameron."

Maybe Arvel had meant *gangrene*. The ride had patches of chipped paint, slightly bent handlebars, a dry and rusty chain, plus a seat with more cracks than a thirsty riverbed, but it also had a sturdy frame and would get the good soldier where he needed to go.

He should never have gone anywhere with Cameron. This was all his own fault for disobeying his instincts yet again. How many times was he going to let his supposed best friend drag him into the mud? He should have parked the Corvette (the *unit*) in the stable and had a quiet night in with his mother as planned. Or better, he should have driven straight to the launch site and then walked the ten miles home rather than travel one inch with Cameron Boone.

Everything Cameron touched turned into chaos. There was an old adage from before the war: *Those who don't understand history are doomed to repeat it.* Now it was a Temporal Recon mantra.

No soldier worth his unit would have ever allowed something like this to happen.

Jack pedaled away on the decrepit bike, his mind already whirring faster than the dusty wheels beneath him. He could radio in and have Jessup send a unit to recover the Corvette — the responsible and obviously smartest move. But the potential consequences hung above his neck like a guillotine.

A reprimand and off the mission at best if he was lucky, or into the brig at worst. Maybe he even deserved it.

He swiped a rough hand over his sweaty brow and kept riding while he worked out his plan. He would start with finding Farley's hideout. Seedy folks tended to know other seedy folks, and there was a watering hole not too far from where he was pedaling, sordid as a place could be until you got to Old Orlando. A murky pit for the underbelly. A place where information could be bought, and Jack had a few chits to spend.

Biking to the grimy dive was an eternity in the sweltering heat. Jack was a broiling, sweaty mess by the time he staggered through the batwing doors.

He stepped up to the bartender, a man about as welcoming as a circling bull shark, but with an inexplicable aptitude for keeping his finger on the pulse.

"You wanna find Farley, then talk to Sutherland," the bartender grunted.

His stomach clenched. Sutherland hated Jack, thanks to some beef he had with his mother going back since he was a kid. Jack didn't understand it or need to — Sutherland was born to yell *GET OFF MY PLOT!* while lifting weights. He acted like his position in Compliance gave him the biggest dick in the Army.

"Do you know where I might—"

The bartender answered his unfinished question with a nod to the corner. Jack turned and saw Sutherland sitting alone and nursing a drink.

"Thanks." Jack gave the bartender a nod and dropped a chit on the counter, then swallowed hard as he approached the beefy man with a chip on his shoulder that was even bigger than his biceps.

"Fuck off, Jack." Sutherland stared him down before Jack could even open his mouth.

Jack tried anyway. "I need your help. Temporal Recon needs your help. It's for the greater good."

Sutherland curled his upper lip and growled, "Only reason to meet a man like Farley is for nefarious purposes. You telling me it's on the up and up?"

"He stole something, and I need to get it back."

"What could Farley have possibly stolen that — *oh shit!*" Sutherland exploded with laughter. "You lost the time machine! They're gonna lock you up and—"

"*Please,* Sutherland. I need your help." When that didn't seem to be working, Jack tried again, moving right to the man's more mercenary tendencies. "I can get you a reward."

"Is the reward me breaking your face?"

The question caught Jack by surprise, just like the punch flew into his nose from nowhere, a blindside blow that sent him sprawling.

Sutherland was on him with two of his buddies running over to join the beating, all three of them swooping down on Jack like vultures onto carrion.

Knuckles like granite met with his face, flesh yielded, blood and spittle splattered. Each punch a hot lance of pain, igniting stars behind his eyes.

Jack was on the ground tasting iron, his head swimming as kicks jolted into his ribs and turned his breath into stolen gasps. The world swayed, colors bled into his nausea as the blows kept coming.

Then, the light of the door opening, and Cameron soared like a comet into the fray, his eyes flashing and fists clenched.

A hurricane could not have stirred more chaos. He went for Sutherland first, with a bone-crunching punch onto his jaw that sent the man's entire bulk reeling backward.

Two more blows, fast as a rattlesnake, and one of Sutherland's buddies was on the floor, groaning as the air ignited around Jack.

Begrudging admiration seeped through his battered body, a reluctant balm to soothe his pride.

He hated that it was Cameron who had to save him, but that didn't stop Jack from finding his feet, and letting a soldier's instinct take over to dilute the sting of his bruises as he joined Cameron with vigor, landing a solid sock on the jaw that echoed through the bar with the sweet sound of retribution as the remaining thug crashed into an adjacent table.

Neither Jack nor Cameron had any intention of stopping once the brutes were down, continuing to beat all three of them as they attempted to scramble away on the floor, leaving them in a heap that was every bit as bloody as the mess those same men would have left them in.

Jack and Cameron staggered out into the street as Sutherland yelled out behind them, "Wait until I tell the quartermaster you lost your fucking time machine!"

The air was sticky, but the open sky felt refreshing after the carousel of violence. A bead of sweat slid down to mingle with the drying blood on Jack's temple. His body ached, but there was an undeniable satisfaction in every throb.

"Do you have a moment?" Cameron asked, still panting heavily, his own bruises beginning to color.

Jack turned to him in disgust. "Fuck off, Cameron."

Chapter Twenty-One

RJ – 2024

"WE NEXT WENT to the second friend's house. And that's where things got really interesting ..." Cecilia paused, and for a moment it seemed like she might leave her story right there.

RJ leaned forward, dying to hear more. "Cecilia, please continue."

Cecilia settled deeper into the armchair, her gaze fixed on a spot in the distance visible only to her. "There wasn't a space in sight of that second house, so we had to park about a block away. It was in a sedate neighborhood, the kind of place where time itself stopped to smell the roses. Where people were inclined to leave an open window without thinking much about it."

"You found an open window?" Michael interjected. "Isn't that breaking and entering?"

"We canvassed the house," Cecilia continued without answering his question. "My partner at the time, green and eager to make a name for himself, reminded me that we didn't have a warrant. But I wasn't going to listen to him, not after hearing John Titor's name again for the first time since 1975, decades after the most nagging case of my career. It stirred something inside me. My partner didn't know about the IBM heist with culprits claiming that a man from the future was the mastermind. That part was still classified. So he didn't understand why I was hellbent on excavating what had really happened back then. I was almost obstinate in my pursuit to dredge up the facts. I felt like an archaeologist, brushing away the layers of lies over time to unearth the artifact of truth."

"What did you find?" RJ asked.

"The basement was a rabbit hole of madness, walls teeming with conspiracy theory magazines and newsletters, the table strewn with printouts of fervid forum discussions."

RJ cast a glance at Michael; his usually impassive partner was showing interest for sure.

"The feverish highlights and annotations of an obsessive mind," Cecilia continued, a trace of unease flashing across her features. "Manic obsession, with Titor's name plastered everywhere. The man's words were scrutinized, doubted, and yet, paradoxically, idolized."

"What did you find in the basement, *specifically*?" Michael pressed.

Her gaze locked onto RJ, a silent communion passing between them. "And there, in the chaotic jumble, we found the components of a bomb, instructions detailing its intricate assembly, and a hand-drawn blueprint of a downtown building that had no business ever being anywhere near the clutches of such individuals."

RJ and Michael traded another glance: *Shit just got real.*

"We heard the sudden creak of the door opening

upstairs." Cecilia shook her head with the memory. "We barely managed to wriggle out of the basement windows in time."

Her eyes met Michael's, challenging him to challenge her. "We raced back to our car, and peeled out of there, running red lights on our way to that building—"

"What was the building?" Michael shouted into her story.

"—with me and my partner both praying that we'd make it in time."

"Well, did you?" Michael asked when she stopped.

Celia leaned forward.

"Buckle up," she said.

Chapter Twenty-Two

J<small>ACK</small> – 2036

JACK STORMED AWAY from the bar and Cameron.

But his brawl buddy ran up to him and grabbed him by the arm.

"Wait." He sounded dead sober, blood staining his teeth from the bar fight. "You don't have to like me right now, but you definitely don't want to refuse my help."

"You're the last person I would trust right now, Cam." He wiped blood from his own mouth, fists clenching on instinct as if to deflect from any incoming blows.

"And you might be right to feel that way, but you also know that I can help, and that you don't exactly have a surplus of options right now."

The raw truth scraped at his pride and nicked his resolve. Cameron was holding the only lifeline in reach. But Jack was no fool; he knew it might be a noose.

"If this is a trap, or some kind of ambush, I swear on my mother I will take you down with me."

"I know that to be true." Cameron nodded. "But I swear, I only want to help you find the Corvette. I would never work with Farley."

"You mean *again*."

"Not in a million years."

Jack extended a bloody hand. "Lead the way, Cam. But you better not let me down."

After a brief stop to swap their bikes for horses — the bike Arvel loaned Cam was much better than the broken green one, but neither was suitable for chasing after a car — they were riding through the countryside in search of Farley's gang. Jack kept trying to cool off more than he already had, accelerating the process that time usually paved over the course of days or weeks, depending on what Cameron had done to piss him off. This situation was mission critical in too many ways for Jack to stay pickled in fury, so even though he still felt his anger pulled taut like a rubber band ready to snap, in his heart he knew that his friend was not to blame here.

Jack could have said no to any request at any time, from helping Cameron fix the broken axle to taking him for a joy ride in the unit.

And even though he had once run with Farley, that had been years ago, and blaming Cameron for the gang's behavior tonight would be like blaming the sun for yesterday's rain.

Jack also knew in his heart that he had been showing off, and that there was a cost for putting pride in front of his duty.

"Feeling any better?" Cameron finally broke the silence.

Jack turned on his horse. "What do you think?"

"That you looked seriously constipated and now it seems like maybe you took a shit. Emotionally, I mean."

"Thanks for the clarification." But he left it at that.

"So ... feeling any better?" Cameron tried again.

"I'll feel better when we have a lead on Farley."

"We already have a lead on Farley. And we'll know more soon."

"You've been singing that same tune since two settlements back, but all we have so far are a bunch of *NOs*. No Farleys, no strangers, nothing."

"There's no other tune to sing. All those places were stops along the way to where we both agree we might find some answers."

"I guess," grumbled Jack.

"That means I'm right. Come on." He lightly kicked his horse. "We're almost there."

Cameron was right. Jack was just having a hard time being patient with so much on the line. Personally, professionally, and emotionally. Because if he didn't fix this fuckup fast, Jack was never going to forgive himself. But they would arrive at Morningside soon, and if anyone in driving distance could help them with this particular problem, Cameron swore up and down it was the coach.

"We're here." Cam nodded to the abandoned high school in the distance a few minutes later.

"Do you think I can't see it?"

"Maybe I was saying that for me."

Jack looked at Morningside High looming larger as they approached the buildings, all overgrown with weeds and looking perfectly desolate from the outside. The windows were all either boarded up or broken into a handful of shards still clinging to the window frames. Most of the doors were flung open in the wind. Graffiti covered every wall.

"Remember, follow my lead when it comes to Coach showing us around."

"I know how to follow orders, but thank you for the extra reminder," said Jack.

They entered the gym, and the inside was even worse. Silent and dark, illuminated by a thin shaft of light from outside. The air held a heavy stillness, as if this nook of the world had been frozen in time. Basketball hoops were rusty and bent, with broken glass littering the court from one side to the other.

Cameron rapped his knuckles for a secret knock on the locker room door.

It swung open to a woman of contrasts. Large in both size and presence, she was dressed for an apocalypse that had passed long ago, in layers of protective clothing with various weapons strapped to a homemade utility belt hanging low on her waist: a rusty machete, a makeshift slingshot crafted from what looked like bicycle tubing, a brass knuckle-duster with spikes, a dented can of pepper spray, an old, dinged-up police baton, and a weathered but functional set of handcuffs. Her hair was cropped short, and hard years had carved deep lines into her face. Still, she smiled wide while greeting them with a hearty wave before ushering them inside the locker rooms.

"Haven't seen you for moons, Cameron. What brings you here now?" She nodded at Jack. "And who's your friend?"

"I'm Jack, ma'am,"

"Coach."

"Coach," he replied with a nod. "It's good to meet you."

"Likewise and all that. Now get to the good stuff and spill some beans. What brings you here?"

"Jack didn't believe me when I told him about all the crap you've hoarded." Cameron laughed as he gestured around the room.

"*Collected,*" Coach corrected him.

A few of the lockers were open and packed with trinkets. At a glance, Jack saw a red Slinky; a set of decorative magnets shaped like fruits (mostly cherries); a collection of shiny, unused birthday candles; a small snow globe (a smiling sun and palm trees); several stacks of mint condition trading cards; a collection of souvenir keychains from various tourist spots; a tiny, hand-painted wooden sailboat; a large assortment of glossy, polished stones; a bundle of unused, novelty pencils with jumbo erasers; a set of small, decorative glass bottles in a rainbow of colors; a delicate porcelain tea set; and several sets of nesting dolls.

But Jack could only see into three of the wide-open lockers and didn't want to get caught staring.

"So what, I like old shit." Coach gave them a shrug. "Did you know it's my birthday the month after next, so you brought me something from the Franklin Mint?"

"What's that?" Jack asked.

Cameron ignored his question and got right down to it. "Rabbit stole Jack's time machine."

"What the fuck, Cameron?"

"Relax. You want help, this is how we're going to get it. Coach needs to know what she's helping us with."

"He's right about that," she said to Jack.

Coach had been married to Farley a million years ago, before he met Cameron. But they still got on, so Farley and his boys and men still met up with her each year for Christmas, a little for family but mostly for trade.

"You Temporal Recon then?" Coach was suddenly looking at Jack a lot differently.

"Yes, ma'am."

She glared at him.

Jack cleared his throat. "Yes, Coach."

"Do you know all of the things you can do with a time machine?" she asked.

"I have some idea." Jack had no idea how else to answer that.

"You should just go back and take out Bertrand Lyndon." Coach nodded to herself. "Without him, no AFE, with no AFE, no war."

Jack glanced at Cameron.

And then Cameron offered Coach the same reply that everyone always gave whenever someone made that argument. "But that wouldn't actually solve our problem. Because even with Bertrand Lyndon taking one to the temple, another timeline where things didn't go to hell would be created. Nothing would change here in this one."

"And you can't just go around killing people before they commit a crime anyway," added Jack.

"Of course you can, if they are eventually going to kill millions." Cameron smiled, changed his voice to sound like Tom Cruise. "If the precogs see a murder, and we stop the murder, then the murder didn't actually happen, right? But the precogs saw it, so it must have happened. But if it happened, we'd be arresting people for crimes they didn't commit. You see the dilemma, don't you?"

Coach hung her head in sorrow. "The last Tom Cruise movie ever."

"Do you have any idea where Farley might be going?" Jack was irritated, asking a question that should have been the first thing out of Cameron's mouth.

"I have a decent idea or two." Coach nodded while walking over to one of her overstocked lockers. "But you need to see these bumper stickers first. Prepare to laugh your asses off."

Chapter Twenty-Three

JACK – 2036

NEITHER JACK nor Cameron laughed their asses off.

Coach had quite the collection of bumper stickers, which she kept in order of how much they made her want to laugh. The top three stickers on the stack read, WARNING: DRIVER ONLY CARRIES $20 IN AMMUNITION, HONK IF YOU HATE NOISE POLLUTION, and IF YOU'RE NOT A HEMORRHOID, GET OFF MY BUTT.

"That last one gets funnier when you get older."

Once back on the road, Cameron reported that his favorites were HONK IF YOU'VE NEVER SEEN AN UZI FIRED FROM A CAR WINDOW and MY OTHER RIDE IS YOUR MOM.

Jack found the entire show and tell a waste of time, but finally said that HONK IF YOU HATE NOISE POLLUTION was his favorite just to shut Cameron up.

"It's your fault." Cameron laughed at Jack, just like he'd been doing for the last several miles.

"You've made that clear. How was I supposed to know she—"

"Because I told you. Before we got there. A few times on the way, and then once more before we got to the gym. Remember? It was when you said, 'I know how to follow orders, but thank you for the extra reminder.'"

"It's remarkable how well your memory works sometimes."

"It always works, I just prefer that it's working for me," Cameron replied. "Coach is really proud of her piles of shit. And she's lonely since she and Farley so violently parted ways. She treats all that junk like companions. If you'd have just let Coach introduce you to a few of those intimate friends on her terms, we would have been in and out of there. But you had to let her know we were in a hurry, so she made sure we weren't getting out of there any time soon. You're lucky I knew how to react when she showed us that old collection of Lucy and Me dolls or we'd still be there instead of on our way to Coleco."

"How do you even know what a Lucy and Me doll is?"

"I've known Coach for a long time," Cameron said.

"Do you really think that we'll find Farley in Coleco? Because time is not on our side here. Sutherland will no doubt tell the army, or worse go straight to Temporal Recon and report the unit missing."

"I think that there's no one around who knows Farley's habits better than Coach, and if she thinks that's where he'd take the Corvette if he didn't know it was a time machine, then I think there's a better than excellent shot at him being there." Cameron shrugged. "But I'm also a chronic optimist."

Coleco was around fourteen miles from Morningside

High — a ride that was just under two hours by horse. The permanent shanty town was several miles out from the fort where Jack reported for duty, but was exactly the kind of bustling hub that people like Farley and his boys liked to frequent.

Outcasts belonged in the outskirts, and Coleco was a ramshackle kaleidoscope of makeshift structures, built from salvaged materials bearing too many scars. A place made by artists, attracting wanderers, survivors, and traders alike.

Coach had figured that Farley would want to take the Corvette there because that's where he would find the best prices for parts. Though few people in Coleco could ever afford something like the Corvette, the place was filled with eyes that could appreciate such a treasure, and surely someone among the population was likely to know someone who knew someone willing to pay, even if that meant breaking the car into pieces and parts. And once they found the Time Machine inside … Jack didn't want to think about the damage someone could do with it. At least they didn't have the code.

Jack could smell Coleco as they reached the outskirts, the air thick with an alluring scent of sizzling meats and unfamiliar spices. It had been night for a while by the time they arrived, and most of the vendor stalls were closed. Those offering food and drink were lively.

Jack and Cameron tied their horses to the hitches nearest the big bonfire where everyone had gathered to dance near the center of the shanty town.

The citizens were all dressed up, though what counted for finery was slightly different in this place, with bolder colors and more skin. The same mood of fellow-ship and warmth permeated the crowd as Jack and Cameron clung to the fringes, soaking up the music and laughter while observing the crowd, looking for the Farley boys through a series of melodious numbers without seeing a thing.

"There!" Cameron pointed to a boy moving swiftly through the crowds.

"That kid?"

"That's one of Farley's."

"How do you know?" Jack asked. "You said that you haven't been around Farley in years."

"I haven't. But I know his moves. That kid just lifted a billfold from that old woman when he bumped into her. I'd bet your time machine on it."

"Fuck you, Cameron."

"See!" He pointed again, this time at the same boy squeezing past a young couple, holding hands and moving along to the music, not paying nearly enough attention to the little thief in between them.

"I saw it." Jack nodded. "What did he take?"

"Not sure." Cameron was already circling around the crowd, looking to cut the kid off on the other side.

Jack followed.

The boy was either clocking out for the night or onto them — he darted away from the crowd and down one of Coleco's homemade streets.

They followed, Jack so desperate to catch the kid that he pulled several strides ahead of Cameron.

The kid ran faster.

"Wait," Cameron said, still slightly behind Jack.

"Are you kidding? He's getting away!"

"But he knows we're following him. He could be leading us right into a—"

Trap.

Too late. They fell into it anyway.

Cameron caught up to Jack and they stopped short side-by-side in the middle of what counted for Main Street in this place. The kid was staring them down, much too confident for a boy all alone.

They heard the roar of an engine down the road.

Then the boy bolted into a gnarl of shadows.

And the Corvette squealed away.

"What just happened?" Jack asked in confusion.

"That." Cameron pointed.

And Jack turned to see a trio of Jeeps barreling toward them, army logos on their sides illuminated by the moon.

Chapter Twenty-Four

JACK – 2036

JACK SAT in the dimly lit tent, cradling his head, suffering the death of everything he had worked for.

Any dreams of being one of the few humans to experience temporal travel firsthand were dashed. It would be back to tending horses for him, something he deeply loved partly because Jack spent a lifetime believing that he wouldn't be doing it forever.

Tending to the horses now would be a luxurious sentence, but prison nonetheless. His anguish gave way to a sorrowful acceptance as Cameron gradually managed to calm him down.

"We're going to be fine. A month from now, this will be our best story yet. And I'll bet three bags of feed that you'll tell it as much as I do."

"You talk so much, I'll never catch up." Jack shook his head. "Please tell me you understand that we're under heavy guard."

"You call this heavy guard? It's one guy standing outside our tent. This is nothing."

"We might as well be in the brig."

"Says you."

"Says the one of us who actually has some experience here."

"Exactly." Cameron nodded as if Jack had just proved his point for him. "I would argue that your experience here seriously clouds your perspective."

"We deserve whatever is coming to us."

"It's not like we can be sent to jail for trying to recover a stolen vehicle."

"Time machine."

"We didn't do any of the stealing ourselves."

"I let it get stolen by not driving it straight to the launch site."

"And then you beat up Sutherland," Cameron clearly already loved telling this story. "Well, that part was me too."

"I screwed up."

"We screwed up," Cameron said. "So let's fix it by getting out of here."

A storm of conflict roiled within Jack, the alluring call of freedom wrestling with the chains of past mistakes. The rhythm of tending horses, once a comforting solace, now echoed as a hollow requiem for lost dreams. He considered Cameron's words — *one guard, one chance.*

"What are you thinking?" Jack asked. "Or is this another flying by the seat of your pants and hoping for the best kind of situation?"

"We start by looking for a way." Cameron was canvassing the tent, searching for anything that might aid their escape. "Too bad we're not in a supply tent. I could whip up a smoke bomb to distract the guard."

"A smoke bomb?" Jack repeated.

"Sure: fertilizer, sugar, baking soda, and a roll of toilet paper."

"You spend too much time in the library."

"That one isn't from the library. It's a trick I learned from Ma, from during the war." Cameron shrugged. "Probably wouldn't work here anyway, because we'd have to extract the potassium nitrate from the fertilizer and that's a serious pain in the ass."

"That part definitely sounds like the library."

"I have an idea," Cameron said on his way to the tent flaps.

"Care to share?"

"One of us needs to get out of here, so I guess that means I'll be the one distracting the guards. You can cut a hole in the tent and go out that way."

"Should I use my butcher knife or my katana blade?" Jack clarified the situation. "How am I supposed to cut a hole in the canvas without anything sharp?"

"Use your belt buckle."

"That will take forever—"

"Then do it fast. Or here, this will be better." Cameron pulled out a lighter from his pocket and handed it to Jack. "Use this. Burn a tiny hole, just enough to start working it."

"Why do you have a lighter?"

"Who doesn't carry a lighter?"

"You don't smoke," argued Jack.

"What does that have to do with anything? The guard didn't take it from me, right?"

Jack burned the hole and then they started working on widening the aperture together.

"We have to go fast before someone sees—"

"You think I don't know that?" Jack cut him off.

When it was nearly wide enough to crawl through, Cameron left him and walked over to the tent entrance. He lifted the flap without giving Jack a chance to object.

The guard turned around. "Get back in your tent!"

"Do you have a moment?"

Either Cameron's tone or the query itself seemed to catch the guard by surprise — Jack had seen the trick countless times before. Same as usual, though it took the guard longer than typical before he replied with an extremely tentative, "What is it?"

"My buddy and I here can't seem to agree, and we were hoping you could break our tie." Cameron jerked a thumb at Jack. "This dipshit thinks the best way to tie your shoes is overhand, but it's definitely bunny ears, right?"

"I'm sorry?" The guard started. "You need to—"

"I get that you might not have any strong opinions on that one, so how about I bounce over to a question that you guys are probably always mulling over around here: if you could choose any period in history to visit, where would you go and why?"

"Get—"

"WAIT! Don't answer that. You might accidentally say something classified, and I wouldn't want you to get into any trouble on my account. So let's stick to something I wonder about all the time, that you might have more insight into, seeing as you work with Temporal Recon. But is it true that people used to put pineapple on their pizza?"

"Get back in the tent!" barked the guard, now fully irked. "Now!"

But his body had fully turned toward Cameron and away from Jack, thanks to Cameron inching to the side more and more by the sentence.

"OH! Sorry!" Cameron replied. "I was just—"

"HEY!" The guard spied Jack, already out of the tent

and sprinting away at top speed. "STOP! GET BACK HERE!"

Jack darted into the shadows, a phantom flitting between gaps in the patrol. He could hear the guard give chase behind him, raising the alarm, but Jack was already too far ahead. His heart beat a timpani against his ribs, his breath already coming in ragged gasps as he made his escape.

If everything had gone according to plan, then Cameron had likely strolled off the base with his hands buried deep in his pockets.

Chapter Twenty-Five

JACK – 2036

JACK SPRINTED BACK to Coleco without stopping, finally arriving at the hitching posts where he and Cameron had left their horses, chest heaving and gasping for breath as sweat poured down his face.

Cameron was there, leaning against his horse, looking calm and collected.

"So much for you causing a distraction! I was the one who—"

"Thanks buddy!" Cameron clapped him on the shoulder. "Now let's go and get that Chevy."

"How did you get here so fast?"

"I asked someone if they had a moment. And when they did, I requested a ride. I find that most people are accommodating if you give them a chance."

"You tricked me."

"I didn't trick you, Jack. There were two ways that little situation could have gone down. I'm sorry you had to run.

Good thing, though: I might be the people person, but you trained for this."

"This is *not* what I trained for."

Cameron climbed onto his horse. "How many timelines do you think you're uptight in?"

Jack swung a leg onto his mount. "I'm not uptight!"

"So probably all of them." Cameron nodded and started to ride.

Jack followed. "Where are we headed?"

"To find Farley."

"Obviously. Are we just wandering through the night like Don Quixote, or do we know where we're going?"

"Don Quixote's quest was to revive chivalry and protect the helpless as a valiant knight-errant, inspired by romantic tales of heroism that he read and fell in love with. Nighttime had nothing to do with it."

"Okay." Jack landed in the same place he usually did when he felt like quitting on a conversation with Cameron. "Are we headed for a specific location?"

"Yep."

"Would you care to elaborate?"

"I know where the Farleys go after Coleco. Pretty much every time."

"Where?"

"To the buyers."

"And you still don't think they know that the Chevy is housing a temporal unit?"

"I don't think Farley could tell the difference between a Picasso and a finger painting."

"That's hardly the same thing," argued Jack. "Do you know a *specific* place where the Farleys would take the Corvette? Or is this more of that hoping by the seat of your pants sort of situation?"

"It's a bit of both," Cameron admitted.

"Did you read a book at the library about how to speak in vagaries?"

"Nope." He shook his head. "Ma taught me that too."

"Why are you being so evasive?"

"Because you hate Old Orlando."

"Oh."

They rode in silence for a few long minutes after that.

Once a vibrant city bursting with life, Old Orlando now lay in ruins, enchanting theme parks that once hosted a bustling tourist industry now desolate wastelands filled with the worst of humankind. The military was content to leave the disaster area alone, because the human roaches skittering about the ruins stayed busy eating each other alive.

"It's another seven hours at this pace," Jack finally said.

"Yep. Sounds about right." Cameron nodded. "So don't fall asleep."

"I've never been less tired in my life."

"Should I keep guessing the code to your time machine? That should keep you awake."

"No."

Banter was spare as they focused on the dark road before them, Cameron casting a beam from his flashlight. Fatigue finally found Jack as they hit the outskirts, which like Old Orlando itself lay shrouded in a veil of decay. Twisted steel skeletons cast eerie shadows on the ground, rusted frames and roller coaster cars on the track both slowly being devoured by wildlife and vines.

Once-pristine streets were overrun by a sea of flora and fauna rooted in the cracked and creviced asphalt, with abandoned vehicles entombed in the overgrowth. The city was heavy with the scent of rot, punctuated by a sharp tang of rust amid the sweet perfume of blossoming flowers.

"Are we here?" Jack asked as Cameron slowed his horse to a stop.

"Almost." He nodded to a three-story parking garage, where a large sign hung, roughly sheared almost right down the middle and looking one strong cough away from crashing to the ground. It read, *HOURLY, DAILY AND MONTHLY RATES AVAILABLE.*

"How sure are you that Farley is in there?"

"I'm going to be straight with you, Jack." Cameron looked at him solemnly. "I'm not sure at all. But I will say this is the only place I know that it could be. Farley is crap at defense, and this garage offers him protection in a layout he's familiar with. He'll want to make a deal for the Corvette, and I think he'll make that deal here. Unless this location has been compromised, it's our best bet."

They obscured their horses and left them tied, navigating the thick vegetation and debris on foot for the remainder of their way to the parking garage. Up close they surveyed the structure, noting the numerous vantage points that might allow one of the Farley boys to spot intruders.

"You're thinking like a soldier, not a street kid." Cameron walked straight toward the garage down the middle of the road. "They don't need to know we're coming if they have enough of them to hold off any intruders."

Jack and Cameron moved quietly through the garage, following the sound of laughter all the way to the top level, where they ducked into the stairwell to get a better vantage point.

Jack felt a near explosion of relief at the site of the ancient Chevy, intact, on the blacktop. But between him and his prize were a scattered group of tents, cars, and

Farley's ragtag gang. Right in the middle, the large loping figure of Farley himself.

"Are we going to fight them?"

"Can't fight the Farleys." Cameron shook his head. "Those boys are mean and scrappy. Even if I used to be one of them, not a one of them will flinch before killing us both. We need to draw them away from the car, either by offering an incentive big enough or a deterrent that's scary enough…"

The thought dangled as he and Jack considered their options. Then a grin crawled across Cameron's features and climbed high into his voice.

"I have an idea."

Chapter Twenty-Six

RJ – 2024

"BUCKLE UP," Cecilia said, her eyes alive with the adrenaline of remembrance.

RJ and Michael were at full attention as she continued her story.

"We pulled up to the building like hell itself was nipping at our heels. Tires screeching, doors slamming, we were like rockets launched from the car. My partner made straight for the security guard, told him to evacuate the building, call the police, and report a bomb threat made to that address. I tore into the stairwell, those blueprints from the basement still burned into my mind."

The door swung open, and Suzanne returned with the coffee. "If the blueprints from the basement are still burning in your mind, then I'm guessing we're at the—"

"Don't divulge the location!" Cecilia snapped.

"I don't *know* the location because you've never told

me, and I was going to say, 'I'm guessing we're at the part when you find those guys on the roof.'"

"Guys on the roof?" RJ repeated.

Another glance at Michael: *Good shit.*

"The plans indicated that the bomb would be placed on the roof. The chase up those stairs ... I can still feel it. The cold sweat, the fire in my lungs, the echo of my shoes against the concrete. My partner huffing and puffing behind me as he worked to catch up."

She took a breath. "The wind cut into us like a knife when we got there. But sure enough, we saw our three stooges with the bomb. They were trapped for sure, but one of the men was threatening to blow us all sky high. We put our guns down, but I needed to know what it all meant, how what was happening on that rooftop tied to what had happened at IBM, or if it even did. So I asked them *why*."

"And?" RJ prompted Cecilia when she stopped.

"They said they were doing it to stop World War III. They believed that if they blew up this building in Omaha, then the government could never be located there and they were diverting themselves from Titor's timeline, ensuring that they never ended up in his war-ravaged world."

"That's insane," Michael said. "Who was it? The name, I mean."

Suzanne rolled her eyes. "She knows what you mean."

Cecilia continued. "They believed in both Titor and the trolley problem."

"The trolley problem?" Michael repeated.

"It means they were willing to kill a few people now to save the millions in the future," RJ explained.

"Exactly." Cecilia agreed. "Negotiation is more delicate than disarming a bomb. I had to make those men see reason through the waves of fear and panic. I offered the two that were listening a plea bargain, but that last one was a true zealot, ready to go down and take everyone with him. He was also the one clutching the detonator."

"Until one of the other two guys tackled him!" Suzanne couldn't help herself.

"That was our chance. We grabbed our weapons and rushed the group," Cecilia said. "The next few minutes were messy and hectic, but we managed to seize the detonator and cuff all three men. The one who had been tackled spat on his attacker and called both of his former buddies cowards, before he started screaming his throat bloody about how they had doomed the world."

Cecilia's fingers idly traced the rim of her coffee cup, her voice relaxing from the story's climax. "The bomb squad arrived right after that, thanks to the guard downstairs. And they dismantled the bomb."

"It's a good story, but why are you telling it to us?" Michael asked. "The three guys were just a bunch of conspiracy nuts, right?"

"Right." Cecilia turned and looked him in the eyes. "That is exactly correct, Michael. And I am telling you this story for two reasons. I want you to understand how dangerous it is to encourage conspiracy theorists, no matter how harmless the conspiracy might seem to you. But also because what happened on the rooftop that day was the only reason I ever figured out who John Titor really was."

"You figured out who John Titor was?" RJ asked.

She nodded. "After booking the three men, I pulled up my old files on the IBM heist. I remembered the inside man on that job was a John Anderson. He had claimed that a man from the future convinced him to steal the 5100, though he later retracted that claim under pressure. Still, it got me thinking. So, I went through all the Titor posts. Even if the FBI wasn't interested in the truth about a thirty-year-old case, I was."

"And?" RJ prompted her.

"Titor didn't drop many hints about his actual family, but there were two that we did follow up on. One hint was that he traveled back to 1975 for the retrieval of an IBM 5100, and claimed his grandfather was a lead engineer on that team."

RJ knew about that one from the Titor posts. But there had to be more. Something that only the FBI would know.

Cecilia delivered the pay dirt. "A woman named Kat claimed to be Titor's mother. And there was only one man who had a mom named Kat and a grandfather who worked on the IBM 5100."

"What was Titor's real name?" Michael asked after a pregnant pause.

Cecilia smiled, pleased to see that she finally had his full attention. "His name was Jack Anderson."

Chapter Twenty-Seven

JACK – 2036

"YOU SURE ABOUT THIS?" Jack asked.

"Do you want me to say no?"

"We do this, and we'll make a permanent enemy out of Farley."

Cameron looked from the Farley boys (men) huddled around their campfire before glancing over to the Chevy again, then back at his chosen brother. "I only have one family."

Jack swallowed, pleased by the answer yet understandably nervous. His training would kick in, but the butterflies in his stomach were still in mid-rebellion, and in moments like this, they fluttered the hardest, building up enough of a gust to keep him alive through the battle.

"So we're good to go?" Jack was just making sure.

Cameron nodded. "On your count."

Jack swallowed again. "3 … 2 … 1—"

Cameron hit a button on his walkie-talkie. "GO."

The stairwell door exploded open behind them, followed by a familiar roar as Jack and Cameron raced from their hiding place.

Hank exploded out of the shadows and charged the Farley boys, followed by Arvel running wildly behind the crocodile, gripping the beast tightly by its leash as he got dragged through the assault.

The motley crew dispersed in an instant, except for Rabbit — he spotted Jack and Cameron sprinting out from behind the truck and now had them in his sights, hot pursuit with a heaving growl, gaining on them faster than Jack expected.

Rabbit was closer to Cameron and reached out to grab him first, but Cameron managed to dodge the swipe and pivoted a few inches to the side, swerving fast enough that Rabbit turned his attention to Jack.

Rabbit snatched him by the shirt tail and yanked back hard.

Jack somehow found another gear inside him, accelerating enough to make Rabbit lose his grip on Jack's shirt.

But the victory was fleeting. The second time Rabbit yanked him back by the shirt, Jack fell backward and pounded his ass on the ground.

"CAMERON!" Jack shouted.

Cameron kept running.

"CAMERON!" Louder still, but still Cameron ignored Jack in favor of racing for the car. *Jack's car.*

And the temporal unit inside it.

That asshole. Betraying him again. If he got away with the time machine, Jessup would hunt him down and execute him. And Jack would deserve the life sentence in prison he'd probably earned by trusting Cameron.

Jack spun around and clocked Rabbit in the jaw.

Rabbit fell to his knees and let go of Jack.

He roared toward Cameron and the Corvette.

But now the Farley boys were all racing toward Jack.

Cameron made it into the Corvette and frantically tried to start the engine.

Jack was almost there, but Rabbit was only a breath behind him.

The engine turned over just as Jack reached the Corvette, slamming into the car as another engine roared to life behind him. Rabbit tackled Jack a second later, knocking him flat on the concrete. Jack twisted, punching Rabbit repeatedly, finally landing a solid blow on his chin. Rabbit went limp.

But before Jack could scramble to his feet, Cameron floored it, and the Corvette was suddenly hauling ass toward the bottom floor of the parking garage.

Another engine screamed behind it.

Jack raced after both vehicles, praying he wouldn't get shot as he bolted into the stairwell and pounded down to the next level. Then the next.

Disaster struck like lightning as Cameron's tires squealed on the concrete, his exit from the garage blocked by a brigade of military vehicles. The army had tracked them down.

One of the cars behind him veered over in front of Jack, while the other careened toward one of the Jeeps in the blockade and plowed right into it.

Cameron flew by the blockade, making a sloppy left into another part of the garage: a heat-seeking missile in search of the nearest exit.

But that exit was also blocked.

Same for the exit after that.

He wasn't going to make it. And Jack wasn't going to make it to the Corvette before the army or Farley's gang killed them both.

The blockades were sending vehicles forward as a beat-to-shit Ford barreled toward the Corvette. Cameron was stuck in the approximate center of ground floor, with enemy vehicles like torpedoes. There was only one thing left to do, only one possible means of escape. Except that Cameron didn't have the code.

A loud chirp from an angry alarm, then a small light to trigger the countdown as Cameron secured himself in his seat and energy crackled around the car.

He stared out the windshield and the F-150 squealed to a stop several feet in front of him.

I'm sorry, he mouthed to Jack.

The Corvette shimmered, streaks of rainbow light radiating out from the metal.

The air grew heavy with the scent of burning rubber and ozone as a high-pitched whine echoed throughout the garage, like a vacuum cleaner on the fritz.

Motherfucker.

He'd figured out the code.

CAMERON GINGERLY DROVE off of the small mound of dirt he brought with him from 2036 and continued toward the exit, now that the only blockade in the garage was a guard at the pay booth.

He looked around in awe. Most of the parking spaces were now occupied, with vehicles similar to his car, only newer. *A lot newer.* Same for all the concrete and everything else.

The attendant looked at Cameron strangely when he pulled up.

"Do you have a moment?"

"Sure," the attendant said. "What do you need?"

"Can you please tell me what year it is?"

The attendant gave him a strange look. "It's 1975."

Cameron whooped and punched the ceiling.

"Do you have your ticket? You'll need your ticket to leave the garage ... sir ... do you have your ticket?"

No, he did not have a ticket. But Cameron couldn't stop laughing.

Part III

Chapter Twenty-Eight

CAMERON - 1975

Cameron cruised along the highway, an almost luxurious feeling of wind whipping through his mop of hair, as he maneuvered the freshly acquired Corvette with the grace and confidence of a man who had recently accomplished the impossible.

He drove top down as the sun dumped buckets of light onto his gleaming hood. Even after a day and a half on the new old roads, he still felt enthralled.

Unlike the simple threads he had traded a day of labor to Ella Washington for back home, Cameron was now properly dressed for the adventure in his off the rack suit, aviator glasses perched on the bridge of his nose.

The roar of a car engine wasn't exactly rare in 2036, but hearing so many at once in surround sound bordered on overwhelming. The hum of other cars speeding past him, the scent of exhaust mingling with the tang of gasoline, was an intoxicating cocktail that reeked of adventure.

Other vehicles darted in and out of traffic, all part of the landscape instead of the bullseye for thieves that the

Corvette made in his time. Sleek lines, chrome bumpers, and wide grilles adorned the cars around Cameron in a blend of vibrant and muted colors that defined the era's automotive palette. His Corvette was still a rarity, but he spied plenty of fellow Chevys on the road as he passed Impalas, Monte Carlos and Novas, Plymouth Furys and Ford Pintos, AMC Pacers and Dodge Darts — all cars he had read about, and would no doubt know how to fix if he were to find himself underneath one or standing in front of its raised hood.

The landscape changed as Cameron came closer to the city, sprawling suburbs surrendering to urban jungle blooming majestically into the sky. Buildings that shocked his eyes as they clawed for the heavens, glass exteriors reflecting gleaming sunlight.

He passed through a tunnel, then the buzz of city life swallowed Cam without chewing, a sudden cacophony of honking horns, chattering pedestrians, and distant wailing sirens.

His final destination lay a few long city blocks before him, but he would have to walk the remainder of the way. Outside the window, New York was even more overwhelming. The number of cars he had seen on his way into the city had been staggering, but the sheer amount of people milling through the streets now felt like a blade between his ribs. A stark reminder of the billions lost in his timeline.

In Cameron's world, cities were avoided. Still filled with danger, mostly destroyed and often abandoned to savages, like Old Orlando.

But here the city bustled with people like ants on a hill, everyone going about their individual lives while harmonizing with the hectic world around them. A life of civil war and an aftermath of strife had robbed Cameron of the ability to truly understand what he was seeing right now, but the sight was still narcotic and soon enough would become as normal to his eyes as the sunrise and sunset.

Until then, he needed to keep drinking it in.

An Oldsmobile Cutlass pulled into traffic just ahead, leaving Cameron with just enough room in between an almost matching set of Volkswagen Beetles for him to parallel park his Corvette.

He killed the engine and reached into the glovebox, grabbing the wallet full of cash that Jack had prepared for the trip, and that Cam had already used twice, once to get gas and his sunglasses after the fill-up, and a second time on his way into the city when he pulled off the side of the road after seeing a billboard from a place called Salvatore's Suits that read, *UPGRADE YOUR STYLE FOR LESS!*

There were no additional details, until Cameron passed the next sign from Salvatore, this one promising *UNBEAT-ABLE QUALITY AND TIMELESS DESIGNS!* Followed by a written plea for Cameron to *BE BOLD, BE DAPPER, BE CONFIDENT!* Details (finally) came at the last sign, when Salvatore's Suits lay just two exits ahead: *MEN'S SUITS STARTING AT $49.99.*

Cameron dropped his change in the meter, then started on the final few blocks to his destination, craning his neck as he walked, marveling at the skyscrapers while squinting up at the tops climbing into the clouds in a way his eyes had a hard time adjusting to, like a sailor lost at sea, gazing at the stars to gather his bearings.

A dirty-looking world seemed to get dirtier by the step, sidewalks littered with newspapers and soda cans, belching exhaust from passing cars into a dense haze that hung in the air like a dark gray fog. Rows of storefronts each adver-tised something different: an all-night diner with neon signs flashing in the window boasting hot food and endless coffee, while a beat-to-shit pawn shop displayed an eclectic collection of items behind its grimy glass. Adult theaters promised provocative titles with suggestive fonts, three in one block: Carnal Carnival, Pleasure Palace, and Temptation Island, that last one sharing its front walk with a hole-in-the-wall bar that barely seemed to be open, a dim glow from inside almost invisible through the smoke-streaked windows.

Cameron passed a group of men wearing worn leather jackets leaning against a graffiti-covered brick wall, their laughter rolling through the street in an echo as they passed a paper bag with a tall bottle among them.

He was approached by several women, each one in revealing attire, voices all dripping with honey as they asked Cam if he was looking for a good time or needed a little bit of temporary company.

Then he finally arrived at his destination: the pulsing heart of this legendary city, where dazzling lights and towering billboards left him on sensory overload.

Cameron was standing in the middle of Time's Square, 1975, and he had never felt happier.

Chapter Twenty-Nine

RJ – 2024

"A WOMAN NAMED Kat claimed to be Titor's mother. And there was only one man who had a mom named Kat and a grandfather who worked on the IBM 5100."

"What was his name?" Michael asked.

"His name was Jack Anderson," she said.

What should have been a revelation worthy of balloons landed like a lead anchor in the room.

"What about his grandfather's name?" RJ hoped it got better.

"John."

Michael didn't even respond, turning instantly to his phone with a series of furious swipes. RJ knew what he was thinking before he said it out loud.

"Super." Michael rolled his eyes in disgust. "According to the U.S. Census Bureau, 'John' is one of the most common first names for males, and 'Anderson' is the 12th most common surname in America. There are literally thousands of leads here."

But there was surely only one who worked at IBM on that computer at the right time, and RJ could argue the point, but it wasn't worth the bother. When it came to John Titor and anything relating to the time traveler's story, RJ was an eager explorer mapping out uncharted territory, while Michael was a reluctant tourist counting down the days to a departure he never wanted to make.

"If you knew who it was, then why isn't the identity of John Titor more widely known? If the poster wasn't really who he claimed to be, then the secret didn't really need to be kept, did it? And was Titor ever arrested, or no, because technically he didn't do anything illegal?"

"Not everyone agreed with my conclusion." Cecilia shrugged. "And I wasn't the only agent on the case, but I might as well have been. Cowards."

Great, that meant more possibilities for RJ to talk to. "What made them cowards?"

"Was it because they were afraid to chase down a hundred thousand John Andersons?" Michael might have been trying to mutter under his breath, but the words came out plenty loud.

Suzanne shot him a dirty look as Cecilia ignored him.

"Let's just say that some of my fellow agents lacked imagination and thus got caught up in another theory."

"Do you mind if I ask what that theory was?"

Cecilia sighed, punctuating her fatigue with a tired smile. "It doesn't matter. They were wrong."

Michael shot RJ a dubious look.

"Can you tell me anything else about Jack Anderson before we go?"

Another sigh. "I can tell you that this conversation has exhausted me, and that I'm in desperate need of my afternoon nap. If you want my best answers, I suggest we talk later."

"You heard her, boys," Suzanne said, shooing them out of her mother's room.

"What can you possibly be smiling about?" Michael asked when he and RJ were both outside the retirement home, back in the humid Florida air and on their way to the car. "Her punchline sucked almost as hard as her stories. Especially considering the seven years it took her to finally get there."

"I'm thrilled that I have someone to actually investigate now."

"Do you have any more of that *mota* you've been smoking?" Then when RJ didn't respond he added, "How are you going to pinpoint one Jack Anderson among the millions?"

"Thousands," RJ corrected. "At most. And that part is easy."

"How so?"

"Because I'm starting with the one trail we truly have."

"And that is?" Michael replied, still not getting it.

RJ laughed. "Too bad you were so busy waiting for the punchline that you missed the joke."

"Who are you going to investigate?"

"The grandfather who worked at IBM in the 70s."

Chapter Thirty

JOHN – 1975

JOHN ANDERSON WAS HAVING a hard time leaving the apartment this morning.

He gave Etta another kiss on her cheek, the third one in the last five minutes. "I'm going to be late."

"I hate when you tell me that you're going to be late for work."

"I know, but—"

Etta didn't kiss him back, meaning she had not issued her silent permission for him to go. "I know exactly when each of your three trains leaves the station, and I am quite sure you still have another ten minutes to offer your wife before you abandon her for your true love."

"You are my only true love," John assured her with a wide smile. "And I'm not cheating on you with my work if you know all about her. IBM is our ticket to get what we need. To get Junior what he needs."

Junior looked up from the living room floor, where he was playing with a tiny mountain of blocks.

John and Etta were happy here in Harlem. They knew most of their neighbors and had decided to raise a family in the borough. But the job at IBM was more of a godsend than Etta liked to acknowledge. It meant Junior could be healthy again. Would be.

"I'm worried about you," she said.

"I know, honey, but I'm not any safer inside."

"Like hell you're not."

"If I miss even one of those three trains, then I'm in danger of losing my job." He glanced out their window at the remains of a destroyed apartment building across the street. A jumbled pile of twisted metal, broken concrete, and dust that billowed into the house whenever Etta dared to open a window. "Today is the day."

"What if it's not?" Etta asked, even though that was the exact phrase John had been trying to steer clear of all morning. The one doubt he didn't want in his head.

Not when he was otherwise sitting on top of the world. "I told you, there's no one better for the project, and I hope you're planning on frying some catfish to celebrate tonight, because when I come home, it'll be as a promoted man who can finally afford Junior's operation."

Junior looked up at the mention of his name, then back down at his blocks.

"I bet you'd still want that promotion, even if it stole more of your hours away from us and didn't pay you an extra dime."

"Why would you say that?"

"Because," Etta started, with a sadder note than John wanted to hear on the morning of his big day, "sometimes I feel like that computer is more important to you than your real baby."

"My real baby is who I'm doing all of this for."

"No." She shook her head. "Not all of it."

"Do you realize how lucky we are that I have a job at all in this economy?"

"I'd have to be a fool not to realize it considering how often you bring that exact thing up."

"Jobless rates are skyrocketing, Etta. Trouble is coming."

"It's three trains."

"It will all be worth it," he promised.

"Assuming you get the promotion."

"Of course I'm going to get the promotion." John was honestly sick of having to defend himself. "I have the skill and I've made all the sacrifices. Laslo knows it."

"Laslo's also white."

"He's not that kind of man." He was, but John was definitely not about to tell Etta that. Besides, on a project of this scale he would surely get past it to choose the best man for the job.

"I hope not." Her thin smile fell too far on the wrong side between faith and fear.

"I need to go, Etta. Is there any way you can be happy for me today? Happy for us?"

"Even if you get the promotion, how much will that really be for *us*? I barely saw you during the 5100, and you were only a programmer. How much are you going to be around when you're lead engineer on the Synthia?"

John took her hands and squeezed them as he spoke in his gentlest voice. "If Junior is alive, does it matter?"

Etta looked like she had two dozen answers and no time for any of them.

"You have to go." She let go of his hands and kissed him on the cheek. "Good luck. I'm happy for us. I promise. Just also scared."

"You don't need to be scared," John assured her as he started toward the door. "Remember, catfish tonight!"

She laughed as he closed the door, causing John to wonder if that meant he was more or less likely to be enjoying his catfish (with red beans and rice).

He descended five stories of steep steps — the elevator in his building was usually busted, so he got tired of playing wait and see, especially on the way down — and exited onto 125th Street.

Harlem was alive at all hours, but early morning in the borough was especially vibrant, with the aroma of sizzling street food already lingering in the air, at battle with the exhaust puffing out from waves of tailpipes passing slowly by in impatient traffic, loud enough to drown much of the lively chatter from passersby amid the music coming from a nearby apartment playing their Coltrane at a volume that was probably too loud for the neighbors, but just right for John as he hustled toward the train station, walking past bell bottoms, Afros and wide brimmed hats, waving at his favorite vendors, skirting by a group of six kids playing hopscotch across the cracked sidewalks, young enough to have little or maybe even no idea that they were growing up amid the visible scars of poverty and decay. Crumbling buildings, boarded-up windows, and graffiti-soaked walls.

But Harlem was a vibrant artery, with thriving businesses, from the Apollo to Sylvia's Restaurant, the streetscape punctuated by small, family-owned shops selling everything from clothing to vinyl.

Three trains later, John had traded the neighborhood fatigue of Harlem for the gleaming skyscrapers and manicured streets of Midtown.

He stopped to savor the moment upon arriving for work, knowing that today would change everything. Then John entered the IBM building and reported for duty.

Chapter Thirty-One

JOHN – 1975

THE COMPACT, offsite IBM R&D facility was a starkly muted contrast to the world John saw at home. Mighty mainframes and orderly rows of magnetic tape machines lined the walls. Complemented by an omnipresent hum of technology and the faint scent of ozone, this room pulsed with the future like a living, breathing thing. The place felt sacred, and John considered himself among the lucky few, frequently peering into the world of tomorrow.

Amid the symphony of blinking lights and whirring reels, John's colleagues congregated around a cluster of meticulously arranged desks. Despite an early departure and the journey on three trains, John was invariably the last to arrive. Today, he could discern the echoes of laughter and friendly banter even as he reached for the door handle.

"Welcome to the party!" Eddie called out as the door swung closed behind John. "Don was just wondering if you were ever going to join us after work, or if you're always gonna run home to the wifey whenever we ask."

"That's not exactly what I said," Don protested.

"Leave him alone." David was always the one among them most ready for work, besides John, who both woke up and went to bed that way. "How would you like taking a train to Harlem when you're shitfaced?"

John wasn't sure how to take the comment. Was David saying that it would be dangerous for white guys like them to be in Harlem while shitfaced after dark, or that he understood why John wouldn't want to ride three trains home after working a full day and some hard drinking?

Such confusion was a regular thing. John's coworkers were all good guys who treated him well, with all the camaraderie and backslapping he could hope for in what was in many ways a dream job. But none of that changed the fact that John was from a very different world, and always would be.

"It has nothing to do with my wife, though I profess that I do love her with all of my heart," John replied. "A man who occupies himself with the serious business of revolutionizing the computer does not have time to squander in a bar."

"I wouldn't call it a squandering." Dan laughed.

Eddie said, "I bet John goes home and still wishes he was here."

Pete, a wiry man in his late 30s who was mostly Adam's apple, added, "I bet he calls his wife the 5100."

Everyone laughed, including John.

"What do you think he tickles more, his baby at home, or his baby here?" Eddie asked the group.

Another round of laughs.

"So I'm a loving father in both places. That sounds like a good thing to me." John shrugged. "The 5100 is the first truly portable computer — it'll revolutionize the industry. Of course I'm proud of my baby."

"It's really *Carver's* baby," Don interjected.

And David said, "You can be the proud uncle."

"Fine. I'll play uncle for the 5100, but by the end of today I'll be named lead engineer on the Synthia 3700 and then I'll be a daddy on that one for—".

The intercom buzzed and everyone traded a glance.

Laslo said, "John. Get in here when you have a minute."

Then the intercom crackled into silence.

Laslo always meant *get in here right now*, regardless of what he said.

"Looks like your big moment is here ahead of schedule." Don nodded in approval.

Eddie clapped John on the shoulder. "Go get 'em, champ!"

"Don't keep the old man waiting," belted David and Pete in unison, before they started laughing.

John chewed on his bottom lip to keep from smiling too wide as he entered Laslo's office, surprised to see that the two of them weren't alone. There was a portly man John had never seen before squeezed into one of the two chairs facing Laslo's desk.

"This is Frederickson." Laslo introduced the stranger to John with a nod. "Frederickson, this is John. He was invaluable on the 5100 project, and I'm sure he'll be equally indispensable for you on the Synthia 3700."

The bottom fell out of his soul.

John couldn't believe what he had just heard, regardless of how hard his heart was pounding, no longer a steady metronome of anticipation, now a tempest of justified rage.

"But—"

Laslo raised a hand. "But nothing, son. I already know what you're going to say and there's no reason to embarrass yourself by finishing the sentence. Your job is to report for duty, and my job is to make sure that assigned duty is whatever is best for the entire team and the project and IBM at large."

"But I did all my work and—"

"This isn't about the work, son." Laslo cut him off again, leaving him even more confused and crestfallen.

"I have a sick baby at home." John tried to stop himself, but he couldn't keep the pathetic pleas from leaving his mouth. "Do you have any idea how much I've sacrificed for this company?"

Laslo remained unmoved. "Frederickson has already been hired for the position.

Frederickson shifted in his seat. The man still hadn't spoken a word to John, not even *hello*.

"I understand, sir." John bowed his head in humiliated defeat.

"Is there anything else?" Laslo asked.

John swallowed hard and got it over with. "I was wondering if there might be any possibility of an advance on my salary … or a loan to help with my son's operation."

He was about to elaborate on what it was Junior needed, and how much that might cost, but John stopped cold when he saw how the men were both looking at him. Like John had spat in their eyes.

He swallowed again, even harder, gritting his teeth as he delivered an impotent parting line.

"Thank you for your time."

Chapter Thirty-Two

JOHN – 1975

THANK YOU FOR YOUR TIME.

The five words kept repeating in that exact order, over and over like a curse in his mind, from the moment John said them out loud for Laslo in front of his new boss, Fred-erickson, to the end of the day when he was finally clocking out and riding the elevator down to the bottom floor.

Back on the Manhattan streets, the reality of his morning hit him even harder, alongside a chorus of other missives from his coworkers throughout the day, from *How would you like taking a train to Harlem when you're shitfaced?* to Damon's reassurance that he shouldn't worry about losing the Synthia project to Frederickson because, *If you play it right, this means more time for your family and the train rides.*

The very worst of all: Etta's prophetic comment this morning, *Laslo's also white.* John couldn't stand the idea of returning home to tell his wife that she was right. His new job had been given to another white man.

The thought of getting shitfaced before taking a train into Harlem suddenly sounded quite appealing indeed. John took his first train, but wandered away from the station at West 4th Street, eager to escape the day, descending a dirty set of stairs into the cacophonous Manhattan streets.

The city's pulse accelerated around him. The chaos of Sixth Avenue was in full swing, blaring horns and animated chatter filling the air as he made his way past Washington Square Park, alive with sidewalk vendors hawking colorful beaded jewelry and secondhand books. He meandered along Bleecker Street, drawn by the buzz of nightlife and flickering neon signs casting a kaleidoscope of colors on the faces of passersby.

John passed several potential spots for getting shitfaced before he finally stumbled upon a dingy, dimly lit dive bar called Muddy's Corner. A worn facade with chipping paint and a barely legible sign.

He pushed through the creaky door and entered the smoky haze, greeted by a racket of laughter and clinking glasses. He slid onto a tattered barstool and motioned for the bartender while stealing a glimpse around at the regulars. Mostly men, from young to old, with a few ragged women who looked thirsty to forget. The perfect place for John to lose himself until he got home again.

"What can I get you?" The bartender was tall and broad-shouldered with a close-cropped beard, dressed in a dark button-down shirt, vest, and matching trousers.

"Whiskey sour," John replied, wondering if that was what he really wanted but figuring he could also make it up with the second request.

"Coming right up." The bartender dipped his chin at John and left to make the drink.

John was only alone for a moment before a man with dark, wavy hair sidled onto the seat right next to him with enough familiarity and warmth that it almost felt like they were friends.

"Do you have a moment?"

John turned to look at the man, taken almost completely off guard without knowing why. There was something strange about him that had nothing to do with his dress or appearance, though it surely must have had something to do with his eyes, not just dark and brooding but alive with a dangerous curiosity and what John thought of as an odd sense of *knowing* in the microseconds he had to process in between the stranger's question and John's response.

"Of course. What do you need?"

"Right now?" The stranger laughed. "Right now I think I need the same exact thing that you need."

"And what's that?" John asked, suspiciously curious.

"A friend." He smiled as the bartender arrived with a whiskey sour. "The name's John. It's good to meet you."

"I'm John, too." They shook hands, and a current of electricity rippled through his body.

The stranger pointed at John's drink and nodded at the bartender. "I'll take one of those."

The bartender nodded back, then made an about face toward the bottles.

The stranger turned to John. "So what brings you into a shithole like Muddy's on a Monday night?"

John laughed. "What if I told you it was the worst day I've had in a very long time?"

"Then I guess I'd have to tell you that I'm sorry to hear that and invite you to tell me some more." The man made a sympathetic face. "What made the day so terrible?"

"It was supposed to be my big promotion, and Lord only knows how much I deserve both the advancement and money, but my boss gave it to this man named Frederickson instead. White guy, of course. No offense. Not that you're white-white."

"None taken." The stranger raised his hands. "I'm white enough. And Frederickson sounds like an asshole."

John laughed again. Something about this guy really put him at ease. He took a long drink and set his whiskey sour back on the bar.

"How is your baby doing?"

"My baby?" John narrowed his eyes. "I never said a word about having no baby."

"You didn't need to." The stranger smiled as the bartender set his whiskey sour in front of him. He leaned closer to John with a conspiratorial whisper. "Would you believe me if I told you I was from the future, and that I'm best friends with your grandson, Jack? In my time, of course."

"Only if you believe that I'm really from the planet Zeebot, just doing my best to blend in."

"I didn't think so." Another smile. "In that case, let's just say that I'm an interested party."

"Interested in what?"

"Interested in helping you."

John shook his head and took another drink. "No one has ever been interested in helping me without a lot of strings attached."

"Oh, there are definitely strings," the man admitted with a grin. "But they're strings you'll want to pull."

John finished his whiskey and raised his hand for another. "I'm a family man."

"Of course you are." The stranger slapped the table and took an indulgent sip. "And that's exactly why I want to help you. And your family."

"What kind of help do you think I need?"

"You need money, John."

"Everyone needs money."

"Can we agree that you need it more than most?"

"Is it customary to proposition strangers in the future?"

"Most indeed. We have all kinds of sayings about it in my time. *Strangers are just friends waiting to happen, a stranger is a friend you haven't met yet.* And even, *neighbors by chance, friends by choice,* though I guess that last one is different." The stranger shrugged. "Point is, the strength of a community lies in its connections, so where I come from, we are never afraid to reach out and make our human networks stronger."

The bartender arrived with John's refill. He took a big swallow as the stranger ordered a second round too.

"What is it you want from me?" John asked once the bartender left, dubious but still willing to hear this out.

"I need your help."

"Help doing *what*?" John's tone made it clear that the stranger had better have an answer this time.

"We're going to steal—"

"*We're* not stealing anything!" John snapped. "You don't know me. What makes you think—"

The stranger raised a hand to calm him. It shouldn't have worked, but it did. "You're right, man. I don't know you. But I know of you, and I know what you need right now."

"I ain't stealing."

"I hear you." The stranger nodded again, his hand still raised. "And I understand how you feel tonight. But providence might find you feeling differently come daylight, or dusk after another bullshit day with Frederickson thinking he knows better than you down at the office. I wouldn't want to skedaddle outta here without leaving you an easy way to change your mind, John."

"I'm not interested." John sipped his drink, staring straight ahead.

The bartender delivered the stranger's second whiskey sour.

The stranger tipped his head and pulled out a $5 bill, which he dropped on the table. "*Tonight*, you're not interested. But I'll be here at Muddy's Corner tomorrow. If you feel differently around this time tomorrow, then I'll see you then."

No answer from John.

The stranger finished his drink in four gulps, then set his glass back down on the bar and took two steps toward the door before turning back around.

"Simple job. Easy in, easy out, and you'll have more than enough to pay for Junior's operation."

One John left and another got busy boiling with rage at that crazy asshole talking a lot of bullshit while questioning his integrity. After his crap-filled day, he felt flooded with fury.

John was so mad that he had marched two blocks away from Muddy's Corner before the truth hit him like a stubbed toe.

He'd never given Junior's name to the stranger, or said a word about his needing an operation.

Chapter Thirty-Three

JOHN – 1975

JOHN KEPT TELLING himself that he just needed to get through the day.

But only two hours in, it felt like it had been three weeks already.

He and Etta got into it after he got home last night, not just because he came in smelling like whiskey and reeking of a rotten mood. John hadn't managed to get that crazy asshole from the bar out of his head, despite trying to wring the experience from his mind during the sobering walk home.

Etta couldn't take a hint that he wanted to tell her what happened in the morning, so they ended up getting into a frothing back and forth that went nowhere for an hour that felt like it lasted until almost dawn. She kept pleading with him to find another job, and he kept explaining that it wasn't that easy. He had a job, and a damn good one, despite the emasculating bullshit he was forced to swallow.

He barely slept. Three trains felt like six. Every step from the final platform to the IBM frontage required the same effort as one-quarter block of trudging. He slogged to the elevator and made it into work with a smile that felt like he was dragging a Frigidaire across the floor with his face.

John knew that the situation would be intolerable from the moment Frederickson greeted him with a dismissively mumbled salutation before turning his full attention to Don, who in no way needed it. The new boss was a condescending jerk, micromanaging or ignoring him to the point where John felt belittled even when Frederickson had nothing to say.

You just need to get through the day.

The reminder barely did anything for him. John returned from lunch feeling even more agitated than before. Frederickson was heartily laughing with the others until John entered the room, then everyone got back to whatever they were doing, as if he had interrupted their fun. The new boss had somehow managed to decay John's friendships overnight.

Yesterday he'd assumed that Frederickson wasn't qualified to lead the project, and part of the self-loathing John had nursed alongside those four whiskey sours was from the wondering if maybe he really wasn't good enough for the job, and that maybe Frederickson really was the best man to bring the Synthia into reality. But only a half-hour into his morning, Frederickson's ineptitude and arrogance were on display in equal measure.

John was stuck in an unnecessary conference before they finished for the day, discussing the next iteration of the computer in detail, as Frederickson ran through a long list of updates the team had been working on and already knew all about. The new boss addressed each line item as if he had completed the work by himself.

John had almost total autonomy on the 5100 project, Carver happy to take the credit without putting in the time, but his work on the Synthia would obviously be the opposite. Same as with his feelings about Frederickson's general qualifications, John's instinct was turning into fact with an alarming velocity. He cleared his throat, trying yet again to discuss the maintenance mode programming he'd been implementing.

"I've been working on a method that allows BASIC or APL interrupts to read or write directly to the registers." His voice was confident despite the tension triggered by Frederickson's impatient huff when he dared to contribute. "This would enable a regular user to write complex programs directly to RAM, bypassing operating systems and unlocking the potential for intricate automated tasks — anything from traffic control to launching missile strikes."

Frederickson huffed again, this time while narrowing his eyes. "Hell no."

"I'm sorry?" John said.

"I hope you are." Frederickson scoffed. "The Synthia won't have any of that. Our team in Rochester is designing it to use application-style software."

John clenched his fists under the table but chewed on his bottom lip in front of everyone. "I understand your concerns, but I believe this approach could—"

Frederickson slammed his hand on the table. "You will address me as 'sir' when speaking to me, do you understand?"

The room fell silent. John's supposed friends didn't even dare to trade uneasy glances.

His cheeks went hot as humiliation washed over him. "Yes, sir."

John tasted blood and stopped chewing the inside of his cheek.

Frederickson smirked, satisfied by his dominance.

Providence might find you feeling differently come daylight, or dusk after another bullshit day at the office with Frederickson thinking he knows better than you.

And then: *I wouldn't want to skedaddle outta here without leaving you an easy way to change your mind.*

More emotional torture for the remainder of his afternoon.

John usually stayed until 5:20 because he wanted to squeeze as much work into each day as he could, and that still gave him plenty of time to catch his first train. But today he was bouncing on the balls of his heels while waiting for the 5:00 bell. When it came, he threw open the door to the stairwell and ran all the way to the bottom floor instead of waiting for the elevator like usual, sucking in lungsful of Manhattan air as he burst outside the building, because even thick smog was better than the oppressive atmosphere of Frederickson and the men who had been John's compatriots yesterday but were already on their way to something different today.

He thought about Muddy's Corner during all three of his train rides, unable to resist imagining himself sitting on that stool as he neared the bar.

Still, he ignored the impulse and went straight home, stepping through his front door to a piercing cry from Junior, the sound laced with unmistakable pain.

Etta looked over at him, defeat in her eyes as she did her best to console their child, her eyes red rimmed and hollow after yet another day fraught with worry.

John got right to work, his bruised ego momentarily

forgotten. They worked in tandem, Etta easing Junior into his father's arms so she could cool his forehead with a damp washcloth, while singing to their son in a whisper, until his breathing slowed and he finally fell into a whispering sleep.

"Give him to me," Etta said when John stood from the sofa to put Junior in bed.

"You're both exhausted. Let me put him down."

"*Give him to me*," Etta repeated, in a voice that brooked no further argument.

It would take a riot squad to move her out of the rocking chair, lulling Junior back and forth as much as herself, just a few feet from the crib.

"If my baby dies in his sleep, I'm going to be right here with him." Etta's whisper sounded raw enough to give John salmonella.

He looked at her and his baby, then glanced over at the door and swallowed, knowing where he had to go. "There's somewhere I need to be right now."

Then he left Etta, too distraught for a reply.

Chapter Thirty-Four

JOHN – 1975

JOHN WAS ALMOST RUNNING by the time he reached Muddy's Corner, wondering as he entered the bar whether he really wanted to see that stranger from last night waiting for him on a stool.

Of course the man wasn't a time traveler from the future. John just wanted to know if the stranger was crazy enough to believe that he was, or whether he had crafted the lie to inspire John's curiosity and make him want to know more about whatever this guy was trying to drag him into.

John still needed to hear the stranger out, but last night's *hell no* had turned into a consideration now. A desperate need to save Junior from what was starting to feel more and more like an inevitable fate was leaving him shy of options.

Sure enough, the stranger was sitting on his same stool from last night, smiling at John as he entered the bar.

"How did you know about my son?" John started in without preamble. "About the operation."

"I told you. I'm friends with your grandson."

They stared at each other.

Then the stranger shrugged and continued. "Jack didn't inherit the same heart defect as your son, but if Junior doesn't survive, my friend will never exist. And while that won't save your grandson from all the trouble I cajole him into, starting around a half-century from now, it will erase him from your timeline. And I would like to help you with that."

John shook his head: this asshole was out of his goddamned mind.

"I understand that you think what I'm saying is crazy." The stranger shrugged again. "But I see no reason to lie about our situation here."

"Is your name really John?"

He laughed with a hearty shake of his head. "No, sir, it is not."

"What is your name, for our purposes?"

"It's still John." He smiled. "John Titor. And I'm here to help you."

"What do you want from me? How is your little time travel yarn gonna get me an operation for Junior?"

Titor signaled for the bartender and ordered them each a whiskey sour. Then he leaned closer and continued with his nonsense, his voice turned low and urgent.

"We need to steal magnetic tape. In the future, we have the right computer — your IBM 5100 computer if you can believe it — but we don't have the tape required to store all the data we need. I'm talking *thousands* of reels, John. Without a single facility left to produce them."

"Shit, man." John laughed and rolled his eyes. "Was

the time travel story your idea, or whoever put you up to this?"

"The time travel story is the truth, and get this, John..." Titor leaned even closer. "Temporal Recon doesn't even know about this."

"*Temporal Recon.*" John scoffed. "You want my help ripping off a bunch of magnetic tape from IBM? Whoever told you I could get you into the building should have also probably told you that I don't have time for no bullshit and prefer straight lines to crazy talk. Why do you really want the tape?"

"I could make something up, sure. But I feel like that would be wasting time for both of us. We want the same thing here, John."

"And what's that?"

"For Junior to get that operation he needs."

"But only after I help you steal some shit that don't belong to you."

The bartender arrived and put their whiskey sours in front of them before leaving again with a friendly yet unobtrusive nod.

"They put you in touch with the wrong guy." John shook his head. "I don't have access to the amount of magnetic tape you're talking about. At best I could maybe—"

"I don't need you to get me the tape. Just to get us in."

"*Us?*"

"Of course, *us.* Do you think I'm planning to just waltz in and out while you hold the door for me?"

"What's the plan?" John asked.

"There's a delivery coming to IBM in a few days."

"Huh." John snorted. "Maybe you are from the future. Why not just buy the tape? Whatever you're planning sounds more expensive."

"You know the answer to that." Titor gave him a patient smile. "It's not the cost of the tapes, John. It's the proprietary cartridges IBM has custom-made for their computers. The prices on those are ridiculous, but all the cost is internal."

"Have you looked at how much a truckload of the cartridges might cost on the black market? That still might be cheaper." John asked, like he had a single clue as to how the black market actually worked.

Titor laughed and took a sip. "Nobody would want them, because nobody has a warehouse full of IBM computers that would need the cartridges. That's why I'm here shooting the shit with you, John."

"I thought you were here for my son."

"That is why I'm here."

"Not because you're trying to convince me that I should take part in your felony?"

Titor raised his glass with a chuckle. "John, truth is like a skilled tightrope walker, and right now you are watching me gracefully balance both reasons on the high wire of my intentions."

He took a sip.

John sighed, feeling thoroughly lost and oddly found. "So what's the plan, besides roping me into whatever this is?"

"You've seen *The Sting*, right?"

John nodded. "Sure."

"Simple. Just like they do in that film, an old-fashioned heist. But this one's not complicated. Me and my crew will smash into the loading dock and get the truck from there. We could even stop it en route. Although you might make the process there easier."

"Sounds like you don't need me at all."

"In the book of my life, buddy," Titor said, shaking his head, "*you* are a chapter that cannot be skipped."

John sighed again. "So what do you need me for? Exactly."

"I need more than the blank tape. There is also a series of coded cartridges that IBM uses to calibrate their machines."

Of course. Not only did John instantly understand what Titor was trying to do, he felt idiotic for not catching onto it sooner.

"Those cartridges are under lock and key, protected by around the clock security." He shook his head. "I couldn't help you with that even if I wanted to."

"Sure you can," Titor disagreed.

"I don't even have access. That door is only open to senior engineers on the project, all well above my pay grade."

"And that's where you earn Junior's operation, my friend." Titor bowed his head. "You'll need to get access to the keys while me and the rest of our crew pose as shipping employees. We'll all meet at the docks, where you will add the cartridges to our load of blanks, then watch us drive away. You'll have the money you need for Junior and never have to see me again."

"Until you start playing with my grandson."

"You'll never have to see me again," Titor repeated, his voice as sober as his sudden lack of a smile.

Chilling, despite John knowing it was total fucking bullshit. "But then I spend the rest of my life in jail for helping you."

"We can leave you tied up, make it like you had nothing to do with it."

"I still can't figure out how you're going to make money on this."

"I don't need to make money on this."

"Right. Because of the time travel." John scoffed again. "Is your entire crew made of up time travelers, so they don't need any money here in 1975?"

"You let me worry about them."

"And I worry about how to steal the keys for you."

"You do that, and I guarantee that Junior will get his operation."

John stared at the man for an era, until his eyes were dry from needing to blink. He thought about Junior's wail of pain, and Etta rocking Junior to sleep, determined not to miss her child's death. He thought of Frederickson, demanding to be called sir while dismissing John's ideas. And he thought of his so-called friends, refusing to look him in the eye while Frederickson treated him like a second-class citizen.

He hadn't known a person could be this angry.

He shook Titor's hand and said, "Let's get this done."

Chapter Thirty-Five

RJ – 2024

"I FOUND HIM!" RJ yelled into the phone.

"D.B. Cooper?" Michael replied. "Michael Rockefeller? Amelia Earhart?"

"The first two might still be alive, but Amelia would only be bones by now."

"I disagree. I think that Papua New Guinea diet kept her young."

"She would be 125," RJ said.

"How do you know Amelia Earhart's birthday?"

"She's not a him anyway. Can we please get to the reason I called?"

"Tell me how you know her birthday. I'm genuinely curious."

"I don't know her birthday, dumbass. It's simple math. Amelia Earhart was 39 years old when she disappeared in 1937."

"And you don't think that's a lot to know about Amelia Earhart off the top of your head?"

"Can we *please* get back to it?"

"*Si, señor.*"

"Fuck you, Michael."

"Who did you find?"

"I found Anderson," RJ reported.

"Really?" He didn't even sound remotely sarcastic. "*The* Jack Anderson."

"Close. I found out where he was working up until last week. But I called his work and they say he's disappeared. Just hasn't shown up in days." RJ could feel Michael deflating on his side of the call like a punctured balloon. "But I also found his grandfather, the guy who worked at IBM. He's a firsthand witness to corroborate what Cecilia was telling us."

"And he's only a thousand years old."

"Are you being ageist for a reason?"

"Jack would have been better."

"Maybe he told his grandfather where he was going."

"Even if he didn't, maybe that's our angle." Michael now sounded buoyant. "John Titor was active in our worldline as recently as a year ago. Maybe he's just around the corner."

"So you don't hate the Titor idea now?"

"I never hated the Titor idea, I just thought it was deader than another documentary about Amelia Earhart. And now that I know about your love affair with Lady Lindy, I'm surprised you've never pitched a series about her."

"You know her nickname."

"We should start filming the process now," Michael said.

"You're sure? What if we hit another dead end and you change your mind?"

"All I've wanted was for the project to feel like it was worthwhile, amigo. We needed to discover something that nobody has ever had, and now we have that to build on. Either we have found a legit lead on Titor, or we run with the story of the split theories of the FBI. Suzanne's mom—"

"We can't make the story about Suzanne's mom. Holding onto that theory killed her career. We're lucky she was even willing to tell us."

"Well, at least we have a new angle, and a personal connection to it."

RJ narrowed his eyes while switching hands with his phone. "Why does it feel like you're about to say something weird?"

"Not weird. Smart."

"Can you be more specific?"

"I think we might need footage of ourselves to make the moment more dramatic when—"

"What?" RJ felt affronted. "*Why?*"

"Like the big reveal at the end of *The Jinx*," Michael explained.

"You're thinking like a marketer instead of a documentarian," RJ replied. "You know the rules. We make our shit, *then* we decide how to sell it."

"I think those rules are outdated."

"It's a terrible idea, dude. The moment we start bringing the camera around is the exact moment our subjects will start stalling on giving us the preliminary info they need. We'll film it all in an interview later. Like we're supposed to."

"Fine."

"Fine? Just like that..." RJ didn't believe him.

"Just like that. But I want to come with you."

"To interview John?"

"Grandpa IBM, right. Where does he live?"

"Not far."

"Sounds beautiful. Do you know what the property tax is in Not Far? I was thinking about buying a house there after I get a dog. Why are you being evasive?"

"I'm not. I was planning on heading there now."

"Super. I'll be waiting outside for you to pick me up. Anything I should know about Not Far before I leave my apartment? Is there a dress code?"

"I'll be there in a half hour."

"You live fifteen minutes away and you said you were leaving right now. Are you stopping for tacos? If so, can you pick me up a couple, *por favor*?"

RJ killed the call and got ready to go. He'd had zero intentions of stopping for tacos, but it was creeping past lunchtime and Michael had put the bug in his ear, so when his stomach rumbled as he passed a Speedy Eats Chargrilled Burgers, he pulled into line, then rolled down his window for two Double Speedies with cheese.

"This is a delicious betrayal to your people," Michael said as he bit into his burger.

Not Far was just over an hour away, but somehow the drive felt longer. Maybe because he didn't trust Michael's sudden enthusiasm. It had been a long time since they'd both been all in on a project.

"I like that you didn't call ahead of time." Michael nodded in approval as RJ pulled up in front of a tiny bungalow. "Crafty."

RJ knocked on the door twice, with a twenty-second interval in between each knock, before Michael nudged him aside and pounded on the door with his fist.

That worked, much to RJ's annoyance, because there

was a sudden commotion from inside the house, followed by a short fit of scuffling about.

Then the door swung open to an ancient man dressed in a pair of dockers that had seen better days and a tattered but well-loved T-shirt from the Million Youth March, which he would have been way too old for in 1998. The man's weathered face was battered with wrinkles and his eyes were hard and suspicious.

"What do you want?"

"We just had a couple of questions for you," RJ started.

"About your grandson."

"Not interested." He went to shut the door.

Michael put his foot in the doorway as RJ said, "We're not here to waste your time, sir."

"I don't talk to reporters." John went to close the door again, more aggressively this time.

So RJ took a cue from Michael and got right to the point.

"We're really here to talk about John Titor." Then a beat later, while that first bit was still sinking in, he added, "Please, sir."

John Anderson was frozen in thought.

Even Michael didn't dare to hurry this moment along.

For a long yawn it seemed like all three of them were afraid to so much as breathe.

Then John exhaled in a gust. "It's been a minute since anyone asked me about that." He opened his door and stood back to let them in. "You two get settled on the sofa. I'll go make us some coffee."

Chapter Thirty-Six

John – 1975

CENTRAL PARK WAS FRIGID, the trees all either barren branches or comparatively luxurious evergreen. The air kept biting John on every inch of his exposed skin. Only the aroma of woodsmoke was keeping him warm.

"I still don't understand why we couldn't have done this someplace with heat, like back in the bar. Or any bar. Or a library. Coffee shop."

"I told you, the kind of men we're recruiting are more comfortable this way." Titor patted the leather satchel against him like he seemed to do every third sentence or so.

"Right. So we can all run if we see cops. Because we wouldn't want them to know that we were *talking*."

"Our new friends have all learned to be suspicious for good reason. Try to see the world from their perspective."

"*Your* new friends," John retorted. "And no thank you."

"Your grandson is a tight-ass too."

"You know, back at the bar, you made it sound like you had a team already in place.

"I'm from the future, so in a way I did," Titor said, with another pat on his satchel.

"How much longer will this take?"

"We've been waiting for ten minutes…"

"To meet some folks who are so afraid of cops that we need to be out in this witch nipple air. Maybe you can see why my nerves won't stop jangling. You should at least buy me a coffee."

Titor shook his head. "I would argue that coffee is the last thing you need right now."

"Where did you find these people? Am I allowed to ask that?"

"You're allowed to ask whatever you want, John. I am not the boss of you."

"If you're from the future, then I doubt your Rolodex goes back to 1975, and I don't see any *Gang Members Found Here* signs." He looked dramatically around him. "So how does a man from the future assemble a team to help him commit a crime in the past if he doesn't know anyone there?"

"That one is easy." Titor shrugged, then patted his satchel, this time on the way to opening it.

He pulled out a stack of papers and handed them over. John widened his eyes when he looked at them: a mugshot and police record for each of the people they were apparently about to meet.

"I looked up old arrest records in the library." Then Titor clarified. "Old for me."

But the clarification only horrified the first person this supposed John Titor had pulled into his scheme.

"Why would you want to do something so dumb?"

"You mean, travel back in time to a world that smells

like this?" Titor shrugged. "I had no idea what it would smell like until I got here."

"Seriously. Let's say you looked up all of these people in your future library — why would you *choose* to work with criminals that you know *for a fact* got caught."

"You're starting to believe me."

"What?"

"A few days ago your primary question would have been how I got these arrest records doctored to look like they were from the future."

John looked at the reports. The first mugshot was dated November 7th, 1976. His stomach dropped.

"But to answer the question you actually asked, do you have some other way for us to fill out this team?" Titor raised his eyebrows. "If you know any criminals who might agree to help us, I'd be much obliged for the introduction."

John fell thoughtfully quiet. It didn't really matter how Titor knew these men. Even if their impossible arrest records were in his own hands, he wasn't totally convinced they were real. Still, he also understood in that moment how easy it would have been for Titor to have made the same assumption that most or (John didn't want to believe it) possibly even *all* of the white (or whitish) folks he had ever met: assuming he knew a few criminals, simply on account of his being a Black man living in Harlem.

"Thanks for not being racist."

Titor seemed surprised. He nodded back at John with his omnipresent smile, but this time the gesture both looked and felt genuine. "It's not a thing where I come from."

Maybe he really was from the future. John wondered what that world would be like.

The first man in their new crew to arrive was named Tom, though he introduced himself as Goober, which seemed like a silly name for such a hard-looking man. He was dressed in a black leather jacket, blue jeans, and a white T-shirt. He had slightly unkempt hair and a scruffy beard. His eyes looked weary, and his lips were fixed in a sneer. Goober also looked like he'd had a life of labor, perhaps toiling on a farm judging by his young but calloused hands.

Frankie came next. She had a slender build and moved like a gazelle. Her dark hair was pulled back into a tight ponytail. Every one of her fingers had at least one ring on it.

Bartholomew was a greasy-haired slob. Tall and lanky, with a tattered tee, jeans stained from belt loops to cuffs, and boots that were scuffed up from a life lived seriously on the edge. His face was unshaven and gaunt, with sunken cheeks and deep bags sagging under his eyes. Looked like he might sell his mother for a stiff drink.

The final future jailbird (according to Titor) was a man named Gabriel. His slacks were sharp and his shirt pressed. He could have come to Central Park straight from the dry cleaners. His face was chiseled but in no way handsome, and he had a sinister glint in his piercing blue eyes. He carried himself with more confidence — and less bravado — than anyone else in the group.

Titor welcomed them and made introductions all around.

"I thought you were John," said Bartholomew, in a tone of voice suggesting that this doubling of available Johns was pissing him off.

"You can call me Titor." His smile seemed to set all the newcomers at ease, same as it had for John.

Titor told them his bullshit story about the future too, but with new information that he had not shared with John while whispering to him from one seat over at Muddy's

Corner. Probably because he didn't want to scare John away with more of the delusional "truth" until he had his backups all in place.

"And yes, there will be a civil war right here in the United States. Starting in 2005 with the presidential election that year. By 2008 it will be everywhere, and America will be split into five regions."

Bartholomew rolled his eyes when Titor finished. "Thanks for wasting my time, asshole."

He turned to go.

But then Titor said, "Don't you want to know what you get arrested for?"

"Fuck you," Bartholomew replied. "You don't know shit."

"How do you think I found you?"

"Did you look in your momma's pussy and follow the trail?"

"I can see that you're tough," Titor continued, undeterred. "But you're also a mess, and you'll run out of road in 1982 when you're running an illegal gambling den. You're barely street level now, but the Feds will be knocking on your door by the time you go down, and once they start digging, they'll have enough to keep you down for good."

"I guess until then I'll just keep going down on your mother."

Bartholomew walked away.

"Do me," Goober said.

"It's robbery for you, Tom. A job you never should have agreed to do with your buddy Lambert, who promises it's an easy score but lands you three years in Florida State."

Goober nodded like he was happy with the prize in his box of Cracker Jacks.

Titor turned to Frankie next, even though she had yet

to issue so much as a grunt of interest. "You pilfer the wrong pocket one day, and that leads to a grand larceny charge."

"How would that even work?" Frankie replied.

"For the record, this is all bullshit," said Gabriel. "But I still want to hear mine."

"You're the man with a plan until '89. You get saddled with a racketeering charge and lose everything. My best suggestion for you is to keep your nose clean and your ego in check."

"You're a lunatic," Frankie said before walking away.

But Goober and Gabriel were both still rooted in place.

And John wasn't going anywhere until Junior had nothing to worry about, and his Etta could sleep through the night.

"Perfect." Titor nodded with a smile, as if this was all going exactly according to plan. "Goober, you drive. Gabriel, you'll help us inside."

Then the plans got more specific.

And John, despite himself, began to believe.

Chapter Thirty-Seven

JOHN – 1975

THE WORDS *VELVET VIXEN* glowed in pink and purple neon. Heavy red curtains barred the entryway, but the other side of those drapes was the last place in the world that John wanted to be right now.

"Why does it have to be here?"

Titor turned to him with even more mischief stuffed into his smile than usual. "Because *here* is where it has to be."

"That's not an answer." Then: "Are you supposed to be some sort of philosopher in your time?"

"A mechanic." Titor nodded at the bouncer and parted the velvet curtains, gesturing for John to enter first. "After you."

John reminded himself that the next few steps were necessary to save Junior's life, then passed Titor on his way into the strip club.

Inside, the walls were lined with mirrors and the stage was lit with a heavy wash of blue and red spotlights. Music jangled from a jukebox as dancers shimmied on stage, three women in various states of undress. John turned his head away in embarrassment as a tall blonde bent over and began to shimmy out of her panties.

But even averting his eyes from the show, it wasn't like John could avoid the reality of his surroundings: bartenders in tight vests with halos of cigarette smoke around them; a sea of men in bell-bottoms and wide collars, a few too many in garish polyester suits; a DJ spinning records; the place had a goddamned disco ball; it was seedy and gross and—

"This place is fantastic," Titor finished with the opposite thought.

"I can't tell if you're kidding."

Titor shook his head. "Of course I'm not kidding."

But his expression still suggested otherwise.

"What about this place is fantastic?" asked John.

"Just that it exists, my friend." Titor clapped him on the shoulder.

"I'm a married man, taking a night away from my wife and baby. This is the last place I want to be, and you still won't give me a reason why we needed to meet *here* of all places."

"We have a few more details to figure out, and it's better to go where we won't be recognized. We've been to Muddy Corners twice. A third time would be a mistake considering what we're planning."

"And the only alternative to our usual bar is a strip club where…" John couldn't finish his sentence, instead gesturing at a man snorting coke off of a stripper's gyrating thigh as she gave his buddy a lap dance.

189

"SHOW US YOUR PUSSY!" someone yelled behind John.

"The rest of the guys will be here soon," Titor replied with a non-answer, pulling a Kodak Instamatic 110 out of his pocket and taking pictures.

John followed his sight path to a well-dressed man (silk instead of polyester, and with a modest-sized collar, compared to many of the shirts on men inside the Vixen) getting an aggressive lap dance. By the look on the man's face, he seemed ready to blow.

"Are you some kind of pervert or something?" John asked Titor. "What are you doing taking pictures like that? What are you going to do with them?"

"Everything is valuable to someone." Another non-answer. "There's Tom."

Titor nodded to the man standing at the entrance to the Velvet Vixen, drinking in the sights like a man finding water in the desert.

"I think he prefers Goober," said John.

A beat later, Gabriel appeared behind Goober.

Titor motioned for them both to follow his lead, then ushered John into a corner booth in the deepest recesses of the club, mercifully away from the chaotic sounds and ungodly sights.

Goober and Gabriel made it to the table moments later, but Goober looked supremely disappointed. "Why do we need to sit all the way back here?"

"Because none of us want to be seen," Gabriel answered for Titor. "That should include you."

"I ain't looking to be seen so much as looking to look," Goober replied.

Then Gabriel again: "You can look all you want after Titor tells us his plan."

A few minutes later, they were layers into it.

Gabriel was the opposite of Goober, fastidious in his thinking and often asking clarifying questions, but never just to hear himself talk (like Goober) or to derail the conversation.

He gave Titor a nod as he finished detailing their strategy. "So, we need access to the loading bay where we'll steal the cartridges coming in on the truck, and access to the data center where the series of coded calibration cartridges are kept to complete the mission. Security is tight, but not impossible, and the loading bay can be accessed by this guy's Ruscard."

Gabriel nodded at John.

"The name is *John*," he interjected, then wondered why he felt the need to clarify his name to a known criminal. Back to Titor: "Is there any other way for us to get access?"

"I love that you're in *us* mode, John." Titor gave him a nod of approval. "But the answer is *yes*. Good news is, there's no additional risk for you here. Because IBM was an early adopter of the Ruscard system, they never asked to track which photo ID cards accessed which doors. No one will know whose card was used."

John shook his head, ignoring Titor's use of past tense. "I'm having a hard time believing that the security is as weak as you're saying."

"They don't see it as weak," the supposed time traveler explained. "Your Ruscard is supposed to be backed up by a visual check of the image, but there's no guard stationed at the loading bay. We should be safe."

"*Should*," John repeated, though it sounded much different coming out of his mouth.

Titor continued. "You'll go into work like normal, then slip your Ruscard to me via the lobby bathroom. I'll use it to get inside the loading bay, where the three of us will capture and tie up the workers."

Gabriel looked thoughtfully sober, and Goober, eager to get going.

"How can I give you my Ruscard and still get where I need to go?"

"We'll get to that."

"Can't wait," muttered John.

"Getting into the data center will be harder. Any Ruscard can access the outer office of the data center—"

"I won't have *any* data card if you have mine."

"—and once inside the data center, there's a door leading to the data storage area. This requires a Ruscard from one of the primary engineers, and has a traditional lock and key. The key is held by a secretary—"

"Carol," John cut in.

"—who keeps it inside her desk in the data center and only uses it after a visual check of the photo ID on the Ruscard. Cameras cover the entire area. So even if we get past the 'no primary engineer Ruscard' problem and the 'needing *Carol's* key' problem ... whoever sneaks in will be caught on camera."

"So is this part where—"

Titor raised a hand to stop John from talking. "I have a plan."

"Of course you do." John thought of Junior again.

Titor gave him a nod. "You'll call an engineer to your desk to fix something—"

"Like what?"

"Surprise me." Titor gave John a reassuring smile. "I just need you to make the call at around 11:30 a.m., and make sure they send an engineer to fix the problem."

Goober snorted. "Maybe you could ask them how many engineers it takes to screw in a lightbulb, then tell them that they can only have the answer if they come down and get it in person."

"I could call down and report having problems with my microcode emulsion system." John ignored Goober, nodding to himself. "Or maybe my punch card instructions aren't writing to the ROM board…"

"The answer is 'one.'" Goober was clearly pleased with himself. "But they need a whole team to calculate his efficiency."

John gave him a look, surprised to learn that Goober knew enough about engineering to make the joke.

Titor ignored him. "When the engineer arrives, John will offer the man a Coke, dosed with a substance that will give him the insta-shits, so he'll have to run for the bathroom."

"The what?"

"The runs."

"Is that even safe?" John asked.

"You know I made that joke up," Goober interjected.

"Safe? Yes." Titor nodded. "Fun for the engineer?" He shook his head. "Not in the least."

"What is this substance, and how will I get it?"

"I've got that covered. Just make sure that you slip the Ruscard off of the engineer. The secretary — Carol — takes her lunch break at noon with the other office girls, every day."

"How do you know that for sure?" Gabriel asked.

John had been wondering the same thing.

"I've been watching the building," Titor replied, nodding again at John. "If you go to the data center then, Carol will be gone. And the keys will be on her desk. You can use the engineer-level Ruscard to slip into data storage, change the labels on the cartridges, and retrieve the ones we need. Then you can slip out again, with no one the wiser."

"What about—" John stopped mid question when he saw that Titor had turned his attention from what had to be the most important conversation in his life to what seemed like an infinitely more trivial photo opportunity as that same well-dressed man from earlier was being pulled into a private room by a brunette dancer who looked an awful lot like Natalie Wood.

"What were you saying?" Titor asked John once he'd finished taking the picture.

"What about the cameras? You said you had a solution."

"Indeed I do. You can turn off the distribution amp to the cameras on your way to the data center. That will freeze the cameras, so they'll show a still image of people sitting there working."

"That isn't going to fool anyone for long," argued John.

"Doesn't need to," Gabriel replied, fully getting the plan. "Point is to keep it from recording you accessing the restricted data storage room. Titor needs to protect your identity to make sure you don't talk. So you can probably stop worrying."

Titor nodded at Gabriel with a half-grin, then turned back to John. "After retrieving the cartridges, you'll head to shipping and receiving. Trash the engineer Ruscard on your way to picking up the package you sent yourself as the excuse to be there."

John nodded along with his instructions.

"You'll slip me the cartridges and get your own Ruscard back, then—"

"I'll 'discover' the tied-up employees in the stockroom." John actually smiled.

"Right." Titor smiled back. "You'll raise the alarm to

remove any suspicion away from you, then meet at the rendezvous point after you finish talking to the police.

"I do have to admit that this really does sound like a perfectly thought-out plan." John leaned back into the plush upholstery with a heavy gust of relief. "What could go wrong?"

Chapter Thirty-Eight

JOHN – 1975

ON HEIST DAY, John's heart felt like it might pound right out of his chest.

"Are you okay?" Etta asked.

"I'll be better if Frederickson gets hit by a bus, but other than that, I'm good." John found his very best smile, but surely she had to know he was faking it.

"Is he still that bad?"

John let his face fall and told her part of the truth. "Even worse."

He pulled her into an especially long hug, before planting a lingering kiss on Junior's forehead.

"You *sure* you're okay?"

"I just love you." John nodded. "And you're right, I'm working too much. Not getting the promotion was a bitter pill to swallow, but a needed reminder of what's important."

"I'm glad to hear that." Etta was trying not to cry, but one fluttering eye gave her away.

John said his goodbye, then took the stairs down to the first floor and stepped onto the bustling New York streets, oblivious to the city around him, consumed with what he would soon have to do.

Step one was stressful enough. Sweat stained his shirt as he replayed the plan over and over in his head, and more as he showed his Ruscard to the guard at the main entrance, trying to keep his nerves in check. He clutched his gut once inside, feigning a stomach bug as he hurried back past the guard to the lobby bathroom.

He hid the Ruscard in the tank of the single stall, his hands still trembling as he was gripped with paranoia that Titor wouldn't be able to find it.

Back to the lobby, rubbing his genuinely unsettled stomach while softly moaning. Fumbling with his briefcase, pretending to search for his Ruscard while holding his breath.

Relief washed over him as the guard waved him in out of sympathy.

Reaching his desk, John tried to focus on his work for the few hours before the rest of their little heist (went to shit) happened. But it was impossible; his head was ringing. *Danger, danger.*

He had worked so hard to get where he was, avoiding every wrong avenue that had led his friends and cousins to jail or worse. And now, here he was, on the brink of committing a crime far more serious than petty theft.

Minutes crawled through a tempest of fear, doubt, and anxiety. Every glance at the clock left him feeling defeated by how slowly the dial had moved.

A half hour until noon, and his heart was a hammer losing control on a nail.

But no one was looking at him. John's colleagues could give a shit what he was doing.

It was time. So he swallowed hard and picked up the phone. Dialed engineering.

Then he hung up the phone as soon as someone answered.

Dumbass. Where was his head at? He hadn't even disabled the emulation input station on his desk.

John was too worried about what might happen to the engineer. What if the drug did something worse than sending him into an hour of torture in the bathroom?

And John also kept thinking about the Synthia, amid many flutters of rage that he had been passed over for his promotion. He wished that things had gone another way with Laslo, instead of one asshole handing the promotion over to an even bigger asshole.

Right now, while mustering the courage to play his part, John was wishing that he had never met Titor.

He opened a drawer and pulled out the picture of Etta and Junior she had lovingly framed for him. He had promised to put it on his desk so they would always be in sight, but seeing them and not being with them had begun to hurt so much that he eventually dropped the photo in his drawer and tried to forget about it.

But right now he needed the motivation.

He looked at the clock — ten minutes late.

John picked up the phone again, right as the door to Frederickson's door exploded open.

"Anderson!" snapped the boss.

John looked over, thinking he might be just on edge enough to snap that pompous head right off of Frederickson's shoulders.

"Can you explain your thinking on keeping the BNC connector on the back of the 5100?"

"I explained it in great detail already, sir." John scrunched his eyebrows, knowing this would piss off the boss but not caring. "Did you not see it in the report?"

"Are you an idiot, Anderson?" Frederickson glared at him.

"No, sir, I am not." John shook his head.

"Then please explain to me why we're including something on the 5100 that is both entirely unnecessary and ludicrously expensive?"

"That was my call, sir. The BNC connector makes it so the 5100 could be connected to a standard TV—"

"I know what it does. But the *cost*, Anderson. *The cost.*"

"It's not—"

"Even if it was free, it's disloyal to IBM and the computer industry as a whole: computers and televisions are like chocolate and garlic, Anderson."

"Sir, with all due respect, we should be giving people what they *want*."

"Not when it cuts into our profit margins! The Synthia 3700 won't have a BNC connector — that's for damn sure."

Frederickson droned on while rage stirred inside John, but he could barely focus on this back and forth.

His mind was on the engineer, who needed to get here *now*.

What if that ten minutes he'd spent in the grips of his own cowardice became the thing that cost Junior his life? The argument kept going, and now the clock was moving too fast.

Stop it.

He glanced up at the clock again. It was already noon, and almost too late. He needed the engineer incapacitated before Carol returned from her lunch break at one.

"Are you listening to me?" Frederickson was two feet from John and jabbing a finger at his ledger.

No, he wasn't. And yet John somehow made it through the next several minutes on autopilot.

At a quarter after the hour, Frederickson left with, "By the end of the day, Anderson."

John had no idea what he needed to do before the end of the day when it came to Frederickson, but he was crystal clear on what he needed to do for Titor *right fucking now*.

He poured some of his own Coke on a punch card, then jabbed it into the slot in his station several times. Then he tried a clean card and the machine got stuck.

He dialed engineering.

"I'd like to report a problem with my microcode emulsion system," John said, then delivered additional details when prompted, smelling his own sweat as he made his way through what felt like an interrogation instead of a few simple yet necessary questions to get him the help that he 'needed.'

"An engineer will be sent to fix the issue promptly."

He hung up the phone, his hands clammy and his breathing shallow, trying to calm himself while waiting for the engineer's arrival. *Nothing weird here at all — I sweat like this all the time!*

And still no one was looking his way.

John reminded himself that Junior's life was on the line and got ready for what came next.

The engineer was prompt as promised, but John could read him like a Time's Square billboard before the door closed behind him. The man was a hiccup away from retirement and wore his disdain for the way things were changing like a uniform.

"Sorry about the trouble," John said.

"If there's never any trouble, then I wouldn't have a

job." Wally gave him a smile that was just as tired as his line. "What seems to be the problem?"

John explained the issue, same as he had on the phone, this time with pantomimed visuals while Wally narrowed his eyes in what could have been suspicion but was more likely disappointment.

"I'll get right on it." He nodded, looking like he wanted to call John an idiot.

"Thanks. I sure appreciate it. Are you thirsty? Can I get you a Coke or anything?"

"Sure, kid." Again, it looked like Wally wanted to say something else.

John got his special Coke and handed it to the engineer.

Instead of saying thank you, Wally scoffed. "My job is to fix what's broken."

"Thank you," John told him again.

"You're one of them engineers whose job it is to try and fix things that *aren't* broken, isn't that right?"

"I'm not sure I follow?" And he definitely didn't have time for this bullshit.

"I don't understand what's wrong with keeping a computer in one place."

"Microchips are getting smaller and—"

"Making computers portable is a fool's errand." Wally grabbed his Coke and took a sip, followed by a trio of hearty swallows.

"Maybe so." John nodded. No reason to argue with him. Best to get the engineer talking and separated from his ID.

John got closer, positioning himself within grabbing distance of the card strapped to Wally's belt. "You are right that shrinkage will lead to a big sacrifice in performance and overall functionality."

"Exactly!" Wally was suddenly over the moon, smiling at John as he took another sip. "You can't have that kind of complex circuitry, with all the vacuum tubes and cooling systems in a compact device. It just wouldn't work."

John reached out and almost nabbed the card, but then Wally turned around and took another sip of Coke.

John added: "Not to mention the costs. Miniaturizing components is expensive."

"Damn straight it is," Wally agreed.

Just as John slipped the card from his belt.

Perfect timing.

Wally's face was suddenly awash with embarrassment. His eyes widened as he swallowed a lump of realization. "Well, kid, it looks like I'll have to—"

Wally didn't even finish, his eyes getting even wider as he turned around and bolted toward the bathroom.

Now a quarter to one, he barely had time to get the rest of the heist done and save Junior.

John was drenched in sweat as he approached the closet, turned off the distribution amp to the cameras, swiped into the data center, then hauled ass to open Carol's desk, muttering a string of curses and prayers under his breath that the drawer wouldn't be locked.

He finally exhaled with relief while yanking the drawer open. It wasn't locked.

But the next breath got stuck in his throat.

Because the drawer was empty: *no keys.*

Chapter Thirty-Nine

RJ – 2024

"HOW DID you feel during the heist?" RJ asked John.

Michael leaned forward. "And when you're done talking about your feelings with my partner, I would love to know more about your reasoning for going along with this thing in the first place. I mean, you were a programmer at IBM right at the dawn of computers changing the world. You were on the frontlines, and you had *some* idea of where this would all take us." He waved a hand around the room, perhaps to indicate the old man's wi-fi. "Why would you risk losing all of that, especially when you had a sick child?"

RJ gave Michael a dirty look. "I think he explained that."

"Your partner thinks I'm crazy," John said to RJ with a laugh. "I would think I was crazy too. You're both right." He nodded. "I did it to save Junior, of course, because

Titor didn't need to be telling the truth about time travel for me to get paid."

"But by definition, the guy was an unreliable narrator," Michael argued.

John answered with a shrug. "You never met him."

"What's that supposed to mean?" Michael asked.

"The man was enigmatic," John replied with a wistful smile. "I found him equally curious and off-putting at first, but the more time I spent with him, the more captivated I became. He really did seem like a man from another time and place, and sure, it could have all been an act. But isn't it a beautiful possibility to believe that something more or different or beyond our realm of understanding could really exist? That's why I wanted to work at IBM in the first place."

"So he was a conman," Michael continued, "who knew exactly how to push your buttons, same as any conman worth his grift would know how to do."

"Maybe." Another shrug. "Probably." Another laugh. "But whatever you want to call him, John Titor could not only convince a person to do something, that man could make 'em damn sure that it had been their own fool idea in the first place ..."

John stopped, apparently lost in thought.

RJ glanced over at Michael only to find that his partner was already eyeing him expectantly. After a full minute, the old man was still staring into space.

"What happened at the heist?" RJ finally asked. "I know that the situation went south, but I would love to hear the story of what actually happened from you."

RJ pulled out some printouts from old newspaper headings. The first one read, *IBM Lead Engineer Orchestrates Daring Heist, Leaving Hostages and Injuries in its Wake.*

RJ read aloud from the article. "In a shocking turn of events, a lead engineer—"

"They never let me be lead engineer. Only it probably sounded better that way in the papers."

"—lead engineer at IBM has been exposed as the mastermind behind a high-stakes heist, resulting in multiple employees held hostage and at least one individual hospitalized due to the severity of their injuries."

John scowled, seeming to take great offense at an old allegation that he still heard now as a slur and an insult.

"That hospital bit ain't true." He shook his head violently. "Never was. That was the same engineer I was telling you about, Wally with the outdated opinions. He went home with stomach cramps after drinking the Coke. Not the hospital. I was worried enough that might happen, so I know damn sure it's a lie."

"We believe you," Michael said, then rolled his eyes at RJ when John wasn't looking.

"How about this one?" RJ showed John another headline: *IBM Scraps Project Amid Security Fears; Russian Liberation Front Suspected of Involvement.*

"In an unprecedented move," RJ read, "IBM has decided to abandon its upcoming project due to mounting concerns over security breaches, with growing suspicions that the recently exposed mastermind was hired by the Russian Liberation Front to infiltrate the US computer systems."

Another scowl. "Do I look like a man who was hired by the Russian Liberation Front?"

"I have no idea what such a man would look like," Michael said.

"To be fair, the Russians could have approached anyone. And they might have seen you as more sympathetic to their cause than the rest of your colleagues."

"Why? Because I'm Black."

"Yes, sir." RJ nodded.

John nodded back, seeming to agree with him.

RJ picked up another clipping. He didn't need to read this one, seeing as the picture was worth at least a thousand words: John getting carted off to jail.

"So you did what you were supposed to do with Wally and got to Carol's desk before the buzzer, but there weren't any keys in the drawer when you got there. How else did the heist go south? Could you not look for the key because Carol came back from lunch early?"

"Nothing ever really went wrong." John sighed. "Turned out, I just didn't know the real plan."

Chapter Forty

John – 1975

JOHN'S RIBCAGE felt like it was closing in around his heart.

So much for Titor's intel. Carol must have taken the keys with her to lunch, so now John had no way of getting into the data storage room.

He was sunk. Continuing on with this fool's errand was stupid. He was going to get caught if he didn't bail right fucking—

But John *couldn't* bail now.

He didn't need another glance at the clock to know that the downstairs loading bay heist had already happened. The two loading workers were tied up and waiting for him.

Titor was waiting for him.

Junior was sick, and there wasn't anything in the world more important than saving him. If there was even the slimmest chance that his actions right now would keep his son alive, John had to keep going forward.

He looked at the security screen next to Carol's desk. The workers were frozen, so it was now or never. Even if he could no longer do the job quietly, so nobody ever even realized that the cartridges were gone, John would still be able to get the cartridges and get out of the building. Earn Junior's life even if it meant surrendering his own.

Because of course the police would know that there had been an inside man.

Though, so far there wasn't anything to indicate him specifically. An engineer had been called upstairs to help him fix a little problem, but so what? That wasn't proof of anything. John would simply fail to find the tied-up employees and steer clear of any suspicion entirely.

John had a lifetime of experience with that.

He glanced at the clock again, afraid of what he was going to see: ten minutes to one. There was still a chance he could pull this off.

A good chance. John told himself what he needed to believe, grabbing a letter opener off Carol's desk and using it to jimmy open the data room door.

His hands were so slippery from the sweat that he dropped the letter opener twice, once before he got the door open, and again right after he swung it wide.

His eyes darted around the room, mostly to make himself feel safe before charging over to the cartridges. His hands shook as he grabbed them, and his heart made laps. No need to relabel the dummy cartridges. There was no hiding the broken door.

He dashed back into the outer room on his way to the loading bay.

A flash nabbed his attention.

He hesitated, glancing at the security screen now

springing back to life. The workers were still all tied up, but John could see Titor, a trucker's cap partially obscuring his face as he sneaked out of the closet, after clearly having just returned power to the distribution amp for the cameras.

John could also see himself, standing in the data storage room where he absolutely should not be and could no longer claim he never was, adjacent to the broken door. His arms full of his stolen loot.

Panic tightened like a knot in his chest.

John needed to run but couldn't tear his eyes away from Titor on the screen, using John's Ruscard to swipe into the room where the precious IBM 5100 — his other baby — was stored. His eyes widened in horror as Titor lifted the entire portable computer and turned to face the camera.

Then with a mocking yet somehow charming doffing of his cap, while still covering his face, he sprinted from the room.

Adrenaline flooded John's body. He braced himself to run and—

Carol entered the room, her eyes widening with shock as sirens inside IBM started to scream.

John had been caught red-handed, with nowhere to go but down for the supposed time traveler's heist.

Chapter Forty-One

RJ – 2024

"IT DOESN'T SOUND like you were caught red-handed so much as set up," RJ said. "What happened to everyone else?"

"You mean it didn't say in any one of your articles over there?" John nodded at RJ's file folder full of printouts.

"Of course I read all of the articles, sir. But I'd like to hear everything in your own words."

"Not much of a documentary if we're just reading articles out loud," added Michael. "Or are we turning this into a podcast?"

John turned toward RJ, intentionally away from Michael, and not for the first time. "Goober and Gabriel got overpowered in the loading bay after Titor never showed up with my Ruscard. They tried to break their way in. The cops collected 'em, and figured they were a couple of hired thieves."

"But not you," RJ said.

"But not me," John repeated with a nod. "I was the inside man, and therefore the mastermind behind it all. I got carted off for an interview with the Feds."

"What made them think you were the brains of the operation and not just someone the actual mastermind was puppeteering?" Michael asked.

"You saying I couldn't have been the brains?"

"You worked for IBM," Michael clarified. "Clearly you could have been the brains. I'm asking you what the Feds thought."

"That I was the brains. The 5100 was my baby. One of the agents was convinced that I'd stolen it for a competitor. Digital Equipment Corporation or Honeywell. Another thought I just wanted to keep the computer for myself. Like I could have done anything with that equipment in my apartment. The department as a whole was convinced that I intended to sell the machine to a foreign power."

"Which foreign power?" RJ asked.

"Germany or Russia, depending on who you asked."

"You didn't use the time travel defense?" Michael raised his hands, playful yet slightly mocking. "I swear it wasn't me — a man from the future told me to do it!"

John kept talking to RJ. "I'm sure I sounded like a lunatic, raving about a man from the future recruiting me. But yes, that's exactly what I said."

"Did they ask you why the future had invented time travel but for some reason needed shit technology to ..." Michael made a face. "Why did they need shit technology again?"

"Shit technology?" John had finally had enough. "Portability, all-in-one design with a built-in display, keyboard, and tape drive. Preloaded software and multiple programming languages. And a motherfucking BNC connector on the back."

He practically ended with a harrumph.

"They all thought I was nuttier than a bag of cats in a tornado, and if some of 'em had gotten their way I would have ended up in the loony bin instead of spending the next two decades in Rykers."

"Twenty years?" RJ repeated in shock. "Why such a long sentence?"

"It didn't start out that long." A bitter chuckle. "Prison is the hardest place in the world to get out of, because the powers that be just keep finding more and more reasons to keep you there."

A chill slithered through RJ's body. He shrugged it off, reminding himself that this could all just be crazy talk. John was an old man with a hard life lived behind him. He might not have been all there to begin with back in '75, he was definitely several notes shy of a symphony.

But if he wasn't…

"So what do you think went wrong with the plan?"

"I told you, I don't think anything went wrong with the plan. I think that Titor was keeping me in the dark about his true objectives and had no intentions of ever looping me in."

"Did any of the feds believe your story?" Michael asked.

"Only the one I liked." John smiled at a memory. "Agent Trainor. Cecilia Trainor. She was a woman who knew how to listen."

"Listen, or believe?" Michael said.

John ignored him.

"What part of your story do you think got her to pay attention?" RJ asked.

"I'm sure it was the cap. That wasn't just my story,

Cecilia saw it on the video. Titor doffing his hat right before he disappeared with the computer."

"What does that prove?"

This time, John gave Michael an answer. "I'm not sure it proves anything. But Cecilia found it hard to see Titor as a garden variety hired thug after that. She might not have believed a word of his story as I told it, but Cecilia believed that I was telling the truth about what Titor said to us, and that I got roped into the whole thing instead of making it up."

"All because he took off his hat?" Of course Michael sounded incredulous.

"He also plugged the distribution amp back in so that we would all get caught."

"So he could keep the loot all for himself," Michael theorized.

"And where would he sell that loot to?"

"Digital Equipment Corporation or Honeywell. Maybe the Burroughs Corporation," RJ answered before Michael, to prove his objectivity.

"Titor would've needed to have those relationships established before the heist. No way anyone would touch the 5100 after our job made the papers."

"So why did he do it?"

John shrugged. "I don't know why that man did anything."

"What happened to Frederickson?" RJ already knew, but he wanted Michael to hear it from John. "And the Synthia computer?"

"I don't know about Frederickson, probably given some other project he hadn't earned. But the Synthia—" John leaned forward in his seat. "That never went forward. After the theft of the 5100, it was deemed too risky to continue. Some government people intervened."

"We know Cecilia. Would you like to know what she said about you?"

RJ wanted to sock Michael in his asshole face. He had a knack for popping the champagne before the party began.

"You know Cecilia?" John narrowed his eyes at them, seeming to work out whether or not this was a positive development.

"She's my girlfriend's mother, actually," RJ admitted.

"You don't say…" John was clearly trying to determine what that might mean.

"Cecilia thinks that Titor is your grandson, Jack."

"Ha!" Then he actually laughed. "First off, my grandson doesn't have the wiles to do what Titor did. He is the consummate straight man. Even harder to argue with, Jack has the wrong skin tone."

John touched his face and started to cackle.

It almost felt performative, and made RJ feel less than sure. Skin tone was much harder to see in old security footage, and all they had to go on was a hand. John could be selling them a story right now. More and more, RJ was wanting to believe it.

"Where is your grandson now?" Michael asked.

"Jack'll be back when he wants to be back." John ended with another harrumph.

"Do you have any theories about who Titor might have been, if not your grandson?" RJ asked, without adding the codicil, *Assuming this story isn't utter bullshit.*

"It was too big a question for me to have any theories. But fortunately I didn't need any."

Michael again: "And why is that?"

"I asked Titor the next time I saw him, but that wasn't until 2000," John added, like the first half of his sentence wasn't a bombshell.

"The next time you saw him?" RJ and Michael repeated in unison.

"That's not my story." John shook his head. "If you wanna know more, you'll have to talk to my daughter-in-law, Katherine."

Chapter Forty-Two

CAMERON – 1975

IT WAS a month after Cameron successfully executed the heist in 1975.

His heart hurt for what happened with John, but when an entire timeline was in the balance, he had no choice. Cameron should have left this time weeks ago, but he needed to stick around and make things right. And there was too much heat on John's apartment on and after that fateful day at IBM, so he had needed to wait it out.

Cameron knocked on the door, then again when no one answered. It swung open midway through his third attempt. John's wife, Etta, was standing on the other side of the threshold, her shoulders hunched and head bowed, red and puffy eyes, hands shaking as she tried not to collapse with grief and defeat.

"Can I help you?" Etta stared him down, her eyes losing their sorrow to the sway of suspicion.

"Do you have a moment?" Cameron asked in a velvet whisper, and with the hypnotic sway of a pendulum.

She stared at him, transfixed for a beat before she found herself.

"No, I do not." Etta started to close the door.

"It's for John."

"John is in jail!"

"For John Junior," Cameron clarified. "For your baby."

"I know who John Junior is," she snapped.

But Cameron had her attention. He handed her an envelope.

After a tentative second, she snatched it out of his hand.

Etta opened the envelope and found it full of pictures: a man in a fancy suit, strutting around in what looked like a strip club. She looked up from the pictures to meet his eyes.

"Why are you giving me an envelope of dirty pictures? What's this supposed to mean?" She shook the envelope angrily in her hand. "And what the hell does it have to do with my son?"

"It's a gift from John. I promised that I would get this to you."

"And what am I supposed to do with this?" Etta looked one sneeze away from sobbing.

"Go to New York Presbyterian Hospital any time after noon on Thursday this week. Let Dr. Philips know that you've been told he's agreed to do Junior's surgery pro-bono, then give him the envelope."

"That's blackmail. I won't have any part in it."

As she shoved the envelop back at Cameron, Junior started screaming on queue in the background.

"That may be true, ma'am, but by the sound of things,

your baby is in pain, and those photos can stop all that hurting."

Etta glared at him, her bottom lip quivering.

John looked deep into her eyes and spoke with an unwavering conviction. "Your fragile child will not always be fragile. He has a lifetime of happiness and wonder ahead of him. One day, your son will find a love so profound that it will shake the foundations of his world. He will have the most incredible children, each one a testament to the miracle of life itself. Now, isn't that a future worth fighting for? Even if it means tainting your conscience?"

Etta looked behind her at the crying baby, then back at Cameron. "Thank you."

"Thank *you* for your time." He nodded.

Then he hit the road for his long drive back to Florida, where he pulled into a dark parking lot where there was no one to witness his time machine activating. A quarter century later, Cameron got out of the Chevy and walked toward the massive metallic ball in the distance, radiating an ambient light that cast a summer hue over the surrounding plaza despite it being the dead of winter.

The ball stood suspended by a chain of metal scaffolding rising to the sky, its surface etched with intricate designs awash in multicolored lights, dancing through the plaza like fireflies in the night.

"5 ... 4 ... 3 ..."

Cameron was at Epcot Center in (not yet Old) Orlando, where the new year was ringing in—

"2 ... 1 — HAPPY NEW YEAR!" bellowed the crowd.

And the year 2000 was here.

Part IV

Chapter Forty-Three

2000

CAMERON STUMBLED through a darkness that was like a thick blanket around him. He could see his own hands, but only barely, when they were right in front of his face. He felt his way along the walls, but everything blended together in an endless void of black.

"I know you can hear me, Kat!" Cameron yelled again. "YOU NEED TO STOP!"

He heard her shuffling, and grappled along the wall toward the sound.

"I'm still John, Kat! Nothing has changed."

No answer.

Cameron called out again, softer this time. "Please, Kat — can you answer me?"

He found his way to the bathroom.

Down into the cabinet under the sink where he kept one palm pressed against his seeping wound, while the other dug around in hopes that he might find a flashlight. To his delight, his fingers closed around some candles and a box of matches.

Cameron lit the candles and called out to Kat again. "I'm in the bathroom."

Then he removed his palm from his stomach, glancing down at blood dribbling from the laceration before he inspected it further, inching closer to the candle and squinting at the wound as he clenched his fists and curled his toes in agony.

Assessing the injury left him with ugly yet indisputable good news: the laceration had only grazed his liver. A severe wound, but one he could probably survive.

He reached for the bandages with shaking hands and a sinking feeling that the blood would seep through them. He grabbed a towel instead, pressing it firmly against his skin to staunch the flow of blood as—

Footsteps thundered past the bathroom door and jolted him to attention.

Adrenaline pumped hard enough to momentarily dull the pain and send him springing into action, gritting his teeth as he flung open the door, then stepped cautiously into the seemingly empty hallway.

Shadows taunted him with their darkness, but the hallway seemed otherwise empty.

Cameron finished dressing the wound, then took the candle back out into the hallway.

He sneaked down the dark corridor toward Kat's bedroom, hoping that he had been right about the sound of her footsteps and where they had taken her.

He paused at the doorway, perking his ears and leaning ever so slightly into the room.

But he heard nothing.

"Through the ages we all wander, chasing shadows, dreaming yonder..." Cameron started to sing. *"Grasping dreams and fleeting sighs, we yearn to touch the boundless skies..."*

Then Kat leaped out of the dark, brandishing her knife at Cameron.

Chapter Forty-Four

RJ – 2024

"THAT'S NOT MY STORY." John shook his head, insisted as he looked at RJ and Michael as though shocked by their surprise. "If you wanna know more, you'll have to talk to my daughter-in-law, Katherine."

Michael grimaced. "Why can't you just—"

"At least we have another lead to follow." RJ wanted to leap out of his seat. Was Michael seriously not excited about this latest development, or just playing the part of his usual dick self?

John shook his head again. "Kat won't talk to you."

RJ smiled. "Maybe she would have said the same thing about you."

"I'm sure she would have. But either way, she ain't gonna talk, at least not without me around." He shrugged. "Even if she would, Kat lives out in the boonies. You'll never find the place without me." '

"You're welcome to come," RJ offered.

Michael shot him a look, but RJ ignored it. What else was he supposed to do?

"I'll make us some snacks," John offered in lieu of saying yes.

He was moving much faster at the end of their conversation than he had been at the start, and less than ten minutes later, John had changed his clothes to a pair of old blue jeans and a flannel shirt, both looking much newer and cleaner than what he had on. His snacks were rice cakes and applesauce.

"You can keep your snacks," Michael told him on their way to the car.

"You mind if I ride shotgun?" John asked.

"Sure thing," RJ replied, to his partner's annoyance.

Kat Anderson did indeed live out in the boonies. It was well past afternoon when they left, and a two-plus-hour drive through long stretches of mangrove swamps to get there. The sun was setting throughout their final leg, smearing the sky with orange and pink as RJ pulled up to Kat's small house, hidden among the trees and brush. White clapboard walls with an anemic chimney shooting like a stalk of sugarcane from the shingled roof. A wraparound porch and shuttered windows probably once made the place seem warm, but empty and closed the home appeared mostly abandoned.

"This place definitely looks like it'll be worth the drive," Michael snarked.

"I'm glad you know how to judge a puzzle by looking at just one piece of it," RJ replied as he got out of the car and slammed his door.

"I'm glad you learned to memorize fortune cookies. It makes talking to you a lot more fun."

RJ ignored Michael and turned to John. "Are you doing okay?"

Though the old man had seemed almost energized while leaving the house, and stayed somewhat chatty throughout the drive, the weight of their trip seemed to have suddenly caught up with him. Even in the dusky light, the weathered lines wrapping around his eyes seemed deeper than before. His gaze was now downcast and his posture slumped.

"You go on ahead." He offered RJ a tired smile. "Kat will have heard the car. She'll be looking for answers fast." An even more exhausted attempt at a grin. "I promise I'm right behind you."

Michael was already walking. "You heard the man."

He knocked on the front door as RJ sidled up beside him and opened his mouth. But it swung open before he could call Michael an asshole.

"What do you want?" Kat asked without a note of grace in her voice.

"Good evening. My name is Ramon Jimenez—RJ— and this is my partner, Michael Atlas. I have to apologize for his poor social graces."

That line or another one like it had disarmed a count- less number of people before RJ tried using it on Kat Anderson. But he had never known the line to be so inef- fective.

She had a strong jawline with full lips and intense eyes, deep brown with flecks of gold. Hair tumbled down onto her shoulders in unruly curls. Her body was toned. She clearly took her gym time seriously.

"Who are you? And what do you want?"

"We're documentarians. We would like to talk about John Titor if you have just a minute."

"I've never heard of him." She went to close the door in their faces.

But John appeared behind them. "It's fine, Kat. You can trust these boys."

"*You* brought them here?"

"Maybe it's time to tell the truth, dear…" He looked at his daughter-in-law for a long while, letting his eyes do most of the work before he finished the thought. "Maybe Jack—"

Kat looked back at John in silence.

And RJ realized that he was holding his breath.

Kat didn't break the quiet, but she did step back and open the door all the way, with a little nod to invite them inside.

Chapter Forty-Five

K<small>AT</small> – 2000

KAT ANDERSON NEEDED TO SCREAM.

Instead she held her four-year old daughter close to her heart and squeezed her tight.

The doctor's office had a sterile chill to it that no blanket could warm, but Kat still rocked slowly back and forth in the hard-backed chair, doing her best to add some heat to the moment as fluorescents hummed overhead.

"It's a murmur," Dr. Sullivan repeated.

"I heard you," Kat told him.

"Do you understand what that means?"

"Too well." And she sure as hell didn't need him to say it out loud. She'd always known it was possible Junior's condition could be passed on to their children, but hearing the words was like the hammer finally falling.

Her head was spinning and that scream was still stuck in her chest. Her entire world had tilted on its axis. A harsh ringing reverberated in her ears, drowning the rest of Dr.

Sullivan's words. Amelia was mostly oblivious, her tiny hands fiddling with the buttons on Mommy's blouse while Kat's heart echoed the beat of her daughter's faulty rhythm.

Heart murmur. Those two words pounded in her head as a relentless drumbeat. The abnormal sound of Amelia's heart was a cruel symphony of turbulent blood flow. Images strobed through her mind: Amelia lying listless and pale, confined to a hospital bed; medication, restrictions, surgical interventions, a childhood tainted by the specter of heart disease.

"Is there a pamphlet or anything? Something I could take home and read later … maybe some literature to help me explain everything."

She rocked Amelia back and forth harder for emphasis.

"I have just the thing." He gave her a sorrowful smile before leaving.

The door was only open for a beat before it swung back closed, but in that long second, the hallway outside was bustling. Now Kat's harsh reality seeped through the walls. Anxiety was rising like a tidal wave to swallow her.

She had to control her emotions, or Amelia would feel it too. And sure enough, tiny creases formed on her daughter's forehead.

"Are you okay, Mommy? You look *so* sad."

Kat tried to project a perfect image of calm.

"I'm good, sweetie." She kissed Amelia's forehead. "I'm just thinking about what the doctor told us about your heart being special."

"You'll still tell me later like you said?"

"Of course I'll tell you later." She kissed Amelia's forehead again.

Most of Kat thought it would be better to not say

anything until all of the tests were back, but the rest of her wondered if she was being a coward.

Kat started to sing, the song she had been working out but couldn't quite untangle the choruses from verses yet.

"There's a whisper in the willows, a secret in the pines, it's the ever-spinning tale of our lady, Mother Time. Through the hours and the ages, as the sun and moon take flight, a dance as old as dawn itself, bathed in pale moonlight."

"I like it when you sing that, Mommy."

"I like it too."

The familiar melody soothed them both, until Kat stumbled and faltered through a few clumsy lines that didn't quite fit in with the rhythm to her second verse, before starting back in on the chorus. *"Oh, time, you relentless river, you wax and you wane, unseen hands upon the clock, in sunshine or in rain…"*

And that was where she always lost it.

Kat started the song over as the door creaked open and Dr. Sullivan entered the room, his face still a mask of professional sympathy, though true concern did gleam in his eyes.

He offered her a handful of pamphlets. "These should help."

"Thank you." Kat felt lost, like she should hug him goodbye.

But that wasn't appropriate.

"Let's go, kiddo." Kat rose to her feet and held out a hand.

Amelia took her mother's hand and they left Dr. Sullivan's office together.

Kat loaded her into the car, then drove to the grocery store on autopilot.

She blinked a few times and found herself in Safeway without any memory of the drive over, but Amelia was merrily skipping alongside the cart, so all must have been right with the world.

And yet, all was most certainly *not* right with the world.

The grocery store was awash with sterile fluorescence as she pushed her cart through the aisles, numbly scraping the colorful arrays of produce with her gaze as she moved from perimeter to interior while Muzak played inoffensive instrumentals as a soundtrack to her insensate performance.

"BARNEY!" Amelia belted out as Kat reached for a box of dinosaur mac and cheese.

She pushed the cart, not sure of where she was going, only feeling slightly alive again thanks to a chill tickling her senses in the refrigerated section, the humming cooling units in a low drone one layer under the Muzak.

To the freezer section. A frigid Siberia of frozen pizzas, microwaveable meals, and ice cream.

Kat grabbed a box of Stouffer's lasagna. She loved to cook, but ever since last year, she'd found quick dinners a small comfort.

"Can we get ice cream?" Amelia asked.

No answer. Just the cart squeaking against the glossy tiles until Kat stopped in front of the ice cream and grabbed a half-gallon of Dreyer's chocolate chip from the cooler.

Amelia squirmed in her seat.

Kat kept pushing the cart. Past the frozen tundra, into the dry goods, the air warming around her enough to tune out again. Tony the Tiger grinned at her from a box of Frosted Flakes while Cap'n Crunch saluted with his spoon. The Honey Nut Cheerios Bee buzzed on his box, oblivious to the tumultuous present they were lucky enough to have now that Y2K was only—

"MOMMY!"

Kat looked at Amelia.

"Why aren't you listening to me?"

"Sorry." Still not an answer.

The checkout loomed and temptations were manifold. Candy bars and gum, brightly packaged and within easy reach. Amelia snatched a Snickers bar.

"Can we get this please? You said that—"

"Sure."

Shock tore through Amelia's expression as she dropped her candy bar into the cart. "Can we get one for Jack, too?"

"Jack can't have candy yet." Kat unloaded her cart, eyes drifting to the tabloids, lurid headlines like a siren call to the bored and curious. There was apparently trouble in paradise for Brad and Jen, which Kat cared about *not at all*. Same for Star's exclusive with the latest *Survivor*.

The final total blinked on the register. Kat swiped her card.

"Do you think we got enough ice cream?" Amelia asked.

Then Kat was outside again with another minute missing, worry for Amelia pulling her through the world like a Red Flyer getting dragged by its handle.

Kat parked in her driveway ten minutes later, right as Rob Thomas and Santana were finishing "Smooth." She forced herself to remember the last three songs on the radio before killing the engine, and felt relieved when they came to her: "Bye Bye Bye," "Yellow," and "Oops! ... I Did it Again" ... again.

"COME IN!" Maggie called out from inside when Kat knocked on her neighbor's door.

She opened it to a living room filled with a hodgepodge of Beanie Babies peeking out from glass cabinets. Jack was parked on the carpet in front of a television set the size of a large bookcase playing a VHS tape of Barney, the purple dinosaur's cheerful song grating against her raw nerves. It hurt that her son didn't look over, but warm relief flooded her when she scooped him up and he gurgled an approximation of *Mommy*.

"Thank you, Maggie!" Kat called out, already on her way out the door, Amelia stealing a glance back at Barney before the door closed behind her.

A trio of middle graders whizzed by on rollerblades, wheels *click-clacking* on pavement as they crossed Maggie's lawn back to their house.

"Are you okay, Mommy?" Amelia asked as Kat carried Jack into the house and got him situated in this living room play area.

"Everything will be fine," she replied, on her way back outside to unload the groceries as Amelia tagged along.

She opened the trunk and pulled out a bag in each arm.

"Me too!" Amelia yelled and grabbed a bag — the one with the ice cream — from the trunk.

But it was much too heavy and she dropped it on the driveway.

Groceries spilled everywhere.

Kat wanted to scream, and that was before she saw the stranger.

"Let me help you with that," he said.

Chapter Forty-Six

KAT – 2000

KAT WAS NO LONGER NUMB, nor in autopilot, suddenly on full alert as the stranger gathered her groceries into his arms and carried them inside the house — where Jack was alone in the living room with the TV already on — without even asking.

The man hadn't even introduced himself!

"Who is he, Mommy?"

"Get in the car and lock the door," Kat replied, dropping both grocery bags back in the trunk so she could more easily run to the front door.

She got to the front porch just as the stranger was leaving her house.

"I set everything on the counter in there. Sorry that happened to you — looks like you had your hands full." His sunrise of a smile disarmed her.

"Thank you for your help." Kat stepped onto the porch as the man stepped off of it. She felt instantly better with the imbalance in their height difference settled.

She waved to give Amelia the all-clear.

"My name is John."

But Kat wanted the stranger gone, not an introduction.

Amelia scampered past him then parked herself behind Mommy to survey the situation. Kat took her hand and crossed the threshold back into the house, safer on the other side of the door.

"Do you have a moment?" the man asked.

No, she absolutely did not. Nor did Kat feel good about any of this. She needed to get this stranger — whose real name might or might not be John — off of her porch.

And yet his smile was still disarming, and the request reasonable, especially after he repeated it.

"Do you have a moment?" he repeated.

"Get in the house, sweetheart," said Kat to Amelia.

"But—"

"*Now.*"

Amelia knew better than to argue with that one.

"What do you want?" Kat asked him.

"This will be hard for you to believe."

"Not a great opener." She shook her head. "You have ten seconds to—"

"I'm from the future."

She actually laughed. "Tell me: is it more like *Blade Runner*, Skynet, or *The Matrix*?"

"None of those." The stranger shook his head, his expression remarkably sober. "The little sprite that just scampered into your house is named Amelia. And the adorable little boy on the floor in there is named Jack."

Had she said Amelia's name out loud?

A chill ran through her.

"Look. I don't know what—"

"Like I said, it's hard to believe. But for the sake of the moment you agreed to give me, I'd like for you to know that your son grows up into a fine man, even if he is a stickler for the rules."

The stranger smiled again, and Kat had no better word for it than *genuine.*

"What do you want from me? Why are you here?"

"I know about Amelia's condition, Kat."

"What condition?" she asked with a trembling voice, wondering if she had said Amelia's name.

"The one you found out about today."

"Stop it." She shook her head. "Why are you doing this to me?"

"Her heart murmur, Kat."

His answer only upset her further.

"I would like permission to show you something. Is that okay?" The stranger stared at her patiently as she considered the impossible story he was trying to sell her.

What was his angle? What did he hope to get from her, and what made him think he could get it by telling her something so ludicrous?

"Why are you here?" Kat asked him again.

"It will help if you see what I would like to show you. Will that be okay?"

She couldn't find the yes inside her, so she gave him a tip of her chin.

He pulled out a book from inside his jacket pocket and handed it to her — an ancient copy of *The Talented Mr. Ripley.* She accepted the book with trepidation, but once it was in her hands, he pulled Exhibit B out of his pocket: a necklace, exactly like the one around her neck, one of a kind because it had been crafted by her father.

"What the fuck?" Now Kat was angry. "What are you trying to play at?"

"I'm not playing at anything." He shook his head. "I can imagine how hard it is to believe what I'm saying right now, but I promise I'm here to help you."

"I have a real life with real problems, buddy! You can't—"

"John."

"—come to my house and start fucking with me. I don't know where you—"

"Kat." He raised both hands, palm out.

But it was the way he said her name that stopped her, uttered with a quiet yet fiercely confident familiarity that she couldn't un-hear.

"I'm here to help you. To help Amelia."

"Get the fuck out of my house."

"I'm not in your house, Kat."

"Then get the fuck off my porch! You have ten seconds before I call the cops. Thanks for your help."

She slammed the door.

"Now can you tell me who that was, Mommy?"

"Someone who doesn't belong here." She glared out the window at him.

But the stranger wasn't going anywhere. Instead he parked his ass on her porch.

Kat turned on *Bear in the Big Blue House* and said, "Please stay in here with your brother."

"Is everything okay, Mommy?"

"Everything is fine, I promise, but I need you to stay in here with Jack."

"Okay, Mommy." Amelia turned her attention to the TV as her brother giggled up at the screen.

Kat headed toward the kitchen to call the cops as promised, but stopped as she was passing the front door because the sound of the stranger singing outside snagged her attention.

"Oh, time, you relentless river, you wax and you wane. Unseen hands upon the clock, in sunshine or in rain. Oh, time, you're the healer and the thief in the night. Stealing moments as you mend, in shadows or in light."

And something inside her broke, tears streaming down her face. Before she knew what she was doing, she had already opened the door. "How do you know that song?"

"You taught it to me a long time ago."

She hadn't even finished the song, but she recognized his version as true. As the song she would one day finish.

"That's impossible."

"If I were standing on your side of that door, I would think the same thing."

"You have to tell me why you're here," she pleaded. "This isn't kind, what you're doing right now."

"Again, I understand why it feels that way." The stranger gave her a conciliatory nod. "But I'm here to do you a kindness, nothing less. On my honor. And where I come from, that means something."

"What kind of kindness?"

"I want to help Amelia."

"And what do you want from me?"

"Just a place to stay."

"You can't stay here." Kat shook her head.

"I can't stay anywhere else."

"Because you're from the future."

"Yes, ma'am." Another tip of his head.

"What if I don't believe you?"

"I expect that you don't. I'm sure you're trying to figure out where the trick is, and what the punchline might be. Have I been following you for a while to know what I know, and when I know it? And if so, what do I want, since it's not like you have much of anything to give me?"

Kat kept staring at him.

"I don't need you to believe me. I just need you to trust that I mean you no harm. Long enough for me to work on something for myself, for all of us really, to help us out in the future."

"How long until you prove you can help Amelia?" Kat would do anything for a real solution, even if it meant listening to the mild rantings of a certified lunatic.

"I can't answer that, other than *as soon as I can*."

Kat took another long look at him before finally answering. "I have a tent that can be pitched out back, but you better believe that every one of my doors will be double-locked and triple-checked. I sleep with a loaded gun by my side, and I have the police on speed dial."

"I believe all but one of those things and can assure you that's plenty." The stranger smiled again, nodding as he gave her his full name. "Titor's the name. John Titor."

Chapter Forty-Seven

KAT STOOD in the kitchen doorway, her still suspicious gaze fixed on the man who called himself John Titor — there was a less than zero percent chance he was telling the truth about his name. She was increasingly surprised by what she was seeing.

Despite her certainty that he was lying about his identity, Kat's senses wanted to insist that he was telling the truth about everything else. That didn't mean he was really from the future, only that he might be delusional, assuming her instincts were right.

But did delusional equal dangerous? And had she already made a colossal mistake opening her door to this man?

Something deep inside her reassured her again that all was okay. Warm light from the table lamp cast a mellow glow on Titor's face as he sat on the carpeted floor, knee-deep in the world of her children while teaching them some kind of game, his hands moving about in exaggerated gestures, fingers wiggling in the air, laughter (genuine like his smile) echoing around as it rebounded against the living room walls. Amelia giggled as she attempted to mimic his movements. Jack couldn't even come close, but he kept clapping his hands and laughing along with his sister.

It all made her miss Junior a little too much. That hollowness inside Kat that had been borne upon his death only grew more cavernous as she heard Titor's laughter and was reminded yet again of how much better her life had been with Junior in it, before sudden adult death syndrome had stolen her soulmate away last year.

And now Dr. Sullivan was telling her that Amelia had the same goddamned heart condition.

And how was she ever going to pay for her treatment?

Reality kept getting grimmer, and even Kat's wins were feeling like losses. Amelia's diagnosis had added an unbearable weight to her already-leaden shoulders. She had just started a new job last month, but that glimmer of hope came with a caveat. Her health insurance wouldn't kick in for another two months.

Amelia couldn't wait that long. Her little clock was already ticking.

Kat considered going into the living room but felt safer keeping her eyes on Titor from the room full of knives, in case she needed one all of a sudden.

Titor stretched his arms, laughter subsiding as he picked up the remote and turned the TV on. But not to *Bear in the Big Blue House*. He started channel surfing with a smile, spending five seconds or so on each channel before moving onto the next one.

It was making her nervous, but Kat didn't want to say anything. Yet.

But then he stopped on *The 'Burbs*, a movie starring Tom Hanks that Kat had seen a half-dozen times since her first viewing in the theater a decade ago. It was one of Junior's favorites, but the stuff they loved about it — taking the mundane setting of suburban America and flipping it on its head — was lost on a four-year-old and a baby. At their age, the paranoia and suspicion would be too intense.

"The children are much too young for this movie."

But on-screen Art fell through the porch, flailing around before crashing through the rotting wood, and Amelia exploded with laughter at the antics onscreen.

Kat sighed, guilt for the murmur she didn't cause still chewing at her insides. "It's fine."

Instead of turning it off, she got out the TV trays and brought them into the living room so they could all watch the movie together.

"This is called The 'Burbs," Kat told her daughter. "Your daddy really loved this movie."

"Did you see it in the movie theater together?" Amelia asked.

"No." Kat shook her head. "This movie came out before we met."

"When can we go to the theater again?"

"You just went to the movies with Grandpop a few weeks ago."

"I mean with *you*, Mommy. We haven't gone to the movie theater since *Tarzan*."

"What is the movie theater like?" Titor asked Amelia. She looked back at him, seeming unsure of how she should answer, so he added, "I've never been to one."

"YOU'VE NEVER BEEN TO A MOVIE THEATER?" Amelia couldn't believe it.

"Of course Mr. Titor has been to a movie theater. He's just kidding with you."

"It's a big, dark room where everybody watches a movie at the same time so they can all laugh and say stuff at the same time too," Amelia explained, just in case.

"Your mom is right. I *have* been to a movie theater, but not since I was just a bit older than you."

Amelia blinked like the idea of not going to the movies for thirty years was incomprehensible.

"What was the last movie you saw in the theater?" Titor asked.

"TOY STORY 2!"

"Not so loud." Kat touched her temple.

"Sorry, Mommy!"

Jack laughed.

"What was *Toy Story 2* about?" Titor asked.

"Have you seen the first one?" Amelia chirped, narrowing her eyes at him.

He shook his head. "I have not."

"It's even better than the first one!" Amelia declared before answering his question, with the longest run-on sentence Kat had heard from her daughter so far. "There's this cowboy named Woody and he's the bestest friend of a spaceman named Buzz and they're from the first movie but they didn't like each other at first until they teamed up to scare Sid, because he's a really big bully and mean to all his toys so really the toys were just sticking up for themselves and not being mean, but I know you really only wanted me to tell you about Toy Story 2 so in that one Woody gets stolen by a mean man who smells like pickles and old socks and he wants to sell Woody to a toy museum in Japan because something about collections, but Mr. Potato Head can take off his parts and Slinky Dog is sooooo stretchy and Rex the dinosaur is afraid of everything but Woody finds out that he's on a TV show that's even older than from Grandpop's time, that's what he told me in the car, and Jessie is a super cool cowgirl and Bullseye is Woody's horse because they're both from the old show too, and Woody is sad because Jessie tells him about how her kid, Emily, left her and she was really, really sad and then she sings a song about it and I got really sad and Grandpop put his arm around me and I told him that I didn't want my toys to be sad…"

Amelia finally lost her wind, but after she sucked in another breath, it seemed she lost her desire to finish. "And then Woody goes home to Andy and Jessie and Bullseye come with him."

"That sounds like the best movie ever made," Titor said.

Kat smiled.

"I like going to the movies with Grandpop because he always gets the real popcorn!" Amelia declared.

"What's fake popcorn?" Titor asked.

"Mom makes popcorn at home and puts it in a little bag for me. Plus she makes lemonade."

Kat felt herself flushing, but it was hard to justify the cost of concessions when tickets to the movies themselves were so expensive.

"We'll have to go to the movies and buy some popcorn." Titor offered Amelia a definitive nod.

But Kat shifted uncomfortably in her seat.

Titor caught the movement and turned back to Amelia. "Where I come from, nobody ever treats their neighbors poorly. People help each other out, even if they're weird." He glanced out the window. "Though I guess it helps that nobody lives quite this close together anymore."

"Why not?" Amelia asked.

"Because there are a *lot* less people."

"I think it's time for bed," Kat announced.

Jack was already sleeping, and Amelia had an overwhelming day and she knew not to argue.

"Hello?" Kat said to Titor, apparently lost in thought, staring at an old wind-up record player sitting next to a stack of records.

He looked over with a wistful smile. "In the future, that's your pride and joy."

She wished he hadn't said that.

Titor headed out to his tent with a farewell smile and a promise that he only wanted her family to be safe, then she tucked her children into bed.

They weren't even there for five minutes before she brought them both back into her room.

Then she locked the bedroom door, tucked a chair beneath the doorknob, and slept between her babies.

Chapter Forty-Eight

KAT – 2000

KAT WOKE UP EARLY, but it was Saturday with nowhere to be, and she wasn't in any hurry to acknowledge her backyard guest. Amelia knew better than to ask about him, but it looked like she had to pee, the way she kept bouncing all about instead of blurting all of her questions in regard to Mr. Titor.

Kat prepared a full breakfast before waking Jack, who seemed to be sleeping even longer than usual. Everyone was full of pancakes and dressed for the day before Kat finally opened the back door.

Titor looked up at her with a patient smile.

Kat pulled the sweater tighter around her body, like armor against her vulnerability.

"Would you like some breakfast?" she called out to him.

"I'm starving." Titor held his smile, patting his stomach as he approached the back door. He paused before entering and made a wild gesture to encompass the world around him. "And today is a gorgeous day for a grand adventure!"

It was a beautiful day, the sky already a brilliant blue and dotted with fluffy white clouds. Not exactly warm, but the breeze swaying a tall row of palm trees in the distance was by no means cold, and her backyard garden was vibrant with color.

"Smells amazing," Titor said as he went inside.

Kat followed and closed the door behind them.

"Good morning, Mr. Titor!" Amelia skipped into the kitchen.

He winked at her. "It's John."

"What are we doing today?"

Kat had been wondering the same thing. "Are you working on the plan we talked about?"

"What plan?" Amelia wanted to know.

"A plan to have fun!" Titor's excitement was infectious. Amelia and Jack had both caught the virus last night and seemed determined for Mommy to start sharing their symptoms.

"What kind of fun?" Kat shot Amelia a silencing look.

"There are so many things about the 1990s that I can't wait to check out. I was hoping we could all go to this magical place I've heard of. It's called *the mall*."

"It's not the 90s anymore," Kat replied. What the hell was wrong with her?

"According to the calendar," Titor sort of agreed. "But according to the culture, it's definitely still the 90s. Which makes right now the perfect time to ask if you happen to have a flannel top."

"I left it at a Pearl Jam concert."

"Did you really?" Titor appeared delighted by her answer.

"No." Kat shook her head. "Not really."

"What's a Pearl Jam?" Amelia wanted to know.

"It's music, honey."

"What kind of music?"

"The kind that sounds like raccoons breaking into a garbage can," Kat replied.

Titor said, "We could start ticking off my to-dos with a trip to the mall for that flannel."

"Can we go to Sanrio?" Amelia asked.

"What's Sanrio?" Titor scrunched his nose, like he might be able to figure that one out if he thought about it hard enough. "

"It's where Hello Kitty lives with all of her friends."

"How fast can we get there? We need to say hello to this kitty."

"How fast can we get there?" Amelia repeated his question for her mother.

The answer was less than twenty minutes, but even those few minutes in the presence of Titor's exuberant energy felt like an hour on a roller coaster. His head was constantly swiveling, eyes wide as he absorbed the passing cityscape. Even the billboards that irritated Kat seemed to interest him.

Once at the mall, he was even more of a whirlwind, parading across the bottom floor, then running up the escalator in the wrong direction while wildly laughing.

"It's all so glorious!" Titor exclaimed, still not breaking character.

And Amelia laughed every time.

"You've really never been to a mall?" Kat was beyond dubious.

"Everything that people have at their fingertips in your time." He looked wildly around in disbelief. "And you take it all for granted."

"I'm not sure that I take anything for granted." But as the words left her mouth, Kate knew they were untrue.

Titor pointed to Hot Topic. "I'll be right back."

"Are we going too, Mommy?"

"Definitely not." Kat shook her head. "Do you want an Orange Julius?"

"YES!" Amelia exclaimed.

Jack clapped.

Titor was just coming back out of Hot Topic by the time they returned with a strawberry Orange Julius to split among the three of them. The time traveler could buy his own for all she cared.

"Do you like it?" Titor pointed to his brand-new flannel, in checkered shades of black and gray.

"Why didn't they have any colors?" Amelia asked.

"Maybe this is better?" He pulled out a Dragon Ball Z T-shirt from his bright yellow bag and handed it to Amelia. "Much more colorful."

"What is it?" She looked at the shirt.

"Something I thought you would like."

"Thank you?" Amelia seemed unsure.

"You'll grow into it," Titor assured her.

"Where do you get your money?" Kat asked. "If you're from the future."

"Jack packed the money."

A strange answer, and yet it was another earnestly delivered sentence that sounded suspiciously like the truth.

"And you couldn't have used it to stay at a hotel?"

He shrugged. "There's only so much of it."

Amelia yawned. "I'm tired."

Kat was worried — did Amelia's fatigue indicate a symptom of her illness, or was she just as exhausted by Titor's energy as her mother was?

Her admitted fatigue didn't stop him from pulling the

children into a photo booth, squeezing the three of them onto the seat while Kat stood outside, and eagerly showing her their goofy faces on the strip of photos with an infantile grin.

"Mind if check that place out?" Titor pointed to a GameStop.

"We're here for you," she reminded him.

He dashed off to the video game store and Kat killed time buying two tickets for the little train that traveled around the mall in an unimpressive circle while waiting. She watched it round the bends while replaying their morning and trying to experience it all through the eyes of someone who had truly never been inside a mall.

And again she told herself that Titor had one hell of an act.

But despite knowing the end of her song, and about Amelia's diagnosis, there was a trick at play here. Kat didn't know his true story, but she still felt sure that he did want to help them.

"Anyone hungry?" Titor asked when their third time on the train came to an end.

"What did you buy?" Kat nodded at his bag.

"A magazine." He sounded astounded with himself. "It's filled with articles about different games to buy. Or ones that are coming out. Have you ever heard of Final Fantasy?"

"No. Sorry." Kat shook her head. "You're ready to go home and eat?"

"Aren't we going to eat at the food court?"

She shook her head again. "You don't want anything at the food court."

"I want Subway!" Amelia announced. "Or Cinnabon!"

"You can't have either of those."

"What's that second one?" Titor asked. "The cinna-something?"

"It's a cinnamon roll that could double as a free-weight."

"Sounds delicious." He might have been salivating.

"Can we please get Subway?" Amelia begged.

"Fine." Kat relented, got sandwiches for the three of them, then grabbed a seat and waited for Titor to finish making his rounds through the food court, with full stops at Chick-fil-A, Burger King, Auntie Anne's, and Cinnabon.

"This is delicious." His eyes were as glazed as the cinnamon roll as he bit into it.

He looked sick soon enough, and a third of the way through his feast, Titor started holding his stomach.

"I think I'm done…" Titor could barely finish his thought and looked like he needed to vomit. He glanced around the mall again, but disgust had finally entered his eyes. "We can go now."

He was half asleep just a mile on the road, but bolted up in his seat, suddenly wide awake as Kat was passing the Mangroves Links golf course.

"PULL OVER!" he bellowed.

She followed the order, alarmed as Titor opened his car door and raced across the street.

"GATOR!" he shouted over his shoulder as her ran onto the course, grabbing a club from a bewildered golfer before rushing over to an alligator sunning itself by a pond.

Then he beat the gator to death as Kat covered her children's eyes, and tried to soothe Amelia's riot of sobbing.

Chapter Forty-Nine

RJ – 2024

"JUST GIVE ME A MINUTE," Kat said after closing the door behind her unexpected guests.

She didn't wait for either RJ or Michael to respond, just took John by the hand and led him into the living room. Already ancient before they knocked on his door earlier that day, the man seemed to have aged a decade since.

Kat settled him into a large armchair in front of the TV, then kneeled down beside him and started whispering something that neither Michael nor RJ could hear, though both of them leaned ever so slightly forward to see if they could get something.

She aimed her remote at the TV and started flipping through channels until she landed on Nick at Nite where an episode of *Gilligan's Island* instantly put a smile on John's face.

But then he started to drool, and RJ had to acknowledge that the doddering old man was hardly a reliable witness. And the way Kat was barely tolerating their presence, maybe it wasn't such a good idea for them to be here in her house at all.

"Either of you want a cup of coffee?" Kat asked as she passed them on her way back into the kitchen.

"It's too late for me." That was Michael's way of saying it was time to get the hell out of there.

"I'm good." RJ smiled.

She gestured toward her kitchen table. RJ and Michael each took a seat.

Kat dragged a chair away from the table and sat several feet away from them. "You're documentarians. I assume you have a list of questions?"

"It's more like a conversation." RJ smiled again.

But Kat wasn't having it. "Then converse."

"Your father said that you met John Titor around the year 2000?" RJ asked.

Kat glanced into the living room and then back at her interrogators. "You mean my father-in-law? The man in there suffering from dementia?"

"Yes." RJ had no idea what else to say.

"I have no doubt that he now believes the story he made up about the time traveling man, because he's old enough and has told that tall tale enough times by now to make it true inside his head."

"Why would he make it up?" Michael asked.

"Junior said that his dad always felt a lot of guilt around what happened at IBM. He participated in the theft of the computer he built and sold to America's mortal enemy. He invented a story about a man that made him do it, and then in later years, after the whole John Titor internet hoax happened, he simply attached his own story to it, and slowly over the years convinced himself that it was a truth he had always believed in. The time-traveler morphed into John Titor."

"He seemed utterly convinced that Titor set up the heist," RJ argued, though he was probably just proving Kat's point for her. "And he seemed to be telling the truth."

"What makes you say that?"

"I've interviewed a lot of people, ma'am."

"And my father-in-law spoke with conviction. Like I said, I do believe that John Titor has become his reality, but there's never been a shred of evidence to back up his claim. In fact, it seems to be the other way around."

Michael this time: "What do you mean by that?"

"Whoever invented the John Titor legend used the old IBM heist as a way to ground his story in reality and make it more believable."

John laughed in the living room. Then Gilligan said, "I'm not just a boulder, I'm a bowling ball!" onscreen and John laughed again.

RJ, Michael, and Kat were all looking at the old man in shared contemplation.

Until RJ finally broke the silence.

"Are you saying that John Titor didn't visit you? You've never met him?"

"I appreciate what you are trying to do here. The internet hoax made for an interesting legend and my father-in-law's story is especially compelling, because so much of it is true. But there was no time traveler behind the heist." Kat sighed. "Just a man who broke the law and his own moral code, because that was the only way he could save his son. And thank God he did."

Another long beat of silence, this one broken by RJ. "Thank you for your time. We'll be getting out of your hair now. But—"

"You have one more question before you go," she finished for him.

RJ nodded.

Kat nodded back.

"Can you tell me anything about Junior?"

Her eyes got glassy and far away. "Junior passed in 1999."

Michael looked curious.

"I understand that," RJ continued. "But before he did … was there anything worth mentioning for this story? In appreciation of what we're trying to do."

"He had a life full of love before he left me with our two beautiful children." She shrugged and wiped a tear away. "I don't know what more you want me to say."

"Can you tell me where Jack is?"

"No." Kat shook her head. "I can't."

"Can't or won't?" RJ asked.

"He left without telling me. I have no idea where he is."

RJ studied her, more than half sure she was lying. He and Michael stood to leave.

"Should we take John back with us?" RJ asked.

"I'll take care of it," Kat replied.

John barely noticed.

Chapter Fifty

KAT – 2000

KAT never drank coffee after noon, but she was already on her second cup and considering putting on another pot to brew. Caffeine was the last thing she needed, but making the coffee and inhaling the aroma as she sipped it was grounding her.

She felt furious at Titor and didn't know what to do with her anger. Watching him beat that alligator to death might have been — surely had to be? — the most terrible thing she had ever witnessed in real life.

He just stood there dazed, staring at the lifeless gator in a bloody mess at his feet. Kat had shouted for him to run, and hurry back into the car — and surely that had been the wrong move? — so she could haul ass and get the hell out of there before an unexpectedly terrible situation got even worse.

Now she was potentially implicated in a third-degree felony. Alligators were protected in Florida. And that wasn't the least of it. Kat felt scared, more frightened down to her bones than she cared to admit. Because if she confessed that truth even to herself, then she would have to march into the living room and grab Titor by his collar before shoving him out of her house.

And yet, despite her entire body bristling to do exactly that, she couldn't risk losing a chance to help Amelia.

She was trapped in her own rage as she watched Titor from the kitchen, trying to reconcile seeing him transform into a different person with the nagging sense that she could still trust him.

It wasn't just the help for Amelia, because Kat would be certifiably insane if that was enough to sway her. That goddamned song kept scratching at her. It was *her song*, and she knew the ending was right the second she heard it, new yet familiar like the scent of a fresh batch of cookies wafting from the oven. Titor didn't even need to sing it in key; the second she heard the words rolling out from his throat, Kat felt swallowed by something in between synchronicity and fate that she didn't understand.

Of course she didn't believe in time travel, but her hard-working mind had a hard time conjuring up other ways as to how that man in her living room could know the end of a song that she hadn't written yet.

But it was still an epic journey away from tangible proof.

"Can I have a cup of that?" Titor pointed to her mug of coffee.

"You really want caffeine this late?"

"Not especially." He shrugged. "But I would love to join you."

Kat went to the cupboard and pulled out a mug, then emptied the carafe to fill it a third of the way. She handed him the mug without replying.

"I understand that what I did was upsetting."

Titor spoke in a gentle voice, trying to soothe her with the explanation she'd refused to hear on the long and silent drive home, broken only by the occasional chirping from Amelia, because no matter Mommy's frothing mood inside the car, her innocent nature was hard to squelch.

"There was a reason for what I did." He shook his head. "I'm not crazy."

"Even if you have a reason, you're probably still crazy."

"I understand why you would think that too." He offered her a smile, but she refused to take it.

"What reason could you possibly have for beating an alligator to death? It wasn't doing anything to you."

"Gators have done plenty where I come from."

"What's that supposed to mean?" It was frustrating to feel both furious and interested in his stupid stories about a future that didn't really exist.

"Gators were taking their territory back because so many humans were dead," Titor said as if the statement meant nothing. "And with all the flooding, gator attacks kept getting worse and worse until we started banding together and actively hunting the gators. It was the only way to protect our young."

"*Protect our young?*" Kat repeated, aghast yet not understanding. "What do you mean by that?"

His face was painfully sober. "After the nuclear war."

"*Nuclear war?*" The repeated phrase left her with a whisper.

"So much death…" His words sounded far away but his eyes were still with her. "But worse than the body count, survivors were … affected."

"Affected how?"

"Kids are rare," Titor replied in a voice of defeat.

"Because not everyone can have them, our communities work hard to protect their young."

"Can Amelia have children in the future?" A ridiculous question with an answer she desperately needed to know.

A strange look washed across his face, delivering the simple reply with a barely perceptible shaking of his head. "She hasn't yet." Then, before Kat could respond. "Would it be alright if I helped you with dinner?"

She was surprised by the question and happy for the help.

They cooked in silence, and paired well in the kitchen, with him seeming to anticipate her moves, as if the two of them near a stovetop was a familiar dance that only one of them recognized.

Dinner was mostly quiet, with Kat stuck in her thoughts, Jack babbling as he played with his food, and Titor joking around less than usual, though Amelia still laughed at his every attempt.

"Is there any more ice cream?" she asked after dinner, even though Amelia knew exactly how much ice cream there was.

"Do you want to know if there is more ice cream, or are you actually asking if you can have some?" Kat smiled at her.

"Can I have some?"

"Sure."

"Can I eat it in front of *Blue's Clues*?"

"Sure," Kat said again.

"Why are so many of your shows about blue things?"

Amelia giggled, but Titor's face was perfectly sober. Kat wasn't sure whether or not he'd been kidding. Jack started clapping as Steve came onscreen in his green striped shirt and the big blue dog trotted out behind him.

"Sorry, kiddo, but it's bath time and bedtime for you."

Kat scooped Jack up from the floor and started toward the bathroom.

"I'll catch you up on what happens," Titor said.

Kat smiled without meaning to on her way out of the room.

Despite being wide awake and ready for *Blue's Clues* just a few minutes ago, Jack was already nodding off as she dressed him in pajamas after his bath.

She heard the TV go off, followed by the faint sounds of Titor talking in the living room. She had to get back in there. But Jack whimpered when she turned to leave.

So Kat brushed a knuckle against the slope of his nose, a motion that usually accelerated how quickly she could get him to sleep.

His breathing turned steady after one last little gurgle, then she returned to the living room.

"...are still dangerous to people where I came from. We're supposed to hunt them if we see them, so I thought I was helping you and your mom."

"Why are the alligators dangerous?"

"Because of the war."

"I don't like your stories about the war." Amelia shook her head, but then encouraged him further. "Why did the war start?"

Kat wondered if she should intervene.

"It all started because of hate," Titor replied.

"Like I hate broccoli?"

"Imagine if you hated broccoli so much that you convinced half of the country that they would be better off without all the people who liked it." Titor looked down at Amelia for a beat, waiting for his words to sink in, and again Kat felt an urge to intervene but he started up again before she made her move.

"There was a man named Bertrand Lyndon who got

some Americans to believe that they would be better off without the others. So, there was a civil war, followed by an actual world war—"

"I think that's enough," Kat interrupted.

Amelia looked back at her mother, then returned her attention to Titor. "What did the bad guy do to the people he didn't like?"

"Have you ever heard of genocide?"

"TITOR!"

"Is that like a genie that grants you wishes?" Amelia asked.

"I think your bedroom is calling." Titor ruffled her hair. "Let's save this discussion for another time."

Like never.

"Can I help you clean up?" Titor asked after Amelia was in bed.

"I think I'd rather be alone." Kat's smile would barely stick to her face.

"Understood." A defeated half-grin, then he was out the back door to his tent outside.

Kat left the dishes for morning. Put Jack and Amelia both in her bed so she could sleep in between them again. Then got ready for bed and locked the door, but this time she left her chair under the desk where it belonged.

Chapter Fifty-One

KAT – 2000

KAT BARELY SLEPT.

Though inspired by a snoring child on either side of her, she never managed to do much more than drift off for an occasional spell, until another errant thought startled her awake and she felt compelled to slip out of bed and quietly make her way to the window, peeking out to check on Titor yet again.

The man was still in his tent every time, moving about and making shadows inside.

And he stayed there the next morning as she got up early to occupy her mind by scrubbing the house down and making omelets instead of pancakes for breakfast. By the time Kat was finished, she almost felt better, thanks to her plan.

The aromas should be bringing him to the back door shortly. She would serve him up and they could have another little heart to heart about what he really wanted.

Titor was saying things that had been hard for her to hear, but the best way to get through this situation with a genuine understanding of what was happening to Kat and her family might be to let the man talk and listen without judgment until he reached the end of his story.

Maybe even ask a few questions that assumed he was telling the truth.

Apparently, the scents weren't as inviting as she expected, because Kat could see Titor still moving around in his tent but making zero efforts to leave it.

She opened the back door to make her meaning clearer.

Several minutes later, he came inside. The children were still sleeping, but Jack would be waking up with a cry any minute, and Amelia would scurry into the kitchen already chattering moments later.

"Good morning," Kat said as he entered.

"Morning." A simple nod. "I'm sorry again about yesterday."

"We can move on from that." Her smile felt awkward. "I made you breakfast."

"Thank you." Titor glanced at the plate but didn't move toward it. "I need to take care of some things this morning."

"Where are we going?"

He shook his head. "I don't need a ride."

"What kind of errands do you—"

"Future stuff." Titor's tone was almost a warning.

So Kat couldn't get the *what future stuff?* out of her mouth.

It was unsettling how much he had closed himself off to her overnight.

"You have nothing to worry about," he said.

"Worry about what?" Amelia asked as she entered the

kitchen, apparently beating her brother to the new day for a change.

"How about we all meet at the movies later?" Titor grinned, his demeanor changed in a blink, right back to the one that always got her daughter giggling. "It will be my first real movie going experience. Dibs on buying the popcorn. The whole adventure is my treat."

"I'm not sure that—"

"Nonsense. I only have a place to stay thanks to you. Really, it's the least I could do."

"PLEASE MOMMY!"

Jack woke up with a scream.

"PLEASE! CAN WE SEE STUART LITTLE?"

"*Please Mommy*," Titor joked.

"I have to get Jack." Kat left the room.

She was barely even gone before she got back, but that was still enough time for Amelia to show Titor how Movie Phone worked, and for them to get both a time and location for *Stuart Little* playing at the Regal 8 that afternoon.

"Okay," Kat finally agreed, though she was still far from mollified.

Titor disappeared on his mysterious errands for the future, assuring them both that he'd be at the theater in time. Amelia asked her what time it was on six separate occasions in between breakfast and when they finally piled into the car and headed for the theater to wait.

Wait they did. Showing up early because Amelia would have it no other way made what would have been a short wait feel longer, but after more than a half hour of loitering in front of the theater it was finally five minutes until showtime. And still no Titor.

Kat broke down and bought tickets, fuming because it was an expense she couldn't afford and would not have justified. But it was a new movie and people were still showing up for tickets. Amelia made her ask the lady at the box office how many seats were left three different times, and after the last query she knew it was either now or never.

Five minutes later he still wasn't there.

"Are we going to get any popcorn?" Amelia sounded even sadder about the possibility of not having popcorn than she had about maybe missing the movie.

"Of course we are." Kat led her children into the theater, starting to worry less about her broken budget and more about Titor.

It was ten minutes past start time and probably at the end of the previews by the time Amelia was hugging her bucket of oil-drenched kernels and Kat was shuffling her and Jack toward theater #6.

Titor came running into the Regal and right over to them. She swallowed a knot of something at the sight of little red flecks all over his shirt. Was that blood?

"What happened to—"

"No time!" He had the audacity to grin at her. "I've always wanted to see a preview!"

But the trailers had ended, and the movie was starting as they settled into their seats.

Amelia started munching on her popcorn as Kat leaned over and whispered to Titor. "Why is there blood on your shirt?"

"Don't worry," he whispered back. "It's not mine."

"That's not an answer," she said, finding his reply even more troubling.

That time he didn't respond.

"*Titor!*" she whisper-shouted.

A loud shush came from behind her. He looked over, but instead of answering her, Titor said, "I'll see you after the show."

"Where are you going?"

"*Fight Club* is playing in theater seven. Do you know how many people in the future would kill to see *Fight Club* on the big screen?"

He left without waiting for her answer.

And Kat was left nursing that thought … about people in the future killing to see *Fight Club*. Hyperbole, of course, but it still opened the door to a bigger and uglier question.

Would Titor kill?

And even more important: who had she let into her children's lives?

Chapter Fifty-Two

KAT – 2000

KAT BARELY SLEPT for the third night in a row, this time getting out of bed as dawn broke to cast a blushing orange glow across the kitchen.

To hell with pancakes or omelets, she thought on her way to the stove, putting on a pot of water with oatmeal instead. That suited Jack's tastes just fine, and Amelia would love it once she got to add her raisins and brown sugar, and Kat needed to get on with her (work) day and prove to herself that she didn't give the slightest of shits what Titor thought about her ability to make a decent breakfast.

She turned on the stove, then went to the window, peeking outside in shock as she saw that Titor was not only gone from her tent, the tent itself was neatly packed up and resting by the back door.

Another surprising pang as she wondered if he was really gone for good.

The sound of a key in the lock made her jump, still

unreasonably paranoid thanks to her now departed visitor, who apparently might not be so departed after all.

But instead of John Titor she saw John Anderson, her father-in-law, here to mind the kids, just like he always did for three days a week while she worked as a receptionist at Serenity Health Solutions.

He closed the door behind him and looked over to the kitchen with a concerned smile. "You okay, honey? You don't look so good."

She braced herself for the usual argument as he held out an envelope in offering. "John, I can't—"

"I'm tired, Kat." He gave her another smile, but this one was indeed fatigued at the edges. "So how about I just leave this here on the table for safe keeping and forget to take it when I leave?"

He set the envelope of cash on the kitchen counter and turned to her with sharp lines of empty etched into his expression. "You want to tell me what's wrong?"

She was trying to find the words when the patter of tiny feet disrupted her rhythm, and Amelia bounded in, rising and shining before Jack for the second day in a row.

"Grandpop!" she squealed in delight while flinging her arms around his knees.

"There's my bucket of sunshine." His voice rumbled with age.

But Amelia didn't reply, already on her way to the window. She peeked outside, then turned back around, her face creased with concern. "Where did he go?"

"Where did who go?" John wondered out loud.

"He put the tent away," Amelia observed. "Does that mean he's sleeping inside tonight?"

"Oh…" John seemed to get it.

But he was getting the wrong thing.

"It's not like that." Kat wasn't sure how to finish, and

her silence was even louder now with the only other sound coming from oatmeal boiling on the stove.

"What is it like?"

"We were helping someone out for a bit. But he moved on now." Kat turned her back to John and started stirring the oatmeal while ignoring the heavy sense of Junior's dad trying not to judge her.

She was midway through manufacturing an explanation when Amelia made everything harder by chirping through a flurry of announcements.

"Mr. Titor came from the future after there was a lot of war there, first a civil one and then a real one, and he wanted to help me and Mommy got mad at him when he beat up an alligator so bad that he made it dead."

Kat turned around from the stove in time to see her father-in-law's shocked expression.

"Titor?" he repeated.

Amelia gave him a vigorous nod.

Kat echoed the gesture with far less enthusiasm.

John looked like he was about to pass out.

"Why don't you go and wake up your brother," said Kat.

Amelia looked at Kat like she was crazy. "I'm never supposed to wake him up."

"Today you have permission."

Amelia didn't need another word, scrambling out of the kitchen without another word.

"What is it?" Kat asked the second they were alone.

"Same first name as me, I assume." A definitive nod. "John Titor, am I right?"

"How did you know that?"

John collapsed into the nearest chair with a sigh. "I knew a man calling himself John Titor once."

"Really?" An otherworldly sensation tore through her

body. And even though there were a dozen questions that could have easily nudged in front of it, Kat found the most urgent one to be, "When?"

"In 1975." He looked ashamed of the coming story but relieved to be telling it. "Titor's the reason I went to jail and missed out on most of Junior's life."

"I thought it was the Russians?"

"Only because that's what everyone was most inclined to think." Another long sigh, this one with a shake of his head. "I stopped telling that story years ago, though. No one ever believed me." His bark of a laugh sounded bitter. "Not that I blame anyone for thinking I was crazy about that."

"Crazy about what?" Though, of course, Kat already knew.

"Titor said he was from the future, got me to play along with his heist on the promise that he'd help Junior while setting me up to fail."

Kat opened her mouth to ask a question, but John was too quick.

"What did this guy look like?" he asked.

"Give me a minute…" Kat grabbed her purse from the counter, shoved a hand inside, and withdrew the strip of pictures that Titor had taken with her children at the mall.

He eagerly snatched the photos from her hand and stared down in wonder. Even making silly faces in each of them, the truth appeared perfectly clear to John.

"That's him," he confirmed with an authoritative nod. "Same guy, and not a goddamned day older."

Kat shook her head. "That's not possible."

"That's what I thought. But guess what? It is." John's expression turned dark. "You can't trust that man. I only let him in because I was desperate to save Junior and—"

Kat burst into tears.

"What is it, Kat?" He was out of his seat and wrapping an arm around her.

"Amelia…" She shook her head and drew a breath, searching for the words. "It's like we were always afraid of … the doctor confirmed that she has Junior's condition."

"And Titor told you he could save Amelia."

She nodded, tears still leaking from both of her eyes.

From the other room Jack started crying too.

"It's like making a deal with the devil," grunted John.

Jack cried even louder, and some ugly sliver of instinct frosted her heart.

"Amelia?" Kat cried out, then bellowed before her daughter had a chance to answer. "AMELIA?"

Kat ran to get Jack, scooping him up from her bed, but there was still no answer by the time she got there.

And still no Amelia.

Not in the bedroom.

Or anywhere else in the house.

Chapter Fifty-Three

KAT – 2000

KAT PRACTICALLY TORE the house apart while looking for Amelia but couldn't find her inside or outside. She and John split up to investigate. He went to Maggie's, while she took Jack and drove around to the handful of places in the neighborhood that held Amelia's perennial interest.

She checked both playgrounds, the one she called Jeep Park because of the pretend metal Jeep by the swings, then the one she called Mango Park because it was easier for Amelia to say than Mangrove Trail.

The community pool didn't open until eight and was therefore mercifully empty. Kat's heart skipped a beat with the grisly image of Amelia floating face down. The library was closed, and the houses of the few friends Amelia had in the neighborhood all looked perfectly still.

Kat wasn't willing to knock and ask any of those mothers for the same reason she had sent John to Maggie's, playing the absent-minded grandpa who didn't know any better.

She hurried back to the house where John was waiting, then got oatmeal to go for the three of them before scurrying outside again to load Jack into his car seat while John assumed position sitting shotgun.

They went to the mall and circled the parking lot until 9:00 a.m., when the doors finally opened.

John took custody of Jack to give Kat a head start as she raced inside and looked wildly around the mall, with none of the wonder she had felt when witnessing that same space through Titor's eyes. Even with the place just opening it was already too loud and too garish.

And much too big. If Amelia was at the mall, how would Kat ever find her in all of that space?

She spied a security guard and ran over to him, but John was already asking about Amelia when she got there.

"Sorry." The guard shook his head. "I've been here since six this morning and haven't seen your daughter, or a guy like the one you're describing."

Kat felt like a popped balloon as they kept on looking.

The photo booth was empty, and the train only ran on weekends.

"Where to now?" John took the cue that they were leaving as Kat made a mad dash for the exit.

"The movie theater."

She burned rubber to the Regal 8, even though there wasn't anything showing for another two hours. No cars in the parking lot other than hers circling, and no sign of Titor or Amelia.

So they drove to Mangrove Links, where Kat told a rambling and rather gruesome version of what had happened when Titor killed the alligator with a golf club to the weathered but spry manager of the course.

"We definitely haven't seen that asshole," he replied. His deep tan and squint lines seemed to exaggerate the anger in his memory. "I can guarantee that if he does come back, we'll be calling Fish and Wildlife faster than my foreman when he sees fungus on the greens."

They checked the neighborhood again: parks, pool, library.

Then back to the Regency 8.

"Sorry lady," said the box office clerk. "We get a lot of dads and daughters here."

"He's not her father." Kat was mad enough to spit. "Two tickets to *Stuart Little*."

"That's already started."

"Two tickets to whatever is starting right now then." She gritted her teeth.

"What about him?" The clerk pointed to Jack.

"He's two years old. There's no charge."

The clerk narrowed her eyes as she printed the tickets. "$12."

Kat paid and bustled inside, dipping in and out of theaters, including *Any Given Sunday, The Talented Mr. Ripley, and Magnolia*, plus both theaters where *Stuart Little* was playing, and finally into *Fight Club*, feeling murderous with the certainty that Titor had introduced her daughter to an orgy of violence. For the second time, if she counted the alligator.

But when Amelia wasn't in the theater Kat, wished it was otherwise, regardless of the trauma that movie would have given her.

"Maybe it's time that we call the police," John suggested once they were back outside the theater.

"She's only been gone since this morning."

"You don't think that's enough?"

"The police won't." She shook her head. "And besides, I wouldn't even know what to say."

"Maybe you could start with something like, 'My daughter is missing.'"

"It's lose-lose, John." Kat wanted to cry. "If I say she was taken by a man from the future, they'll decide I'm incompetent and take both of my kids away from me. But if I tell them that I have absolutely no idea who the man I let stay in my house for several days is, I'll get the same result."

"Are you sure?" John asked, looking anything but.

"If she's still not here by dinner time, I'll take the risk and call the cops. But for now, we're on our own."

"Whatever you say." He nodded, but it looked like John was thinking something else.

They scoured the area surrounding the theater, once more to the mall after dropping Jack off at Maggie's with a casual excuse and a wilting promise before checking back at home and then all around the neighborhood again. Still nothing.

Kat was pacing the living room when a storm darkened the sky ahead of schedule.

"I'll go back out and take another look before it gets too bad out there," John offered to a backbeat of thunder.

"What about after it gets bad? I need to get Jack from Maggie's before you go. Don't leave in case she calls."

John nodded, but gave her no other reply.

Maggie was clearly curious, though she handed Jack over while keeping the questions in her eyes.

Kat came back home even more defeated than before, drenched by the sky that had just opened up on her. Another boom of thunder, big enough to shake the house.

"There is one more thing I can tell you about Titor."

John put a hand on her arm in an obvious attempt to make her feel better.

"What is it?" His tone filled Kat with a new hope she could hear in her voice.

Jack started crying.

"It's what happened *after* I went to jail." John swallowed, his eyes calm but his breathing excited by the secret he'd been holding inside for a quarter century too long.

Jack cried louder.

"I'm sorry." Kat sighed and drew a deep breath. "Just give me a minute. I need to get him in something dry."

She toweled him off, put Jack in his playpen, then came back out into the living room and said, "What happened after you went to jail?"

"Titor came by my apartment to see Etta, and if he hadn't, I'm pretty sure that Junior would never have survived childhood. He really did help, just like he promised, and despite what he did to me, I've never believed that Titor was a bad man. Just that there was something about what happened that I could never understand without seeing all of the pieces."

Kat stared back at him, not knowing what to think.

John gave her a clue. "I know it's hard to believe, and I'm not saying that we shouldn't be worried, but I do think that Amelia is safe, wherever she is."

"Maybe—"

But that's all Kat got out before the storm killed their power and all the lights died, plunging the house into darkness.

"GODDAMIT!" she yelled instead.

Jack started crying again.

"I'm going to go over to Maggie's and see if she has power. You call in the outage." John turned around and headed out again. Kat had made it to the kitchen when she heard the front door slam.

She felt around toward the counter on her way to the phone.

"Do you have a moment?" said a voice in the dark.

She jumped at the sound, but a second later Kat was gripping the hilt of a butcher knife and whirling around to face Titor in the shadows.

Chapter Fifty-Four

RJ – 2024

RJ AND MICHAEL stood to leave.

John barely noticed, ignoring them to ask Kat for help with a defeated growl. "Can you make me some coffee? The buttons never work right for me."

"Of course, John." She turned to see them go. "Would you care for a cup? It's a long drive."

"We're good," Michael answered for them both.

"Thank you so much for your time." RJ smiled at Kat.

She barely smiled back.

John had his back to them, with zero intention of turning around.

"Where's the nearest Starbucks?" Michael said as RJ started the engine. "Never mind, how would you know? I'll check the app, I bet there isn't one for like ten trailer parks from here."

"I thought you didn't want any coffee."

"Since when have I ever not wanted coffee? I didn't want *her* coffee."

"You're such a snob." RJ shook his head and put the car into drive.

"I'm not even being a snob about the coffee, even though it probably tasted like brewed dirt. I just didn't want to be in that shack anymore. The old man's crazy was making me claustrophobic."

"Old doesn't equal crazy."

"You're absolutely right. But that guy was *mucho loco*. Please tell me that you've had enough of this nonsense to move on from it."

RJ wasn't delusional; he knew perfectly well that the nail was already in the coffin on this project, but it had been fun to feel inspired again and he wanted to stoke the dying embers in whatever ways he could, before the flames were gone forever.

"I think our next step is to try and find Jack Anderson. Maybe we could even go back to Kat's and push that angle harder? It sounded to me like she was lying."

"You can't be serious!" Michael didn't give RJ even a second to answer. "Look. It's been really fun getting into the shit with you again. Genuinely. Digging in and really looking at a story is our jam, and I appreciate that you made me see that again. But there's nothing here and both of us know it. Our only lead came from an old lady in an elder care facility who refuses to be interviewed on camera, and the story that John told us can't be corroborated *at all*."

"You don't know if—"

"We would *never* even get it past Legal. Besides, even if we were to find Jack Anderson, there's nothing connecting him to Titor except his *abuelo's loco* heist story."

"That is a terrible use of *abuelo*."

"I love the sound of your accent," Michael said.

"It's not an accent. That's what correct pronunciation sounds like."

"Point is, our only link is a dud. But the good news is that I get it."

"And what do you get?" RJ asked, suspicious like Michael had trained him to be.

"I get what this is, or was. This was never really about John Titor at all. By the way, there's actually a Starbucks in this little sphincter of Florida ... it's like five miles from here."

"You really don't want coffee this late. You're not even driving."

"Four miles, actually."

"What were you saying about our John Titor project never really being about Titor at all? And please continue telling me in your most self-important tone, because without that I'm not sure I'll be able to absorb enough of your infinite wisdom."

"The Titor project was all about you," Michael declared.

"About me?" RJ turned to look at him.

"Or *us*. You were right." He nodded. "We needed this to rediscover the joy in our work. I hear your issues with *Gator Gitters*, a hundred percent. You're fully off the project with all of my support."

"Thank you. I mean that."

"Our next step is to find something new. A story we can really dig our teeth into, just like in the old days."

"Like what?" RJ asked.

"Whatever lights you up like Titor did. I'm glad you wasted our time, because it brought us back in sync."

Michael laughed and RJ felt suddenly lighter.

But after Starbucks, followed by a long drive of back and forth without landing on any ideas that either one of them was excited about, let alone both of them, the place felt suddenly empty. Stupid as it all might have been, the Titor project had filled RJ with purpose for the short spell when he had been allowed to indulge his interest.

He had been truly, genuinely, deeply excited about the Titor legend, and that was the type of enthusiasm he had never known how to manufacture. Michael was so much better at feigning interest in whatever subjects were best for growing their business. RJ struggled, half of the time feeling like a failure because he wasn't better at doing that same thing himself, and the other half feeling like a winner for being the one willing to follow his creative North Star.

RJ had the daunting task of figuring out what came next, and hated both ideas they'd come up with: a docuseries focused on people with dying jobs telling the stories of why they persisted in their vanishing professions, or a docuseries about following a team of scientists conducting long-term field research in extreme or remote environments: the Antarctic, a rainforest, maybe the Sahara — RJ didn't want more than a quick visit to any of those places.

He got home to find Suzanne on her laptop, swallowing the last of her wine as he entered. RJ wanted to tell her the news, but stirring up the truth from his stomach felt too much like the end of things for now.

So instead he got his own glass and filled it with pinot grigio before refilling Suzanne's.

"I have news." She took her glass with a grin.

"Did you win something? It looks like you won something."

"I've been thinking about something my mom said in her interview."

"Oh yeah?" RJ was definitely interested.

"Yeah." Suzanne nodded, smiling wider. "Remember

when she said that the FBI had another theory? Well, I finally got in touch with the agent who worked with her."

"Seriously?" Now RJ was grinning too.

She nodded again. "He was a junior agent when they were researching Titor, but he was there for it all and is therefore someone who can help to explain the alternate theory."

"Do you know if he's willing to talk?"

"He is, but only off the record."

RJ was excited by the lead, but Michael had already pulled the plug on the Titor project. "Did the agent say who Titor was, according to the alternate theory?"

"No name." She shook her head. "But he did confirm that it was all a hoax."

Now RJ really didn't know how to feel.

"The hoaxer was some college kid," Suzanne finished.

The excitement was already seeping back into him. It would've been more fun to raise the possibility that Titor was real, but that it was a college prank? That was a new angle no one had ever hit before. Even Michael would see it.

"You have a meeting with the agent tomorrow."

And RJ grinned, thinking, *Just in time.*

Chapter Fifty-Five

Kat – 2000

KAT WAVED the knife in front of her, not knowing if Titor was close enough for her to cut him, and not even sure if that's what she wanted if so.

Lightning flashed, illuminating his frightening form.

Her eyes adjusted enough that she could see him approaching, though his steps were slow. He was a large man, and even his usually playful mop of hair right now looked electrically menacing.

"AMELIA!" Kat cried out.

No answer.

"Where is my daughter?" She waved the knife in front of her again, but Titor stood stoically in front of her.

"She's safe."

That wasn't an answer.

So she bellowed, "WHERE IS MY DAUGHTER?"

Kat swung toward the sound of footsteps in the hallway and another flash illuminated Amelia as she entered the room, frightened, trying to assess the scary situation unfolding in the dark.

She came up behind Titor and reached out for his hand.

"Come to me, Amelia." Kat started to cry. "Please."

But Amelia looked scared. *Of Mommy.*

"Put the knife down, Kat," Titor said. "I can explain."

Jack started screaming.

She couldn't see Titor's smile in the dark, but Kat had seen it enough to last her a lifetime in the last few days, and right now in the blackness of her mind, his charm was menacing.

"What did you do?" Kat demanded.

"With Amelia?"

"Back in 1975! You sent John to Jail. Why?"

"I helped him. I saved Junior's life."

"You set him up. Again, *why*?" Kat kept clenching her fists not to scream, the hilt boring into her muscle and nerves. The questions were coming too fast now. "What do you really want here? Why were you covered in blood the other day?"

Titor wasn't answering, but even in the dark, she could see him assessing the situation, waiting for her to make a move.

She finally reached out and made a grab for Amelia.

He went for the knife, but Kat saw him coming. Moved fast and just the wrong way for Titor, who took her blade to the gut.

Another flash of lightning illuminated the horror, blood already gushing from his stomach as Kat pulled the knife out and grabbed Amelia by the wrist.

Jack screamed louder from his playpen as Kat ran into her bedroom with Amelia in tow and slammed the door behind her.

"What's happening, Mommy?"

Kat had never heard Amelia more frightened. She tucked her under the bed and said, "I need you to stay here, no matter what happens, okay?"

"Why won't you tell me what's happening?"

"I KNOW YOU CAN HEAR ME, KAT!" Titor roared.

"I'll tell you as soon as I can. Just stay hidden. And don't say anything, no matter what."

"YOU NEED TO STOP!"

Kat went to the bedroom door and waited for Titor to either pass, or come in and face her knife again. She needed to go back out there. For Jack.

"I'm still me, Kat! Nothing has changed."

Her breathing was thunder, but she couldn't slow her racing heart.

She heard what sounded like him entering the bathroom.

Then sure enough: "I'm in the bathroom."

Moments later, she peeked into the hallway and saw a light flickering from under the door. She needed to sneak past Titor to retrieve Jack.

Kat made it to the playpen, but Jack's screaming kept getting louder as she raced past the bathroom and back into the bedroom.

She pushed Jack under the bed with Amelia.

"You're going to play a game with your sister. Amelia, help your brother play the best game of hide and seek in history."

She stood by the door as light drifted closer.

"There's a rhythm in the rustling leaves, a sonnet in the sand. A testament to yesterdays, slipping through our hand. In the mirror of the moments, in the echo of the chimes, we're just players on the stage, in the theatre of time."

But there was nothing sweet in the tune now. It only sounded menacing, fading down to broken notes by the time she was at his door.

Kat jumped out into the hallway, brandishing the knife, trembling with fear but willing to die if it meant killing this monster and protecting her children.

Titor was fast, grabbing Kat by the wrist and pushing her back into the bedroom then down onto the bed.

"I'm not trying to hurt you," Titor insisted, even though the press of his body declared the opposite. "I just need you to hear me."

She struggled against him, but even with a gut wound, his strength was too much.

"I'll leave if you will just listen to me."

Kat stopped struggling and he relaxed his grip. The knife clattered to the floor.

He picked it up and put the hilt back into her hands. "Keep that on me if it makes you feel safer, but I'd appreciate it if you didn't stick me with it again."

"Say what you need to say."

"Amelia will die without medical intervention. And not just now. She needs an operation immediately, and you can expect another one when she's a teenager. Do you understand what I'm saying?"

Kat nodded, afraid for so many reasons.

"I need you to repeat it for me," he ordered.

"Amelia needs an operation right now, and another one when she's a teenager."

"I think I've done enough, but in case I haven't, you need to move away from here. To somewhere more rural. It doesn't have to be right away, but the sooner you can get away from the city, the better."

She nodded again, suddenly believing him despite the impossibility.

"The next time you see me, this will all make a lot more sense."

Kat was paralyzed, holding the knife in her still-trembling hand.

"You're a really good mom." Titor turned to leave, looking back at her when he got to the door, illuminated once more by yet another perfectly timed flash of lightning. "Don't forget. Bring a gas can with you for when the car dies on the side of the road."

Then he was gone.

Chapter Fifty-Six

2000

THREE MONTHS after that terrible storm where Kat stabbed her time-traveling intruder in his gut, FBI Agent Cecilia Trainor knocked on her front door.

Kat didn't like the look of the woman one bit. The FBI agent on her porch was dressed in a blue tie and matching heels, her hair cut in a professional bob, badge on her belt and gun on her hip. She didn't even need to open her mouth for Kat to know why she was here.

"May I help you?"

"Kat Anderson?" The agent continued only after Kat confirmed her identity with a nod. "I'm agent Cecilia Trainor. I was wondering if I might have a word with your father-in-law. Is he home?"

Cecilia already knew he was home, same as she knew that he had moved in a few months ago, watching the kids during the day while Kat was at work.

She did not know that they were planning to move soon. Somewhere rural.

"I'll see if I can find him," Kat replied, though he was right there in the living room, listening to the exchange with a determined grimace.

John took his time on the way to the door, remembering Cecilia from the old days, but just because she was the only one who had listened to him back in 1975 didn't mean he would give her the time of day now.

"May I help you?" John asked, feigning ignorance when he got to the door.

"Mr. Anderson. Do you remember me? I'm Agent Cecilia Trainor." She knew damn well that he remembered her. Could see it in his eyes and feel it in his posture.

"Good to see you again."

"The circumstances are better." Cecilia smiled and gave him a silent cue with her nod toward the slightly ajar door that she was hoping for an invitation inside.

John recognized the gesture for what it was and declined to invite her. "What can I help you with, Agent Trainor?"

"A man was found stabbed to death in his apartment."

"And that has something to do with me?"

"His name was Bertrand Lyndon."

"I'm still waiting for the connection."

"That name doesn't mean anything to you?" Cecilia asked. "You don't know a Bertrand Lyndon?"

"Never heard that name until you brought it onto my daughter-in-law's front porch."

"We managed to lift some fingerprints from the scene that had an interesting match."

John was defensive but clear: "It couldn't have had nothing to do with me, because I don't know any Bertrand Lyndon."

"The prints matched ones lifted at the scene of the IBM heist from back in 1975. I thought that perhaps they belonged to your partner."

His face fell, but still John refused to talk.

To hell with his woman, he thought.

"You have nothing to say?" Cecilia pressed.

"I could tell you again that I don't know anyone named Bertrand, if that's helpful."

"Or maybe I could bring you in for more official questioning?" Cecilia knew she might be pushing him too hard and too fast.

He didn't disappoint. "So you came here because of some prints that are *not* mine, acting like I should be afraid of you and your badge and your gun? I served my sentence and, for the third time, I don't know any Bertrand Lyndon or anyone else. So I'm going to ask that you get back in your car and drive away from here. Don't come back until you get yourself a warrant."

John closed the door without waiting for a response.

Kat touched his arm, then gave it a squeeze.

Amelia came up behind them and said the words that Kat had been dreading to hear. "Mommy, I feel the feeling."

"What feeling?" Kat asked, though of course she knew.

"The one that Mr. Titor warned me about. The one that means it's time to go to the doctor."

And the one that Kat was now prepared to pay for, thanks to the shoebox she found under Amelia's bed on the night Titor disappeared. Shortly after she stabbed him.

For Amelia, it read at the top.

Inside there were layers of paper with a simple note of explanation on top: *I don't know which one will take off in your timeline, so please hold and use when needed.*

Stock certificates in an array of companies: Microsoft,

Circuit City, Apple, Amazon, Ask Jeeves, and more. Beneath the stocks, there was an impressive stack of cash, and beneath that, Kat's pendant from a future she now understood that she might never see, and a notebook filled with his writing.

A title was scribbled on the cover: *Time Travel 0*.

Part V

Chapter Fifty-Seven

2001

THE CARGO VAN was soaked in testosterone. Nine men and three women, all dressed head to toe in black, from body armor to helmets with tinted visors. Of course their assault rifles were also black, same as the flashlights, radios, gasmasks, and shields. A familiar scene for fans of action-oriented police procedurals, though this group of black-clad warriors had no labels on their van or vests, FBI, SWAT, or otherwise.

They were parked outside a large colonial style house with white clapboard siding and green shutters. A wide front porch with a bright red door, garish string lights linking the porch to the front yard, littered with plastic lawn chairs of every color, surrounded by a trampoline large enough to support the dozens of people bouncing on it. Thumping music rolled out from the home's open windows in a cloud.

Philip stood tall, his gaze riveted on the crew, no need

for preamble with everyone hanging on his every word. "The mark has been tracked to the house where he's holed up. You have clearance to use force, but he must be brought in alive — do you copy?"

A chorus of agreement rippled through the van, everyone nodding along except for a single dissenting voice. Curious at the very least.

"Why?" Aubrey always had questions.

"Our mission is not to question, but to execute. We retrieve the subject alive — he seems to hold significant value for our superiors."

Drake, a man more inclined to actions than questions voiced his concern next. "Wouldn't it be more prudent to wait until this little soiree loses some of its fervor? A few hours from now, these partygoers will be inebriated into oblivion. Snagging the subject then will be cake."

"Is this a bakery, soldier? Are you in the market for cake?"

"No, sir." Drake shook his head, realizing that he had just stepped in it.

"If it isn't my place to question our orders, then what makes you think it should be yours?" Philip glared, pressing Drake, minimizing the odds of any asinine follow-up questions from anyone else.

"My mistake, sir."

A curt nod, then Philip offered the van his remaining scraps of information. "It's a now or never situation. We have intel that the opposition is mobilizing. If we fail to seize the subject immediately, we risk missing our window — regardless of the party. So is everyone with me?"

"Yes, sir!" The chorus came in full.

"Given all the work they've put into this kid already, the risk of going in now beats the chance that we might lose him to the other side. This is barely a tactical situation.

Everyone at the party is a college kid, and most are drunk, probably half are underage. We have a better than excellent chance that the majority will tuck their nuts up under their ass and run while yelling *COPS!* on their way out the door. But I'm sure we can also all agree that our subject is more likely to stay put than anything else."

A round of groans to confirm that the van full of soldiers did indeed know exactly how their subject was likely to behave.

"On my signal …" Philip looked around to make sure that every member of his crew had murder in their eyes. "AND GO!"

The team spilled out from the cargo van and moved in formation toward the house.

It looked like a paramilitary unit storming the frat house, but no one from the black-clad and assault-rifle toting crew received the expected reaction. Instead, cheers rang up around them as they stormed through the front door and waved their guns around. Not a single partygoer appeared to give an iota of shit about the clear and present danger all around them.

The house was a factory of chaos, with the music blaring even louder and a reek of alcohol permeating the air. A mass of bodies writhed like a multi-limbed beast awash in cacophony. Inhibitions were drowned in an ocean of booze and hormones. Couples pawed at each other with grasping hands and hungry mouths, twisted and tangled like mating snakes.

The team finally made its way into the heart of the party where their target (and douchebag prime) was sitting on the center couch like the lord of the manor he believed himself to be.

Jacob grinned, looking even smugger than usual as he loudly whistled and spun his pointer finger around in the air. One beat later, a large *WELCOME FBI!* banner dropped into view from the ceiling.

Jacob blew his party horn and grinned even wider.

But then that smug expression left his dented face as Philip's fist plowed right into it.

Chapter Fifty-Eight

RJ – 2024

RJ SAT in the parking lot of the FBI Tampa Bay field office, looking up at the building's facade and wondering if he should go ahead and call Michael, like he'd been debating doing during most of his drive over, or keep stalling long enough to make himself late for his interview with William Curtis.

Not that it was an official interview.

Which was why he shouldn't feel the need to tell Michael. If it all came to nothing, then there was no reason for him to know about the trip, and at this point RJ wouldn't have to listen to any more of his ridicule. It wasn't even like RJ had gone out hunting for this; the lead was a gift from Suzanne.

And that gift made the interview that wasn't even really an interview more like an obligation. And again, one Michael didn't need to know about.

RJ drew a deep breath as he closed his car door and

walked with more confidence than he felt toward the building. He felt dumb, showing serious interest in a time travel story. Right down to his final source, who refused to identify himself as a source and was only willing to discuss Titor off the record, as a favor to Suzanne.

William had worked with Cecilia for years and apparently considered her family. But he had already warned RJ on the phone that he would never sign off on anything he said officially, because the truth as the FBI knew it could never be aired to the public.

"Just so we're clear, my main reason for agreeing to talk is that I'm hoping to convince you not to continue with this documentary," William had said. "And I think once you've heard the story, you'll agree with me that it's better to let this one lie."

RJ felt better about being in Tampa the second he entered. The FBI's lobby walls were lined with photos of distinguished officers, past and present. At a glance, he didn't think Cecilia Trainor was one of them. A tidy reception desk boasted a single monitor. The place was warmly lit and immaculately clean, but somehow also conveyed a heavy sense of professional danger.

A much cooler setting than the sterile nursing home, John Anderson's house, or even Kat's, though at least her setting was picturesque. The Tampa office was the kind of place that looked great on camera because viewers at home were peeking into the guts of a building where serious shit went down.

The tickle of new ideas felt good. RJ gave his name to the receptionist and let his mind wander into possible pitches for docuseries centered around the FBI that might lead to him interviewing actual agents, with conversations on the record.

An *Agents in Action* show could follow field agents on

active investigations — stalking suspects, running surveillance, making dramatic arrests, interviewing agents and recounting their most perilous cases, close calls, and rewarding wins.

Or maybe a series focused on the FBI's most wanted list, tracking painstaking manhunts bringing dangerous fugitives to justice.

A behind-the-scenes look at Academy training, from grueling physical tests to simulated scenarios.

RJ could even—

"Mr. Jimenez?"

He snapped to attention and looked up at the receptionist. "Yes?"

"Agent Curtis will see you now." She handed him a badge with his photo on it. "Room 2097. That's on the second floor."

"Thanks." RJ didn't tell the receptionist that he already understood how numbering on floors worked.

He stepped off the elevator and walked down a long hallway to 2097. An agent, presumably William, was visible at his desk through the glass. The agent jumped up from his seat when he spotted his visitor and got to the door before RJ could knock.

"William." He offered his hand, and they shook. "Come in, it's good to meet you."

The office was an advert for fastidious agents, with everything neatly tucked into its place. The walls were barren except for his diplomas, certificates, and service awards. Nothing on his desk except a computer. Two photographs on top of the filing cabinet, one with family and another with friends. A rolling bulletin board full of Post-Its rested idly off to the side.

"Can I get you a cup of coffee?"

"I'm good, but thank you."

"I just made it." William laughed with a nod to his Keurig in the corner, sitting at a small coffee station, so tidy it was almost invisible. "The donut shop is pretty good, and I have almond and coconut in addition to cow, if you want milk."

"That's a lot of choices."

William shrugged, as amiable in person as he'd been on the phone. "I like dairy, and the other stuff keeps. Something for everyone. So, coffee?"

"That sounds nice." RJ returned William's smile as they walked to the Keurig.

Maybe after their off-the-record conversation about Titor, RJ could come back and interview Agent Curtis for one of his other ideas.

They made small talk until both capsules finished brewing — William decided that he wanted a cup for himself after smelling RJ's hazelnut.

Then they each took a seat in front of his desk, blowing and sipping as William got right to it.

"I love Cecilia like a mom who doesn't constantly post embarrassing baby photos of me on Facebook or make passive aggressive comments about how I never give her handwritten cards anymore, so I guess that means I love Suzanne like a sister, even though my sister is a disastrous human, which is pretty unfair to your lady considering how cool she has always seemed."

William might not have needed the coffee.

"Anyway, we solved the Titor case years ago. *Conclusively*. I know Cecilia had other ideas, but our tech was plenty good enough by the early 2000s to prove beyond the shadow of a doubt that we had our man."

"And what makes you so sure that you had the right guy?"

"Because he was shit at covering his tracks, and back

then, the general public didn't really understand much about IP tracking."

"So who was he?"

"Again, this is seriously off the record."

"Of course." RJ offered him a reassuring smile. "A journalist always protects his sources."

"Is that the same thing as a documentarian?"

RJ laughed. "Not exactly, but you have my word."

"Well, while I'm sure your word is good and all—" William passed RJ a three-page non-disclosure agreement to sign. He barely glanced at the terrifying consequences of talking, before scribbling his name at the bottom.

"And John Titor was…"

And for the first time in the entire process, someone was finally willing to answer that question without preamble.

William nodded and told him the truth. "John Titor was a college kid named Jacob Lambert."

Chapter Fifty-Nine

JACOB - 2000

MORNING MIST *still clung to the clustered pine trees surrounding the compound as a flurry of scientists bustled about the ashram, their faces all lit with a zealot's fervor; after years of secret experiments and theorizing, the Gateway was finally ready for human trial.*

The egg-shaped contraption of metal and glass stayed housed inside this sanctuary in the woods. A cadre of clandestine scientists had finally finished their life's obsession, building a bridge to the prime dimension — a realm of pure chaos seething beneath our own, frozen in time ever since the first blinking microsecond in-between the Big and the Bang.

Two scientists slid open a door in the egg's burnished surface, one on either side, stepping back as its interior glow cast an azure light on one of the white-robed devotees whose belief they had nurtured stepped forward to stake his claim in tomorrow's history.

The lead scientist rested a hand on the young man's shoulder. "Go now, Seeker, and return borne upon wonders we can only imagine!"

Then the robed man climbed inside the egg and the door sucked shut behind him.

A blinding flash as space and time crackled like lighting.

Scientists gasped in mingled rapture as the egg blinked from existence.

And the Gateway had been opened.

It played out like a movie in Jacob Lambert's mind, albeit somewhat embellished, as Professor Wyght explained the legend of Ong's Hat to his class. Jacob had never heard any of the story before but was instantly captivated. Not enough that he would ever mention what he was learning out loud to even one of his friends, but still Jacob was already picturing himself digging around online to see what else he could find later.

"The rise of digital communication has enabled the proliferation of modern myths and legends in unprecedented ways," Wyght continued. "For most of history, propagating stories required the consent and participation of publishers or media gatekeepers. But the internet has stripped the world of these barriers, allowing narrative to spread organically through online communities without oversight or verification."

Goddammit was the professor longwinded. Why not just say: *The internet lets us spread lies without an editor or fact-checker to stop it.*

"Ong's Hat is a prime example of a primarily digital legend. Its tales of inter-dimensional travel and paranormal experiments arose back in the 80s on BBS and via Xerox mail art, but it wasn't until the rise of online forums that the legend began to build steam. Lacking any factual basis, its popularity was driven solely by a desire for entertainment and pretend, evolving into a shared fiction and cornerstone of internet folklore."

The balls out Ong's Hat story proves that people get hyped about insane stories BECAUSE of how off-the-wall they are.

"In the past, we relied on traditional media to separate truth from fiction. While often imperfect, the presence of editors, fact-checkers and subject matter experts at least filtered out the patently absurd before it reached the public." Wyght shook his head as he looked out at his audience like a sage. "But no such safeguards exist online. Rumor and reality now spread at equal pace, and the distinction between them is increasingly blurred. This new paradigm enables creative expression to flourish unrestrained by physical limitations or social restrictions. But it also grants fictions a weight and immediacy that can sometimes eclipse truth, reality becoming whatever anonymous individuals decide to invent and communities choose to believe."

Truth moves faster than bullshit when no one knows who's talking and anyone can say they're an expert.

"The internet's power to extend reality only reinforces how much we construct it from shared stories. Legends like Ong's Hat persist not despite but precisely because of their implausibility — and our hardwired human tendency to weave fragments of fact and fiction into a narrative whole, regardless of how fantastical the result. Humans crave wonder, and we hunger to submerge ourselves in fables that reveal new meaning about our world, or perhaps transport us away from the one we know too well."

Humans are hardwired to construct meaning from myths, because reality sucks.

He looked around the room as Wyght droned on, expanding simple points into masturbatory paragraphs. Jacob was bored right the fuck out of his nutsack, and the last thing he wanted to be doing was listening to the professor jizzing his blather across the room. Jacob would love it if Wyght would just talk about Ong's Hat, or digital myths in general, without all the fifty-cent words that only stood in the way of his audience's interest and understanding.

Renner was trying to get Jacob's attention, nudging Harley in the ribs and nodding at him. It didn't matter that they were all the way across the room, Jacob knew exactly what they were talking about. And it was still bullshit. He had exactly zero interest in going on a stupid ski trip. Ski lifts were overpriced death traps run by underpaid and underwhelmed idiots.

Besides, he couldn't ski, and Jacob sure as shit wasn't getting lessons, or going on bunny slopes in front of the guys. So fuck the whole thing wholesale.

What? Jacob said with his expression, aiming it at Renner and Harley, both looking over at him.

He knew what, but even Wyght's droning was better than that nonsense, so he returned his attention to the front.

"And the beautiful thing is, people fell for the story of Ong's Hat — hook, line, and sinker." The professor laughed while pressing a button on his projector remote. A photo of him fishing with what Jacob could only assume was a paid acquaintance (he definitely didn't have friends), appeared on screen as Wyght chuckled again. "I guess you could say that people took the bait…"

The room was awkwardly silent in the absence of laughter.

He cleared his throat and continued, somehow managing to stay pleased with himself. "This is my friend and fellow professor, one of the group of young men behind the Ong's Hat game. He asked me to play a scientist. Now, I bet you're wondering what this story has to do with today's class, other than knowing that Old Professor

Wyght here had his hat in the internet's first widespread urban legend."

Another expectant pause that failed to deliver.

And still the professor held his smile. "Your assignment is to take any old folklore or myth and reexamine how that legend could be done online today in a way that perpetuates and supports the old story."

Wyght was still a windbag narcissist who cared more about how cool his students thought he was than actually teaching the class, but that was still a cool-ass assignment. His wheels were already turning, thinking of ways he might alchemize old myths into something new.

Jacob had three decent ideas competing for brain space immediately: Create a basic website dedicated to investigating the "real" events behind famous myths like Atlantis or Bigfoot, with pictures, eyewitness accounts, and heaping dose of speculation, then promote the site on message boards for traffic; launch a MUD or MOO where people could go on text-based virtual adventures in a world inspired by Greek mythology, Arthurian legend or other folklore; or build a found footage website around some sort of fictional artifact that had "recently been discovered".

"That was so fucking stupid," Renner said after class.

"Totally," Jacob agreed, though not really.

Harley nodded. "It was like a balls sandwich with extra balls."

Jacob laughed. But Harley was also an idiot.

"So are you coming on the ski trip?" Renner asked. "Or are you going to be gay?"

Jacob had no idea what homosexuality had to do with their possible ski trip, but that was par for the course among his friend group. "For the last time, your mom liking anal doesn't make me gay."

"Are you going on the ski trip?" Harley's turn, because clearly they were in this together.

"I can't." Jacob shook his head. "I have plans that involve April's pants around her ankles and her face—"

"Why don't you just bring April up the mountain?" Harley tried.

"Tell you what ..." Jacob nodded like he meant it. "If Renner promises to bring his mom, I'll come. Both on the ski trip and on her tits."

"Dude," Renner said as Harley started laughing.

"I promised April that—"

"Fuck you, man!" Renner cut him off. "You promised *us.*"

"I never promised to go on a skiing—"

"But you promised to help plan our senior prank, and that's where we'll be talking about it," Renner kept arguing. "The ski trip is practically a requirement of being in Omega Theta Pi. Apparently, Travis has something amazing planned, so your vagina has herpes if you can't be there."

"Have you considered changing your major to law?" Jacob glanced back at the photo of Professor Wyght and his supposed friend as the barest germ of an idea rooted in his mind.

He needed to think up something that would outshine Travis.

Chapter Sixty

JACOB – 2000

JACOB'S FAMILY only lived seven miles from campus, though he often wished his childhood home was at least a hundred miles away.

He dumped his overstuffed laundry bag on the floor of his old bedroom and fell face first onto the bed, headphones on and *Californication* blaring in his ears — definitely the Peppers' best since *Blood Sugar Sex Magik*.

Four bars into "Otherside," his mom knocked on the door and poked her head inside his room to render the knocking irrelevant. "How were your classes this week, hon?"

Jacob grunted, but she didn't take the hint.

"That's very interesting! I think I read an article about *mgrmphrup* just last week. I'm not asking you to talk about B-Law. How about your Folklore and Contemporary Culture class? Are you still enjoying that one?"

He removed his headphones and replied in a tone that clearly broadcast his irritation. "*What?*"

"Are you having a hard time listening with all that Slim Shady in your ears?"

"I was listening to the Chili Peppers. And Slim Shady isn't his name."

"Then why does he keep saying that's his name, over and over and over, no matter how many times I asked you to please turn out it down? You know, the song that starts, 'Hey kids, do you like violence?' and then something about nails in eyelids?"

"I know the song, Mom. But his name is Eminem. Slim Shady is a character."

"I doubt his name is really Eminem."

"It's Marshall Mathers." Of course Jacob had to explain the moniker because sometimes his mother acted like her brain was a ball of rubber bands. "It's his initials, M and M: *Eminem.*"

"That's very clever. I can see why he's so popular."

"It is clever. *He's* clever."

"Oh, I can tell. He *does* seem very clever. I'm glad that Mr. Mathers could curse his way to stardom."

"Did you want something?"

"I wanted to ask you how you were enjoying your Folklore and Contemporary Culture class, but now I'll move on and just let you know that dinner will be ready in ten minutes. And ask you to please tell your brother."

"Why can't you tell him?"

Mom stared at him.

"Fine," Jacob said.

He started "Otherside" over, played it twice, then dragged himself off of the bed and walked one room over to pound on Rudy's door.

Jacob's twelve-year-old sibling was a freak of nature, a

real pimple on the ass of popular culture. The kind of kid who believed that brains trumped social skills — just one in an infinity of reasons that he had the charisma of a soggy noodle, and a personality like pepper spray to the face.

And hilariously, considering that Rudy was in all ways a load that their dad should have flushed, he looked at his older and much wiser brother like he was the village idiot.

The door swung open to his sniveling little glare.

"What?" Rudy snapped.

"Mom wanted me to tell you that it was time for dinner, and I thought you should know that even if you're finally starting to sprout some hair on your balls, no one is ever going to see it."

"Your reliance on raucous revelry as a substitute for substantive discourse highlights the stark contrast between our intellectual wavelengths."

"Okay, freakshow. See you at the table."

There were only three settings when Jacob entered the dining room for dinner.

"Dad working late?"

"Again." Mom nodded. "But I'm actually okay with it. We're going to Cancun for a month in May. And no, you can't have a party here. Aunt Helene will be watching Jacob."

"Got it. No party."

"She'll be watching him, *here*."

"I heard you, and I get it," Jacob said as Rudy entered the room.

"Perhaps she's reiterating her statement because you either display a flagrant disregard for established guidelines or have consistently demonstrated an intellectual deficiency preventing their retention."

"You do know you're twelve, right?" Jacob took a seat.

"We were probably learning to count at the same time."

"It's a miracle you got to three, considering there are only two people who love you."

"There are more than two people who love him, Jacob," Mom admonished him. "Please be nice to each other. For once." She gave them a smile as they started to eat. "For me?"

Jacob tried to comply. "Hey, Rudy, have you ever heard of Ong's Hat?"

"Of course. And don't tell me you believed that shit."

"No swearing at the table," Mom cut in.

"Why would I believe it?" Jacob rolled his eyes at Rudy. "I thought it was interesting, and exactly the kind of nerdy crap you've probably filled a sock or two over." He turned to Mom. "I didn't swear."

"You might as well have."

Rudy said, "Clearly there are several people behind Ong's Hat."

"Are you talking about your ass?" Jacob laughed.

"Ong's Hat is an elaborate hoax, meant to propagate virally. The perfect mix of fringe science, paranormal encounters, and utopian ideals designed to titillate those seeking hidden or forbidden knowledge, while evading critical scrutiny."

"I bet you titillate yourself while thinking about—"

"JACOB."

Rudy turned to their mother. "His facile dismissal reveals the narrowness of his thinking." Then back to Jacob. "Have you noted the strategic anonymity of their authors?"

"I have noted that you have the anatomy of a Ken doll."

"Stop it. Both of you. Jesus." Mom changed the

subject. "Your father and I are also getting away this weekend to go antiquing."

"Antiquing in winter and Cancun in the summer." Jacob snorted. "I can't wait to get old."

"You're too cool for Cancun?" Mom asked.

"It was more the antiquing I was objecting to."

"You need to stay here with Rudy," she finished.

"What? Why? What about Aunt Helene?"

"Aunt Helene has plans."

Rudy started snickering.

"I can't. Sorry." Jacob shook his head. "I have plans too."

"You didn't have any plans when I asked you about this weekend yesterday."

"That's before Renner made me promise that I'd go on a ski trip with the guys."

"Oh?" Mom perked up. "Well, I am glad to hear that."

He might have made a mistake. Cheers to getting out of a weekend with Rudy, but jeers to spending it on the slopes instead. And as much as he was totally over everyone in his family, Jacob's constantly working father included, he wasn't the kind of person who would lie to his mother.

Guess I'm going skiing.

Chapter Sixty-One

JACOB – 2000

THE RENTED mini-bus rolled through thick blankets of snow, snaking up a winding road until Renner reached a roundabout lined with sky-scraping trees dusted in white. Frosted mountains kissed the distance as shadowed skiers slalomed like ants down the slopes.

The ski resort was in its prime time as skiers and vacationers bustled in and out of the lodge. Plenty of honeys were standing in clusters as Renner idled in the mini-bus, waiting for the Tahoe in front of them to pull forward. The interior of their vehicle echoed with whistling, including from Harley and Marcus, even though they were the only two guys dumb enough to bring their girlfriends along on this guys-only trip.

Renner finally parked and Jacob felt nauseous. Now that they were finally at the lodge, he was running out of escape routes. He had never been on skis before, and that truth was about to become abundantly clear to everyone, which meant they would likely be leaving the mountain with Jacob as the subject of too many punchlines.

The mini-bus door creaked open, unleashing an icy blast that gnawed at his overheated skin. Melissa, Harley's girlfriend, faltered on the steps as she descended, and in her clumsiness, Jacob saw a glimmer of an opportunity to navigate through this awkward moment.

He hung back, allowing everyone else to disembark before making his own descent down the mini-bus steps. In a calculated misstep, Jacob stumbled on the last one, clumsily tumbling into the frosty snow.

A string of under-the-breath expletives tumbled out as he landed, and he scrambled to recover, putting on a brave face to shrug off the embarrassment while exaggerating the spectacle.

Everyone looked concerned, except for Travis, peering down at Jacob as he approached his still-prone form, not exactly rolling his eyes so much as letting Jacob know with his body language that he could if he wanted to.

Jacob was wishing he had leaned less hard into his little performance as Travis kneeled in the snow, like he knew exactly how cool he looked in his blue and white ski jacket, Abercrombie & Fitch jeans, and Timberland snow boots. That easy smile and aura of unrelenting confidence, always relaxed and ready for fun. Jacob either hated Travis, or hated how much he wished he could be just like him.

Travis gingerly took his ankle in hand. Looked it up and down, then made eye contact with Jacob for a split second before addressing the group.

"It looks like Jacob won't be skiing with us this weekend." Travis sounded disappointed, but both he and Jacob knew the truth of what had just happened.

A kindness and a cruelty. Jacob had traded the worry

of wondering how to keep his lack of skiing know-how a secret for the incessant shame he felt from Travis seeing right through him.

The group helped him get to the cabin. It was large enough to house all ten of them, including Melissa and Jenny, but the place felt empty once the gang was gone, and there was little to do inside except wish that he'd played a better game than the one that had left him alone.

He'd brought some Saran wrap to rig the toilets with, but now that kindergarten level prank felt about as stupid as this ski trip.

That's what he wanted more than anything else right now — a totally epic prank that would redeem his standing among the guys.

Something smart, maybe even unforgettable.

But after two hours of thinking Jacob still had only the feeling of being alone.

He went back to the bookshelf and perused the titles again, but nothing had changed since the last time. The shelves were still mostly full of spy thrillers and a couple of trashy romances — but not nearly dirty enough to stir his interest. There was a Prairie Home Companion Joke-book, but after spending a few minutes with that waste of pages on his final trip to the bookshelf, Jacob knew better than to give it a second try. Only one of the five jokes had made him laugh. Idiotic puns like, *Why don't scientists trust atoms? Because they make up everything!* Or, *Why did the scarecrow win an award? Because he was out standing in his field!* But, *How does a cucumber become a pickle? It goes through a jarring experience ...* did manage to surprise a smile out of him.

He abandoned the bookshelf and figured he might as well start on some homework. He had his laptop but no internet, so the downloaded Folklore assignment would be a perfect way to pass the time, reading more about Ong's Hat, which eventually led to a nice round of thinking.

The gang exploded through the cabin door a few hours later, Renner yelling much too loudly about how girls at ski resorts loved to show off their tits once they got inside in the warm and could shed all those ski clothes, bellowing with a sense of authority, even though Jacob knew for a fact that Renner had never seen so much as a single nipple at a ski resort before.

They'd started drinking, too much too fast, same as usual.

Melissa must have been trying to prove Renner right because she stripped down to her bra and panties, seemingly just because. Harley didn't mind her parading around because she was showing his friends what he got to fuck.

"Did I miss anything good out there?" Jacob asked.

"We were mostly talking pranks all day," Travis replied, probably because he knew that's what would make Jacob feel like he missed out the most.

"Oh yeah?" Jacob prompted him.

It was an Omega Theta Pi tradition for each of the seniors to pull a prank. The most epic one was declared the winner, and Jacob assumed that even though it was taking him an obnoxiously long time to come up with a kick-ass idea, he would have something mind-blowing soon, and the only other senior standing in the way of Jacob being declared *numero uno* in this category was Travis himself.

"Travis won't tell us his plan," Renner reported.

"He's being a total douche about it," added Jenny.

"I thought girls didn't like the word *douche*," AJ said.

"We also hate queef." Melissa made a face.

"You ladies can all wait to see it for yourself," Travis said, referring to everyone in the room.

But they kept on cajoling Travis to no avail, until the frat brothers finally started repeating their own planned pranks to insinuate they had the best idea and that Travis was stalling on account of having nothing.

Then Travis finally showed his hand. "So, Dean Wilkens acts like he's running Harvard instead of this dump—"

"We go to a good school!" Harley argued.

"—and I can't think of anything that would piss that asshat off more than the diabolical, dirty, and downright hilarious ..."

Travis dramatically paused.

"Do we get to see the movie, or just your preview?" Renner asked.

Travis grinned and continued. "I'm gonna write the dean a heartwarming message on the front lawn using some good old-fashioned bovine excrement — that's cow shit to you, Brad." Travis pointed to the one brother who regularly needed even the simplest jokes explained. "I'm talking thick, hearty, and fresh from the farm. But that's not enough — this prank comes with a twist."

Another dramatic pause, though the punchline was obvious. Even after the grass was cleaned, the fertilizer would have turned the lawn epically green no matter how short the grass was shorn.

"Cow shit is basically superfood for grass. I'll be leaving it green enough to make Ireland look dry." Travis finished to a hearty round of applause, but Jacob figured that was probably just because everyone always needed to slobber all over their fraternity's fearless leader.

Jacob actually liked Robbie's Y2K Redux idea better, sending out an "emergency bulletin" saying that the Y2K bug had struck again, this time targeting the university's grading system and resetting all grades to F.

"How about your idea?" Travis asked.

There was no way he could follow Travis. Not right now. Anything Jacob said would pale in the light of his invisible hold over the brothers. The best thing to do in a situation like this was to sell the sizzle instead of the steak.

"You'll all just have to wait and see." Jacob grinned, escaping the same nudge that had befallen their fearless leader. "But I can promise, this one is going to be *legendary*."

Chapter Sixty-Two

JACOB – 2000

RENNER WAS NAVIGATING the Florida freeways as they made their way back from the airport. The entire mini-bus was giving Jacob shit for not donning skis at any point in the weekend.

"The snowmen got more time on the slopes than Mr. Couch Potato," Harley said.

"He turned chilling out into his own sport," added AJ.

"He's the only person in the world I know who goes to a ski lodge for hibernation."

"I'm surprised you know the word *hibernation*, Brad." Jacob was sick of the banter.

"He was on a mission to study patterns in the carpet," Renner explained. "That's why he was always lying on his stomach with that stupid notebook."

"He was writing porn," Harley opined.

"You don't write porn," argued Brad.

"What do you think romance novels are?" Jacob

pictured his mom's tall piles of Rosemary Rogers, Robin Schone, and Anaïs Nin.

"Your favorite thing to read?" Renner guessed.

"Can we get back to how Jacob's skis saw less action than—"

"He twisted his ankle," Travis cut into what surely would have been another dud of an insult from Brad. "There was nothing else he could do."

Fuck you, Travis.

Jacob could change the subject himself. "Any of you assholes ever hear of Ong's Hat?"

"No. We can't remember a stupid story that—"

"What's that?" Harley asked.

"—Professor Wyght told us a couple of days ago," Renner finished, glancing into the rearview to meet Harley's gaze and let him know he was an idiot.

"What's Ong's Hat?" Travis asked for everyone else.

He could still fuck himself, but Jacob appreciated the opening.

"It's some level ten insanity—"

"Are there only ten levels?"

"Shut up, Renner," Travis said, assuming for some reason that Jacob couldn't have told Renner the same thing himself. "I want to hear this."

Jacob continued. "There's supposedly this town in New Jersey where there was this weird commune of scientists—"

"Isn't that redundant?" Harley interjected.

"—who discovered interdimensional travel. The eggheads called themselves the Incunabula, and they had this gizmo that let people slip into parallel universes."

"That's not real, though, right?" Travis asked.

"Of course not." Jacob shook his head. "The whole thing was a massive hoax. Predating the internet, but then taking off online. A social experiment to see how far these guys could push the story and still have people buying it. They even cooked up a batch of fake documents and interviews, then spread that shit like Brad's chlamydia."

"I DON'T HAVE CHLAMYDIA!" Brad roared in his defense.

"Dude." Harley made a face. "Thou doth protest too much."

Jacob kept going. "You wouldn't believe how many people fell for the story. People were obsessed, digging into every little nugget of 'evidence' while trying to track down this place that didn't exist. Well, actually Ong's Hat is a real place."

"Does it exist or doesn't it?" Travis's patience was somehow *more* irritating.

"Town does, weird commune doesn't. But the whole thing was like a giant game of telephone that could be played by anyone with an internet connection."

"Were they as obsessed as Travis is with Jennifer Aniston?" Renner said from up front.

"He wants to get the Rachel for his next haircut," Brad replied.

"That doesn't even make any sense, dipshit." Jacob shook his head. "You can't add a bunch of hair to a haircut, and even if you could, Travis wants to stick his dick into Jennifer Aniston, not look like her."

"Rude," said Melissa.

Jenny shrugged. "I'd fuck Jennifer Aniston."

No one gave a shit about what Jacob was saying about the internet legend, except for Travis, but this entire minibus full of assholes could fuck itself. This bunch of dim lights might have missed out on the spark of excitement, but Jacob was circling an idea that he felt increasingly certain could be the most epic prank Omega Theta Pi had ever seen.

All he needed was a truly excellent story, and reaching for his notebook again, Jacob was sure that he already had one.

The drive back from the airport seemed to take an eternity, at least whenever Jacob tuned into the inanity of his brothers and the tagalong girls chattering around him. But when he ignored all the jabbering and focused on the potential of his upcoming prank, time disappeared altogether.

Soon the girls had been dropped off and the boys were back home, pouring into the house and dropping their belongings all over the floor to deal with later like the slobs they all were.

"So if nobody has any better ideas than casino night for our end of the year blowout, we should—"

"Fuck your casino night, Brad!" Renner snapped.

Harley started laughing.

Travis said, "Your casino night idea only kind of sucks. The point Renner is actually making is that we need to do something better than we did last year. The casino idea is played out, and therefore, not epic by definition."

"It also just sucks," Renner added.

"That's been established." Travis turned to Jacob. "What do you think?"

"I think I need to take a shit." He saluted to his brothers and headed for the stairs.

Jacob's bowels were perfectly empty, but for once he wasn't interested in planning shenanigans with the group. Not when he had his own mischief to organize.

Alone in his shared bedroom, he opened his laptop and (finally) went online to look up time travel, searching around for some forums in particular. A few minutes later he stumbled upon the Time Travel Institute, filled with exactly the type of forum posters Jacob had been hoping to find.

Over the next few days he read, planned, and worked on his prank. He mapped out the science and filled in plot holes. When he felt ready, he created an account and began to interact with some of the crackpots hanging around on the forum. It only took a moment for them to ask who he was.

"My name is John. I'm 38 and a time traveler from Florida."

Jacob took a deep breath, hoping this would work, before hitting enter on step one of his prank.

Chapter Sixty-Three

JACOB – 2000

TWO MONTHS later and Jacob was at home for winter break, still wishing his parents lived seven hundred miles instead of just the seven away from campus, alongside his usual semi-gratitude at having a mom still willing to do all his laundry.

"Is that all for me?" Mom touched her chest as if flushing from embarrassment before pointing to his laundry bag. "You shouldn't have."

"Thanks, Mom." Jacob kissed. her on the cheek. "Are you making dinner tonight?"

"Jesus Christ, Jacob. I make dinner every night. Can you just please ask what I'm making if that's what you actually want to know?"

"What are you—"

Jacob was silenced by a heavy knock on the door.

Mom was already on her way to answer it.

She opened the door to see a tall man with a strong

build, early twenties, dressed in a navy suit with sunglasses on top of his head. He nodded in salutation.

"Good afternoon, I'm agent William Curtis with the FBI." He showed them his badge.

Mom was all aflutter and stuttering for words until she finally turned toward the stairwell and belted out, "RUDY!"

Jacob looked toward the top of the stairs where Rudy was rushing out into the hall.

But then he stopped at the top of the stairs, stole a look at the suit and tie on the front porch, then made an about face back to his bedroom. Jacob heard the key turn in the lock.

Agent Curtis cleared his throat. "I'm actually here to see Jacob."

Mom turned to look at him with questioning eyes before returning her attention to the front porch. Jacob just shrugged: *I have no idea?*

But he definitely had an idea.

"Please, come in." Mom opened their front door all the way and invited the FBI agent inside, obviously swallowing her nerves as she led them into the dining room and pointed at the table. "Can I make you a cocktail?"

Agent Curtis (of course) seemed surprised by the question.

"I'm so sorry." Mom shook her head, still flustered. "Of course you don't want a drink. How about a cup of coffee instead?"

The agent smiled. "No thank you to both."

Mom took a seat next to Jacob.

"Have you been following me?" Jacob asked.

The agent stared at him, his stony face revealing nothing.

Jacob grinned. "You definitely have. That is *so* cool."

"Why is that cool at all?" Mom asked, out of her depth, just like Donny from *The Big Lebowski*.

"Is this about the time traveler posts?"

Agent Curtis sighed, clearly less delighted by this exchange than Jacob. "Yes. I am visiting you today in regard to the time travel posts."

"What time travel posts?" Mom asked.

"Your son has been posting online as a time traveler from the future," Agent Curtis explained before turning back to Jacob, clearly embarrassed by what he saw as a lowest man on the totem pole type of mission. "We have to follow up on these sorts of things, and there were parts of your story that gave the Bureau a bit of concern."

"There's nothing to worry about," Jacob assured him with a shrug. "I made it all up. I was thinking of changing my username from Time_Travel0 to TiToR — like time traveler, Time Travel-OR. What do you—"

"You're a senior in college, is that correct, Mr. Lambert?"

"That's right," Mom answered for him.

"Can you tell me about your physics classes?"

"*Physics?*" Mom repeated.

"What have you taken? Introduction to Physics? Classical Mechanics? Thermodynamics and Statistical—"

"What was the first one?" Jacob cut him off.

Agent Curtis gave him a polite smile. "Introduction to Physics. Newtonian mechanics, basic thermodynamics, and electromagnetism. It's usually a prerequisite for higher-level physics courses."

"That one." Jacob kept grinning like a smart ass.

"*Just* Intro to Physics?" He tried to clarify.

Jacob nodded. "Just the one."

Mom still looked confused.

"Where did you get your take on time travel?" asked Agent Curtis.

"I got it right?" Jacob was over the moon.

But the agent was stone faced, clearly not getting what he came here to get. "I highly recommend that you stop with this hoax immediately."

"Am I in trouble?"

Mom leaned forward, still confused but clear enough to know she should be extra interested in this particular answer.

"No." Agent Curtis shook his head. "You are not in any trouble."

"So, unless I'm missing something, if I'm not in trouble or doing anything illegal, then doesn't that mean that you can't really do anything to stop me?"

"Jacob!" Mom blurted.

"Your son is correct," Agent Curtis admitted, though he was clearly annoyed.

"How did you know it was me?"

"You didn't even bother to mask your IP address."

"Ah." Jacob nodded. "Rookie mistake. Maybe I should go back in time and mask it to keep you from wasting your trip over here today."

The agent stood, looking from Jacob to his mother and back again. "Fair warning, Mr. Lambert: you would be well advised to not let this little prank of yours get too far out of hand. If it hasn't already."

"Seriously?" Jacob rolled his eyes, failing in every way to take the situation seriously. "What can possibly happen from a bunch of people on a forum believing that there's a time traveler among us? OH NO!" He suddenly cried out, slapping his cheeks like Macaulay Culkin. "People might start paying more attention to the world and appreciating their present!"

"Have a good day, Mr. Lambert." Agent Curtis nodded to Jacob, then let himself out.

"Do you want to tell me what that was all about?" Mom said once the door closed behind him.

"It's about your eldest son having the intelligence of a lepton," Rudy answered, suddenly appearing at the top of the stairs.

"Right. Because a moron could get the FBI to give him a home visit."

"You're saying that like it's a good thing." Mom sounded deeply concerned.

"What sort of techno-barbarian doesn't shield their IP address?"

But Jacob just snorted. "You will *never* get a blowjob."

Mom really gave him hell for that one. Enough that going to his room wasn't enough.

So Jacob went for a walk.

And after two blocks, he noticed the blue repair van following him.

Chapter Sixty-Four

Jacob – 2001

JACOB WAS BACK IN CLASS — not physics, but har-dee-har-har to that one — and could barely focus on a word Professor Wyght was saying. There were too many other more important things on his mind. Like tonight's pledge vote at the frat house, and all the Titor posts he kept writing in his head, which would spill right out of him as soon as he got to the keyboard.

His Titor posts had attracted attention from the goddamned FBI! Maintaining that quality required a level of time and effort that was finally catching up with him. He had been doing his damndest to keep up with the forum, but members weren't as dimwitted as he at first imagined them to be, and with school now back in session, their prompts had been putting him through the paces.

But every minute spent on the project was still fun for Jacob. He loved playing Titor so much that half the time he found himself thinking he really was the man, working full-time to see the world through his time traveling eyes.

Wyght droned on, and Jacob kept thinking about the posts he would respond to later. Titor was getting grilled hard with a crazy spectrum of questions, everything from queries about what the future looked like in general to specifics about the process of time travel itself to deep dives into the physics of black holes. Those questions were the most challenging, and therefore the ones he found most rewarding to answer.

Jacob wanted to reach a larger audience now that his story had been put through its paces, and he was even thinking that maybe he could get Art Bell to do a show about his story if he got enough attention on his forum posts.

But he had a growing suspicion that even after the big reveal, none of his housemates would get how amazing the prank was. A remarkable feat, executed all by himself. Not flashy like that stupid cow shit from Travis, but legendary by default, considering his prank's exponentially more impressive reach, with members of the forum (and people following it) spanning the nation, sea to sea. Plus other places in the world, probably.

Jacob *could* tell his brothers that the FBI came to visit him about his time traveler from the future, but there was an eighty percent or greater chance — according to Jacob — that his brothers wouldn't believe him, no matter how much he swore up and down that it had really happened. One comment about how Jacob was "serving up a steaming platter of fantasy crap," which was what Renner usually said when he thought someone was lying, and the rest of the guys would be all over him.

Jacob was mostly pissed at himself. He should never have pulled that stupid stunt with his ankle when they got to the resort. Travis had been cool to him for the most part since they got back from the ski trip, and had never called him out on the lie about his injury, but it was enough that he knew.

If Jacob's prank was in competition with Travis claiming the title he saw as rightfully his, there was zero chance Jacob could keep his secret without the brother everyone listened to most making a fool of him in front of the entire fraternity.

But maybe there was a way Jacob could goad Agent Curtis into making another visit? The FBI had still been following him in that blue cargo van (not exactly inconspicuous, but slightly better than the sleek black car that had followed before Curtis's visit) ever since winter break.

And what if he could make that follow-up happen at the fraternity house instead of his home, where the genius of this epic prank was obviously lost on Jacob's mother?

He managed to slip in a post before the pledge vote that evening, which he'd almost forgotten about entirely once firmly seated in Titor's headspace. Back at the frat, Jacob had joined the ring of hooded figures as they'd gathered around a circle on the floor in a dimly-lit room, arms raised as they prepared to chant their oath and decide on which pledges to cut — only then could they agree on who got an invite to their next epic party, planned for the following weekend: 90s themed, because Travis had strongly argued that now into the first month of 2001, the 90s were officially retro.

Renner pulled back his hood, but instead of chanting, he snapped at Benjamin, a sophomore brother who came walking through the door. "Hey, asshole! Harley says that you're the dick drip that ate my footlong — is that true?"

"Leave him alone." Jacob lowered his hood. "I'm the one responsible for your footlong, but I didn't eat the stupid thing. I threw it away because it grew more mold over winter break than your mother's—"

Jacob got snatched from behind before he could finish his sentence, interrupting their ritual as his apparent kidnappers dragged him out the front door.

"I'm a fully pledged brother! You can't do this to me!"

The rough hands refused to listen, dragging Jacob down the block, then throwing him inside that same blue van that had been following him and closing the door. He finally stopped thrashing once inside the van, surrounded by men in tactical gear. There was an assault rifle in his face for an extra note of punctuation.

"Who the fuck are you?" Jacob dared to ask.

No one answered.

But the engine started as some kind of sack was slipped over his head.

Chapter Sixty-Five

THE SACK WAS UNCEREMONIOUSLY YANKED off of Jacob's head as they entered a dimly lit warehouse and the door closed behind him. Tall ceilings with dirty walls and a dusty floor. Desks with computers arranged in rows. A whiteboard covered in pictures and scribbled plans was tucked into the corner, but neither the distance nor the light helped him to decipher what those images might mean.

Jacob didn't know if he was relieved to be right or wishing he was wrong as the apparent leader walked up to him in an FBI jacket, all muscle and grimace, looking more like the kind of bouncer that used to confiscate his fake ID and dare Jacob to do something about it than an actual officer of the law.

"We've been looking for you. For a long time now."

"I live at 905 Chestnut," Jacob started. But then the

leader's mouth turned down at the corners and he wondered if maybe he should wise the fuck up and stop smarting off. "Agent Curtis gave me a visit over the break."

"You're the ghost." An odd reply from the leader of this little assault squad, who introduced himself to Jacob by shoving a rifle in his face.

Jacob was about to ask what the hell that was supposed to mean, but with the appropriate words and in a deferential tone, of course, when he heard a sudden commotion behind him. Unsettling, loud, and then uncomfortably louder. Deep and low, a long growl rolling from deep within the throat of a beast he did not want to see.

The growling continued and Jacob forced himself to turn around—

The Rottweiler snarled one last time, baring its teeth as it ran into the room and right at Jacob, until a sharp whistle saved his life, or at least his balls, by bringing the dog to an immediate halt.

What the fuck was this? Was he about to get ripped apart or thrown in jail? This wasn't like *Profiler* or *The X-Files*. It wasn't even *Silk Stalkings*. Jacob was seriously scared shitless and terrified of losing his composure.

But then he finally did. Not knowing where to turn, between the dog that clearly wanted to rip him to pieces with its teeth and the FBI agent with an assault rifle waiting to dress him down.

Jacob fell onto his knees and started to sob.

"I'm sorry ... I'm *so sorry* ..." He choked on his words before he could recover his breath. "I'll never ever do it again. I promise to stop and I'm—"

"No, son." The beefy leader was suddenly smiling wide. "You've got it all wrong."

Jacob looked up at him, recovering more of his breath, acutely aware of the audience of agents surrounding him, the room silent enough that the Rottweiler's quiet panting now sounded loud.

The leader reached down and clapped Jacob on the back before squeezing his shoulder. "I admire everything you've accomplished so far."

Jacob had no idea what the guy could possibly be talking about. What had he accomplished with his Titor posts besides convincing a forum full of gullible dummies that time travel was real? The majority of them were only on a forum like that in the first place because, just like Mulder, they wanted to believe.

And it wasn't like he had convinced the entire congregation. There were plenty of skeptics peppering him with questions and attacking his posts with their artillery of doubt.

Plus all the people who were surely keeping their mouth shut while rolling their eyes at him.

"I need you to promise that you'll keep doing your duty for this country."

"Okay." Jacob had no idea what else to say. "I promise to keep doing my duty."

Another squeeze on the shoulder, then the leader offered his hand. But only after he hefted Jacob back to his feet did Jacob realize that he had pissed himself.

"Don't worry about that," the leader assured him with one final squeeze before letting him go.

"We have a job for you," said one of the nameless agents.

"What kind of job?"

"A big one that can help to save this country," another replied.

"I'm still not sure what kind of job that is."

"Does it matter?" Asked yet another agent. "You either do the job or you go to jail."

Then back to the leader. "The job is hard, and you'll have to prove yourself."

Jacob swallowed. Now they were getting to the keg stand competition part of this conversation.

"I would love to know what the job is." He swallowed again. "Even if I don't have a choice."

"We need you to create a virus," said agent number two.

"What?" Jacob would have been less surprised if they had asked him to organize a bum fight. At least he could have figured that one out. "How am I supposed to do that?"

"A computer virus," clarified agent number one.

Jacob felt a compulsion to shake his head and forced himself to stay stoic. He wasn't their man, regardless of what kind of virus they wanted. And he had no idea what made them think that he could make one when all he had done was make some posts on a forum.

But maybe they were all a bunch of Brads, drifting through life on good looks and connections, and maybe none of these Brads understood how computers actually worked.

"What kind of virus do you need?" Playing along was better than jail. And he might have the wherewithal to figure it out, if he could make it back out of this warehouse.

The leader gave him a nod, clearly pleased to see Jacob bouncing the ball. "We want you to prove yourself with a challenge first. Complete the challenge, and we'll give you the bigger job. Fail, and go to jail."

"How am I supposed to do that?"

"By creating a virus that can get past the university firewalls and wreak some havoc."

That last part was said with a smile. Inviting Jacob to ask, "Any particular kind of havoc?"

"That's entirely up to you."

Jacob liked that answer a lot.

But now he had to figure out how the hell he could create a virus.

Chapter Sixty-Six

JACOB – 2001

JACOB WAS BACK in Professor Wyght's room, sweating through the interminably long class.

He could barely focus. The preparation for the challenge had been intense, and the move to Art Bell's forum had gotten more eyeballs onto his John Titor hoax than he'd anticipated. Between the two projects, he was stretched thin. And neither would count towards class credit.

Ironic that Wyght could probably appreciate Jacob's prank better than just about any professor in the university, and exponentially more so than any of his brothers, if he wasn't a total windbag who only cared about looking cool in front of his class, especially when it came to the female students everyone knew he was always trying to sleep with.

The preparations were all made, and in another few minutes Jacob would be executing the trial job that would supposedly get the FBI to climb off his back, though after doing the math on their last conversation, he had wondered if dealing with the Federal Bureau of Investigation might be a little like dealing with the Mafia, and once they had him, there would be no escape.

A successful virus (or an approximation of the same thing) would only lead the FBI to expect that Jacob could accomplish an even bigger job. But he was used to trading a problem solved now for one hatching later, and this was no different. Jacob's number one aim right now was to get through this next sequence of moments, then he could handle whatever might be waiting on the other side when he got there.

Nothing about this prank had gone as expected so far, and though the fruits of Jacob's labor were abundant, the branches were bare when it came to his fraternity brothers.

He had been shocked to his pubes after getting back to the house and realizing that his brothers all thought they were being punked by another frat (probably Beta Upsilon Tau), and didn't see anyone with FBI on their jacket, meaning Jacob didn't even get props for the kidnapping.

No one believed his story, and it had nothing to do with that sprained ankle bullshit. Without evidence, Jacob wouldn't have believed it either.

He was determined to get this virus thing right but didn't know where to start. As with most research projects, the library should have been square one, but of course the librarian couldn't point him to any appropriate books, and he didn't dare ask a follow-up after his first question made it seem like the librarian might turn him into the authorities for asking.

Jacob spent an hour wandering the stacks, but nothing jumped out at him, and he left in defeat.

There was one obvious place he could go for help, but

Jacob would rather walk across the campus in a pair of 'N Sync pajamas than ask him.

Yet after leaving the library, and wondering what would be worse between the pajamas thing, listening to Yoko Ono's entire discography, or marathoning *Teletubbies*, his mind got back to thinking about the important stuff again. Like the Titor posts. And Jacob realized that sometimes the illusion of having done something was as good as having actually done it.

That's when he decided on a two-for-one, pulling a little prank for himself and the brothers while simultaneously making the agents believe he'd created a havoc-wreaking computer virus as promised.

While it might be impossible for him to create a virus that could break through the university's firewall, every security system had a weakness, and that weakness was usually the human controlling it. Each teacher had their own mini-website as part of the primary university domain. Jacob just needed access to a single login to create chaos on that subdomain. And getting a login sounded a lot easier than breaking through the website barriers. More than likely he would be able to spread his homemade mayhem across the entire website.

He recruited frat brother AJ, first to help Jacob determine which professors would be most likely to have vulnerabilities in their security, then writing down step-by-step instructions detailing everything Jacob would need to do once he had access to the system.

The second part was much easier, and Renner was more than willing to help with any secret mission that involved sleeping with Professor Graubner's TA to get the logins.

"I'll hit that twice if you need me to," Renner offered.

Everyone had done their job, and now Jacob was vibrating on raw nerves, waiting for class to end.

Class ended and he sprinted to Graubner's office, one building over.

"Professor Graubner?" Jacob burst through the door without knocking, huffing and puffing from his run, but well-prepared for this pre-written outburst, speaking with deep conviction and zero pauses — just like AJ had instructed him was the best way to catch Graubner off guard — before the professor could stop him.

"Sorry to barge in here like this, but thank you so much for seeing me, Professor Graubner, everyone I know who's taken your class can't stop saying great things about you, which is what brings me here, because I'm not sure if I should take Business Law — I mean, on one hand your class promises a riveting dissection of the intertwining mechanisms of business and legislation, and I'm sure we could agree that a lexicon of legal jargon could sculpt me into the next prodigy of the corporate world, but then again, that requires grappling with the monotonous march of case studies, statutes, the thrilling history of torts and the less than thrilling reality of Tuesday 8 a.m. lectures."

Jacob paused, but only because he had less breath after running than he did in rehearsal.

"Can we start over?" Professor Graubner smiled. "What's your name, son?"

"Pauly Shore." And then Jacob plowed forward, not sure how much longer he would have to keep going before the next part of his little plan kicked into gear. "Your class could be a launching pad for me — a firm foundation for a future in corporate law, international business, entrepreneurship even. With the understanding of legal implications in business you promise your students—"

"What was that?" Graubner asked.

It was the commotion Jacob had planned, right on schedule. The scream should be coming right about—

"AHH!" the secretary screamed from right outside the professor's office.

"What in the..." Professor Graubner cast an exasperated look at Jacob, clearly hoping that the candidate for his class would be gone before he returned, then darted out into the hall.

It took time to wrangle raccoons, and Harley had freed three of them when he saw the door to Graubner's office close behind Jacob. So the professor would be a while.

Jacob sat behind the computer and pulled out the slip of instructions from AJ. Logged in, tapped out the code exactly like he was supposed to, and logged right back out.

He hit refresh.

And just as AJ promised, the university website now redirected visitors to a wall of vintage porn.

Chapter Sixty-Seven

RJ – 2024

AGENT WILLIAM CURTIS followed up his extremely off-the-record revelation that John Titor was in fact a college kid named Jacob Lambert with enough evidence to make RJ's brain feel like it might explode all over the table, bits of gray matter raining across the piles of printed posts and images of Jacob, the frat, and several scenes from the stories Curtis had been telling him.

The FBI had known the truth about this crazy story all along.

"That really is incredible …" RJ didn't know what else to say, flabbergasted by the whole thing.

And even after this impossible sounding revelation, RJ was still sure he only had part of the story.

"Not as incredible as actual time travel, though," Curtis replied with a laugh.

"Do you mind if I ask something else?"

Curtis laughed again, but it was short and rolled to a

sudden stop at the end. "You do look like something might be bothering you."

"Not bothering me exactly … I'm just trying to understand." He shifted in his seat, looking for the right words so it didn't sound like he doubted the agent's story, so much as needed to see how the elements all came together.

"Speaking as a storyteller," RJ continued, "I'm always looking to understand a character's motivation. And I just can't really see what was driving Jacob Lambert in this situation. His John Titor project had to take a ton of time, and for such a small reward—"

"Says you," Curtis cut him off. "But the Jacob Lambert I spoke with appeared to be getting exactly what he was looking for during his time playing Titor."

"And what was that?"

"Validation." The agent shrugged. "That was Lambert's currency, and the kid was in seriously short supply."

"But there has to be more to it than that. Everything you just told me in your story makes it sound like Jacob was just some dumb frat bro, and yet the Titor posts were all so much more than that."

"So much more than *what?* The whole thing was a prank."

"Sure, that was the intention, but I'm pretty sure I've read every post Titor ever made, and I can confidently say that there is no possible way that some drunken idiot could have written them."

"Lambert wasn't an idiot, nor was he always drunk."

"It's more than that: the science all makes sense, and the detail is too real. You said that Lambert didn't have any of the physics classes required—"

"Apparently he didn't need them."

RJ shook his head. "That can't be the actual solution."

"Lambert was smart. Incredibly smart, as it turns out. Like you said, we can see plenty of proof right there in his Titor posts. But Jacob was also young. I was greener than a Saint Patty's Day parade at the time, and I still had several years on the kid. Do you remember what you were like in college?"

RJ laughed. Indeed he did.

"Care to share?" Curtis said.

"I was just remembering what dumbasses we used to be back in college. Me and my producing partner, Michael. We were inseparable, always chasing some new idea. We would do anything that excited us. Two pawns on a chessboard, blindly following each other into checkmate." Another laugh. "We landed an interview with our university's most reclusive professor, this dude who had been teaching the history of Prohibition. It was a big get. But Michael showed up in a Viking helmet, convinced that it would be a 'fun little ice breaker'. Professor Cranston threw us out of his office."

"Would your partner ever do something like that now?"

RJ shook his head. "Definitely not."

"And if he did want to, would you allow it?"

He shook his head again. "Definitely not, times two."

"And there you have it." The agent shrugged again. "Lambert still had a lot of growing up to do. He took that giant brain of his and aimed it in the wrong direction, working to impress his fraternity brothers instead of using that same intelligence to figure out what he should be doing with his life."

RJ considered his words, and though he could find no fault with them or anything to disagree with, the solution felt hollow.

Curtis gave him a long look, waiting to see if RJ would

break the silence. After a long beat, he finally broke it himself. "Sometimes it's the smart ones who make the stupidest mistakes."

RJ nodded, smelling the end of this story like dinner leaving the kitchen. He wanted to hear the conclusion, then put John Titor to bed.

"When did Jacob realize that the people he was doing jobs for weren't really FBI?

Curtis sighed, clearly disappointed by his own answer. "Sadly, it wasn't fast enough."

348

Chapter Sixty-Eight

JACOB ENTERED THE CAMPUS GRIND, expecting to get in and out with a cafe mocha before class, so he had zero idea that Brutus would be waiting for him, short sleeves rolled up even shorter on his beefy arms as he sat in the corner, casting a cold stare at the entrance.

It had been a full month since his escapade in Professor Graubner's office, and he was starting to think that he might never hear from the FBI again. Maybe the prank wasn't big enough — AJ's code had managed to affect the entire website, which was an epic result for sure, but the redirect to all of those pages filled with vintage porn only stayed up for just under twenty-four hours before it was fixed.

Jacob played it cool, nodding to Brutus as he fell into line, then waiting to order behind three bumbling idiots who were all clearly ill-equipped to order coffee or anything else so early in the morning.

He felt like a dumbass, not wanting to make eye contact with Brutus again until he was ready to join the FBI agent in the corner.

"Good to see you," Jacob said as he sat, feigning confidence in a situation he had not anticipated and had zero control of.

"Is that what you call wreaking havoc?" Brutus asked in greeting.

Jacob held his stare. "Things were pretty bonkers on campus."

"For less than one day."

"It was pretty close to a day," Jacob argued. "And that hack was a *big* deal. It lasted less than a day because of the emergency shutdown. Web admins were forced to do untold damage after that. Dean Wilkins called the cops, looking to charge whoever was responsible for the incident with charges of pornography involving minors, because there are some students on campus who are under eighteen. It was a public relations nightmare, and has already led to increased security measures, meaning we could never do the same thing again. So I'm not sure what—"

Brutus raised a hand to stop him. "We are aware of the consequences of your trial run and are willing to accept those results as proof of your eligibility for the bigger job. But I disagree about whether you could do the same thing again. We are all quite confident that if a repeat performance was necessary, your student body would be subjected to all that ancient bush as many times as you wanted them to be."

Jacob was as delighted to hear that he was ready for the next challenge while simultaneously and quite suddenly needing to shit his pants. He had no idea what they want him to do next, or how he could ever possibly pull off whatever it ended up being. The last job was executed by way of spit and ingenuity. Surely that strategy would run dry for whatever came next.

He would have to find a way to lure them back to the frat house. Or else use the secret weapon that gave him the chills just thinking about it.

"How can I be of service?" Jacob asked.

"We would like you to help us solve a problem."

"That's why I'm here. Though I did come because this place makes a killer cafe mocha." He took a sip.

"We have a traitor in our midst."

"Like in *Enemy of the State*?" Jacob got no response from Brutus and added, "It was made by Ridley's little brother, the *Top Gun* dude. It kicks more ass than it should considering it has the Fresh Prince of Bel-Air and Denise Huxtable in it."

"While using the agency to access bank accounts owned by known criminals, we believe that someone on our team was siphoning money away from criminal organizations and putting it into their own pockets. We can't use any of our internal teams to research the problem without risking the traitor getting alerted."

"Oh." So this was motherfucking serious.

"We need someone from the outside, someone with exceptional computer skills. A hacker, frankly."

"And what is it that you want this hacker to do?" Jacob wanted to gulp.

"We need our volunteer to plant a second virus in the bank's system. One that tracks down the first virus and reroutes the money back to our government where the appropriate parties can decide what to do with the assets."

"Why don't you just have me delete it?"

"Because deleting the virus isn't enough." Brutus shook

his head. "Our aim is to expose the mole and highlight the problem so we can bring him to justice."

"You know it's a *him*?"

"The odds are good." A thin smile before he continued. "We aren't in the business of helping to fund criminal organizations. We need to collect evidence and follow the money to see exactly how far it goes. Simply stopping the mole means killing our best lead."

This wasn't *Enemy of the State*, it was *Internal Affairs*.

He took a long moment to consider before shaking his head. "I'm out."

"You're *out*?" Brutus repeated. "That's not the way this works."

"You used the word 'volunteer' earlier." He shook his head again. "I don't volunteer. I'm not comfortable going any further than I already have."

Jacob wasn't just in over his head, he was like a guy trying to explain *The Matrix* after one too many Jell-O shots. There was no way in hell he could ever get into a bank system to launch a virus, and even if he could, that was more than just a prank, it was a goddamned felony charge. Even working with the FBI, the potential for implicating others or truly fucking up his own life was as real as the sweat on his ballsack right now.

Brutus was apparently ready for his argument, offering Jacob an indifferent shrug. "We can still prosecute you over the college website incident, and considering the child pornography charges they'll slap you with, you'll go down for a long time, and stay down with a sex offender rap on your record for life."

"I did that for you! Isn't that like entrapment or something?"

"You hacked the website to prove yourself. No one on

my team ever directed you to engage with pornography. Your orders were to 'wreak havoc.'"

"Exactly: *my orders.*"

Brutus grinned at Jacob like a total fucking asshole. "There is no paper trail, which leaves you shit out of luck, Lambert. We'll take you down for the website redirect, and then we'll take you down for everything else."

"Like what?" Jacob wanted to scream.

"How about we stick to violations of the Computer Fraud and Abuse Act. Like spreading computer viruses or malware, fraudulently obtaining personal information, distributing pirated software and copyrighted content, defacing websites, cracking password files … do I need to go on?"

Brutus was still smiling, breaking his gleeful sneer only to recite a line of allegations that sounded rehearsed. Jacob swallowed hard as the full realization of what was happening here hit him like a full keg falling onto his foot.

The FBI really did think that he was a hacker called The Ghost. And Jacob had just realized who The Ghost was. His secret weapon wasn't a secret at all.

Jacob had no choice. He *had* to do this. Even if it meant going to jail.

"Just tell me what to do next," Jacob finally said.

"You're a good man." Brutus reached over and clapped him on the back, just like he used to do in the old days back in that warehouse.

Jacob anticipated the squeeze on his shoulder, and Brutus didn't disappoint.

He gave Jacob directions for what to do next, then left him alone with his cafe mocha, late for a class that no longer mattered.

Because until this was over, *nothing* else mattered.

Jacob drove seven miles with his heart pounding the entire way. Marched inside the house and straight to his stupid little brother's bedroom, even though Rudy really wasn't stupid at all.

The Ghost was infuriating, but far from dumb.

"Rudy!" Jacob pounded on his door. "We need to talk!"

Chapter Sixty-Nine

JACOB – 2001

JACOB WAS IN HELL, with no one to blame but himself.

The metaphorical flames were licking his balls as he looked around the fraternity house at his brothers, waiting for an opening to plead his case. They had gathered to go through the entire list of remaining recruits, to choose their final lineup ahead of the Welcome to Hell party where they would be officially inviting them into the brotherhood.

Jacob's foot kept bouncing up and down, tapping the floor on repeat as his gaze made yet another circuit of the room, wondering if he should just go ahead and get his interruption over with. This was some serious Tom Sawyer shit, and he needed every brother in the house to help him whitewash miles of fence for the FBI. The bullshit and backslapping was finally over.

Travis cleared his throat. "Should we get started?"

Jacob raised his hand. "I've been thinking about our group prank. So real quick before we get going with the final selection, could we talk about what we're going to do?" He didn't wait for an answer. "What if we pulled off something *beyond* epic. Something so seriously righteous that Homer would want to write a poem about it?"

"Not Simpson, Brad!" Renner remarked.

"Didn't we already *do* our prank?" Harley asked. "Porn all over the university website wasn't epic enough?"

Jacob shook his head. "Not epic enough to be our official senior prank."

Renner could not for the life of him understand what the hell Jacob was talking about. "But the raccoons!"

"And the porn!" Harley brought up his favorite part again.

"So much porn." And then since he already had the floor, Brad added, "And I know who Homer is, Renner!"

"I've gotta agree with the guys," AJ said, because of course his code had made the prank possible. "I'm not sure that we can get our shit to be any more epic than porn taking over the university website."

"I agree that it was epic." Jacob did have to give them that. "But there is a difference between epic and *truly legendary.* We still have time to do something even more incredible. The prank to end all pranks. One that will be talked about for years, no, for *decades* to come."

"Do you have an actual idea, or are you just showing us your tits?" asked Renner.

"Did Brad write that line?" Harley wondered out loud.

"I do have an idea." Jacob nodded. "But it involves everyone. This is an 'all of us' prank. It's the sort of thing that can't be done alone."

"How can we help?" Travis asked.

Jacob gestured around at all of the Hell Party decorations. "First, we're going to need a new theme."

Everyone leaned forward.

And he told them the plan. Or at least the version that he needed for them to know.

The day of the job came too fast, but Jacob was as prepared as he could possibly be, and almost optimistic that he might actually be able to pull the impossible off in front of his fraternity brothers and the FBI. His life had become seriously cinematic.

Jacob was at the bank with a check from his mom for a whopping $50 that gave him a good enough reason to be there. The other pocket held his true intentions: a floppy disk filled with a virus that would help the FBI to catch their mole.

His right arm was linked with a girl named Zoe. They had never met, but Jacob was assured multiple times that she could be trusted. After April told him in no uncertain terms that he could fuck the hell off.

"Dude," Renner had said, "She's like if designated driver was a personality."

Still, Jacob had only told her what she needed to know to execute her part of the plan.

They approached the teller window together after a final traded glance.

Zoe pitched forward when they arrived, right onto the glass.

"I…" She didn't finish her sentence, and the *I* was mostly just breath. "I feel faint…" Zoe managed before becoming obviously unsteady on her feet.

"Are you okay?" asked the teller, her throat ripe with concern. "Here."

The teller already had a bottle of water, cracking it open before handing it across the partition to Zoe. She reached for it, but then fell dramatically backward, knocking the water everywhere.

Jacob was instantly on his knees at her side, shouting

into Zoe's face. "Baby, wake up!" He looked frantically around, as if the gathering crowd of concerned customers might actually move to help him.

He looked back down at Zoe as her eyes fluttered open.

Then she burst into tears, sobbing loudly as her shoulders trembled.

So Zoe was not only trustworthy, but one hell of an actress.

A bank manager came rushing over just as Renner and AJ entered the bank.

They both looked around uncertainly, then assumed their position at the end of the line once that bit of pantomime was behind them.

"Can you bring her into my office?" the manager asked Jacob.

"Of course." He made himself sound worried and indebted. "Thank you, sir."

Travis entered as Jacob and Zoe followed the manager.

"My name is Gustavo." Inside his office the bank manager was all smiles and apologies. "I'm so sorry this happened to you. Is there anything I can do to help?"

Jacob donned his most defeated expression and produced the check from his pocket. "I just really need to get this cashed, but I can't leave my girlfriend."

Gustavo hesitated for one beat longer than it took for Jacob to start sweating this part of the plan, but then he opened the office called out to one of the tellers. "Roberta! Could you come here, please?"

Roberta came rushing over and Gustavo handed her the check.

"Would you be a dear and cash this for our friend, here?"

"Of course." Roberta nodded then left the office, leaving Jacob and Zoe alone with Gustavo.

The check convincing Gustavo to leave them alone in his office had been a long shot. And now it was onto Plan B.

It was Renner's turn at the teller, but he dramatically slipped on the water spilled by Zoe when he got there.

AJ rushed over to "help" him, but then AJ slipped on the water as well. Landing on Renner with a loud OOF.

"There is no *WET FLOOR* sign in here!" Travis marched over and jabbed a finger at the matching set of frat bros writhing on the floor. "A situation like that is just a lawsuit waiting to happen. And I'm a lawyer, so I can assure you that the inevitable has just—"

Gustavo went rushing out of his office, waving his hands in the air and declaring that such action was unnecessary, though Jacob tuned out the details on his way to Gustavo's computer, where he inserted the floppy disk, opened a key file, then yanked the disk back out.

But it wouldn't budge. No matter how hard Jacob tugged, or how much he sweat, the disk was stuck in the drive, jammed.

He finally managed to wrench it free and reclaim his seat.

Just seconds before Gustavo returned.

Chapter Seventy

HAVING FINISHED the bank part of their epic prank (that was definitely no longer a prank), Jacob and his brothers returned to the frat house triumphant, and to much enthusiastic (inebriated) celebration. While the primary team had been executing their part of the plan at a branch of Chase Manhattan, the rest of the brotherhood had been preparing the frat house for tonight's fiesta and their guest of honor.

Omega Theta Pi always decorated to the nines in their backyard for parties, but now even the front yard was strung up in string lights and scattered with dozens of colorful lawn chairs. Several of the guys had agreed that the trampoline belonged out front as well and had worked as a team to drag it onto the lawn.

The *WELCOME FBI* sign was already installed and rigged for its string-pull, with FBI-themed props and miscellaneous paraphernalia everywhere. Navy blue streamers dangled from the ceiling; flags, signs, and props with FBI logos covered the walls. People were dressed in suits, holding plastic guns and handcuffs, already giddy with anticipation.

Zoe had been flirting with Jacob ever since that morning at the bank. At first, he tried shedding her like a winter coat come spring, but she had done a terrific job with her role in the mission, and an hour before the party Jacob realized that he enjoyed her attention. Enough to trust her with the rest of the plan.

"But if you're not in any trouble, then why are we expecting the FBI to come?" Zoe asked.

"Because we have four kegs." Renner laughed.

And of course Harley joined him.

Then Jacob said, "The FBI is coming because I was supposed to do a job for them."

"You already told me that part. *What kind of job?*"

"They wanted me to create a virus."

"Like on the computer?" Zoe clarified.

"Exactly."

"You know how to do that?"

Jacob shook his head. "Nope."

"Then why did they want you to do it?"

"Because they needed my help to catch a traitor and redirect money being siphoned off back to an account for the government."

"But why did they want *you* to create a computer virus if that isn't something you even know how to do?"

"Because what they don't know will never hurt them," Jacob replied.

"Or land you in jail," added AJ with a nod.

"So what did you do?" Zoe asked, still confused.

Jacob grinned. "I redirected the money to the American Mustache Institute."

"That's not a real thing," Zoe said.

"It absolutely is." He grinned even wider. "AMI is dedicated to protecting the rights of, and fighting discrimination against, mustached Americans."

Zoe stared at Jacob.

Renner answered the question in her head. "He's not kidding."

"It was between that and the SPAM museum."

"The stuff in your email, or the meat?" Zoe asked.

"It's not meat." AJ shook his head.

"The meat-like substance," Jacob clarified. "And there is definitely a museum. Seriously, it's in Austin. Minnesota, not Texas."

"Why is there a SPAM museum?" Zoe sounded insulted.

"SPAM helped win World War II."

Zoe thought that Jacob was kidding, even though he wasn't.

"I still don't understand how you redirected the money to the American Mustache Institute..." Zoe took a second, seeming to consider her ludicrous words. "If you don't know how to create the virus?"

Jacob gave her a shrug. "I barely understand it myself."

"Okay." Zoe reset again. "So you redirected the money from the traitor. Even if you're not taking the money yourself, aren't you still stealing it from the FBI?"

"Technically, yes," Jacob admitted with a nod. "But the FBI set the whole thing up, so it's not like they can really rake me over the coals for it. And it's not like I took the money for myself. I'm giving it to people in need."

Jacob laughed, because American Mustache Institute.

Renner laughed, because he knew that shit was funny.

Harley laughed, because he had no mind of his own.

And AJ laughed, because the chuckling was contagious.

Zoe studied the brothers before she finally said, "I'm impressed. But where's the money now? Because you didn't send it back to the FBI, and now you're on the hook for it?"

"I also sent them a ransom note for the money, telling them to show up at the party or never see it again." Or at least Randy had.

"Cool." Zoe grinned. "When are we expecting them?"

"I have no idea, really." Jacob shrugged again. "But I'm guessing somewhere between any second from now and midnight."

"Like Cinderella?" Zoe seemed to like that idea.

"Sure." Jacob shrugged again.

"We're not waiting for the FBI before we get this bitch started?" Renner asked, doubt creeping into voice as he added, "Are we?"

"I think that would be the mistake of a lifetime," Jacob replied.

"Thank Christ!" Harley marched toward the nearest table full of alcohol.

Hours later, the armed men came storming through the door as expected, waving their guns around and threatening to end the party with violence. But the music was so loud that the men with their assault rifles were barely audible, and the brothers and their guests were all far too hammered to give a shit about the danger they weren't even worried about.

It was all under control, and part of the plan.

Those partygoers that weren't hammered were wasted, plastered or smashed. Jacob himself was sitting on the living room sofa blitzed, half smashed to shit and three-quarters fried. People were making out everywhere, and he had to keep sucking in his breath to keep himself from laughing hysterically at all this chaos by design.

He grinned and twirled a finger as he raised a party horn in the other hand.

The *WELCOME FBI* banner dropped from the ceiling.

He blew the horn and grinned even wider.

Then Brutus reeled back for a punch and socked him in the face.

His head snapped back and his eyes widened in agonized surprise as the fist plowed into him. His jaw trembled before the force of that blow rippled down his neck and into his shoulders.

Blood trickled from his nose and mouth as his face contorted in anguish.

Then Jacob's chaos-by-design crumbled in the face of true pandemonium as another cluster of armed men and women stormed the frat house, dressed differently from the first group and carrying themselves with a more professional seeming breed of swagger.

"FBI!" One of them bellowed. "EVERYONE DOWN!"

And then all hell broke loose.

Chapter Seventy-One

RJ – 2024

"SO JACOB WAS REALLY WORKING for a group of criminals posing as the FBI, and that group had been following the real FBI cybercrime unit tasked with finding The Ghost, a famed hacker," RJ finished, wanting to make sure he understood everything. "Is that correct?"

Agent Curtis nodded.

"And The Ghost was none other than Rudy." RJ shook his head as the agent kept nodding. "Twelve years old. Goddammit."

"After following the trail to his family home and seeing us talking, Philip Parsons, aka Brutus, thought that Jacob was the Ghost and tried to recruit him into a criminal organization that, until we finally collided with them at that party, had a decade of successfully posing as FBI, to the tune of more than a hundred-million dollars."

"That is a staggering story," RJ said.

"And completely off the record," Curtis reminded him.

"Why does it need to be off the record? A hundred million dollars makes this a massive story."

"The Federal Bureau of Investigation is not in the business of storytelling."

"You're *sometimes* in the business of storytelling, right?"

"Parsons believed he could get Lambert working for them by pretending to be the good guys because it was the best play in their book. The 'original' bank virus was them knowing about a rival organization's scheme and attempting to take the money for themselves. The FBI had unintentionally exposed Lambert to the bad guys, so we never ended up charging the kid with anything."

"No consequences whatsoever?"

"The money was easily returned to the non-criminal accounts it originally came from. Rudy was monitored and told to knock it off and stay clean. He became a cybersecurity analyst before there really even was such a thing, and started one of the country's biggest security firms."

"Ghostwatch Security?" RJ asked, aghast.

"Yes." Curtis nodded, seeming almost proud.

"What about Titor?"

"Lambert was told to send Mr. John Titor back to the future and stop posting on the forums."

RJ wasn't sure if he was really missing anything, or simply feeling the same tickles of sorrow that always came when he realized (yet again) that this was the end of a story he wanted to keep hearing more of, thanks to the teasing intrigue of its impossibility.

"I still don't understand why this is all off the record? Why hasn't Jacob ever told his story? After all of this time, and all the online speculation, why didn't he ever claim credit for coming up with John Titor? The Jacob Lambert in the story you just told me would have wanted the credit."

"He was protecting his brother. Sure, Lambert broke a few laws, but The Ghost had written the virus that actually stole the money. And before that, he'd broken all kinds of laws. The FBI agreed not to charge him on the condition that Rudy work for us on the side. His mother loved the terms and begged us to make sure that his work never got in the way of school."

"So the silence has nothing to do with Jacob? It was all about protecting Rudy's identity as the Ghost?"

"Exactly." William nodded. "Or mostly. If any attention was ever brought to Rudy's true identity, he and Jacob would probably be killed years ago. Prior to all of this, Rudy ripped off a lot of dangerous men. The Lamberts are a large family with a lot to lose now. I'm sure you can appreciate why I was hoping to convince you that the world had heard enough of John Titor."

"I can't say I'm not disappointed, but I do understand." RJ gave him a defeated smile. "Do you mind if I ask one last question?"

William smiled back. "Be my guest."

"What about Kat and John Anderson? How do they fit into this story?"

"Lambert believes that they're both hustlers, trying to take advantage of the legend he created."

"But why? What do they have to gain?"

"Plenty of people have tried to capitalize on what he did back in 2001. And I'm sure it wouldn't be difficult to discover the Andersons' motivations if it was worth the effort. But I can assure you, Mr. Jimenez—"

"RJ."

"—you already know the truth."

"Thank you, Agent Curtis." RJ offered his hand. "I really appreciate your time."

"It was a fun trip down memory lane." William

released his grip. "And I appreciate you dropping the story."

"Consider it done." And RJ meant it.

He was in the car for less than five minutes when he gave Michael a call to tell him that he really was honest-to-goodness dropping this Titor business for good.

And not because he had to, but because RJ was finally satisfied. Even if the reality was less magical than the little boy inside of him who still believed in magic longed for it to be.

"It's over," he said when Michael answered.

"Are you talking about avocado toast? Please tell me you're talking about avocado toast."

"John Titor."

"Sorry. I lose track. Weren't we already done with that?"

"For real this time. The mystery has been solved."

"Oh yeah?" Michael sounded genuinely intrigued. "So tell me, Sherlock, who stole the cookie from the temporal cookie jar?"

"I can't tell you."

"Can't or won't?" Now he sounded genuinely annoyed.

"Won't because I can't."

"Someone else in the FBI?"

"The case has been solved. That's all you need to know."

"You're projecting," Michael said. "I never needed any of this. You're the one with the boner for stories we have no way of actually telling. I'm just glad that I finally have my partner back."

"I've always been your partner."

"Then I'm glad I have my buddy. Now let's go make some shit."

"I thought we established that I don't want to make *shit*," RJ said.

"We've definitely established that 'shit' is an affectionate term for the crap that we make. Seriously, though, I have a lead on a new story and it's one that I think you're going to love."

"No more *Gator Gitters*?" RJ asked.

And Michael agreed. "The Gitters can get the fuck out of here."

Chapter Seventy-Two

A SMALL-TOWN SHERIFF sees a man walking down Main Street, carrying a penguin under his arm. He pulls up next to him and says, "You can't just walk around town with a penguin! You need to take it to the zoo right away." The man nods and walks off. The next day, the sheriff sees the same man walking down Main Street, still with the penguin under his arm. He pulls up next to him and exclaims, "I thought I told you to take that penguin to the zoo!" The man smiles and says, "I did, and he had such a good time, today we're going to the museum."

"Fuck you, Garrison Keillor."

Jacob almost considered throwing the *Prairie Home Companion* book into the fireplace, but he could never actually do that. Even though the jokes in that shitheap of pages were too stupid for human consumption, the thought of actually burning a book turned his stomach, and even though he *might* do something that dumb in front of an audience full of his fraternity brothers, they were still out skiing the mountain while he sat in the cabin pretending his ankle was sprained.

So he stuffed the book in Harley's box labeled *Emergency*

S'mores Kit and hid all of the chocolate in the back of the closet. Then he started looking through the mountain cabin again, this time hunting for a place he could let loose the dump he had been working up for one of his brothers to find. An upper decker was much too obvious, and if he could maneuver himself properly into position, a desk drawer might be nice.

He did find two secretary desks, but he didn't think the arrangement of shit would be quite as impressive if someone pulled the lid back on the desk. It would be a lot harder to actually shit inside the thing, and the shenanigans required to cajole or manipulate one of his buddies into taking a look into the secretary desk instead of a drawer felt a lot more complicated.

It wasn't even a clever prank, let alone epic. But he'd hoped that contemplating some smaller pranks would inspire him with an idea for his big senior prank.

He found himself in the cabin's smallest room, surprised to find something in the nightstand. All of the other drawers had been empty, not even a Bible like in a hotel. But this drawer had a beat-up old notebook with the words *Time Travel 0* written in neat block letters across the front.

Jacob picked up the notebook with an electric curiosity and started turning the pages with a burning excitement he could not understand so much as feel like a current suddenly alive inside him.

The entire notebook was filled with words and diagrams, with a few photos tucked into the back.

He got lost in his ideas. Jacob felt himself swimming through what read like an impossibly wonderful narrative. Exactly the kind of Ong's Hat shit he had been looking for. Crazy crap that Jacob could not understand, and he had a sneaking suspicion that the author had no idea either. They were simply making things up.

Like: *I am a time traveler from the year 2036. I am on my way home after getting an IBM 5100 computer system from the year 1975. My "time" machine is a stationary mass, temporal displacement unit manufactured by General Electric. The unit is powered by two top-spin dual-positive singularities that produce a standard offset Tipler sinusoid.*

And, *The displacement machine is a fairly simple device. The basis for time travel is not very complicated. You bend space-time into a donut shape, bring the two sides of the donut together and "pop" through the hole.*

Or, *In the future, there are organized police forces and a national army, but their focus is shifted. People spend more time reading about law and history to understand how things work. I would compare it to the life of a frontier in the American West in the late 1800s.*

Jacob flipped back to the start and read the words, *For Amelia.*

But then the door exploded open and everyone entered the cabin, much too loud, with Renner louder than any of them. "I swear, once these ski bunnies defrost indoors, it's like Mardi Gras in the mountains!"

Renner had never seen so much as a single nipple at a ski resort.

"Like Baywatch on Ice," added Brad.

"No one shows their tits on network TV," Jacob said, the notebook already stashed and a plan for history's most epic prank in motion.

Part VI

Chapter Seventy-Three

CAMERON BOONE TREMBLED as he hid under the table, just like his mother had ordered him to. The walls were scorched and blackened, paint peeling away and dripping down in tattered strips like long fingers pointing at the shattered glass that littered the floor.

The stench of smoke hung heavy in the air as sirens screamed and explosions boomed in the background. Yelling kept getting louder outside.

In all of his ten years of life, Cameron had never been more scared of anything. He put the odds at fifty percent that today was the day he was going to die.

His mother came rushing back into the broken living room and tried to pull her frightened son out from under the table.

But Cameron refused to leave.

"I can't." He shook his head violently back and forth.

"You have to." She fell to her knees and looked into his

375

eyes. "Trust me, Cameron. Everything will be okay. I promise not to let anything happen to you."

He took a deep breath and nodded, taking her hand and letting his mother pull him out from under the table, then outside and down the chaotic street, his smaller feet barely keeping up with her only slightly larger ones.

It was even worse than Cameron had imagined outside. There were so many people, alone and with their families, everyone running, every fourth or fifth home now burning as they passed.

People screamed as they rushed forward in a herd, dodging scattered debris on the street as smoke filled the air from bombs detonating not nearly far enough away in the distance.

The ground trembled underfoot.

"We're going to be okay," Mom promised him again.

"Nukes are coming next!" someone yelled.

"Don't pay attention to him!" She took a second she couldn't spare to look back at Cameron as they ran. "He doesn't know what he's talking about. No one knows what the military will or won't do."

That's what Mom always said when the subject came up, and he wasn't about to argue with her, but Cameron figured that some of these people probably did know what they were talking about, maybe because they had a brother or cousin enlisted, or were even enlisted themselves.

He had been hearing that the war would go nuclear no later than 2008 for sure, and it had already been that year for months.

The home that Cameron felt certain he would never see again was long behind them by the time he spotted a military transport in the distance.

His lungs were on fire and every breath felt like swallowing thorns when they got to the vehicle, a thick metal frame with massive rubber tires, painted in camouflage with a large star on the side.

People were climbing into the vehicle, a few with go-bags but most carried only their hope.

Mom lifted him up toward a gruff-looking soldier reaching down from inside the transport. But once he was safely aboard, his mother was still planted firmly on the ground.

"What are you waiting for?" Cameron wanted to cry, because inside he already knew.

"I can't come with you, Cammy, I only had enough to get you out of here."

His entire body went numb. "No, PLEASE! *I can't leave without you.*"

He was the last one to board, and now the soldier was giving her a look.

Cameron lurched forward, frantically reaching down for her as the soldier held him back.

She took his hand and gave it another kiss. "This is how I'm making everything okay, just like I promised."

"THIS ISN'T WHAT YOU PROMISED!" Hot tears rolled down his face.

Mom looked stoically back at him.

"If you loved me, you would never want me to be away from you!" Cameron continued to sob.

"It's time to go," said the soldier to them both, his voice surprisingly soft.

"NO!" Cameron bellowed loud enough to make his throat ache.

She squeezed his hand for the final time. "Sometimes loving a person means doing the hardest things, and there is nothing in the world that I wouldn't do to save you."

The transport rumbled to life then lurched down the debris-strewn road.

Through tear-filled eyes, Cameron stared back at his mother, standing still as a statue amid the chaos, slowly shrinking as he desperately clung to the railing until the only person in the world who loved him finally faded into a dot, and then nothing.

Chapter Seventy-Four

CAMERON – 2016

IT HAD BEEN eight years since Cameron's mother had ushered him onto that transport away from the battle zone and into places unknown. He still barely ever stopped thinking about her. But sneaking through the library, filthy and starving as he was, made him think about her more than ever.

The shelves stood stark and mostly empty. Cobwebs kissed the corners in the ceiling and the walls were covered in dust. The air was ripe with mildew and decay. No librarians. Only creaking floorboards that announced his presence with every step.

Cameron had seen his reflection in one of the few glass doors still in their frames on his way into the library. He was eighteen and would have looked twice his age with meat on his bones. Gaunt as he was unkempt, his clothes were tattered and caked with dirt. His skin was paper thin and pale, his eyes sunken.

Cameron needed to stay invisible, but the patrolling guard kept getting closer and closer to his hiding spot and the shelves in front of him were too bare for the job of obscuring a grown man dumb enough to try and use them as a shield.

He finally risked pulling an old, dusty book from one of the shelves. He couldn't even see the title, but that had barely ever mattered before. Cameron always wanted to read whatever he could get his hands on.

He had his fingers on the spine for several seconds before he dared to drag the volume down into his hands. Caution made zero difference. Either the sound or the motion snagged the guard's attention.

Cameron clutched the book to his chest and darted out from his hiding place behind the shelf in a mad dash out of the library and into the overgrown field beyond.

A cadre of soldiers was clustered at the bottom of the steps, but they were all more interested in their banter than in chasing a scrawny street urchin into chigger-ridden weeds.

He considered sitting down to read, once he was sure the soldiers weren't going to chase him, but the farmer with the baseball bat striding his way changed his mind. "Get gone, you good-for-nothing hoodlum! You're not stealing bread out of my children's mouths!"

Cameron ran.

Eventually he wandered into a nearby town and found refuge in the shadows of a reeking alleyway. He leaned against a wall of crumbling brick, looking around to make sure he was alone before he savored the opening of his new book with eager yet trembling hands, running his eyes across the pages of fading text.

A commotion nearby caught his attention. He lowered the book and looked around again, still seeing nothing, until the cacophony came closer and his curiosity got piqued enough for him to peek around the corner.

He saw a tall man strolling down the street, dragging a large cart behind him, loaded from top to bottom with more fruit than Cameron had ever seen in one place, at least for the last decade.

"Oranges and apples!" shouted the man. "Hershey's Bars and Jolly Ranchers! Treats and confections from before the war!"

A crowd was beginning to gather around him, appearing from nowhere like moths to the fire of whatever this strange man had brought to their dreary little town.

But as the crowd huddled closer to inspect the merchant's goods, a trio of ragged looking boys kept darting around the perimeter, pickpocketing from the onlookers before disappearing into the shadows of another alley across the way.

Cameron kept watching, until most of the crowd had dispersed, and then he finally made his way over to the man's cart as a potential shopper — not that he had a chit to his name or even looked like he might — and plucked an orange from the pile as if inspecting the merchandise ahead of his purchase.

The tall man was on Cameron like lighting striking a tree, slapping his orange onto the ground, where it rolled into a gnarl of shadows. "What do you think you're doing? You best get your dirty mitts off of my fruit."

"I may need a washing, but my mind's sharper than prickles on a cactus."

"How do you know what a cactus is?"

"I know plenty." Cameron had read the book *Cacti and Succulents: An Illustrated Guide* a few times until he lost it.

"What else do you know?"

"That I have a knack for making people realize they

need what I've got." Cameron really *felt* more than *knew* that one.

The tall man's face slowly split into a mischievous smile that struck Cameron as warm like a campfire. "How long has it been since your last hot meal?"

He went over and plucked the orange from the ground while Cameron considered his answer. Then the tall man handed it over and answered himself. "The answer is too long. Here. You can start with this. Now follow me."

And of course Cameron did.

Chapter Seventy-Five

CAMERON — 2016

FARLEY AND CAMERON made their way down the sun-bleached asphalt, snaking through the town's main thoroughfare. The once-straight road now wound through a disarray of dilapidated buildings with boarded windows and sagging roofs crowding the road on either side. Cameron had never traveled too far from where he was born, but he had still seen a spectrum of settlements, from sad and destitute to practically thriving. This town was in the middle, the air tinged with desperation-laced resilience.

A reedy man, with a pitch to his voice that made him sound like a showman, Farley was larger than life against the somber backdrop, speaking to Cameron like a sage as they walked.

"We're not here to take. We always give whenever possible. Do you see that, Cam? Do you understand what I'm talking about?"

"Yes, sir." Cameron nodded.

Sir sounded appropriate after Farley had given him the best meal in recent memory. Just a small salad made from edible plants, berries, and nuts. For dessert, Farley handed him a candy bar and a wrapped cookie whose label read, *Otis Spunkmeyer.* The date on the package was from before the war, but the cookie still tasted fresh enough, though Cameron only had his memory of the cookies Mom baked every so often to compare.

"We *give* to the people, you see? That's the trick. Knowing how to help instead of being in the way. That's how we survive."

Farley set up shop another two times, same as he had when Cameron first saw him, inviting gathering crowds to his cart of nostalgia: previously loved teddy bears, faded comics with rips that barely mattered, and magazines with glossy stories featuring pretty people who were probably dead. Money and items traded hands as Farley flashed a tooth smile.

Then he would invite Cameron to keep walking with him.

On the third such stop, Cameron spied one of the pickpocketing boys from earlier expertly maneuver his hand into the back pocket of an unsuspecting man.

"Hey you!" A large woman with hanging skin cried out from nearby, jabbing her finger at the boy. "That kid just stole that guy's wallet!"

Farley sprang into action, darting after the pickpocket.

The crowd watched with anticipation as the boy bounded away like a terrified rabbit, disappearing into a warren of broken-down buildings and leaving Farley to decide between chasing him down or safeguarding the cart that carried his livelihood.

"AND YOU BETTER NOT COME BACK!" Farley roared after the boy.

Then he straightened up, dusted his hands theatrically, and returned to the cart as murmurs of approval rippled through the crowd. After witnessing a hero in action, people were happier than usual to spend.

Farley finished his transactions, then he and Cameron kept walking.

What passed for civilization surrendered to untamed fields beyond the town borders. Cameron looked around at an ocean of wild vegetation rustling under the bleakest of skies.

He saw streaks of movement from somewhere deep in the field.

And then the pickpockets emerged, six of them, all wearing grins and dressed all in rags, bounding in a crowd over to Farley and Cameron.

Farley laughed at Cameron's surprise, then turned his hearty smile on the boys. "Well done."

They formed a rough semi-circle around Farley and Cameron, mostly ignoring the newcomer beyond some dirty looks, then one by one, they handed over their takings.

Two minutes later, Cameron was marveling at the bounty of treasures, speechless as he surveyed the pile to take a quick inventory before Farley scooped it all up and stowed the haul into a side compartment on his cart: wallets; loose currency in the form of bills and chits, plus some pre-war cash, not that it was worth much; several different types of medication; three pocket knives; a half-dozen lighters; one small flashlight; two watches; four bracelets; and a package of gum.

Cameron felt sick to his stomach.

"Something on your mind, son?" Farley stared into his eyes, challenging him with a knowing glare.

"What happened to giving and not taking?"

Farley placed his hands on Cameron's shoulders. "In this brave new world here, Cam, family is everything. And *this* is my family." He looked down at the half-dozen children. Dirty as they were, no one looked hungry. "*My boys.* And though you're a man, you can still be one of us if you understand that one unbreakable rule. You'll never sleep on an empty stomach again. Can you follow that one simple rule, Cam? *Farley family first?*"

Farley spoke into Cameron's silence. "Sometimes doing the best for our family means giving instead of taking, and occasionally our survival requires that things are the other way around. Sometimes it's best to show people what they want to see. Whatever gets the family further. You understand me, Cam? Do you want to be part of this family?"

Cameron thought about his mother, who'd sent him away to live while she stayed behind to die. What would she have said to him right now?

It didn't matter, because while she'd loved him, she'd left him without a family to take care of him. Whatever she would have said had died along with her. He was alone now.

If Cameron wanted to survive, he would need a new family.

"Yes, sir," Cameron said.

Chapter Seventy-Six

CAMERON – 2016

OVERGROWN FIELDS TENDED to blend into each other, but Cameron could easily remember the details of the most recent field he had been yelled out of. Just that morning, an old man had chased him with a bat while cursing him for being a good for nothing hoodlum who wanted to steal bread out of his children's mouths.

Farley was looking to camp out in the same field, so Cameron told him about the earlier misadventure that put him on the road leading to that alley where he first met Farley's acquaintance.

"Perfect," said Farley with a nod.

"Why is that perfect?" Cameron asked. "Didn't you hear what I said?"

"It's called an object lesson, son." He nodded at a house on the other side of the field. "Follow me."

Farley knocked on the door twice. Moments later, the

same farmer who had threatened Cameron opened the door and eyed them both in suspicion.

"Do you have a moment?" Farley asked.

The way those five words rolled out of his mouth struck Cameron as hard as they hit the farmer. He felt an unfamiliar but nonetheless wonderful awe rippling through him as Farley donned another blue-ribbon smile to somehow disarm the farmer entirely. His rigid posture relaxed, shoulders loosened and arms now idle at his side, the brow that had been furrowed just moments before was suddenly open and curious.

"Would it be a terrible inconvenience for you if me and my boys made camp at the far end of your field tonight?" Farley's face withered, as if in an attempt to maintain his composure. "We'll just be the night, and no trouble while we're here."

"How many boys are we talking about?"

And Cameron could hear Farley's unspoken lesson loud and clear: *the farmer was already halfway to a yes.*

"Eight of us total, including me and my son here." Farley laid a fatherly hand on Cameron's arm. "We take care of the boys as best we can, none of them have any other family, but with six additional mouths to feed, we don't have much in the way of payment. But even if there were sixteen of us instead of the eight, we still wouldn't ever take anything for free, so I'd appreciate it if you'd let me fill a little gap in your life with something from my little mercantile on wheels."

The farmer appeared to be thinking.

"How about some citrus?" *Make them picture it, son!* "A full crate of oranges for you and the Mrs. — or twice as many oranges for yourself?"

An hour later, Farley and the boys had their tents set up

in the field with a big screen rigged to a projector, running off of the farmer's generator.

After delivering the crate of oranges, Farley surprised him with a small box of chocolates, still shrink-wrapped with old-fashioned lettering that read *See's*.

"Underpromise and overdeliver, Cam," Farley said once out of earshot.

"But those chocolates seemed valuable." He understood basic barter currency, and an unopened box of chocolates was a more generous offering than what appeared to fit the nature Cameron had witnessed so far.

"Says you. But only because you don't know what I have planned. And it got us the use of a generator." Farley gave him a sly grin, and ended up underpromising and overdelivering himself.

As twilight gave way to the dark, Cameron found himself in a huddle of boisterous boys beneath a flimsy canopy tent. Only Rabbit's pint-sized face was pinched with suspicion, the one boy who let it be known on his face how unhappy he was to have Cameron joining the crew.

They gathered around an old projector Farley had somehow coaxed into life. Its flickering beam illuminated the otherwise-darkened field as the screen sprang to life and opened a window to the yesterday lost forever when Cameron was only a boy.

The Sting was an old-world classic, though Cameron had never heard of the two tricksters in it until the magical movie was playing in front of him. Even though he was already an adult, he still stared at the screen thinking how much he wanted to be either one of the two leading men in the movie when he grew up. Robert Redford and Paul Newman both had charisma Cameron could almost smell like oranges in the air.

The plot unfolded in a chaotic ballet. Conmen scamming the rich and ruthless, maneuvering through perilous games of cat and mouse with a showmanship that Cameron found thrilling.

He was pulled into the cinematic current, feeling the characters as their emotions reverberated within him, living with their struggles as though they were his own throughout the entire two hours of runtime. Movies were like diving into a dream, he thought.

For the first time in too long, he fell asleep with a full belly and a (canvas) roof over his head, slumbering amid the comfort of newfound companions and a foreign sense of belonging, safe as Farley turned their night into a double feature.

Cameron wanted to see the second film, but tendrils of sleep crept into his consciousness and turned his eyelids despite his intentions.

Soon he was snoring, still with the library book that he knew would never be returned tucked under his arm.

Chapter Seventy-Seven

CAMERON – 2018

CAMERON'S next two years passed in a blur.

His initiation into Farley's gang fell into a helter-skelter routine, and Cameron quickly grew accustomed to the peculiarities of a wonderfully unconventional lifestyle. They roamed from town to town as a family, less as vagabonds than as a troupe of traveling entrepreneurs. Bartering, storytelling, and getting by with a blend of guile and charm.

Cameron's new normal was made even more buoyant after the gang acquired a seafaring vessel that Farley referred to as "solid like a stone in the belly of a mountain," despite it clearly being a hodgepodge of parts.

But the boat did give them the mobility to move up and down the coast selling oranges and wares amid a promise of safety — an escape hatch in the event of trade gone sour.

The vessel became vital, often moored to a lonely dock as the gang dispersed into the coastal towns to barter and charm their way through another quiet heist of a town's collective belongings.

In the evenings, they returned to their anchored refuge, where stories and laughter mingled with the gentle lapping of waves against the hull under the glimmer of stars.

Cameron once considered himself a quiet young man, but only because he had been living in fear for so long, and never had anyone to teach him the words that opened a person like putting a key in their lock. Farley had versed him in the art of storytelling, and Cameron had grown into a skilled negotiator, his charm like a moonbeam luring in the tide.

He understood the power of a smile, and the easy swaying of a person's behavior with a smartly placed compliment or heartfelt appeal. From walking the cart like he had seen Farley do the day they'd met, to suggesting strategy, Cameron had gone from simple pickpocket to vital cog in the operation.

Even while thriving in his new role, Cameron could see that he lacked Farley's refinement, a subtle artistry finessed through decades of practice. The gang moved fast enough to bury their shortcomings in front of an audience and were smart enough to stay steps ahead of suspicions and backlash, thanks to their excellent use of misdirection.

Whoever pushed the cart would 'notice' the pickpockets in action — a gasp, a shout of surprise, a chase — and the townsfolk would join in, their attention diverted and vigilance compromised. By the time those townsfolk discovered their empty pockets, Farley and his gang were long gone.

The script was always the same, same as with all of the

movies Cameron watched whenever he possibly could — always a theater of clever distractions and subtle cons.

On land or sea, he felt at home with his new family.

But even after two years, he and Rabbit still barely got along. He was still the youngest in the group, and incessantly envious of Cameron, who he saw as skipping to the front of the line. They nursed an uneasy camaraderie, because there was no other way to share in Farley's spoils as rival siblings under his mentorship.

Cameron's charm was a magnet that made admiration like steel, but if he was a silver-tongued diplomat who could pacify and negotiate, Rabbit was an armed soldier, forever on the offensive, living his life like he was climbing a mountain face, always clawing for either respect or attention, and often both at once. Rabbit spat venom and stole anything not nailed down. He yearned for a father's approval that Cameron's closeness with Farley had stolen from him.

The gang kept heading south until the landscape slowly morphed around them and the air thickened with humidity. Terrain became a muggy sprawl of swamps and everglades. Houses stood on stilts, like giant birds perched on thin wooden legs.

"Why do the houses all look like that?" Rabbit looked over at Cameron in obvious hopes that his rival also had no idea.

"So they can avoid flooding when the hurricanes come," Farley said.

Rabbit had his reply ready to go. "Nothing worse than a hurricane this far south."

But Farley disagreed. "Sure, hurricanes come barging in like uninvited houseguests to turn the world topsy-turvy, then drown it in water, but they aren't as bad as the gators you never see coming — all teeth and no manners."

"There ain't no gators anymore." Rabbit scoffed.

"You better hope not." Farley's words were ominous in the quiet countryside.

Evenings were haphazard as the family gathered to share stories, out loud most often, or silently while watching movies whenever they could access a generator. Even Cam was talked into reading from the books he still stole from every ancient library he could break into. But the nights were never silent.

Farley was a born bard, regaling them with tales of his youth. He spoke of grunge and its thrumming heartbeat, from the raspy angst of Nirvana to the beer-soaked emotion of Pearl Jam. He would wax lyrical about every movie he could remember the plot of, from *Thelma & Louise* (he loved to recite the beats of that movie, but neither Cameron nor any of the others had ever seen it) to *Jurassic Park* and *The Matrix*. Cameron had seen both films twice each since joining the boys. He had never seen the TV shows *Seinfeld* or *Friends*, but Farley kept promising that they would eventually find some DVDs. Same for *The X-Files*. Most of the boys believed it would happen, especially after they finally found the "Very Necessary" Salt-N-Pepa CD that Farley swore they would eventually get one day.

He cherished all of Farley's nostalgia, but movie nights were his favorite, and films from the 90s were the best by far. *Fight Club*, *Pulp Fiction*, even *The Lion King*. But Cameron's cinematic education was also steeped in the classics, from *Taxi Driver* and *The Godfather* to *Casablanca* and *12 Angry Men*. He had even seen an ancient black and white movie without any talking, starring a guy named Charlie Chaplin.

It was almost fitting, and certainly planned, that the night after Farley screened *Lake Placid* — featuring a giant,

30-foot-long man-eating alligator terrorizing the people around a lake in Maine (which was much better than Cameron expected it to be given the premise) — the gang got to wrestling with some gators themselves.

Chapter Seventy-Eight

CAMERON – 2018

SUNRISE FOUND the gang gathered around a large, roughly drawn map, set carefully on a rustic wooden table Farley had scavenged from a nearby cottage.

They had gone without food for a few days, and it had been a while since Farley's last shower or shave, but even grizzled and weather-beaten, he seemed more alive than ever, standing with his sharpened stick, eyes gleaming and focused.

The gang huddled around him, their youthful faces eager, trusting, and scared.

"Listen up, boys," Farley started with a slap of his stick against the map. "We've been hired for a clear-out. Not our usual kinda job. Today we'll be going toe-to-toe with some gators."

"Gators?" exclaimed several boys in unison.

Farley nodded. "A congregation of 'em."

The table exploded with a song of fear and excitement.

Farley silenced them with a raised hand. "It's dangerous and dirty, but the pay'll keep us in food and drink and fuel and even some movie nights. So who among us isn't with me?"

Of course everyone was with Farley.

So he proceeded to outline his plan, tapping the map with his stick as he spoke. "We'll be pushing the gators from the sound wall over here to the pen. A man named Richmond will be dispatching the gators from there. While another man, Guillermo, will be paying us."

"Just tell us what to do," Cameron said.

"I ain't scared of no gators," added Rabbit.

Farley marked a swampy region surrounded by an estuary and turned to Cameron. "You and Rabbit'll lead the charge. Rest of you boys are flankers. Try not to kill 'em, our job here is to herd 'em."

Two hours later, the gang was wrangling alligators in what Cameron could only describe as an anarchically mortal ballet. A chaotic waltz between man and nature, where every misstep equaled a potential plunge into the gnashing jaws of a cold-blooded predator.

But the boys worked with an almost impossible synchrony considering they had never wrangled gators before, circling the area on foot, driving the beasts toward the pen, working them like pickpockets in a crowd.

Cameron and Rabbit took the frontlines, prodding and luring, fear masked by adrenaline.

Cameron watched with a terrible sense of awe as a particularly large gator lunged at Rabbit with snapping jaws, only to be deterred by a lightning-fast jab from the end of his pole.

The growing crowd of onlookers was keeping a safe perimeter, but a beast broke free amid the pandemonium.

Its murky eyes were trained on a local as the gator bolted toward him.

A man about Cameron's age, his face a mask of terror as the reptilian mass lunged—

A woman — his sister judging by the looks of her — leaped into action, grabbing a thick stick and rushing to his defense, plunging it down repeatedly onto the alligator's head.

The creature should have retreated. Instead it fixed the woman with its steely gaze and made a guttural sound in warning before it—

Cameron jumped to the woman's defense. A jolt of adrenaline surged through his body as he pushed off the scaly adversary and made a dash toward the woman, the gator's wild rhythm matching his desperate pace through the mud.

He lunged with a roar, wrestling the gator away from her. His body coiled with strength, fingers locked around the creature's jaws as he drew a blade from his belt and stabbed the gator through the skull, over and over until the beast finally stopped thrashing beneath him.

Cameron stood and turned toward the woman, eager to bask in the glow of her acknowledgment.

But she was lying on the ground, her chest heaving as she gasped for breath.

"Stay back!" Her probable brother shouted at Cameron, pushing him away. "I need to get her to the doctor!"

"Let me help!" Cameron called out after him.

But the man had already scooped her up from the ground and was disappearing into the distance.

Cameron turned back to the dead alligator. "Well, that didn't go as planned."

He caught a glint in the dirt, then reached down to

retrieve a delicate necklace from the ground, its chain shimmering in the waning sunlight.

The young woman's necklace.

With the cool metal nestled into his fist, Cameron couldn't shake the feeling that this was the start of something he didn't yet understand.

Chapter Seventy-Nine

CAMERON – 2018

FARLEY and his boys settled in, sticking around town longer than anywhere else they had ever stayed before. This place was different, and for the first time, the gang decided to dig a well instead of constantly searching for water in the desert.

They were welcomed in Zephyrhills, having proven themselves adept at wrangling gators. It was a big win-win for everyone; the alligator menace was significantly dimmed, and the meat was plentiful.

Now locals regarded the Farley Boys with gratitude more than suspicion.

Still, Farley's intentions were clear from the start. "Scope out your marks if you must, but no takin' until our last night here. Can't risk any of you getting hauled off to the barracks. We're here to help for now, so no trouble."

They spent their days hunting, trading, and helping out wherever they could. Cameron couldn't curb his fascination with the woman who had braved the gator. He learned that her name was Amelia, and hoped he would run into her whenever he went into town. Then one day he finally did, catching sight of her dark, curly hair in a glimmer of sunlight as she moved between market stalls.

"Amelia!" Cameron called out, approaching her with the necklace she'd lost in battle.

She turned toward him, her expression more neutral than grateful, and her eyes almost impatient.

"You dropped this." Her necklace dangled from his fingers.

She took it. "Thank you."

Cool and indifferent. The kind of woman who could stare down a gator.

Cameron's curiosity had gone from piqued to starving for answers, so he followed her home, trying and failing to engage Amelia in the kind of small talk that had served him so well for the prior two years. Cameron couldn't tell if he was really annoying her, or if it was all part of an act he was determined to see the other side of.

Amelia seemed well and truly done with him by the time they arrived at her simple single-room house, built on stilts like all the others in this recently rebuilt community. The man Cameron had seen during that melee with the alligators was indeed her brother, and Jack beamed at the sight of him, before inviting Cameron into their cozy abode for lunch.

He accepted with a hearty handshake, then followed Jack up the ladder and inside to a warm space filled with old furniture and new quilts, the air pregnant with the scent of a meal in mid-preparation from their mother, Kat, merrily cooking in the kitchen.

Amelia moved about the small space with an air of

visible strength that Cameron found alluring. He forced himself not to stare before lunch.

They ate alligator étouffée around a battle-scarred table. The dish was missing bell peppers, though Cameron would have never known without Jack telling him so. That alone accounted for ten percent of the conversation. Jack was a lightweight when it came to banter, and Amelia kept playing mute.

He liked them both. Jack was kind and earnest. Amelia was sincere despite her seeming indifference to him, and she remained a puzzle he wanted to solve. Cameron kept stealing glances around the room whenever he felt sure that his spying might go unnoticed. Casing their place was a habit that filled him with guilt, though that inner disgrace was grated away by the reality that the Andersons had nothing to steal and could therefore stay clear of the hitlist of thefts planned for their final night in town.

But then Cameron saw it, nestled in the far corner, nearly hidden by the shadows cast by a sputtering gas lamp: a vintage windup record player and two tall stacks of records, one on either side of it.

His heart sank while trying not to stare at something he knew for a hard fact that Farley had been searching for. Not just the player, but every record in that stack would be a glittering gem to Farley. Cameron could hear him in his head: *Bad music is still better than no music, my boy!*

"Those are my pride and joy," Kat said when she saw Cameron eyeing the records, before turning to look at Jack and Amelia in turn with a laugh. "Other than my actual pride and joy, of course."

Did putting the Farley family first mean hurting other families?

Amelia finally started talking, but Cameron felt so sick,

he excused himself by saying that he was expected back at camp.

A gnawing doubt chewed through his conscience as he walked. The low murmur of the boys laughing and chatting prickled his ears before he broke through the shadows of the tree line and into the sound of a crackling campfire that painted the clearing and its shadows in shades of gold and orange.

Rabbit sat slightly outside the circle with a faraway look in his eyes, raising his head with a sneer as Cameron approached. "Find anything good?"

"Just a family with shittier stuff than we already have." He moved past Rabbit to join the huddle around the fire. "What's this?"

Cameron pointed at the screen where a man in a vivid orange tuxedo and hair in wild tufts was attempting to yank his foot free from a frozen pole as a second man (his tux was powder blue) bumbled frantically about in the background, all while a tiny dog in a knit sweater yapped like a town crier alerting the populace.

"It's called *Dumb and Dumber*," said one of the boys.

"And it totally lives up to its title," added another.

He tried to enjoy the movie, but he kept feeling Rabbit's stare at the back of his skull.

But Cameron was wrong. Because when he turned around to check, he saw that Rabbit was staring out into the night, toward where Amelia and Jack were living with the treasures that Cameron was suddenly intent on ensuring the Andersons could keep for themselves.

Chapter Eighty

CAMERON – 2018

CAMERON VENTURED into town at least once during the day over the next several days, each time with a cluster of flowers plucked from wild blooms that dusted the outskirts of their campsite. Bouquets were mostly tickseed, sunflowers, and goldenrod, according to the pictures and labels he remembered from *A Field Guide to the Everglades.*

He tried to hand Amelia his freshly picked offering every time, and was met with the same strain of lackadaisical acknowledgment. A soft smile brushing her lips, born more out of politeness than genuine pleasure.

"You know our place is sick with sunflowers," she would say while barely meeting his eyes. "It is nice of you, though."

He was entranced by her indifference. But just when Cameron was considering ways to double down on his efforts at capturing more of Amelia's attention if not her affection, Farley announced that it would be their final night in Zephyrhills.

"We'll be hitting every house in the town," he informed his boys with a nod while sketching a rough map into the dirt. "We take slightly more than we can possibly carry, then make for the road before dawn."

What he really meant was *every house with something of value*. Cameron was relieved to see that Amelia's home had not made the list.

Something had changed inside him, and the pull at his conscience he usually felt when secreting away things that did not belong to him had turned into a violent tugging at his soul. It had been a long time since Cameron was truly starving, so the excuses he made for himself back when he lived on berries, and was therefore willing to do anything for a full belly, were now more than two years behind him.

But he held his tongue, realizing that he was now biding his time while waiting for an escape from Farley as they sneaked into homes to fill their sacks before slipping away like smoke in the wind.

When their fates took a hard turn after breaking into the home of an old man, Cameron thought, *serves us right*.

"Now wait a minute there, good sir ..." Farley raised his hands, confident that he could talk his way out of yet another hairy exchange. "I'm sure we can talk about—"

"What do you want to talk about?" The man cocked his gun. "How about we talk about you expecting me to be at the tavern and my home to be empty tonight? Sound good?"

He jabbed his gun at Farley and—

Wrong move. Farley reached out and snatched the weapon away from him.

A scuffle ensued but didn't last long.

"Tie him up." Farley nodded at Rabbit and went right back to filling his bag.

A minute later, they were all outside.

"Ramblers, let's get to rambling," Farley said.

"We gotta hit one more place," Rabbit announced.

Cameron swallowed, knowing exactly what the scoundrel was doing. "No more stops. We gotta get out of here."

"One more stop," Rabbit pressed.

Farley turned to Rabbit.

And Rabbit explained. "The Anderson family's got a windup record player. Just like you're always looking for."

"That ain't true." Cameron shook his head. "I even had dinner with—"

"He's sweet on the girl, same one that got attacked by that gator. That's why he was lying to protect them." Rabbit grinned, and Cameron could see that Farley knew right then who was telling the truth. "I saw the record player with my own eyes."

Farley narrowed his eyes at Cameron but kept any thoughts to himself. "Looks like we have one more stop."

The man sounded grimly determined, suspicion percolating alongside his anger.

Cameron ran for his life. Not from danger, but toward it, his heart thumping out of control in his chest, fear mingling with desperation as he worked to outpace the young men he'd once considered his family.

A predatory moon hung low in the sky, soft light casting hard shadows across the forest floor.

Cameron ran faster, making a mad dash for the Andersons, pounding his knuckles raw on the door when he got there.

It swung open to a frightened Kat.

Cameron panted, "They're coming. Do you have any weapons?"

"Who's coming—"

He pushed his way inside as Jack and Amelia appeared behind their mother, both armed, Amelia with a knife, Jack holding a hammer in one hand and a Phillips screwdriver in the other.

"Bad people. And they mean to do terrible things." Cameron felt a chill hearing that ugly truth leaving his mouth.

He tried to explain, with no time to turn himself into the hero, spilling his guts without thinking, admitting to his part in Farley's nefarious plans.

Kat had plenty of questions, same for Jack and Amelia at her side, but Cameron shushed her before the first one could make it out of her mouth, nodding into the distance as a chorus of footsteps echoed through the stillness and Farley came marching into view with his troupe of boys.

Rabbit grinned like a wolf approaching a paddock as he looked up at Farley with vindication. "Told you he turned Judas on us."

Farley stood rooted, his hard gaze drilling into Cameron.

The Andersons stood behind him, surely wondering what this stranger had brought to their doorstep.

"You broke our code." Farley spoke in a heavy voice, leaden with the weight of betrayal. "You broke my trust." A glance up at the Andersons. "You chose them over us. So now you're on your own. You have no one, and no home waiting."

"I did what I had to do." Cameron stood tall and kept his voice steady. "I stand by my choice."

The gang rumbled from a huddled silhouette as Farley lifted a hand and beckoned Cameron down from his perch.

NIAMH ARTHUR & SEAN PLATT

Boots thudded against the decking as he descended the ladder to stand before Farley.

Only one of Cameron's heels had hit the ground before Farley punched him in the gut. He doubled over, breath caught in his throat, gasping as his former father figure delivered several swift kicks to his ribs.

Pain bloomed in his side, radiating outward like a wildfire.

Farley bent down to his crumpled form, his face a stark mask against the moonlight, and low voice bleeding out from his lips in a whisper. "You better sell it, boy."

The kicks kept coming, but Cameron knew he was getting off easy.

Chapter Eighty-One

CAMERON – 2018 - 2020

TIME EBBED and flowed through the Anderson home, carrying Cameron in its tide as it rolled inexorably forward. Amelia was clearly reluctant to fully welcome him into her life, but both Kat and Jack were hospitable enough to make up for it. They had immediately offered the home that Farley had assured him he'd never find.

The creaking floorboards felt familiar fast. Same for the ever-present allure of Amelia, with her flinty gaze, armored in a chainmail of indifference that left him longing for her attention.

Cameron continued to offer her wildflowers, but she refused his bouquets more often than not, with a soft smile that rarely reached her eyes.

He persisted. Something about Amelia's stoic demeanor stoked the embers in his heart, drawing him closer.

Cameron found himself nursing his wounded pride after yet another disappointing attempt with Amelia when Kat came over and sat beside him on the couch.

She patted his knee with a knowing smile. "You are a patient man."

"They say patience is a virtue. I would argue it's more a survival skill."

"It's not you, and it isn't your fault." Another pat on Cameron's knee before Kat folded her hands and leaned back against the cushions. "Amelia is … complicated. Not her fault either."

Cameron turned. There was something sad and urgent in her voice, words leaving her lips like pus from a wound.

"Amelia has a heart condition. Just like the one her father had. My Junior." She wiped a tear away. "Losing him left a scar for both of us. *All of us.* But Amelia sharing his condition makes her afraid of loving and leaving someone the way he left us. I'm sorry to tell you that as sweet as you are, Cameron, and as much as I would love to tell you that things might be different someday, I'm not sure you'll ever really have a chance, no matter how hard you might try."

"Amelia's been guarding her heart, and I've been trying to win it. Someday there will be enough time in between us that she'll be able to see things right."

Two weeks later, Cameron and Amelia were standing in a soft wind under a full moon, its soft glow illuminating her silhouette. Instead of his usual blather, he basked in the silence. Tonight was the night, Cameron had told himself over and over while stirring his courage in front of the slightly cracked mirror.

Amelia finally broke the quiet. "If you came out here to say something, you should probably get to saying it."

Cameron held her gaze instead of flinching away in

fear of the usual rebuff. "Life is short, Amelia." His voice was barely audible over the rustling leaves and a nocturnal chatter of insects. "No one knew that better than my mother."

"Your mother?" Amelia repeated. "You've never mentioned her before."

"That's because it's like someone squeezed lighter fluid on my heart and lit it on fire every time I think about her." He needed a breath. "I was ten years old when she gave her life for me."

Amelia blinked in surprise.

"Sure, it hurts to talk about, but I barely ever stop thinking about my mom, and all of those memories are good. Despite the pain still feeling fresh, I would never trade an escape from the hurt for the years of her loving me. It's the memories of my mother that keep me going. And the only thing worse than loving and losing someone ... is never having loved them at all."

Their breaths hitched as the world itself seemed to hold its breath.

The air was electric, charged with an intensity that tingled his skin.

Amelia moved forward and grabbed a fistful of his shirt in each of her hands.

Then her lips were on Cameron's, hesitantly tender as he drew her closer to his body, meeting Amelia's kiss as she started to sob and their shared breaths fell in sync.

Love blossomed into shared whispers and stolen moments.

Amelia was his solace and he was her sanctuary, their life together a balm for those wounds that time refused to heal. They would lie under the shade of a tree, fingers braided as he spoke of legends and lore gleaned from his ample time in the library. She would listen to every word.

But Cameron only told Amelia about the stories he read, most from a long time ago, never mentioning all the tall stacks of titles he tore through while trying to understand her condition better. Driven by a desperation to escape the shadow looming over their joyful life, he pored over medical texts in search of a miracle, skimming jargon and studying diagrams of the human heart. Denying survival rates. Researching ways to help her, despite the impossible odds, considering an operation would necessitate a hospital where open heart surgery could be done in a modern world with no such luxury.

Cameron left his research at the library, returning home where they shared stories and music, including his favorite composition — a song Kat had started writing two decades earlier, before the war, and had tinkered closer to a perfection she would never achieve.

It was the soundtrack to their evenings. Cameron and Amelia often joined Kat as she sang, their voices harmonizing with hers in a way that sounded both beautiful and bittersweet. Jack thought he sounded too nasal to join them.

Cameron loved to regale the family with recitations of movies he'd seen, and Kat was usually able to fill in the missing gaps when he had a hard time remembering.

Nights were a tapestry of story and song, but Amelia's condition was still a predator they could never outrun, licking its chops while lurking in shadows.

The day finally arrived when his songbird fell silent, and the tree under which they held hands stood as a lone sentinel to guard over her as Amelia went back to the earth.

Her absence left a hollow void inside him, echoing with the memory of her laughter and the ghost of her touch.

Amelia slipped away with the grace she held in life. But

her absence left a deafening silence, and a scar on the skin of his existence.

Only time could heal the festering wound inside Cameron.

But not at all in the way that he expected.

Chapter Eighty-Two

CAMERON – 2035

THE AIR REEKED of grease and rusted metal as Cameron tinkered in the dimly lit workshop. Many years of messing with all of this old machinery had gradually turned him into an expert beyond his age in these parts. Despite the grime and manual labor, he felt deeply satisfied as ancient gears sprang to life under his touch.

"Cameron!" Morris barked from across the space. The owner of Machine Fixes by Morris — an on-the-nose name if ever there was one — sounded like a grizzly bear growling, but he was really more of the teddy variety.

Cameron turned his attention from the old projector he was delighted to be no more than one more hour away from finishing and met the man's gaze.

"You ever consider wearing my logo on your coveralls full-time?" Morris didn't wait for Cameron to answer, never did. "Your hands can make rust sing. You're the best young man with old machines I've ever worked with."

"I speak their language."

"So will you consider it?"

"I consider it every time you ask me," Cameron replied with a nod. "But my answer is still the same. I can't get tied down." He shook his head. "So long as I'm still working for Orbital Wire, and am in charge of maintaining the wireless nodes, I'll need to stay on the move."

"Always the nodes." Morris smiled through his grumbling, but Cameron heard genuine envy stuck to its edges like gator meat in his teeth. "You're wasting your talent, son."

"How many times have I helped you out for free, Morris?"

"Plenty. And I thank you for that."

"I'm not asking for your gratitude. The point I'm making is that I'm happy to be here whether you pay me or not, though of course I prefer the latter. But being here can't be my job, no matter how many times you ask me."

"Ain't you done with that yet?" Morris teased him, pointing at the projector.

"Any minute now."

"You been saying that for two weeks."

"This time I mean it."

"You said 'no more than a day' when you dragged that thing in here," Morris grunted.

"Looks like I was wrong." Cameron adjusted a cog, then flicked a switch. Light cut through the gloom in a beam to project flickering images on the wall.

"Well, shit. So what now? You planning to sell that thing?"

"Not a chance." Cameron shook his head. "Tonight we're watching *The Usual Suspects*."

He could barely contain his excitement, all the way from Machine Fixes by Morris back to the Anderson homestead. He would have bounded up the ladder if not for the heft of his projector.

Surprise! was on his lips but Cameron felt the emotion for himself instead. This was not to be a quiet evening with just the three of them.

He entered to find Jack holding hands with Delilah — Cameron was almost sure that was her name — a woman he and Jack had seen a few times in the marketplace over the last couple of years.

"You remember Delilah," Jack said.

"Hi!" She gave Cameron a wave.

Kat followed suit from the kitchen.

And Cameron thought, *Shit.* He had planned on premiering one of his favorite films on their new (ancient) projector, along with an important conversation afterward. Something he had been dying to discuss with Jack for a while now.

He wanted to celebrate his buddy's new assignment, while confessing his plan about how they could work as a team to save the world, or at least their timeline, and the most important person in it. Or who had been in it.

But clearly that would not be happening tonight.

Kat must have sensed that Cameron was looking for a moment alone with her son. She called out from the kitchen. "Why don't you come over here with me, Delilah? We can let the boys catch up for a moment."

Kat waved again and then walked toward the stove.

Jack followed Cameron toward the door. "Why do you look like that?"

"Like what?" Cameron asked when they got there.

"Like someone dropped your baby."

"I have no idea what you're talking about."

"Sure you do," Jack disagreed. "You finally finished fixing that projector, so I'm guessing the only reason you're not rambling on and on about whatever movie from 1999 you wanted to watch tonight is because I brought Delilah home to meet Mom."

They descended the rope ladder and continued their conversation on the ground.

"Congratulations on your new job," Cameron said.

"I still can't believe the TRU is willing take a chance on me."

"The Temporal Recon Unit is lucky to have you, J. I hope someone there is saying they still can't believe that Jack Anderson is willing to take a chance on the TRU."

Jack laughed, but it was easy to see that he didn't really mean it. "You still look like someone dropped your baby. I was hoping that you would be happy for me, man. It's a big night. I want us to celebrate."

"That's why I'm here. With a projector and a movie. From 1995, by the way."

"Is that why you look disappointed? You couldn't find anything from '99?"

"I have an opportunity if—"

"An opportunity for what exactly?" Jack asked.

"I was just about to say before you interrupted."

"Maybe. But not before a lot of preamble, where you build your case as to why I should be excited about yet another ride on your roller coaster of last-minute miracles and near-disasters. I was just hoping you could get to the good part so we could go back inside and watch the movie."

"Imagine if the Synthia 3700 never existed," Cameron blurted out the first part of his plan.

Jack looked back at Cameron in confusion. "What?"

"If the Synthia never existed, then neither would the AFE."

"Again, *what?*"

"And if the AFE never came about, then the civil war won't happen and the world war and the nukes will never drop."

"What are you actually saying, Cameron?" Jack's voice now had an edge to it.

"You have the power to rewrite the past. So why stay here stuck watching reruns, when we could be reshaping the world instead?"

"That's not how the TRU works."

"Maybe it could be."

"The role of the Temporal Recon Unit is to go back in time and retrieve what we need without disrupting the timeline."

"You sound like a textbook," Cameron argued.

"Even if I were to go back and change those things, it would only create an alternate timeline where *I'm* in a world without the war, but it wouldn't change anything for any of us here. You would still be stuck here where all of this—"

"This is a shitty timeline anyway. You shouldn't even want to live in it."

Jack sighed. "This is about Amelia, isn't it?"

"She's your sister. Don't you want her to live?"

"Everything happens for a reason, Cam. Including what happened to Amelia. And on some other timeline out there, she *is* still alive."

"We could be doing more." Cameron clenched his fists. "Why are you fighting me on this?"

"Because what you're saying is not practical or possible." Jack smiled to soften his words. "Even more than usual. Now come on. Let's go back inside and watch *The Usual Suspects*. Even I have heard of that one."

"Verbal is Keyser Söze," Cameron replied.

Before he walked off into the night.

Chapter Eighty-Three

CAMERON – 2036

A YEAR LATER, Cameron was obsessed with his plan.

He never mentioned it to Jack again after the night he'd spoiled *The Usual Suspects* for him. Instead, Cameron needed courage to execute what he felt increasingly sure he would be able to do.

Starting with his plan for the perfect heist. After several months thinking and rethinking the plot until he had ironed every last wrinkle out of it, Cameron finally had an out of time robbery to execute.

Next, he needed to assemble the proper elements so that his heist would move like gears in a machine. Names and public files for the ex-cons Cameron would require in his future-past of 1975, details about John Anderson Sr., and comprehensive records of publicly traded companies that experienced boom times in the early 2000s.

Once Cameron had everything he needed, and the entirety of his net worth liquidated down to the chits in his pocket and the valuables in his backpack, he enlisted some help from Coach, Farley's ex who now dealt in weapons, among other things.

Then he set out to find Farley and make his former father figure and the boys (mostly all men by now) an offer they couldn't refuse.

He left Zephyrhills after hearing rumors that the old gang had made camp in Old Orlando. The whispers were true, and *old* was the operative word. One and a half decades looked like a lot more than a quarter century on Farley's now-haggard face. It appeared that he had been playing double-or-nothing with Father Time and losing. Same for Rabbit, now in his early thirties. There were three younger boys now traveling with the gang of grown men, but the vibrant eyes Cameron had seen in his time had blinked out long ago.

But bygones were bygones, and Farley was pleased to see him. Even Rabbit was willing to help him out, for a price, just as Cameron had suspected.

"That's everything I have in there." He unzipped his battered backpack and showed the gang their prize.

Several fabric-wrapped bottles of alcohol; specialty soaps (Farley had always loved them); antibiotics; a pouch full of seeds; several knives, a hand-cranked radio, a miniature solar panel; four rolls of duct tape; and the jewel of Cameron's collection, a loaded revolver, its grip worn smooth from use.

"Plus just under twenty-five hundred chits," he added.

"How *under*?" Rabbit asked.

"A hundred and eighteen under."

"Good enough," Farley replied, before Rabbit could get another word in. "Or almost good enough." A sly grin. "You still live with them folks back in the swamp?"

"Not for a long while now. But I occasionally make their acquaintance."

Farley nodded. "You make it long enough to get me that windup record player and you can have all the help you want."

"Plus that backpack and all your chits," Rabbit added.

"Does it sound like I need an articulator?" Farley snapped at Rabbit before turning back to Cameron. "Do we have a deal?"

"We have a deal." Cameron extended his hand, and they shook.

He returned to Zephyrhills and went to Kat's place next.

"Is this one of your elaborate jokes that's going to take me a while to understand?" Kat asked.

Cameron shook his head. "I promise I'm not playing with you."

"You want to travel back in time and steal the IBM 5100…" Kat waited for him to nod. "So that IBM will be scared out of ever producing the Synthia 3700. And you think that'll stop the AFE from ever forming."

Cameron kept nodding.

"But why not just steal the Synthia?"

"It'll be too late if they are already making it. Steal it, and they'll just make another one. I have to make them decide to never launch the project in the first place."

Kat shook her head. "Even if I thought what you were saying is possible—"

"Of course it's possible."

"—it wouldn't be fair to Jack. He'll get kicked out of the Temporal Recon Unit. And I'm sure you know exactly how hard my son had to work for what he's accomplished, and exactly how long he's been dreaming about being a part of TRU."

"You're right, Kat. This isn't fair to Jack. But won't it be worth doing anyway? If it means Amelia having a life?"

"She already does have a life. Somewhere. In some other timeline."

"But not with me." It was barely a whisper.

A tear rolled down Cameron's cheek, and then Kat was crying too.

After a long moment that she clearly needed, the answer left her in a heaving whisper. "*Of course it's worth it.*" Kat caught her breath and wiped at her tears. "But I'll never believe you." She shook her head. "In the past, I mean. You'll need some way to convince me."

Cameron already knew that, but it was a relief to see her already on it.

"I was planning to give Jack my *The Talented Mister Ripley* book. And my necklace."

"Those are just objects," Cameron argued. "Are you sure that will be enough?"

She thought for a moment, then offered him a decisive nod. "Failing that, you can always sing one of my songs."

"'Echoes' oughta do it."

"That's the one," she agreed with a smile. "The record player is going to hurt."

"I know. And I'm sorry."

Kat put on some Sam Cook to say goodbye, both to the record player and to Cameron, and they danced around the living room to "A Change is Gonna Come."

Then they walked outside together, climbed down the rope, and stood under the stars to say their real farewell before the false one they'd have to perform in front of Jack later.

"So this is it?" Kat asked.

"Just about." Cameron nodded. "I imagine it's the last time we can be open about it anyway."

"Jack has explained it all to me. I know how it works."

"Time travel?"

"Timelines," she clarified. "I know that it's impossible for you to ever come back to my worldline. I understand exactly what kind of goodbye this is."

Cameron opened his arms, and Kat fell into them.

"Thank you." She hugged him tight. "Please take care of my little girl."

"From the second I have her and for the rest of my life," he promised.

And over the next few days, he paid Arvel to make sure that Hank kept Jack under the truck, got the time machine's code from Kat after she plied it out of Jack, returned Farley's wink as he stole the Corvette, then finished moving the pieces around on his timeline-altering board by taking the unit into the past, to the precise point where he could start changing history back in 1975.

Chapter Eighty-Four

CAMERON – 1975

CAMERON FOLLOWED John Anderson for days before finally making his move and "accidentally" meeting him on a neighboring barstool in Muddy's corner.

He finished his drink in four gulps, then returned his glass to the bar as he made to leave in the aftermath of his offer. "Simple job. Easy in, easy out, and you'll have more than enough to pay for Junior's operation."

By the time they were meeting Goober and the rest of Cameron's band of criminal misfits in Central Park, he felt like fate had smiled on his operation. And when buying $100 worth of McDonalds stock, the broker had to ask Cameron why he was laughing.

"I'm just imagining a world conquered by Big Macs and Chicken McNuggets."

"What's a McNugget?"

"Eight more years, then the world changes forever." He grinned. "You might want to buy $100 of Mickey D's for yourself. But no matter what, don't ever actually eat the McNuggets."

Cameron had so meticulously planned the heist that the only difficult part was manipulating John to do what he needed him to do, though the manipulation was necessary, and fun to get away with once he learned to compartmentalize the guilt.

He used John's Ruscard to access the rear exit to the IBM building after plucking it from the front and leaving Cameron exactly one flirty exchange with the mailroom secretary away from his ascending to the proper floor.

"Is it always so warm in here, or is it just that you have such a welcoming presence?" Cameron asked the secretary like he meant it.

He checked to make sure John was in the data room, then flicked on the cameras.

He apologized under his breath about what had to be done before heading into John's computer lab and lifting the IBM 5100.

Then he returned to the camera's eye line again, this time doffing his cap for the viewer, mocking the ease in which he was executing his heist to further confuse the viewer, keeping his face covered as he sprinted through the building.

Cameron boarded the humming subway with the 50-pound computer tucked under his arm, the precious artifact an ironic antithesis to the graffiti-splashed scenery rushing by outside the window.

After a series of transfers, as carefully mapped as the heist itself, he surfaced in a nondescript suburb, the subway buzz replaced by birdsong and the distant laughter of children. He followed the sound to a throng of pre-adolescents playing a spirited game of baseball on a nearby field.

"Do you have a moment?" Cameron asked as he

approached the pitcher. The entire team turned his way, but he walked straight to the batter. "Would you mind if I borrow that bat for a moment?"

The kid handed it over as if hypnotized, then Cameron hoisted the IBM 5100 onto a clear spot and drew a deep breath before swinging the bat down onto the computer. The machine made a CRUNCH as sparks flew off into the air like defeated fireflies.

The children hollered with joy and stood in line for their turn.

One by one, they swung, the bat colliding with the machine as their laughter crescendoed with every fresh hit, the IBM fragmenting until it was finally reduced to a clutter of pieces.

Cameron gathered the pile and heaved it all into a nearby dumpster as he passed by without stopping, abandoning that alley amid gales of still-laughing kids behind him, walking toward a stately Victorian embellished with an unlocked wrought-iron gate a few blocks away.

Down a mosaic of cobblestones to the front door, with a wraparound porch skirting the ground floor, complete with rocking chairs and swings for the most leisurely of afternoons. But there was nothing lackadaisical about the way he pounded his fist against the wood.

The door swung open to a man standing in his foyer dressed in silk pajamas.

"Do you have a moment?" Cameron asked.

The words disarmed the man, like they always did. He went from looking like he was about to yell *What the hell do you want?* to "I'm sorry?"

"You don't have to be. So long as you do the right thing. You are Mr. Philips, I presume?"

"*Dr.* Philips," the surgeon corrected.

"Exactly." Cameron nodded as he pulled an envelope.

full of pictures from his jacket pocket. "And Dr. Philips probably doesn't want anyone seeing these pictures of himself at the Velvet Vixen."

The surgeon tried to snatch the envelope from Cameron's hand. "No, sir." He shook his head. "You can't have them back. *Yet.*"

"You want money? I have plenty of money."

"Obviously," said Cameron in disgust. "You ever do any pro bono work? Or do you need every dime to pay for your pool men and gardeners?"

"Pool *man*," Phillips corrected. "There is only one of them."

"It must be hard."

"What do you want from me?"

"I want you to take a pro bono case. A little boy named John Anderson Junior. You fix his broken heart, and you can have the pictures back."

"Look buddy, I don't know who you—"

"Who's at the door?" called out a female voice from somewhere behind him.

"Mrs. Philips, I presume?" Cameron grinned. "Maybe we should—"

"John Anderson Junior," the doctor hurried. "Pro bono. You got it."

Chapter Eighty-Five

CAMERON – 1975

A FEW WEEKS LATER, Cameron found himself dressed in a suit, armed with a fake sidearm (it was really a BB gun) and an equally artificial badge that looked real enough to get him past the security at IBM, despite the heist that should have left everyone in the building under an even more vigilant guard. Instead, it appeared that no one believed lightning could possibly strike the same place twice.

"Do you have a moment?" Cameron asked the security guard.

"That is my job," he replied, though it looked like the guard had wanted to say something else before those four words left his mouth.

Cameron flashed his badge. "I'm here to see Mr. Laslo."

"Is this about the 5100?" The security guard shook his head. "Never mind. Of course it is."

"What do you want?" Laslo growled without even giving the supposed agent a greeting. John had been right to hate this guy.

"I'm Tyler Durden with the CIA." Cameron showed Laslo his badge.

"What do you want from me? I didn't have anything to do with what happened here. Except that I was pretty sure John Anderson was no good from the start, and I'll admit to my guilt for not following my gut in that instance."

"We're requesting that IBM halt any and all work on the Synthia 3700."

"I'm sorry to hear about the objection, but I am afraid that the CIA has no authority to tell IBM what it can and cannot develop or manufacture. At least not without a lengthy legal process. Or have things changed in America in a way that I am unaware of?"

"I know the secret of the 5100."

Laslo raised his eyebrows.

Cameron continued. "There's an interface between the assembly code surrounding the ROM exterior, and the 360 emulator hidden beneath it."

"How do you—"

"The 5100's emulator gives your programmers access to the functions of the larger non-portable IBM mainframes."

"What are you saying?" Laslo almost sounded scared. Maybe defensive.

"This theft was clearly perpetrated by a foreign power hoping to access top secret information stored on those mainframes. And the Synthia 3700, being based on it, incorporates the same flaw. You need to redesign from scratch."

"You found out who Anderson sold the unit to?"

Cameron nodded. "A man going by the name of M.

Night Shyamalan. One of the most dangerous men in the world. He'll sell secrets to the Russians same as he'll sell them to the North Koreans. It makes no difference to Shyamalan. You ever heard of The Green Mile?"

"No?"

"Of course you haven't. And you don't want to. There are secrets we at the CIA keep so that good citizens such as yourself can sleep at night. Now. My superiors won't allow me to leave this office until IBM agrees to halt any and all R&D in regard to any machine sharing the emulator's functionality."

"I can't just—"

"*In writing*," Cameron pressed. "Unless you want me to call Malkovich."

"Who?"

"John Malkovich." Cameron swallowed hard, now feigning fear. "My boss. Please don't make me call him. That won't be a good thing for either one of us."

"I'm honestly not even sure if—"

"Do you want to know what will happen if IBM moves forward with the Synthia 3700?" Cameron wasn't about to wait for Laslo's answer, leaning forward and whispering the true secret instead. "The American government will be overthrown before a civil war destroys our nation and sends us into a third world war. Cities will be bombed and become uninhabitable. Families will be torn apart. Life as we know it will end, and the entire nation will get blasted back to the 1800s in terms of our technology. *None* of your computers will matter."

"How could you possibly know any of that?"

"That's just one possibility," Cameron admitted with a shrug. "But none of them are good. So what am I going to tell Malkovich? Have I done my job, and can I report that IBM will do what's right for this country and scrap the

Synthia, or will he need to come down here and convince you himself?"

Laslo cleared his throat. "What happens if he comes down?"

"John Malkovich is the final act in a play. If he steps onto the stage, it's curtains for everyone at IBM. Do you really want to be a part of that drama, Laslo?"

No, Laslo did not.

Chapter Eighty-Six

CAMERON – 2000

KAT HAD BEEN TRYING to entice Cameron inside the house with all kinds of delightful smells for a while, and now that he had finally finished his preparations, he was finally ready to go inside.

"Good morning," Kat said as he entered.

"Morning." Cameron gave her a nod. "I'm sorry again about yesterday."

"We can move on from that." She returned his nod with an awkward smile. "I made you breakfast."

"Thank you." He glanced at the plate but didn't move toward it. "I need to take care of some things this morning."

Kat looked at him. "Where are we going?"

"I don't need a ride."

"What kind of errands do you—"

"Future stuff." She obviously didn't like that he left it at that, so Cameron added, "You have nothing to worry about."

Amelia entered the kitchen with a question already halfway out of her mouth. "Worry about what?"

"How about we all meet at the movies later?" Cameron suggested.

After a fair amount of protest, Kat finally relented, then Amelia helped him to settle on *Stuart Little* playing that afternoon at the Regency 8.

That gave Cameron plenty of time to take care of his future minded agenda, starting with the selling of his McDonald's stocks and investing in the new ones that would pay for Amelia's second surgery, with some left over to make sure that Kat would be okay in the future.

That left one more task in the past before his mission would be complete.

Cameron took a cab to the home of a Mr. Bertrand Lyndon, the man responsible for obliterating his timeline.

The facade of Bertrand's home did exactly what it was supposed to be doing by hiding the monster who was living inside. Painted in a pleasant butter yellow with a white picket fence around a lucky clover-colored lawn and large tropical plants lining the gravel driveway.

Cameron pounded on the door with his right hand while gripping the knife behind his back with his left.

The door swung open.

"Bertrand Lyndon?" And then when the man replied with an uncertain nod: "I've come here to kill you!"

Bertrand tried to slam the door, but Cameron shoved his foot in the opening and pushed his way into the house.

Bertrand fell on his ass, but after a fear-soaked whimper, he managed to scramble back up onto his feet and run for his life.

Cameron gave chase to his prey with a wide smile,

ready to correct the future by becoming a man out of time yet again.

"What do you want?" Bertrand cried out, barricading himself on what he mistakenly saw as the safe side of his sofa.

But there was no safe side for Bertrand Lyndon right now, and there never would be again.

"I already told you. I came here to kill you." Cameron also needed to hurry. The paperwork at TD Waterhouse had taken much longer than he imagined it would, and now he was late for *Stuart Little*. He hated to keep his family waiting on him.

"Why do you want to kill me?" Terrified as he must have been, Bertrand's query dripped with curiosity. "What did I ever do to you?"

"It's not what you did to me," Cameron explained. "It's what you did to the world."

"What did I ever do to the world?" Bertrand sounded aghast.

"It's what you're going to do," Cameron amended his accusation.

Anyone in any time could have heard the core of truth in his voice. At the very least, Cameron must have believed in what he was saying. But Bertrand didn't know what to make of it.

"What am I *going to do*?" His bottom lip trembled as he corrected himself.

"You're going to use the Synthia 3700 to steal information from the government—"

"Use the *what?*"

"—and start the American Federal Empire."

The truth dawned on Bertrand's face like a shadow from a thunder cloud.

He had just said something out loud that Bertrand had

only been thinking about, and Cameron could see that truth in his eyes.

Somewhere deep in the recesses of Bertrand Lyndon's mind, his crimes had already been committed. So no matter what year they were in, Bertrand was out of time.

Cameron grinned at his unintentional admission. He gripped his knife tighter.

"You allowed millions of people to die by fracturing our nation and preventing them from putting forward a united front."

Bertrand swallowed. For the last time.

"You ruined the entire world. Given the chance, you'll do it again."

"No—"

Cameron repeatedly plunged the blade into his chest, Bertrand's face twisting into a snarl, sour hatred for what the man had done stinging his eyes as he stabbed.

Bertrand's scream pierced the living room as blood spattered the ground and walls.

Then into a pool as his life drained away.

Cameron bolted out of the house, late for family time at the movies.

Chapter Eighty-Seven

CAMERON – 2000

Kat wanted him gone, and she was clearly past the point of no return. No amount of charm would turn the tide now that she smelled danger all over him.

So Cameron left the tent before dawn and neatly packed it up and set it against the house by the back door.

But only after he was a mile down the road walking toward the Corvette and his final leg of this adventure did he realize his mistake and make an about face back toward the Andersons.

He had forgotten to leave the notebook for Amelia, and that wasn't something Cameron was willing to let go of. He had filled it with stories about the future and his life. An out of timeline gift tying the future and present in a bow.

Cameron planned to sneak back inside the house and leave the notebook in Amelia's bedroom, but as he crept up to the front porch Cameron could hear Kat talking to her father-in-law, the two of them discussing him in the living room.

John's voice sounded much older and more ragged —

that heist from a quarter-decade ago had only been a recent event for one of them.

"In 1975. Titor's the reason I went to jail and missed out on most of Junior's life."

Kat said, "I thought it was the Russians?"

"Only because that's what everyone was most inclined to think." John sighed. "I stopped telling that story years ago, though. No one ever believed me." An acidic laugh. "Not that I blame anyone for thinking I was crazy about that."

"Crazy about what?"

"Titor said he was from the future, got me to play along with his heist on the promise that he'd help Junior while setting me up to fail — what did this guy look like?"

"Give me a minute…"

Then moments later: "That's him. That's the same guy, and not a goddamned day older."

"What are you doing out here?" Amelia asked, suddenly behind Cameron.

He spun around to face her. "I was—"

"Are you a bad man?" She crossed her arms and glared at him.

"Do you think I'm a bad man?" He smiled as Amelia steeped in his question.

"No." She finally shook her head after a few beats of serious consideration. "Why is my mommy being so mean to you?"

"I promise on my life that I am not a bad man. But your mom does have her reasons. Your heart will tell you the truth, Amelia." He put his right hand over his own. "So in your heart, do you believe me?"

Amelia nodded.

"Do you want to go for a walk with me?"

She nodded again, then together they walked to a

weathered wooden bench, its surface almost wet from humidity, the pergola above climbing with vibrant green leaves and twisting vines.

A pleasant setting if not for the threatening sky, already too many shades of gray as the wind started snapping amid the scent of rain and the distant rumble of thunder.

"Don't be mad at your mother," Cameron said. "She's only trying to protect you."

"What is she trying to protect me from?"

"Things she doesn't understand. Did you know that my mommy saved my life?"

Amelia shook her head. "No."

"She wanted me to be safe and happy. The same is true for your mommy. That's a mother's job. It's one of the reasons that mommies are so important."

Cameron looked around the park. "My mom took me to this same park once. It wasn't as pretty as it is now, but this same bench where we're sitting right now was here."

"Oh." Amelia obviously didn't know what else to say, perhaps instinctively understanding that her role right now was to listen, so she could understand better in the future.

"There's nothing more important in this world than family. Sometimes they won't understand why you do the things that you do, but the answer is always because you love them. Do you understand that?"

Amelia nodded like she had no other choice.

Cameron kept going. "Your heart is special. Not only does it always know the truth, it also works harder than other hearts."

"Why?"

"Because you're so strong and brave, and so able to love others, that your heart has a hard time keeping up."

"What does that mean?"

Cameron wrapped his arm around her. "You're going

to out-love your heart, Amelia. But don't be scared. Because your heart knows the truth, and one day it will whisper that truth to you. When that day comes, and you feel that feeling in your heart, tell your mommy that you need a doctor *immediately*."

"Okay. What will it feel like?"

"Can you imagine if there was a little birdie lost inside your chest, fluttering around while it tried to fly out?"

Amelia squinted in concentration then said, "I think so."

"Good." Cameron glanced up at the darkening sky. "Ready to go home?"

She nodded back. "Will I ever see you again?"

"I promise that you will."

"When will I see you?"

"After you move to the mountains."

Amelia smiled. "We're moving to the mountains?"

"You're going to *love* them. More than just about anything else in the world. Now let's—"

That's all Cameron managed to say before the sky opened up to a downpour. Bright white streaks of lightning illuminated the navy-blue sky as rain fell like beads from an infinite necklace. Thunderous booms echoed in the distance.

"It's okay," he reassured her. "We'll stay here until it stops."

But Cameron was wrong about how fast the storm would pass, and when the rain came in sheets and began to pelt the pagoda even harder, he finally covered her up in his jacket and carried Amelia back to the house.

Then he tucked her into bed and wandered back into the kitchen where he waited for Kat. The front door opened and she entered with John.

He waited for the right moment to interrupt them, but

then the choice was taken away when the storm killed the electricity.

"GODDAMIT!" Kat bellowed in the suddenly dark house as Jack started crying again.

"I'm going to go over to Maggie's and see if she has power. You call in the outage." John turned around and headed out again.

Kat entered the kitchen, feeling her way toward the phone.

"Do you have a moment?" Cameron said.

Kat spun around to face him, butcher knife in hand.

LESS THAN A MONTH LATER, Kat's world fell askew from its orbit as she processed Amelia's words.

"My heart feels like a little birdie trying to get out, Mommy."

She rushed Amelia to the hospital. The surgery that was a marathon of waiting.

Kat paced the corridor, fluorescent lights casting a sickly glow across the sterile environment. Softly humming machinery and murmured conversations among the medical staff amid the steady beeping of monitors were a soundtrack to her life on standby for news.

The surgeon eventually emerged, mask pulled down around his neck, eyes warm enough to dim her worry.

"She's strong." He smiled. "The surgery went well. She needs plenty of rest, but your daughter will make a full recovery."

Amelia started talking as she convalesced, not about toys or cartoons, but about mountains. So Kat rented a small cabin to escape their prior life. Cocooned in an evergreen embrace with a view of soaring mountains, their tops often shrouded in clouds, Amelia slowly recovered.

But when they finally returned home, Kat hadn't known to bring the notebook Titor had left for Amelia. The one her daughter had been poring over every night and carefully tucked into a drawer by the bed in cabin. Amelia had sobbed until Kat finally promised that they would get the notebook back.

She called the rental company in a panic, but even after passing Kat onto the elderly owner — whose sand-paper voice sounded as rugged as the mountains themselves — insisted that no book had been found at his cabin. There had been other renters through since they left on their long drive home.

"Checked the whole place, top to bottom and twice, ma'am. Didn't see a notebook in any of the drawers, or anywhere else. I even checked every book on the bookshelf to see if maybe it was stuffed between a couple of volumes. Looks like someone had their way with my *Prairie Home Companion* joke book, but other than that I found nothing amiss."

Kat sank into her chair, the absence of Amelia's note-book hitting her like a physical blow. A hard knot tangled her stomach. She had lost the thread that tied them to Titor, the peculiar man who had (in a twisted way) saved her daughter.

Looking at Amelia, now radiating health in their living room, a wave of gratitude for the enigmatic man from the future washed over her.

Chapter Eighty-Eight

JACK WAS WORKING as a software developer, designing, writing, testing, and maintaining the source code of software systems for Nimbus Network Systems (a company focused on designing advanced cloud-based solutions for big data processing and analytics) in the year 2024, when Cameron came to visit.

Jack's job could not have sounded more boring, but it certainly seemed to suit the man's personality.

"Do you have a moment?" Cameron asked, after the receptionist delivered his message and this worldline version of Jack appeared in the lobby.

Jack's face softened with curiosity and perhaps even awe. He nodded but said nothing out loud as Cameron identified himself.

He didn't have Kat's pendant to prove his identity, only her song, though after singing a few bars and disarming his best buddy from one worldline over for good, he offered the apology he had carried through both decades and days to deliver.

"I'm sorry, Jack." Cameron clapped a hand on his friend's shoulder. "In another life, I did something terrible to you. To another Jack."

"I know the legend about you." He swallowed. "About John Titor. Grandpop sees you as the Anderson Family's personal genie."

"Even after he went to jail?" Cameron asked.

"Titor always showed up to save the day just when we needed him." He shrugged. "Even if the price we had to pay was high."

"Too high?"

"I suppose not, seeing as you saved both my father and my sister's lives." Jack stared into his eyes. "Hell, I wouldn't even be alive if it wasn't for you."

"I'm not sure about that," Cameron said.

"I think you are." Jack gave him a nod. "Aren't you going to ask about her?"

"Ask about who?"

"You know who."

"You could mean Kat." But when Jack didn't respond, Cameron added, "How is she doing? Is Amelia happy? Is she married?"

"Would you like to ask her?"

"I couldn't do that." Cameron shook his head. "No, thank you."

"You'll travel through time to save my sister, but you won't drive a few more miles to see her in person?"

Once he put it that way, Cameron had no other choice.

"Come on." Jack tried to sweeten the deal. "I'll drive."

"How about I drive instead." Cameron grinned. "We can take the car I stole, after Temporal Recon assigned it to you. It's a Corvette. *Much* better than a DeLorean."

They laughed on their walk to the Chevy, and kept going as Cameron drove, with an easy banter that had somehow survived between worldlines.

"I'm afraid to see her," Cameron admitted into a lull in their conversation.

"*You*, scared?" Jack laughed again. "I don't believe it."

"What could you possibly be scared of? *You've traveled through time*. Your courage is legendary, though now that we've finally met, I'll have to admit that the legend feels a little … exaggerated."

"Oh, does it?"

"I think that my mother and grandfather both mistook your cockiness for courage."

Cameron laughed. "Maybe you're right."

"Either way, it worked. Whenever Amelia or I have ever needed to do something hard in our lives, we always ask ourselves: *what would John Titor do?*"

"Well, that's embarrassing." But Cameron was smiling.

Discussion turned to movies from 1999. Cameron was appalled and intrigued to learn that Neo had been played by Keanu Reeves in this worldline (an actor he had never even heard of) instead of Will Smith. Jack had just started to tell Cameron about a movie called *American Beauty* from that same year that he had never heard of (but wasn't sure if it was missing from the timeline or of no interest to Farley) when the car died.

"When was the last time you gassed her up?" Jack asked after Cameron pulled over to hug the roadside on a rural stretch flanked by Florida swampland on either side, just after dusk. After traveling through half a century, the Corvette finally suffered a temporary death due to lack of fuel.

"The year 2000." Cameron pointed at an alligator in

the distance. "I imagine it's still illegal to kill those things here."

"So far as I know," said Jack.

Cameron shook his head in disgust. "That's something else your worldline got all wrong."

Jack explained the plot of *American Beauty* on their way to the nearest gas station, and soon they arrived at Homestead Gas & Goods, an old-fashioned store filled with a lot of old-fashioned merchandise.

Jack approached the counter while Cameron looked around to see what sundries might line the shelves of a lonely Florida gas station in the year 2024.

A frenzied man hurried into the store and looked at the clerk. "Excuse me, sir, do you have a phone I could use to call a tow—"

"Right over there," said the clerk as he gestured to the wall.

"Thanks." The man walked toward the payphone as Cameron approached him.

"Excuse me. Do you have a moment?" Cameron asked, hoping the man might settle an argument between he and Jack about the most popular movies of 1999.

The man turned around but was too frantic to really see beyond his own situation. "I'm sorry—" He held up a finger.

Cameron nodded and the man turned back around.

"I need a tow. I had a blowout ... I'm outside of Homestead Gas & Goods ..."

Cameron returned to his conversation with Jack. "*Wild Wild West* is a masterpiece."

Jack finally got the stranger on the phone to participate after giving him a thumbs up indicating that Cameron was wrong about the color blue in *The Sixth Sense*.

He walked to the counter. "Excuse me. Do you have a moment?"

"Too many of 'em, buddy. How can I help you?" The clerk gave him a smile. "I'm not sure that you need any more gas than you've already got."

"I was hoping you could give me directions. I'm looking for a Coral Snake Road."

The clerk gave Cameron directions and sold him a bag of something called Gator Bits that seemed suspiciously like Sugar Smacks, along with some gas. Then he and Jack walked back to the Corvette.

They made easy conversation as they drove up the mountain, making a left at the top onto Coral Snake Road until they stopped in front of a cabin in the woods.

The chimney sent spiraling smoke into the air as they parked.

"Are you ready?" Jack asked his out of time companion.

"As I'll ever be," Cameron replied.

He knocked on the door and it opened to Amelia, offering a man out of time the shyest of smiles.

And he gave her his sloppiest grin. "I am John Titor."

"I know," Amelia said.

And then she grinned right back.

Chapter Eighty-Nine

RAMON – 2024

RJ — no, *Ramon* — glanced at the gas gauge and decided it was finally time to fill up. He was paranoid about gas now with Titor's warning like an echo in his head. Ramon might be overcorrecting, but if so, he didn't give a shit.

He decided to pull over at the next station and kill time by checking in with Michael.

"Are you on your way to *Running With Wolves*?" Michael asked when he answered the call.

"I thought we were calling it *Running With the Pack*."

"I like *Running With Wolves* better. It's more commercial."

"You can't just say something is more commercial every time you want to get your way. I suggest we split test that."

"So you want to pick your projects *and* name them?" Michael laughed. "Fine. Like I give a shit. *Running With the Pack* it is."

"Maybe." Ramon laughed. "The more times I say it out loud, the more I like *Running With Wolves*."

"Makes sense. It is better. Where are you?"

"I'm about to stop for gas."

"So specific. It's like you gave me your longitude and latitude. Are you headed to interview the Norris kid or not?"

"Yes."

"Great. I have some paperwork for you to fill out when you get back."

"I'm pretty sure that filling out the paperwork is your job," Ramon said as he parked in front of a pump. "So how about you do it for me?"

"Because I'm not RJ, and the form I'm filling out asks—"

"Use Ramon. I'm not RJ anymore either." Ramon opened the trunk, deciding that he should fill up the gas can as well. It was a long drive to the Norris place. "I'm ready for people to start calling me by my real name."

"Fine, Ramon. Aren't you fancy."

"It's fancy to use my real name?"

"Depends. Are you going to use the accent mark or whatever it's called?"

"A diacritic." Ramon noticed a gift-wrapped box in the trunk next to the gas can. Then he picked it up and eyed the box with curiosity on his way back to drop it on the passenger seat.

"See, *fancy.* I bet nine out of ten people don't know that word. *Muy bueno.*"

Ramon ignored him. "I should be there in another three hours."

"Tell the boy I said, *'Awwoooo!'*"

"He's not a kid anymore."

"Once a boy raised by wolves, always a boy raised by wolves," Michael argued with a self-satisfied chuckle.

"I'll give you a call when you I get there." Then Ramon realized that talking to his business partner might be the last thing he wanted to do after a couple of hours alone with his thoughts. "Or I'll text."

He killed the engine, filled the tank, and added a gallon to the gas can just in case.

Then he got back in the car and noted the package still sitting on the seat beside him and called Suzanne.

"Thanks for the gift."

"You mean the box I put in your trunk?" Suzanne didn't wait for an answer. "That wasn't from me. It came in the mail yesterday. When I saw it was wrapped..."

"What is it?"

"I just said it wasn't from me."

"Why is it in the trunk?"

"Because it's for you," Suzanne replied.

"Again, why the trunk?"

"You kept going on and on about the gas can, so I figured it was only a matter of time before I surprised you. Congratulations on not even lasting the day." She laughed. "So, are you going to open it? Never mind, I can hear you tearing the paper."

Ramon looked at the card, taped to an old notebook. It was a note from Agent Curtis: *Jacob asked me to pass this along to you.*

"It's from Jacob," Ramon reported.

"Jacob who?" A beat and then, "Lambert?"

Ramon's heart was pounding much too hard for him to answer Suzanne as his eyes took in the rest of the card and what was underneath it.

There's just one universe, and we're living in it. Or there are many, and the paths untaken in this universe have been taken in another. Everything is everything. But so is nothing.

Ramon looked at the unassuming notebook in his hand, Time Travel 0 inscribed on the top. He sat down and flipped it open to the first page where the inscription read *For Amelia*, and he began to read.

For some, it told a story of hope, describing a better future where community trumped competition and humanity rediscovered a way of being that they'd lost in the modern age.

For others, it was an epic romance, the tale of a man so devoted that he would move worldlines to protect the woman he loved.

For others still, it was a mind-bending story that proved reality is more malleable than we generally believe, and that one man's heroics could save the world.

For Ramon, it was all of these and more. A story about the power of story, about how legends are born — and how they die after serving their purpose.

Everyone he had interviewed needed to believe in something.

Just like Ramon.

Just like Titor himself.

And with the prize in his hand, he thought:

We're all John Titor.

Acknowledgments

This book would not have been possible without the collaborative efforts of Mark Grande, Rob Meyers and the team at VERSUS. Not only did they contribute to the story throughout the entire process, the origin of the idea belongs to them and we couldn't have done it without their help and support throughout. *Thank you.*

Our sincerest appreciation to the team that brought the final product together: Bonnie Johnston for editing, Jen Turrell for preparing the book for publication, and Dan Van Oss for the stunning cover design. A special acknowledgement as well goes to our tireless proof reader (and catcher of many of the mistakes that can slip into a final product) Dale Baromen.

Thank you to the entire Sterling & Stone team for your brainstorming, ideas, and support. With particular thanks to Sawyer Black, who's knowledge of 1970s technology and the legend of John Titor was indispensable.

Special thanks to our family and friends who stood by and supported us (even when time travel was proving to be a nightmare to crack).

Every novel owes its existence to countless people, and we know we would never be able to thank them all, but a special thank you definitely belongs to TimeTravel_0.

Whether an elaborate prank, an internet experiment, or an honest account of one man's journey through time, we owe the ultimate appreciation to the person behind the legend that inspired this story and the collective of people who kept the legend alive.

Thank you reader for giving us a small slice of your time and remember: bring a gas can with you when the car dies on the side of the road.

About the Authors

Niamh Arthur (pronounced Neeve) is the CEO and Genre Trends Specialist at Sterling & Stone. She moved to Ireland at 18 to attend the renowned Drama and Theatre Studies program at Trinity College Dublin, where she focused on film studies and wrote a senior dissertation on how cultural ideologies are expressed in modern Hollywood film. She went on to study marketing with a focus on audience response, psychology, and brand bonding.

After more than fifteen years running a successful business teaching entrepreneurs how to use story to connect with an audience Niamh realized that she was missing her favorite part of storytelling: fiction. She leapt at the chance to join Sterling & Stone as CEO and as Sean's writing partner. She uses her deep understanding of emotional triggers, audience response, genre, and commercial trends to ensure stories hit the mark and create long lasting impact on the audience.

After 20 years in Ireland she now lives in Colorado with her husband and two children.

Sean Platt has always been an entrepreneur, but knew he'd rather tell stories. When his wife bought him a laptop for his birthday in 2007 he dropped everything to start writing fiction.

Since making the leap, Sean has written hundreds of

novels (including the international best-sellers Yesterday's Gone and Invasion), penned dozens of scripts, and founded the IP Incubator Sterling & Stone where more than thirty storytellers work together to create world changing IP. Sterling & Stone's stable of writers come to Sean for ideas, mentorship, and "better words."

Originally from Long Beach, California, Sean now lives in Austin, Texas with his wife and dog, Fisher.

Also By Sean Platt

The Dead World Series

Dead Zero

Dead City

Dead Nation

Dead Planet

Empty Nest

The Beam Series

The Beam Season One

The Beam Season Two

The Beam Season Three

The Beam Season Four

The Beam Season Five

Robot Proletariat Series

En3my

Robot Proletariat

The Infinite Loop

The Hard Reset

Cascade Failure

Reboot

The Tomorrow Gene Series

Null Identity

The Tomorrow Gene

The Tomorrow Clone

The Eden Experiment

Karma Police Series

Jumper

Karma Police

The Collectors

Deviant

The Fall

Homecoming

Yesterday's Gone

October's Gone

Yesterday's Gone Season One

Yesterday's Gone Season Two

Yesterday's Gone Season Three

Yesterday's Gone Season Four

Yesterday's Gone Season Five

Yesterday's Gone Season Six

Tomorrow's Gone

Tomorrow's Gone Season One

Tomorrow's Gone Season Two

Tomorrow's Gone Season Three

Available Darkness

Darkness Itself

Available Darkness Book One

Available Darkness Book Two

Available Darkness Book Three

WhiteSpace

WhiteSpace Season One

WhiteSpace Season Two

WhiteSpace Season Three

Z2134

Z2134

Z2135

Z2136

The Dream Engine Series

The Tinkerer's Mainspring

The Dream Engine

The Nightmare Factory

The Ruby Room

The Pandora Core

The Engine Convergence

Stand Alone Novels

Burnout

The Island

Crash

Emily's List

Pattern Black

Devil May Care

The Secret Within

The Sleeper

Last Night Never Happened

I Am John Titor